CW00687524

BOOK TWO

TRANSFORMATION

A NOVEL BY

ABBY WYNNE

First published in 2022 by Praxis Publishing
www.praxispublishing.ie

Edited by Elizabeth Henry, , Niamh Deveraux and Ian Wynne

Source ISBN 978-1-9163627-4-1
Ebook Edition 978-1-9163627-5-8

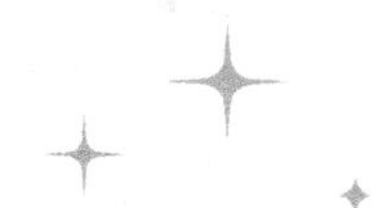

For Ian

DISCLAIMER

This is a work of fiction. None of the techniques in this book are designed to be utilised by any reader. In other words, you are not encouraged to use any of the techniques in this book with others or on upon yourself.

The information provided in this book is designed to provide an insight into the subjects discussed. Not all opinions offered here are those of the author. Conflicting information may have been delivered from time to time at the author's discretion for the purposes of the story, delivered from the point of view of a character.

This book is not a training manual. If you wish to become a fully trained psychotherapist, Reiki practitioner or shamanic practitioner you are encouraged to find a teacher or school in your location that is appropriate for your training needs.

This book is not intended as a substitute for the medical advice of physicians. For diagnosis or treatment of any medical problem please consult your doctor. The author is not responsible for your or any specific health needs and is not liable for any damages or negative consequences from any treatment, action, application or preparation to any person reading or following the information in this book.

If you are interested in learning more about the techniques or want advice on your healing process, you are invited to read the author's non-fiction books, listen to her podcast or find her via social media, or her websites www.abby-wynne.com and www. abbysonlineacademy. com

BOOK TWO

TRANSFORMATION

A NOVEL BY

ABBY WYNNE

We are many stories many lifetimes all happening
in different dimensions at the same time,
and even in our complexity
there's no possibility the human mind could put the
puzzle together when we are but insects compared
to the continent of a single piece
made for the hands of another being
who could accidentally squash us while reaching for the sugar,
as they drink their tea and read the paper in a shaft of sunlight
on a Sunday morning.

— From: Planting the Seeds

CHAPTER ONE

Marissa's whole body was shaking uncontrollably and she was drenched in sweat. It was 5am and it was still relatively dark outside. She could see through her partly open curtains that the sky was tinged with moonlight and a faint orange glow from the streetlamps. Her bedside light was on, her bedroom was empty, she was alone.

She heard a scratching at the back door. *Thank Goodness! Tobermory! You're back.* She felt so heavy. She pulled her mind into the room; as her eyes got used to the light and her mind tried to focus on letting the cat in, her trembling body began to release some of the terror. She lifted herself up, but her body was slow and not responding the way it normally would. The visitation had knocked her sideways.

No, that wasn't real. Not real at all. I must have made up the whole thing.

She shivered. Tobermory's scratching became more urgent. She brushed her hair out of her eyes, threw off her duvet and swung her legs over the side of the bed, resting there for a moment. The hard floor beneath her feet was comforting. The scratching at the back door got louder.

'Coming, coming, baby,' she said, grabbing her cardigan and managing to stand up.

The coldness of the wooden floor helped ground her but her body was still trembling. She shuffled to the back door and slid open the bolt on the cat-flap. The large black cat came straight in and wrapped himself around her legs, purring profusely, which was quite the opposite reaction to the previous evening. He brought a layer of cold air with him, chilling the bare skin of Marissa's legs, and the sound of his purring helped her feel more awake and more present. She liked it. She opened the door completely and stood there, allowing the cold air blast against her face. She decided she needed more cold things, hard, real things, things that reminded her she had a body.

She stepped outside in her bare feet and pulled out one of the deckchairs, opened it up and sat down into it, facing the magnolia tree. She pressed her feet into the ground one at a time and felt the stones and gravel beneath, the breaks in the paving stones, the sharpness of their edges pressing sharply into the soles of her feet. Her head was still in some kind of lucid nightmare, yet her body was here, outside in her garden. Or was it? Where was she? In her body, or out of it?

I am here. And I don't want to think about it. At all. Ever again. It didn't happen.

She sat, her body shivering, but she didn't mind the cold. In fact she craved it. It seemed to instil a stillness inside her. The sticky sweat down her back had dried off and her body temperature was beginning to come back to normal. She watched the condensation of her breath in front of her face, knowing that she didn't want to go back into the flat just yet. Maybe not ever.

Tobermory had followed her outside. He jumped up onto her lap. That was new – normally he didn't like the strange folding contraptions that were deckchairs. Marissa would tease him, saying deckchairs were beneath him, and then she would laugh out loud at her own joke. But now he settled onto her and she appreciated the weight of him, and his apologetic claws, as he manoeuvred himself into position. It was another sensual reminder that she was here, she was real and she *was* safe, even though she wasn't believing it just yet.

Marissa started petting the sleek black cat. His purring became louder and reassuring. His whole body vibrated on her lap, calming her down. But looking down at his face as she stroked him, she realised something was different. A thin streak of white ran across his face from his right cheek, up and over his head, then across his left ear, right to the tip. *Has he been hit by lightning? That white definitely wasn't there before.*

Tobermory looked up, green eyes wide, still purring. His pink tongue popped out of his mouth and he licked his nose. Marissa looked at him. *Is this my cat?* She cradled his head in her hands and turned him to face her so she could study his new white fur. She touched it. It was coarse, not as soft as the black fur tufted around it. Tobermory shuddered as if he didn't want her touching it so she pulled her fingers back.

Tobermory lifted one of his paws to his mouth and began cleaning it, and then the other paw, while still looking at Marissa. She threaded her index finger around his long black tail to check and yes, there was the familiar twist, the kink that he always had. *He definitely must be my cat, but this white fur?*

They sat there, breathing together, Marissa's shivering dwindling until it came in smaller and smaller waves and then eventually left altogether. A different kind of shivering took over: her teeth started to chatter from the cold.

The sun was coming up. Marissa wasn't hungry, but she fancied some tea. *Normalitea.* She gathered the cat in her arms, but as she stood, Tobermory gently dropped to the ground. Marissa shook herself – arms, legs, hands and feet – it felt good bringing the life back in. She made her way to the back door. Tobermory went into the kitchen ahead of her and leapt up to his favourite spot on her armchair.

The flat was significantly colder than usual. Marissa shivered again and put on the kettle, then went into her bedroom and unexpectedly caught her breath as she stood in the doorway.

This was where this being, this man, this thing, had been standing only an hour or so earlier. How did he find me? Does he really want my soul?

Her mind started racing once more and her heart started beating faster in response. Just thinking about it brought back all of the terror she had just managed to dissipate. She jumped when the kettle switched itself off with a click.

Strangely, she noticed her low-level anxiety wasn't present. Underlying everything was a sense of deep calm. This didn't make any sense at all. But somehow she had become divided. Part of her seemed to know what to do, as if it had been waiting for this moment for years, but the Marissa part, the human part, was really freaking out.

Of course I'm freaking out, I met a demon. Yes, that's what he was. No more doubt on that now. But what now? If he really wanted me, wouldn't he have taken me already?

She went back to the kitchen and made tea, then took the hot steaming drink to the sofa and sat down, curling her legs underneath her. She felt the heat of the mug seep into her fingers and she started to warm up. She wanted to contact Matt, but she felt she needed to calm her mind herself, rather than depend on him. He had just slotted into her life all of a sudden and he had done so much for her already. So many new things happening all at once, it was overwhelming.

Putting the tea down on the table, she reached underneath to the shelf and felt for her angel cards and shamanic oracle cards. They felt like old friends. Just looking at the picture on the cover of each pack helped bring her back to her centre. It had been a long time since she'd drawn a card. She adjusted her position on the sofa and opened the boxes, stacking each deck on the table in front of her. She felt more drawn to the angel cards so she held them in her hand for a few moments, then cut the pack and spread the cards face down onto the table. As she took a breath, she noticed one card was slightly out of place. She picked it out without disturbing the others and turned it over. *Haniel – Courage.* Relief flooded through her body. She pulled out another card. *Raziel – Mysteries.* She hadn't met Raziel before, so she picked up the booklet and read about him.

> *Archangel Raziel is the Angel of Mysteries. He is a wizard and an alchemist and holds the key to unlocking many of the secrets of the Universe. Call on Raziel when you need new spiritual insights. Ask him to refine your psychic abilities and help you tune into your own sense of Divine magic.*

Marissa closed her eyes. *Archangel Raziel, Archangel Raziel, Archangel Raziel, am I safe?* She breathed out and felt stillness around her. She felt her heart slow down and a deeper layer of tension leave her, tension she hadn't realised she was holding. She kept her eyes closed and allowed her body to sink into the sofa.

She was still holding the card when her alarm went off in her bedroom about forty minutes later. She woke with a jump. She hadn't touched her tea; it was cold, and a sticky film of milk was gathering on its surface. She put the cards back into their boxes, leaving Raziel and Haniel out on the table top, and put the boxes away on the shelf under the table.

Sunlight was pouring in through the window the birds were singing. The back door was still open and Tobermory hadn't stirred from the armchair. He was awake and looking directly at her, his tail swaying as if he was concentrating on something. *Almost as if he's been standing guard while I slept.* His new white streak was glowing in the sunshine. He seemed like his usual self, perhaps a little more alert than usual. It made Marissa think of a movie she had seen in which a bodyguard had jumped out to prevent his ward from getting hit by a bullet. *Maybe he took a hit for me?*

Marissa got up and stretched her body, she really did have to get up and get ready for work. She went about her morning ablutions, taking an extra-hot shower and enjoying the contrast from the cold she had craved earlier. She took her time, and moved slowly. On the way into work everything looked different, almost glassy. It was as if she could see through everything; her day to day life was a fabric of existence that wasn't real. Her bus took its usual route but it seemed as if everything around her had slowed down and Marissa was looking at things for the first time – sad, tired faces of people driving past, lines of people queuing up for coffee, shafts of sunshine reflected on shop windows, rubbish bins with refuse overflowing, parents hunched over as they walked their children to day-care.

She got off the bus a stop earlier than usual and went to buy a coffee in a place she liked to go to sometimes before work. Everything inside seemed to be in high-density colour – the yellows were yellower, the greens greener, the paintings so vibrant the people portrayed in them were about to jump out and get into the queue with her. She felt a rush of vital energy flow through her; yes, it was good to be alive. She *was* alive! It was her turn at the counter, and instead of her usual cappuccino, she spontaneously ordered an extra-hot caramel macchiato and a chocolate muffin. *I always wanted to try one of these – heck, what am I waiting for?* She walked the rest of the way into work, stopping now and then to sip cautiously at her too-hot beverage, relishing the sticky sweetness of the syrup on her tongue. She smiled at everyone she saw in her building, they smiled back when in the close confines of the elevator, and that felt good too. When she got to her desk she sat down, unwrapped the muffin and switched on her computer. Everything seemed surreal. But she was alive. And she felt good. Her phone beeped a text. It was Matt.

Hello love, sorry again I couldn't b there last night. I'm free tonight, pizza @ mine @ 6?

Marissa hesitated. She wasn't sure if she wanted to trek all the way out to Dun Laoghaire. She was at work already, she'd have to go home first and back out again ... or would she? That would be the old way of thinking. She could just pop into Penny's at lunchtime and pick up a toothbrush and new PJs ... no, wait. Tobermory. And his new white stripe. He needed her. *What to do? I don't think I want to spend tonight in my flat, though. I'm not ready yet. And it would be nice to see Matt.*

Hi! Sounds good, got to run errand first, 7.30 ok?

Gr8! Cu l8r!

Marissa chuckled. Text shorthand wasn't like Matt. The sound of her laughter seemed to come from somewhere outside herself. After a few bites she realised that she wasn't really enjoying her muffin, it had looked so appealing but it was quite dry inside. She swept the remains of it into its napkin, gathered up the crumbs and put it all into the wastepaper basket.

She brought her awareness to the computer screen and opened up her emails. As she started to focus on work-related things they felt so foreign to her. She didn't remember the last time she had been to work. *So strange, I'm sure it hasn't been that long... Oh yes, I was in Clifden only yesterday. It feels like I stepped out of time. Did I?* She tracked it back in her mind. *Yes, that's right, I was in work Friday morning, so it's only been two days really. It is so strange how weekends in Clifden seem to last for two months!* Then she remembered coming home, going to bed, then waking up on the sofa. She felt butterflies start up strongly in her belly and was glad she hadn't finished the muffin after all.

Thinking back to Clifden felt better. Marissa remembered the shamanic work she had done with Séamus, with the group, and how intense the healings had been. She remembered Zaad's smile, his white teeth, his sparkly eyes. *Ah, yes. The fire ceremony.* Thinking about that felt good. It was an anchor point, a milestone in space and time. She remembered the heat of the fire on her face, the vital sense of being alive. Recalling it helped her orient in the world once again, be more present. *But no, that's not it. I'm missing something.*

She looked at her calendar for the week to see if what she was missing was in there. *Last Tuesday I was at college. That's right, I did my assessment and it went very well. Thursday I was in Cabra. Her heart leapt. Cabra – the last time I saw Martin. I saw that demon that night in Martin, didn't I?* It all started coming back to her, like pieces of a jigsaw puzzle slotting into place. Matt had stayed the night on Thursday. Then she remembered the healing she had with Séamus, on the sofa, in the main room. *When did that happen? Her body tensed up again. What did he do to me? Was it really only yesterday? It feels like years ago. Did he have something to do with what happened?*

It didn't bear thinking about. She felt herself becoming more and more anxious the more she thought about it. It was too confusing, the timelines were getting mixed up in her mind. She decided to focus on what was in front of her. She'd see Matt later that evening, she could tell him everything and maybe it would make more sense then.

By lunchtime Marissa had managed to get a bit of work done and had mostly pushed aside what had happened, but now and then dark images would creep back in. Each time she got wobbly, she brought herself back to her memories of the fire ceremony.

As she walked to the shop for lunch, she practised her mindfulness exercise. *There's a red car, the traffic lights are green, there's dog poo on the street, buds coming up in the garden there, a crisp packet flapping in the breeze...* She chose her usual tuna sandwich and decided to eat it outside as the air was chilly, but it was bright and sunny too. She sat on a bench close by her office and smiled at her work colleagues as they rushed by, some of them acknowledged her in return.

Sarah came walking towards her like a breath of fresh air. She wore a furry white winter coat with a white scarf and a white hat to match. She looked like a Russian princess. She also wore white mittens and had a bag slung over her arm from the local shop with her lunch inside.

'Can I sit with you?' she asked.

'Of course,' said Marissa, shifting across the bench to make more room.

Sarah sat down and sighed, then took off her mittens, putting them on the bench beside her. She rustled in the bag to get her sandwich out. Marissa had hardly eaten any of hers.

'You're all in white,' said Marissa, 'and mittens too. All new?'

'Yes,' Sarah said. 'You like?'

'You look amazing. Are you planning a trip to Russia now? I never liked mittens myself.'

Sarah giggled. 'No, I guess I do look a little Russian with the hat.'

'And your blonde hair,' added Marissa, with a grin.

Sarah ignored this and looked at the sky for a moment. 'A trip to Russia *could* be interesting...' She unwrapped her sandwich. 'The mittens are very annoying though, I agree. I'm not able to do anything when I've got them on. But they are warm, probably better for a Russian winter, not a damp Irish one. My mother bought the whole lot for me for Christmas so I thought I'd better wear it at least once. I like the coat scarf and hat, but the mittens, they just aren't practical at all.' She sighed and took a bite of her sandwich.

When they finished, they threw their rubbish into the bin (including just over half of Marissa's sandwich), then walked back inside together. They threw their coats (and hat and mittens) aside and went to the canteen to get tea.

'You were in Clifden this weekend, weren't you?' said Sarah as she added milk to her brewing tea, leaving the teabag in the mug.

'Yes.' replied Marissa, stirring hers to draw out the strength.

'How did it go?'

Marissa stiffened, then relaxed a little as she focused on the good things she experienced. 'It was great fun, actually. Lots went on, and I'm still trying to make sense of it all.' She hoped Sarah wouldn't pursue this line of conversation.

'Any nice men?' said Sarah with a wink and a smile.

Marissa relaxed a little further. 'Ha, ha, yes, they're all nice, but I have Matt now, so I'm not looking.'

Sarah raised an eyebrow, flicked her ponytail and said, 'I meant for me!'

'Always you with the men,' said Marissa flippantly as she poured her milk. Smiling, she suddenly realised she sounded like her own mother and grimaced.

Sarah laughed. 'Only teasing. You look exhausted, though. You must have been very busy.'

'That's one way of looking at it,' replied Marissa.

They walked back to their desks. Sarah's was at the other end of the open-plan office so she waved and mouthed 'Bye' as she walked away. Upon sitting down, Marissa tried again to focus on emails. Twenty more had arrived since she had left for lunch. She looked at the clock. *One minute at a time. I guess that's all I can do right now.*

+++

Marissa stood outside Matt's in the rain and rang the bell. It was just after 7.30pm and as dark as midnight. Marissa had managed to keep herself busy all day and avoided thinking about difficult things, but as soon as Matt opened the door and she saw his beaming happy face, her strength of resolve fell away and she crumbled.

'Hey, love, hey, what's going on? Are you okay? You don't look okay... Come in, tell me everything.'

He ushered Marissa inside and closed the door behind her. They went into his living room and he took off her coat, removed her bag and sat her down on the sofa. The room smelled like warm cheese. The pizza had been delivered and was lying there open with one piece missing. Matt looked at it and then up at Marissa with a child-like guilty look on his face.

'I didn't know if you wanted meat or not, so I just got plain. But that doesn't matter. What's going on?'

Marissa burst into tears. Matt put his arms around her and held her for several minutes until she composed herself. He offered her some tissues. She couldn't speak, so instead, she took out her phone and showed Matt a photo of Tobermory that she had taken just before she had left the house.

'Jeez, what happened to Tobes? Is he okay? What happened?'

Marissa sniffed, and gathered herself before answering in broken tones. 'I don't know what happened. I'm so confused.' She started to cry again.

Matt waited patiently for her, then said 'What can you tell me? Start there.'

'Tobermory disappeared last night as soon as I came home from Clifden, it was as if he didn't want to be near me.'

He nodded.

'Then this morning he had this white streak on his head. But that's not why I'm upset.' She told Matt a little bit about Clifden, about the session with Séamus, and partially recounted her 'dream' of the night before, and her terrifying experience when she woke.

Matt sat patiently and listened, giving her his full attention, pushing aside his desire for more food.

'And only then, when I was sitting outside in the night air, that's when I noticed. Tobermory's fur I mean. Like I said, he had been avoiding me all night, then suddenly he was there, on my lap, as if he was protecting me. Looking like he'd been struck by lightning. I don't understand it and I'm scared. And confused too. That thing, he ... it ... said it knew where I lived, Matt. It called me by my name. I don't know what to do. I don't know if it's real, or if I'm making it all up. But the white on his head is real, you saw it yourself, here.' She thrust the phone at him again, he took it and nodded his head. She looked at him with pleading eyes. 'Can I stay here tonight?'

Matt scratched his head and finally succumbed to another slice of pizza. He took a large bite and seemed very thoughtful as he chewed and swallowed.

'Let me get this straight. Séamus called this presence a demon, and he, it, showed up at your flat last night, in your bedroom? He jumped out of your dream? So he's real then? He could be here, with you now?'

Marissa shook her head. ' No, no. No, I don't think he's here, I can't feel him. I haven't felt him since Tobermory came back to me in the garden. I hope he's gone, but I don't think he's gone for good.'

Matt was still figuring it out. 'Of course you can stay here tonight, but this is more serious than just tonight, isn't it? If it did really happen, we need to know what to do if it happens again. You should call Séamus, you should ask him.'

Hearing him say 'we need to know', gave her prickles down her back. Marissa felt very grateful, and less alone than before. But when Matt mentioned Séamus, she felt a crushing weight on her chest which mirrored the feeling she had experienced during the healing session with him.

'No, I don't want to,' she said and shuddered. 'I felt paralysed when he worked on me. On the sofa in Clifden. I can't believe it was only yesterday.'

After a moment, she continued. 'I felt the same paralysis in my room later last night, when that being, the demon, was there. I don't want to even say that word, Matt, it's like it is giving him power. But that's what I think that he is. Or it. That's what Séamus called it, anyway. I don't know much about this, and I certainly don't want to summon it back again. I need to talk to someone, though, I really do. Someone who can help. You're right, I can't just expect that this will go away. But I don't want to contact Séamus, not just yet anyway.'

'What about talking to Dolores then?' Matt suggested gently.

'Oh! Yes of course, I didn't think of Dolores! Yes, of course she might be able to help, or at least point us, me, in the right direction.' Marissa turned to Matt with a smile of relief. 'I really appreciate your support with this, I really, really do.' She leaned into him, putting her arms around him and squeezing him tightly. Then she pulled away and said, 'But I don't know if this is your fight, your problem. It's definitely mine, but I don't want to bring this to you or involve you directly if I can help it.'

Matt nodded and smiled back. 'Well, I'm here for a reason, and I do believe all of this is happening for a reason. We might not know what that reason is just yet, so we will have to grapple blindly in the dark for now. At least we do have each other. I mean, you do have me – I'm here.'

Marissa suddenly felt drained and exhausted. Knowing that Matt was there gave her space to release some of the tension she had been unknowingly holding.

'Let's watch some mindless TV and finish this pizza,' suggested Matt. 'You're staying here tonight, so you can get some sleep. I'm on watch now and we can contact Dolores in the morning.'

CHAPTER TWO

'Have you got an iron, Matt?'

Matt was in great form, singing and brushing his teeth at the same time while hopping from one foot to the other. Marissa couldn't help but laugh. He put down his toothbrush and smiled at her, toothpaste bubbles fizzing over his lips and trickling out of the corner of his mouth and down his chin into his beard.

'Iron? No, sorry, I've no need for an iron.'

'Oh well,' said Marissa, not really surprised as she examined her crushed blue skirt and jacket. 'I'll have to get one for next time.'

Matt grinned at the thought of a next time. 'What about tonight – are you coming back here?'

Marissa stopped in her tracks. She hadn't thought that far ahead. She had college that night, and Tobermory needed her to feed him. Travelling all that way back to Matt's that late wasn't really an option.

'Can you come to me?'

Her voice sounded like she was begging him and she didn't like it. She looked at the floor. Matt came up to her, pressed himself into her and kissed her cheek softly. He put his index finger on her chin and lifted her face to his.

'I'll see what I can do. I don't want to leave you alone for a night just yet. Perhaps if I spend tonight at your place it would help you settle back in there again.'

'Yes, perhaps.'

Marissa kissed him back and checked her watch. 'I have to go or I'll be late. Thanks for last night. Hey, how much do I owe you for the pizza?'

'Don't be silly – you only had two slices, don't worry about it. See you at your place later. What time?'

'I'll be finished class at 8.30. Is 9.30 okay? It takes about an hour for me to get home.'

'Yes, of course. I'll drive over. I'll be there.'

'Thank you Matt, I really appreciate you.'

'I should hope so,' he said with a smile.

Such a big teddy bear, I do feel safe when he's around.

There was a big sales pitch with a major client planned for the end of the week, all the sales team were being called in to help. Preparations preoccupied Marissa's mind for most of the day. She absorbed herself fully, dulling down any flares of anxiety or difficult thoughts. She was taking it an hour at a time, a minute at a time, without checking the clock, moving, drifting almost disconnected from herself, to prevent herself from revisiting that night, that room, that face. At one point, as she was standing by the photocopier, she thought she saw the flicker of a shadow moving on the wall and her heart leapt, but when she shook her head and looked again, it was nothing.

I've got to get a hold of myself. Maybe this whole thing didn't even happen. Maybe I'm making it all up.

Dinner was a sandwich, a packet of Tayto and a Diet Coke which she munched while on the bus to college. This was actually more than she had eaten in one sitting in the last twenty four hours. The bus jaunted on its merry way through the traffic as she finished the last crumb, wiped her hands on her coat and crumpled the packaging a ball and shoved it into her bag. When it was time, she pulled herself up and out of her seat, navigated her way down the narrow curved staircase and pressed the 'stop' button. Once the bus doors opened she stepped out onto the pavement and got her bearings. She walked tall through the gates of the school, entered the building and went straight to the canteen.

Her friends were at a table by the window. Ronan and Yvonne were in deep discussion about the assessments, Yvonne looked quite anxious, but Katie seemed relaxed. *She must have already had her assessment?*

Marissa pulled out the ball of packaging from her bag and stuffed it into the over-full bin, then went to the sink to wash the smell of crisps off her hands. She got a seat at the table beside Yvonne.

Katie smiled at her. 'Hey, Marissa, how was your weekend? They've not finished the assessments yet – we have the last few to do tonight.'

She brushed it off and changed the subject. 'It was good, thanks. Hi, everyone! Yvonne, have you had your assignment yet?'

'No, not yet,' Yvonne shook her head and looked down at the table. 'Mine's tonight, I'm first, actually. And I'm a little nervous.' She was turning a sweet wrapper around in her hand, wringing her fingers together.

Ronan turned to her. 'You'll be fine, stop worrying about it. Here, have a biscuit.'

'Don't worry about it, Yvonne,' Marissa said. 'You'll be great. All you need to do is listen to what your client says and reflect it back to them.'

'Yes, you make it sound so simple, so why am I always thinking about what I should be saying next?'

'I don't know. Maybe you could spend more time listening to what *they* are saying instead of listening to your own thoughts?'

Yvonne blushed and looked back down at the table again. Ronan's eyes were wide and he looked astonished. *Oh no, did I say something wrong? What did I do?*

She looked at Ronan questioningly to see what the damage was and caught a glint of pleasure in his eye and a small curve of a smile at the corner of his mouth. She smiled back, then he nodded towards Yvonne and raised his eyebrows to remind her that a smile would certainly be thought of as inappropriate. The smile vanished from her face, then Ronan winked at her, which made her want to laugh out loud. Yvonne, however, was now completely distraught, so Marissa got up quickly before she upset Yvonne further and went over to the boiler, and poured out a cup of tea that she really didn't want.

She waited a little longer than usual before coming back to the table, and when she did, she swept away the crumbs from somebody else's snack before placing her chipped cup down in front of her.

Ronan had deftly changed the subject by asking everyone what they had done over the weekend, which was exactly the subject that Marissa wanted to avoid. Marissa stared at the tea bag floating in her milky tea hoping that he wouldn't put the focus on her. She stared deeper into her cup and was reminded of an image they had seen in a class on Freudian psychology. A large glacier had been floating in the ocean, two-thirds of it underwater. The part above the water represented the part of yourself that you showed to other people, the part beneath, the greater part, represented the part that you never shared.

Whatever about hiding this from other people, there's a big part of me right now that I don't want to see for myself.

She still couldn't bring herself to look at Ronan so she turned the mug around to see it from a different angle. On it were the words: 'You can't have flowers without rain' and a picture of someone sitting in a garden under an umbrella, with sunflowers beside them reaching up to the sky. In the sky there was cloud, with rain coming down from it and a yellow-orange sun half-hidden behind it.

You can't have light without dark. The thought came in unbidden and was immediately unwelcome. She shivered and tried to push it away. *Well, maybe squeezing a little more darkness out of this tea bag wouldn't be so bad...*

Yvonne seemed to have recovered and was telling a story about taking her niece and nephew to the zoo and being yelled at by her sister-in-law because she had taken them to McDonald's on the way home.

'How was I to know they had banned them from fast food?'

It really seemed that nothing was going right for her.

Marissa looked for somewhere to dump her tea bag, Ronan quietly passed an empty saucer over towards her and she gratefully picked out the tea bag with deft fingers and plopped it onto it.

Emmet arrived, bringing his good humour and a blast of cold air in with him. 'Hello, folks,' he said with a smile, rubbing his hands together. 'So! Last night of assessments! It will be great to get this all over with so we can get back to the real work.'

Barbara came in behind him, her face sullen and unenthusiastic.

'Hi, Barbara,' said Yvonne. 'Are you tonight too? Or did you manage to do your assessment on the weekend?'

'Yes, I'm all done,' Barbara acknowledged. 'It was almost better than going to the dentist.'

Yvonne shivered and appeared to shrink a little more.

Emmet went over to get himself a biscuit and noticed that there was a sheet stuck up on the wall with the schedule for the evening. 'Yes, folks, assessments until 8 tonight. I hope you're ready for an evening filled with fun and frolics!'

Marissa wandered over to cast her eye over the sheet and avoid Ronan, and saw her name was down as a client for the third assessment. Her heart sank. The last thing she felt like doing was talking about something that was bothering her. Particularly today. *There's my pattern again. I really should make an effort.*

They were in with the other group again so there was a mix of people she did and didn't know, which made watching the assessments a little more interesting. Marissa watched Yvonne's session with Clara from the other group. She was willing her to do well, and it did seem that as hard as her advice had sounded, Yvonne had taken it on board. She wasn't as fidgety as usual, she looked interested in her client and she even asked, 'Can you explain what you mean by that?' to go deeper into the emotions. When she stood up, she smiled, knowing she had done well, and smiled directly at Marissa, showing that all was forgiven. During the next assessment session Marissa tried to decide what she would talk about when it was her turn to be the client. *What about talking about Eli and the family dinner? It is a continuation of the issue from before, and at least it is a real thing. Or the situation at work between Lucy and Sarah, I could pretend I'm Sarah? No, I need to keep it real.*

The clapping in the room brought Marissa back to the moment and then it was her turn to be up in front of the group. *I don't like this. It's harder for me to be the client than the therapist.* She smoothed her hair back and sat down, breathing to centre herself before the 'therapist' began. He was a tall man from the other group with glasses and ginger hair which fell in curls around his face. She hadn't met him before but had noticed him in the canteen a few times. Tonight he seemed hesitant and nervous. She tried to remain calm so it would be easier for him. Everybody wanted everybody to do well and it felt good to know that they were all rooting for one another.

The ginger-haired man started the session with an introduction. 'Hello there. I'm Peter. Nice to meet you.'

'Hi, Peter. I'm Marissa.'

'We have fifteen minutes together, um, perhaps you'd like to tell me about something that is upsetting you? Um... Perhaps I will be able to help you with it.' He crossed his legs and folded his arms, then unfolded them again, looking uneasy.

Marissa took a breath. She felt a wall inside, a brick wall building up in her; the words and the feelings that she really wanted to talk about had surfaced from the deep and were behind it. *Perhaps they weren't that deep.* The wall she was building to block them out was so high, it was impossible to climb. She was putting all of her energy into the wall that words wouldn't come. She opened her mouth, then closed it again. *Why can't I talk about what's wrong? Why do I have to always feel stuck like this when I'm a client?* She looked at Peter, no she really didn't want to be sharing something like this with him. She imagined the wall turning into a large black box, containing all of the difficult heavy emotion. She pushed it aside and sent it outside of the room. There was a small relief in that. She looked around her and could feel everybody's eyes on her, waiting for her to begin. Peter was getting agitated. She had to say something.

'Peter, hi. Yes, something happened in work and I think I'd like some help with it.'

Peter relaxed in his chair, his face softened and a lock of ginger hair fell into his eyes and brushed against his wire-frame glasses. He ran his hands through his hair and pushed it back from his face.

'Yes, of course, you can talk about whatever you want to here. It's your space.' He smiled, relief showing plainly on his face.

'Thanks. There's this person at work, her name is Siobhan...'

Marissa managed to slip out of class without being confronted by any of her friends who would want to know who Siobhan was, and why she never told them about what was going on in her job. When she got off the bus she walked to her flat and Matt was there, outside, waiting for her. She smiled with relief.

'I didn't want you going into the flat on your own tonight,' he said, 'so I got out of my Tai Chi training early so I'd be here to meet you. Jim will get the notes for me.'

Marissa was so happy to see him. She felt a heavy weight leave her and her whole body relaxed. 'Hey, thanks. I really have to move past this.'

She reached into her bag, took out the key, opened the door and went inside. Matt came in behind her and as she felt for the light switch, he put his arms around her from behind and held her tightly. She sighed and turned around to face him, turning the light on and then wrapping her arms around him.

'Thank you for being here. Really. It means a lot to me.'

Matt smiled and kissed her on the forehead, then on the nose, and on her cheeks. It felt nice. Tobermory wound himself around her legs and mewed loudly, as if cranky with her.

'Tea?' she asked, 'I still have to feed Tobermory.'

'I'm all tea-ed out,' said Matt, peeling himself away from her and taking off his coat. She took hers off too and they hung them up on the back of the door. Marissa locked it and pulled the bolt across. *Not that that will make any difference to that, Thing...* She shivered and went into the kitchen to get the cat his food, followed by her very hungry cat.

Matt went over to the bookshelf in the living room and browsed the titles. 'You go ahead if you want a cuppa,' he suggested, pulling one down off the shelf and opening it.

Marissa shrugged her shoulders as she tore off the top of the packet of wet food and squeezed it into Tobermory's dinner dish. Her cat mewed with gratitude. 'I'm tea-ed out too. We had assessments tonight, they seemed to go on forever. I'm so tired now.'

She tidied up the kitchen things and plopped down onto the sofa and Matt sat down beside her, leaning into her. Tobermory had finished his meal and was licking himself clean.

'You were right,' said Marissa, 'I'd have been too anxious here on my own tonight. But I need to figure out what I can do so I can be here on my own tomorrow.'

'Did you contact Dolores?' Matt asked.

'Oh shit! No. What with the sales meeting and class, I totally forgot.'

'Well, I brought two things that might help – at least I hope they'll help.' Matt reached down into his bag and pulled out an old, black leather-bound book. He pulled it up onto his lap and opened it to the table of contents. He turned to Marissa. 'I borrowed this from a mate of mine. I thought there might be something in here that could help.' He turned the book to show the cover to Marissa. She couldn't see it, so she leaned into him, his closeness making her feel more secure.

'*Occult Spells, Warding and Witchcraft*,' she read slowly. Marissa's eyes opened and she snapped back into the room. She turned to Matt, touched the cover of the book and said, 'Now this sounds like something from Harry Potter, only for real!' Marissa laughed. 'Wow, I didn't know there actually were books like this.'

Matt seemed relieved at her response. 'Oh yeah, this stuff is real, alright. My friend, he was reluctant to give it to me, but I told him it was an emergency. He did stress it wasn't for beginners and that we shouldn't be meddling in this type of thing, but I reckon it's too late for that.'

Marissa sat back into the sofa and remembered the warding spell that Séamus had taught them in Clifden. She shivered again. *Is shamanism to blame for this? It might be worth exploring... Why didn't I think to ward the flat?*

'Do they have a warding spell in there?' she asked. She got up from the sofa and went into her bedroom to search for her notebook. The memory of that particular lesson seemed fuzzy and unclear to her, as if her mind was in a fog, yet she was certain she would have written down enough information to remember what to do.

'Yes, they do!' shouted Matt excitedly from the other room as he turned the pages of the book.

Marissa looked everywhere for her notebook – in her bag, on her desk, under her bed... She eventually found it inside the empty backpack that she had thrown up on top of the wardrobe. *Strange, I* know *I put it on the desk. I don't even remember putting it in my backpack.* She noticed Tobermory was looking at her, head cocked to one side. She smiled at him and opened up the notebook. He arched his back as she turned the pages to find the information she was looking for. All she had written down was: *'Warding: do the walls, the ceiling and the floor too.' Nothing else.*

Nothing else? That's not like me.

She cast her mind back to the lesson but it was harder than she expected, as if parts of the memory had just vanished from her memory banks. She remembered they had got up and drawn something in the air, a symbol, many times, in many directions, floor and ceiling too. But what was it? She couldn't remember it ... ah yes, Séamus had told them not to draw it in their books. She did remember you needed to draw it white and then imagine it turning red. *Or draw it red and imagine it turning white?*

'Here, look,' said Matt, coming over to her with the book open in his hand. 'This says it's a banishing symbol.'

Marissa jumped at his voice and proximity to her. She stared at the symbol that he was holding out to her. It seemed to go in and out of focus as she looked at it. She felt dizzy and had to look away. Nausea filled her stomach. She breathed out, felt the ground beneath her. *I've got to do this. Jeez, it's just a drawing in an old book...* A cold shiver went down her back. She closed her eyes and retreated somewhere deep inside herself.

She found herself inside a cave, alone. A symbol made of circles and triangles was etched on the wall. It was moving slightly when she looked at it, and as she looked it drew her in, feeding off of her attention. It began to move a little faster, and faster again until it was spinning, it set itself alight and seemed to be on fire. But it didn't affect her, it was just something in the cave. She moved away from it and looked around to see what else was there. She noticed a wooden, oval full-length mirror which seemed entirely out of place. She walked towards it and the symbol lifted itself off the wall, it was a buzzing ball of fire now, it followed behind her.

Standing in front of the mirror she saw herself in her school uniform staring back at her. 'I survived years without magic,' she said in a hollow voice to her image in the mirror. 'I can do it again. It's too much. Too real.

I can't do it. Sorry, Marissa.' The girl in the school uniform started to cry. The emotion became too real, too strong, too much. The image vanished and she was back in her body in the room with Matt.

She brought her awareness back to the room, and there was the page, but the symbol on it looked glassy now, as if it was mocking her. She ignored it and read the banishing prayer that went with it. *No, that's not what I want. It's not right at all.*

'It's not what we did in Clifden, I don't remember what we did, actually, and this is probably more powerful. I feel a bit sick, Matt. I think I should sit down. Are you sure this is good? That we should be doing this?'

They went back to the sofa and sat down. Matt cocked his head on one side. 'I remember learning somewhere that the power comes more from the intention behind the words, more than the words themselves. But Derek, my mate, he said that symbols were very powerful and we needed to be very careful about which ones we worked with. Sometimes just looking at a symbol could activate it, and they had a life of their own. Now I think that is scary. And we certainly don't want any more scary tonight.'

Marissa felt the nausea subside as she focused on the bookshelf and not the book. Matt was still looking expectantly at her.

'I'll ask my guides,' she said. 'I think that's the best thing to do.'

Matt nodded his head and Marissa tried to look at the banishing symbol once more. The nausea started again. She closed her eyes and tried to focus, tried to journey. She felt Matt's hand on her leg, she relaxed.

She was on the lakeside. The scene was fuzzy, like trying to tune in an old television. She waited a few moments, concentrating on her feet in the image in her mind, but there was no improvement. She walked towards the edge of the lake, willing herself deeper into the image.

Her two medicine women were already there, waiting for her. She heard the waters behind her breaking with a splashing and a hissing, spitting noise, and saw the sea serpent was there too, its glistening silver and turquoise head had risen up from the water, his big face and kind eyes were looking directly at her. Something in her image stabilised and she felt safe, then.

'Is this the right thing to do? This symbol from the book? This banishing? How do I protect myself?'

The women looked at each other. They seemed to be in disagreement. Emelda the Navajo, was shaking her head, whereas the Peruvian woman, who was yet to reveal her name to Marissa, looked very serious. Instead of her usual blue hat she was wearing a man's boater and she had a cigarette in her mouth. The sea serpent hissed loudly. They both looked to Marissa and the Peruvian shaman woman spoke first.

'Marissa, we are the ancestors. We can only do so much for you. We are almost certain that he is gone for now. But we may be mistaken. Use the banishing spell if it makes you feel better, but you do not need anything more for the moment. You have much to learn before you can take on an adversary such as he.'

Emelda walked towards her. 'Be careful of any symbol,' she said. 'Perhaps it is best not to use this one – you do not know where it came from or what was the intention behind it. We have never seen it before. We,' she nodded over to the other woman, 'do not always agree, but we agree on this – we are asking for an intervention on your behalf. It is done. Ask Matt what he has for you in his pocket.'

Marissa nodded, wondering what Matt had to do with this.

The Peruvian shaman smiled, showing her black teeth. 'You must be careful. We know that you are not given more than you can handle. But you must trust your instinct. Listen to your body – your body has done this many times before, your body knows. Listen to the "no" and do not cross this sensation.'

Marissa nodded again.

The sea serpent hissed loudly, there was an urgency about him, as if he had something more to tell her. But she didn't understand, so she smiled and bowed at him, placing her hands in prayer position in gratitude. He nodded at her, then disappeared back into the waters. She she felt herself coming back to the room.

After a moment Marissa turned to Matt and said, 'What's in your pocket? My guides told me to ask you.'

Matt blushed, then pulled away a little. 'How did they know? Hang on...' He put his hand in his trouser pocket and pulled out a dark blue stone about the size and shape of an egg. He handed it to Marissa.

'It's for you. I went out in my lunch hour and visited the Angel Shop and asked Mairead if she had anything I could give you for support and protection. She said it was lapis lazuli, the stone I mean. It sounds like a poem I had to study when I did the Leaving Cert.'

Marissa remembered the poem by Yeats. It was obscure, yet she was still drawn to it. She looked at the blue stone in her hand, still warm from Matt's pocket. It was quite beautiful, with large patches of deep blue etched with lines of gold and grey, speckles of grey and white and a few white spots, but mostly swirls and lines of gold, grey and a beautiful rich blue. She moved it in the light and saw the gold glinting.

'Mairead said that she felt this was what you needed. It will help you anchor into your deeper wisdom.'

Marissa nodded as she touched the soft polished stone, rotating it in her hand. It felt snug in her palm. She felt a wave of relaxation rush over her; it was almost like getting into a hot bath. She was much calmer than she had felt, well, since she had seen Martin the week before in Cabra.

'Yes,' she said. 'I do feel better.' She turned to Matt and smiled. 'Thank you. I'm calmer now. I think I'll hold onto this stone for a while.'

Matt looked at her and smiled. The relief in his face was palpable. His eyes softened and glistened with emotion. 'I'm so glad it has helped. I really am worried about you.'

'I trust my guides – they've been right every time. They must have told Mairead which stone to get for me. Lapis lazuli – what an unusual name, and what a beautiful, unusual stone. Thank you, Matt. I hope it wasn't too expensive?'

Matt blushed. 'You're worth it. And I know Mairead wouldn't sell me a dud!'

Marissa laughed. 'Of course not. Thank you, love.' She reached over and kissed Matt on the cheek, but he had turned his head, so she got his nose instead. 'It's late now and we both have work tomorrow, so let's go to bed, the three of us – you, me and the lapis lazuli!'

It was dark. Marissa was walking down a corridor which glimmered from the light of torches which hung on walls so high they seemed to touch the sky. She was barefoot and wearing a pink silk tunic embroidered with gold edgings. She stopped walking and touched the wall, engraved upon them were carvings – shapes and figures, different sizes, different symbols. She ran her fingers over and into them, noticing there was gold inlaid on some of them. The light of the torches danced, giving life to the figures, making them seem animated. She traced the etchings once more then pulled away, looking up to see if she was outside or inside, if it was daytime or night-time, but she couldn't see the sky.

She heard someone whisper, 'Come along, we're going to be late.'

She followed the others – for now there were others – as they went down the corridor and emerged into a large chamber, also lit by torches, with many people in it.

The chamber floor was strewn with red and pink roses, whose smell was astonishingly beautiful and strong. The quality of the light inside the chamber was very different from that of the corridor as it was more open and much brighter. The walls had etchings on them too, and in the stronger light, Marissa could see they were hieroglyphs.

On a raised stone platform in the centre of the chamber was a large white marble bath filled to the brim with a white milky substance. Rose petals, leaves and small sticks were floating on top, almost spilling over and onto the floor. It was quite beautiful, Marissa had never seen anything like it.

As Marissa observed the room she realised all the other people there were women. They looked almost identical, they wore white dresses with gold trimming and had long, thick black hair piled up elaborately in different styles on top of their heads, thick locks of hair held in place by golden clasps. They were all wearing gold necklaces, gold bracelets and gold rings which were inlaid with deep blue stones. 'Lapis lazuli!'

The women's faces were heavily made up so it was difficult to judge their ages; thick black kohl pencil adorned their eyes, deep red blusher on their cheeks. Blood red lipstick and sparkling green paint on their eyelids made them seem regal. Three of them turned towards Marissa and started to remove her clothing. Marissa wanted to struggle but her insides said, 'Yes, this is what is supposed to be,' so she allowed them remove her pink tunic. She was naked beneath it. One of the women held out her arm and Marissa wrapped hers around it and was led to the bath. Another of the women brought a wooden step over to the bath and Marissa was encouraged to step up onto it and get into the bath, which she carefully did.

Marissa sank into the warm milky liquid and nobody seemed to mind that some of it sloshed onto the floor. It was blissful; every muscle in her body relaxed as soon as the liquid touched against her skin. The liquid seemed to penetrate her, as it entered her body it soothed and released the deeply held anxiety and fear she had been carrying. The woman who had led her to the bath stood behind her and placed her hands on her shoulders. 'Deep breath,' she said, and Marissa took a breath and held it and the woman pushed her under, the volume of her body forcing even more liquid and petals to slosh out of the bath and spill out onto, and be absorbed somehow, by the floor. She could hear the women around her clapping their hands together and whispering. It wasn't scary anymore, it felt like an initiation, a baptism. The hands were removed from her shoulders, but Marissa stayed under, enjoying the sensation of being completely covered in the warm, nourishing liquid. She felt her mind relaxing too, just like the muscles in her body. It felt like being inside a womb, safe and warm. She felt the presence of the women around her and she wasn't in a rush to leave. But she needed to take a breath, so she eventually surfaced.

The women laughed. Their laugher sounded like bells tinkling and Marissa smiled. She felt safe. She stretched out in the bath, admiring the length of her limbs, how they seemed longer and harder than they usually were, hard as if she had been in training and was now stronger than she expected to be, battle ready.

'Come now, let us dress you.'

Marissa was reluctantly helped out of the bath and taken over to a corner of the chamber where she was patted dry with sumptuous white towels. Scented oil was poured all over her body. It smelled of roses. The women rubbed it into her skin as she stood there vulnerable and naked, allowing them to do it. She felt their gentle loving touch as they made sure not one patch of her skin went uncovered. Marissa stroked her own arm and discovered it was soft to the touch, not sticky. The oil had been absorbed completely into her skin and she was completely dry.

One of the women brought her a new robe. This one was white. She gently lifted it over Marissa's head and it flowed smoothly over her whole body. Golden bracelets were placed on her wrists and her upper arms, she was given a large golden necklace with a pendant shaped like a cross with a loop at the top, and golden rings were placed on her fingers, rings without stones, just pure gold with hieroglyphs similar to those on the walls.

Marissa was taken to a golden chair and invited to sit, which she did. The women adorned her hair and painted her toenails and fingernails a dark blood red. They made up her face to match theirs with kohl and powders. Leather-thonged golden sandals were placed lovingly on her feet.

Everything was vivid, lucid, clear... It didn't feel like a dream, or a shamanic journey, it felt very, very real.

Once the women were happy with how Marissa looked they beckoned her to follow them out of the chamber, leaving everything else behind.

They walked down the corridor in procession. Some of the women in front had picked up small baskets filled with rose petals and were strewing them on the floor with every step. As Marissa followed she could hear the women's soft singing echoing off the high walls. Their shadows danced in the torchlight.

This time Marissa could see that the hieroglyphs covered the entire wall. She craned her neck once more to try to see the apex, but the walls were so high up, and in this light, it was impossible.

The procession came out of the corridor and entered a large bright chamber and the singing, oh the singing, it was marvellous. The sound echoed off the stone walls and the stone floor. It was uplifting, raising Marissa's spirits, making her freshly washed and oiled body tingle right through to her bones.

As the procession moved into the centre of the chamber she saw a giant throne made of marble; it was engraved with beautiful glyphs of the sun, the moon, the Earth, animals and unfamiliar symbols. The throne was completely embossed with gold. Standing beside it was the most beautiful woman Marissa had ever seen. She was tall, taller than everyone else; the throne had obviously been made for her. Words could not possibly describe her beauty. On seeing her Marissa wanted to throw herself down on the ground and grovel at her feet. She was about to do it when she noticed that the other women in her procession were actually doing it. She knelt, ready to lie down and prostrate herself in front of this, well, goddess. She must be a goddess, for she was immense and magnificent, with unearthly beauty and such power.

The goddess smiled and waved her hand in the air. The music stopped and the chamber fell silent.

'Tori Scarlett Lightbringer, I call upon you, my priestess of Isis. Have you returned to us, my sweet one, as this Marissa Tori Rosenthal?'

For a moment Marissa didn't realise she was being addressed. Then something in her head clicked, as if a switch had flicked on, and a part of her woke up. She suddenly knew where she was and she knew who this was, and she answered loud, proud and clear, 'O Great Mother Isis, yes it is I, returned to you once more.'

She heard her own voice and felt disconnected from it, an observer in her own body.

'At last, girl – I thought you'd never come back to me! Get up off the floor, come over here, let me look at you!' The goddess sat down on the throne and waited patiently, with a warm smile on her face.

Marissa, with great difficulty, peeled herself up from the floor. The other women had also risen. Feeling their eyes on her, Marissa felt very small as she (or was it her?) walked in front of everyone to stand at the great goddess's feet. Only here could she comprehend the sheer size of this chamber and the size of the remarkable, beautiful goddess who was now right in front of her.

'My, my, you have shrunk,' the goddess said. 'This is not my Tori Scarlett Lightbringer! I do not recognise you. What has happened to you?'

She knelt down and looked into Marissa's face. She blew on her, and Marissa started to cry, and just like Alice when she ate the mushroom, she started to grow larger. She grew until she was three-quarters of the size of the goddess herself.

'Ahh, that's better. I can see you better now. Tell me, how is life on Planet Earth these days? What can I do to lighten your load? I see I need to remind you of who you really are. Well, I am here now, so it will all be set to rights.'

'I was recognised before I remembered myself,' said Marissa, then something opened in her heart and she felt a rushing of regret.

The goddess looked very serious. 'This is a real problem,' she said, nodding her head. 'We need to rewind a little bit, give you some more time – Marissa, isn't it? Your incarnation?'

'Yes, I am Marissa,' said Marissa, puzzled. It seemed as if she was answering not just as herself but as two different people.

'You have brought her here with you? That is some amazing feat! How did you manage to do that?' asked the goddess.

Now Marissa was truly puzzled. 'Yes, she is here with me, she is I and I am she, she awakened and so I could not leave her behind.' The voice came from her mouth, but it didn't feel like her voice.

'Tori, my darling,' said the goddess, 'we will have to help little Marissa remember she is one of my greatest champions. How will she be able to hold that in her tiny heart?'

She laughed, and her laughter was loud and strong and rippled out many frequencies and vibrations. It shook the whole chamber and echoed and reverberated around the walls, the torches flickered and Marissa noticed for the first time that the chamber was triangular, a pyramid.

'I'm inside a pyramid?'

The goddess stopped laughing and faced Marissa, looking at her with her gentle and kind eyes. 'Yes, my love, you are inside the greatest of all pyramids in my lands of Egypt. You are my high priestess, my light-bringer, my champion. You will remember eventually. And as my Tori says, you have been recognised. So I need to help you. And I have come. Or should I say, you have come to me, and I am grateful for it. Your guides have done well. We have much work to do.'

'Who is Tori?'

'Why, she is you – is that not your name?'

'Erm, yes ... middle name...'

'So there you are. Are you going to argue with a goddess?'

Marissa became worried she had done something wrong for the goddess looked stern, but then she started laughing again. Marissa relaxed and started laughing too, but she still felt a quiver of tension.

'It is good that we meet,' the goddess told her. 'Your spirit ancestors are powerful women. I admire them very much. But they are not goddesses, like me. They are brave, they came and found me and told me what was going on. Now I have come. I am here. Now we have met. Now you have been cleansed and you are clear of influence. I must next consult my teacher and together we will decide how you must proceed. But for now, you are protected. That demon-spawn son-of-the-devil will not be able to find you or remember who you are, or know that you are incarnate, for now. But this will not last forever. And in the meantime, we must gather strength.'

'Now child, I must go – Thoth awaits. It has been a blessing and a gift to see you again. All you need to do is call my name and I will be there.'

Isis stooped down as Marissa had started shrinking again. She blew on her face and then kissed her forehead. 'We will prevail if we are strong,' she whispered and then she vanished, leaving Marissa with a feeling of loss. It was as if a massive part of herself had left with the goddess. She noticed she had shrunk back to the same size as the other women in the room. One of them came up to her with a goblet of wine. 'Drink,' she said.

Marissa drank, then everything went black.

She woke up shivering and cold. Matt had taken the duvet and was snoring in the bed beside her. The sky was dark. She looked at her phone: 4.33am. She got up and stretched and there was the thud of something heavy hitting the floor. *The lapis lazuli!* She had been holding it the whole time, she had dropped it on the floor without realising it. She got down on her hands and knees, felt around for it and found it again. Her hand was stiff from being wrapped around it, but she still wasn't ready to let it go.

Matt hadn't stirred notwithstanding all her noise. Marissa grabbed her cardigan and the throw from the sofa and went to sit in her chair in garden in the dark. Tobermory came with her, his white streak catching in the moonlight as they stepped outside.

Marissa pulled on her cardigan then dragged out the chair and opened it. Then she wrapped the throw around herself and sat down, and Tobermory, for the second time in his life, leapt up onto the deckchair. He settled down on her lap, started purring immediately and fell asleep on her. His presence was comforting.

So much to think about. But how do I feel? And who is Tori Scarlett Lightbringer? Is she really me?

CHAPTER THREE

Marissa woke up feeling stronger in herself, if a little cold, and stiff. She was still in the deckchair outside. Tobermory, sensing she was awake, stretched and leapt down from her lap, and waited patiently for her at the door. Matt hadn't even realised she'd gone; when Marissa went into the bedroom and took off her cardigan, he stirred in the bed and turned onto his side.

Marissa ran the shower and got in. the hot water brought her body back to life. As she washed herself she remembered sinking her body into the big milky bathtub filled with rose petals. Her limbs didn't seem as long or as toned as they had been in her dream. *Was it a dream? A journey?* She wasn't sure. All she knew was that she felt much happier than she had felt in a very long time. *Demon? What demon?! He could go take a running jump. No demons are welcome here. No more!* She smelled the suds on her body, then looked at the label on her shower gel. It said 'freshness', but it didn't smell of anything much. She resolved to get herself some rose-scented soap or something similar next time she went shopping. Wrapping a towel around her head and another around her body, she brushed her teeth. She could hear Matt moving about in the bedroom.

'Hey, Matt, will you leave that occult book with me? I want to take another look at it when I have some quiet time.'

'Sure. And you'll contact Dolores today, won't you, and get her to take a look at you?'

'Promise. I feel different today, though, stronger. I dreamed I was inside a pyramid and met the goddess Isis. She spoke to me. It felt so real.'

'I love it when that happens,' he replied, coming over to her and kissing the back of her neck.

Marissa shivered and smiled. 'Isis said she would look after everything,' Marissa had strength and certainty in her voice, for the first time in a very long time.

Matt smiled at her. 'As long as you're feeling better, love, that's all I'm worried about. Hey, I've got to run – I've my car with me, but the traffic is starting to build up. I'll call you later? You're okay to be here on your own tonight?'

Marissa didn't hesitate. 'Yes. I've got my lapis, I've got Tobermory, I've got the goddess, and I've got your book to read. I'll be just fine.'

Marissa was still feeling happy at work. Around 4pm she got very hungry, though, and realised that she hadn't eaten very much in the last few days. She decided to visit her parents after work and catch up on the latest news, and maybe get a home-cooked meal while she was there.

As she walked around the corner towards their house she noticed that there was a different car filling up the narrow driveway. She rang the doorbell, still puzzling over the car, and her dad answered it. He was preoccupied, in conversation with someone in the kitchen and had a bottle of unopened wine in his hand. He turned to her and smiled widely. 'Oh, hello, love! Great to see you! Come on in!'

There was loud music and talking coming from the kitchen. *There's obviously more than one person here.* Marissa stepped over the threshold, wondering what was going on. A loud pop and a fizz came from inside and then clapping. *Not wine – champagne! What are we celebrating?*

She could hear her mother's laughter, and when she stepped into the room, she saw her her father pouring the champagne into glasses. Uncle Lou and Aunty Naomi were there, Marissa smiled, delighted to seem them, they seemed delighted to see her, too.

'Come in, Marissa. Would you like some champagne?' Her dad looked through the cupboards for another champagne glass, to no avail. He held a small glass in his hand and asked apologetically, 'Will a tumbler do?'

Marissa nodded, still puzzled and now very curious. Bernie poured the last of the champagne into a small whisky tumbler and placed the empty bottle on the countertop. Then he turned to the group, lifted one of the glasses and said in a loud voice: 'A toast! To Louis, for once more taking us out of the fire! This time I tell you I have absolutely no guilt whatsoever in accepting this grand gift, this fine gesture.'

'Hooray, hooray!' said Rose, looking as if she was drunk even before she lifted the glass to her lips. Naomi was beaming. Louis raised his glass in return, as did Marissa, and they all drank together.

'What did I miss?' whispered Marissa to her dad as Louis and Naomi clinked glasses with Rose once more.

'Can we tell her?' asked Bernie, turning to the others.

'Of course! We work hard so our children can bask in our glory!' said Louis, moving over to embrace Marissa.

'Hello, love,' said Rose to her daughter. 'Your Uncle Louis has ensured that we are now completely out of debt, and have a little gelt put aside for a getaway too! Isn't that wonderful news?'

Marissa didn't think she had heard correctly. She untangled herself from her uncle and put her glass down. She remembered he had said there would be more money coming, but to take her parents completely out of debt? That was something else altogether. She looked at the faces in the room, seeing their smiles so bright they almost lit up the world, and she realised they were serious.

'Wow!' she said with a sideways grin, as it sank in. 'That's amazing!' She looked around the room again. She hadn't seen her father's eyes so bright in many years. He reached out to her mother, who took his hands, and they squealed like children and started dancing around the kitchen. Louis clapped his hands and Naomi hugged Louis and invited him to dance with her too. Marissa was overcome with emotion. Never had she seen so much joy all in the one room – the joy of these adults she loved so dearly. To see them here, so relieved, made her realise how much stress her father must have been under all these years, how hard he had had to work to make ends meet. She knew how jealous he had been of his brother, who seemed to make money without even raising his little finger. But here he was, dancing with her mother, who also looked happier than she had seen her, maybe ever. Their happiness brought tears to Marissa's eyes, big hot fat tears trickled down her cheeks and onto her shirt. Her father, with a brightness in his smile that had been missing for so long, her father, who had protected her when she was in crisis, who would do anything for her, oh yes, he deserved this, especially at this time of his life, even if the money had come from his brother.

Slowly raising her glass and what was left in it, Marissa caught Louis's eye and said out loud, 'To Uncle Louis, the hero of the family!' She smiled, then everyone laughed, even her mother, and they all clinked glasses and drank once more.

'Well, it's not really me,' Louis said, suitably bashful, 'it's consumerism – people just want what I have to offer. Luck! It could change, but I did a few deals, I bought a few companies, sold a few companies, turned a few coins, and now we are on the pig's back, so to speak.'

'A kosher pig!' shouted out Bernie, still dancing.

'Yes, of course! The only kind of pig in Ireland!' said Louis, and they fell about laughing.

I wish Eli could have heard that!

After phoning Eli and getting him and Carol to come join the celebrations, they went to the local restaurant, ordered whatever they wanted, and Louis told them the story (again) of how he made his first million. Then he told the story of how he was on his way to his second million. All the while Eli had his hand on Carol, making sure she was comfortable and had everything she needed. The baby wasn't due for a few months yet, but she was showing, and the family in their joyfulness seemed to finally accept it. Plenty of wine was had, plenty of declarations of love were made, and plenty of gratitude was offered to Louis.

After the food Marissa realised how exhausted she was. When her father suggested ordering another bottle of red, she professed a need to finish an assignment for college, got up and kissed everyone, even Carol, made her excuses and left them to it. She walked back to her flat, full and happy, still trying to process the news and what it meant.

Her flat was peaceful. The book Matt had left behind seemed to glow on the coffee table, but she didn't feel the need to open it. The two angel cards were still on the table too, just as she had left them the day before. Raziel and Haniel. *Dear sweet Haniel.* She suddenly felt so much affection for Haniel that she said out loud, 'Thank you, my lovely angel, for helping me, for keeping me safe. Please watch over me tonight so that I sleep well in my flat, in my space, in my room.' There was something powerful about saying this out loud. She nodded, it felt right, so she said more words out loud: 'This is my space, my flat, my bedroom. No dark energies are welcome here. I say no. No!'

She suddenly had a desire to get her drum so she followed the urge and took her drum down from the mantelpiece, where she had left it. She took out the beater from inside it and started to beat it softly, saying, 'No!' over and over again, becoming louder as she felt her intention growing stronger. She beat the drum in each of the four corners of the living room, over the sofa and by the fireplace. She stood at the kitchen sink and beat it, making the cutlery jump on the draining board with the reverberations. She beat it from the floor to the ceiling, agitating the dust and the dead air, clearing and claiming her space. She became firmer and more certain with every beat. She marched into her bedroom, banging the drum more loudly than she would have dared to on a day when she was worried about the people upstairs. '*No! No! No!*' she shouted as she banged. She even banged the drum in the *en-suite*, by the toilet, the shower... She looked at herself in the mirror and something seemed to have changed. She seemed older somehow. She peered at herself, still banging her drum, but the work was done. It felt complete. She softened, her beating softened, her 'No' softened to a whisper, but stayed strong in its intention.

She went around the flat once more and banged above her desk, then she stood at the spot where the demon had been. She banged her drum once more very loudly here, and then jumped with surprise as there was a banging on the ceiling almost right above where she standing. She laughed! *Just a minute more.* She banged again in response, and then took the drum and one more loud '*No!*' to the garden door. But she felt it wasn't needed. Instead, she opened the door and felt the cold evening air fresh upon her face.

Marissa stood at the threshold, looking at the sky, luminous with light pollution, listening to the neighbourhood children refusing to go to bed. She smiled, thinking of her father's joy earlier that day, her mother's face as they danced. She stepped out onto her deck and sat down on her chair, still holding her shaman's drum. This was her sanctuary.

There was no sign of Tobermory, so Marissa sat with a drum on her lap instead of a cat. It had been a wild ride, she didn't know where she had been but she felt like she was back now. Back in her power, back in the moment, back and ready to face the world. She felt protected and strong and she had reclaimed her space as her own.

She put her hand in her pocket and felt the Lapis egg. Taking it out, she turned it in her hand, looking at the glistening gold sparkling in the dimming light.

'Thank you, Isis. I am so grateful for your help.'

A quiet voice inside her said, 'You're welcome.' *Where was that coming from? My mind? Or was it inside my heart?* She felt a warmth in her stomach which rushed through her whole body. 'Child of mine, you are safe, for now.'

Safe and reclaiming my space. Yes, my drum has spoken. She realised that she had probably upset her upstairs neighbour, but it had to be done. *Thank you beautiful drum, and thank you beautiful white bison from where the drum hath come.* She'd leave her neighbour a note or something tomorrow to apologise for all the noise. Or not.

Her phone started to ring inside the flat. 'Oh, that must be Matt!' she said out loud. She got up and went in, placing her drum gently on the sofa. She reached for her handbag and felt for her phone deep within it, then pulled it out. It *was* Matt.

'Hello! How are you doing? Do you need me to come over, or are you okay?'

You sweet man. Marissa looked at the time. It was pretty late, but she was doing better than okay.

'Hi, Matt, you're so good to think of me. I'm good, really I am. I just was banging my drum in my flat, in each room. I think I was claiming back my space. I felt Haniel here with me and I feel much happier in myself now.'

'Oh good! I'm so tired but I would have come over anyway, like, if you needed me. You know, I do think you need to feel safe, though, on your own. It is your home, after all.'

'Yes, I agree.'

'Did you contact Dolores?'

'Oh! No! I totally forgot. Again! I'll do it tomorrow, but actually, Matt?'

'Yes?'

'I don't know if I want to tell someone else, now that I feel better. If I tell the story again, I might call it all back. I'm feeling good right now and I think I'd prefer to keep things as they are. But hey, I promise I'll talk to her if I get upset again.'

There was a pause on the line before Matt replied. 'Okay, love. Well, you know you can tell me anything, and I'm here if you need me.'

There was a silence on the line. Marissa thought about telling him about the dinner with her family, about the money and the celebrations, but then decided not to. He didn't know much about her family yet and she was tired, too.

'I'm doing fine. Really I am. I'll text you later, or tomorrow?'

'Yes, okay, tomorrow is good. Text or call me then. Sleep well, Marissa.'

'You too, Matt, sleep well.'

Marissa hung up the phone, packed away her cards, put away her drum and put on the kettle. She got into her pyjamas and put on her cardigan. There was a mewing at the window – Tobermory was looking inside from out on the window ledge.

'Hello, lovely cat,' she said, letting him in. He strode onto the worktop flicking his tail, the silver streak on his head glistening in the light. *I wonder where you've been, what you've sacrificed for me. I do truly appreciate it.*

Going through her cupboard Marissa found the tin of tuna fish she knew was at the back of the shelf. She stood at the sink with Tobermory's dinner bowl and opened the can, poring the liquid into his dish, then scooping out the meat with a fork. 'You deserve the best,' she said, and put it down on the floor at her feet.

Tobermory jumped on the food and ate every scrap, lapping up all the liquid, then he sat and cleaned himself. Marissa watched him with a smile on her face and a heart filled with love.

CHAPTER FOUR

Marissa woke a few minutes before her alarm went off and remembered tonight she was in session in Cabra that evening after work. Her heart leapt, then a sudden calmness pervaded her body. She deliberately stretched out her legs, reached her arms up to the sky, and said softly, 'No more of this, all is well and I am safe.' She sat up in bed and reached over to her desk for her counselling notes to refresh her mind on the sessions she was due to have that evening.

Fiachra – two sessions left, new girlfriend, new job, seems happy now.
Cliona – anger issues, working on relaxation.
Martin...

There were no notes for Martin. Just reading his name sent a shiver down her spine. *Was it really only a week ago?* At the faint touch of a memory of what happened the last time with Martin, a heaviness crept into her stomach and she started to feel trapped. She stood up and opened the window. Breathing in the fresh morning air brought her back into the moment. *I suppose I don't have to see him again if I don't want to. They did warn me about him, that he was difficult... But that feels like giving up. He's really a nice guy and it would upset him if I quit on him. No, I won't give up on him. It's not his fault he's got a demon hanging about.*

Another involuntary shiver rippled through her body. Marissa threw down her notes and closed her eyes. *What do I want? No, it's too soon to decide. And I know this – I'm not throwing in all of my training for nothing. I'm not going to stop my client work for some ragamuffin who's trying to scare me.*

By the time Marissa got to Cabra she was resolute in her determination that nothing was going to get in the way of her client work. She entered the building and shook off her umbrella, then walked confidently down the corridor with her head held high. She turned the corner under the archway and went up the back stairs. The higher she got, the softer her footsteps became, as marble was replaced by wood, and then by carpet. Her room, Room Three, was in the loft.

The air on the top floor felt close and musty, there wasn't very much ventilation unless the skylight window was opened, and in February it was still too cold. It had been raining profusely that night, so she couldn't open the window for sure, or the rain would come in. The door to Room Five was ajar so she peeked in. There was a man inside, he looked about twenty five and was wearing a dirty white T-shirt, old jeans and runners. He was swivelling in the chair, hands folded behind his head as if he owned the place, looking up at the ceiling. He swivelled in Marissa's direction, saw her, and smiled.

'Hi there!' he said, breaking into a grin. He got to his feet and extended his hand. 'I'm Dave. Who are you?'

'Marissa,' said Marissa, wondering if this person was a client or a therapist. *Not my client anyway...* 'I'm in the room next door.'

'Great!' Dave said, still smiling. 'I've just started my client sessions. I'm doing a master's in counselling psychology. What's it like working here?'

'Erm, yeah, I like it. I think it takes a bit of getting used to, though. And sometimes the clients don't show up. It's annoying that, but I guess it's par for the course when it's low cost.'

'Yes, fair call,' said Dave, shrugging his shoulders nonchalantly. Marissa wondered if he was the therapist type. *This isn't something you take up as a hobby, you really need to have a calling to be a therapist. He doesn't look like he has one...* Dave was smiling at her, as if waiting for her to continue the conversation.

'Anyway,' she said, brushing away her judgemental thought as soon as she caught it, 'maybe I'll see you later then.'

Marissa gratefully opened the door to Room Three and went in, turning on the light. She draped her wet coat over the radiator, hung her bag on the back of the door, and then closed the door behind her. She took a moment to sense what the energy in the room was like, but she didn't feel anything off. *I should have brought my drum. I could reclaim this space just like I reclaimed my flat.* She moved around the room, straightening the pictures on the wall, blowing the dust off the table and rearranging the books and candles. *I guess that's another way of claiming space...* She chose one of the chairs and sat down, then lit a candle. She felt strangely peaceful, considering how upset she had been the last time she'd been here. *I've got this.*

There was a knock on the door. Marissa jumped, then looked at the little clock on the table. *It's too early for clients. Who is it?*

The door opened and it was Dave.

'Sorry to bother you – hey, nice room! Looks just like mine. Funny that. Anyway, do you know where the kitchen is? I'm dying for a cuppa.'

'It's complicated. Actually, I wouldn't mind one myself. I'm a little early, so I'll come down with you and show you for next time.' Marissa got up from her chair and led Dave down the corridor, down the back steps, through the ground floor and into the kitchen.

'Jeez, I'm glad you came with me – I'd never have found it, it's like a labyrinth in here.'

Marissa smiled as she filled the electric kettle, dug out two mugs from the cupboard and popped a tea bag into each. 'I hope you don't take milk,' she said, looking in the fridge and frowning. 'It seems this one is out of date.'

'Oh crap,' said Dave. 'Yeah, I take milk. Sugar too. Is there any coffee?' He went to the cupboard and pulled out an old packet of digestives, some honey and a newspaper. 'The honey might work.'

'What's counselling psychology?' asked Marissa, as she waited for the kettle to boil.

'I'm doing a psychology degree and there's an option to study counselling. It helps psychologists become more accessible to people. I think, anyway.'

'Oh,' said Marissa, 'I always wondered about the differences between psychotherapy, psychology, psychiatry and counselling.'

'Well, I'll find out about counselling now that I'm in the proverbial hotseat,' said Dave, rooting around in the drawer for a spoon that looked clean enough to dip into the honey pot. 'Do you want some honey too?'

'I'm grand, thanks, I got used to having it black.'

The kettle clicked off and Marissa lifted it and poured the boiled water into both cups.

'You know, I've heard many different definitions of each of those and I'm still not sure what sits right with me. Anyway, nice talking to you. I'm going to head back upstairs, I've got some prep to do before my clients come.'

'Clients? You've more than one tonight?' asked Dave, stirring the sticky substance into the hot liquid.

'You probably should have taken the tea bag out first!' laughed Marissa.

'Yes, I was just thinking that,' he said and grinned.

'I've got three tonight,' Marissa said, 'if they all show up. Even when they're in process with me, if they feel like they're doing okay, they won't come in.' The wind picked up outside, they could hear the echo in the walls.

Dave nodded his head in agreement. 'And when the weather is as bad as tonight I'm sure staying home and watching TV is much more attractive than bracing the weather and spilling your guts out to someone. I've been waiting for almost an hour now, wasn't sure if I should hang on, but after listening to you I should probably go home. But this tea, well, it's made the whole experience of being here tonight worthwhile. And, of course, meeting you.' He looked up at her with a cheeky grin.

'Thanks,' she said in a noncommittal way. 'Well, got to go. See you next time.'

Walking back to her room, trying not to spill her tea, Marissa was grateful for the distraction Dave had provided. Just before she entered the room she felt a wave of anxiety flood her stomach, lapping over her legs like prickles and rushing up her chest, making her feel woozy. She breathed it out then opened the door, put down her cup and moved her coat which was a little dryer, from the radiator onto the hook on the back of the door. As soon as she sat down her mobile beeped a text from Matt:

> Hi love, just checking in, hope u had a good day. Happy Valentines - sorry didn't get u anything, will make it up 2u, promise.

There was a soft knock on the door and Marissa looked up. 'Fiachra, hi. Great to see you. Come in.' She switched her phone on silent and put it back into her bag.

'Oh, you just made tea? I'd love a cup.'

'I've not had any yet – here, you can have mine. There's no milk, though. Do you take it black?' *Feck it, you're not supposed to have tea in a client session, this is off to a bad start. Oh well, I guess anything goes tonight.*

'Actually yeah, that would be lovely, thanks. Are you sure?'

'Certainly. Do come in and sit down. How are you this evening?'

The session with Fiachra was, as Marissa's tutor would have said, mostly roads and weather. She checked Dave's room and he was gone. Marissa felt a little bereft. It would have been nice to have had someone else in the building with her, just in case. *In case of what?*

After the session Marissa took Fiachra's mug down to the bathroom, used the facilities and left the mug beside the sink as she made her way back to her therapy room. Cliona was waiting outside. Her make-up was loud and her mini-skirt was, well, mini. She had chewing gum in her mouth and was making snapping sounds with her lips.

'Hi, Cliona, come in.' Marissa smiled and held the door open, Cliona went in ahead of her and sat down on the chair she had just been sitting in.

'The woman downstairs let me in, so I just came straight up,' she explained.

'No bother.' Marissa closed the door behind her and sat facing Cliona in the opposite chair. 'How have you been? What can I do for you this evening?'

Cliona fiddled with a bright pink lock of hair that had fallen down in front of her face and crossed her fishnet-clad legs in front of her.

'Er...'

'How are things at home?'

Cliona didn't say anything.

This isn't like her. 'Has something happened?'

Cliona shook her head, then exclaimed loudly, 'I can't *believe* it! Of all the things...' then she hid her face in her hands and started rocking her body in the chair. It looked as if she was crying.

Oh no! Marissa wasn't sure what would be better, to probe further or give Cliona some space. She opted for the latter. She sat back in her chair and held her open hands palm up on her lap, an indicator for Cliona to speak. Cliona didn't appear to get the signal, though, so after a few moments, Marissa asked in a gentle tone, '*What* can't you believe?'

Cliona looked up. 'We had it sorted, you and me. I mean, we knew what to do with me, didn't we? And I tried, really I tried, and it was all going so great. Fuck's sake! I can't believe it. I really can't fuckin' believe it.'

There was silence again. Normally Marissa was great with silence, but this time it began to really irritate her and she didn't know why. *Where's my compassion? What is going on with me?* Irritation, hot and itchy, crept like an animal up her legs and into her lower back. It was difficult to sit still – she wanted to stand up and shake it off, but she couldn't. She tried to breathe it out, but it didn't make any difference. She felt as if she had a traffic jam in her head, trying to manage the sensations in her body and facilitate Cliona at the same time. Then Cliona stood up and started pacing around the room, and the sensations left Marissa's body almost as quickly as they had arrived. *Very strange, but that's a relief.*

'Okay. It's hard to say this, but I know I can say it to you, right?'

'Yes, of course,' Marissa said, just relieved to be feeling more at ease in her body. *Was I picking this agitation up from Cliona?*

'Okay. Well, I just did the test, just now like. Before I left the house to come here. My nan is minding Ariana and I had to run out the door, I couldn't look her in the face. Nan, I mean. I don't know what to do. I'm actually shaking right now, look.' She held out her hand, but for all intents and purposes, Marissa couldn't see if it was shaking or not.

Marissa had a feeling around what Cliona was trying to say, but she made space for her to get the whole thing out rather than filling in the gaps or second guessing.

'I can't get my head around it,' said Cliona, pulling her hand back in and continuing to pace the room. She suddenly stopped walking and slapped herself on the head, hard. She turned to a shocked Marissa (who was trying not to show it) and said, 'I mean, of all the stupid, ridiculous things to happen to me. You'd think I'd paid it all back by now, whatever it was that I did to deserve this.' A large tear rolled down her cheek. 'I really don't deserve this. Again! Why again? For fuck's sake!'

The tears were flowing more freely now, smudging Cliona's make-up. Marissa reached for a tissue and stood, handing it to her. 'Please, don't hurt yourself,' she said in a compassionate tone. 'Come back and sit down, and tell me what it is, get the words out.'

'Okay,' said Cliona, blowing her nose and making her way back to the chair. She collapsed into it, blew her nose again and reached for another tissue, using the first one to wipe the tears and the second to wipe away the make-up stains. She sat forward in the chair, then put her head in her hands and her elbows on her knees and looked straight at Marissa. She pulled a white plastic stick out of her bag and shoved it towards her.

'Look at it. I'm fuckin' pregnant.'

Marissa stared at the stick. She hadn't seen one before, bar on TV. She didn't want to touch it, didn't know what she was supposed to be looking at. *But that doesn't matter. I need to stay with Cliona, give her the space she needs to talk about how she feels.*

'I'm just so angry at myself, and at the world.' Cliona put the stick back into her bag and shivered. 'I mean, here's the thing – it isn't Bren's. I know it's not his because, well, because we haven't been together since we broke up that time before Christmas. He wanted us to take it slowly this time and made a point of not sleeping with me.' She started crying again. 'I've been trying really hard, Marissa, doing those exercises you set for me, but I'm so goddamned angry now, there's no way I can relax!' She made a fist with her left hand and punched the air.

Marissa didn't flinch. Not taking her eyes off Cliona, she controlled her breathing and continued to focus on the moment. She said nothing.

Cliona went on, 'It was just the once, I swear it, just that one time. Andy, my brother's friend, he was over around Christmas and we were looking at records. He'd just got in some new vinyl – "Vinyl's coming back," he said. "Ha, ha, well, fuck me," I said, and he did alright. Now I'm totally fucked.' She laughed, 'Would you listen to me? I'm fucked, Marissa. Brendan will leave me again when he finds out, and this time he'll never come back.'

Marissa didn't want to placate Cliona; a counselling session wasn't the place for that. *But where do I go with this?*

'You're right, Cliona,' she said. 'It isn't funny or easy to be in this situation. And it's okay to be angry. So, you've not told anyone else about this yet?'

'No. Like I said, I just did the test. You're the first person I've told.'

'Perhaps you need some time to process the news, to figure out what you are going to do?'

'Damn right I do. Sorry, Marissa, it's not your fault. I just get so angry sometimes, and I'm really angry now.'

'It's great, though, that you are able to see it – that means you can control it better than if you didn't know you were angry.'

'So you're saying I've made some progress? Even though I find myself up the duff, I'm still making progress? Ha, ha, life is so fucked up sometimes.'

'It can seem that way, yes.' Marissa tried not to smile but she couldn't help herself.

Cliona turned to Marissa and looked at her earnestly. 'What do *you* think I should do?'

She took a breath. 'Cliona, you know I can't tell you what to do. But we can talk about it until *you* feel clearer in your mind about what your options are, so you can make a decision for yourself.'

'Well I don't think I can make any decision right now.'

'That's a good idea. Take some time to get your head around it.'

Cliona cradled her head in her hands. 'Oh shit, Marissa. This is the last thing I wanted to be doing right now, having another baby. What will Nan think? "Always you with your drama, always something going wrong in your life..." She's right, too. Why can't I just have a normal life?'

Cliona's hands were clenching, making fists.

'Cliona, I can see you're getting even angrier right now,' Marissa said, stopping her midstream. 'Would you like to try something with me?'

'What?'

'Stand up for a moment. I'll stand up too.'

Both women stood up. Marissa took the cushion from her chair and placed it on Cliona's chair, so that chair had two cushions on it.

'There, it's a punchbag now. Who would you like to punch first? Or what?'

Cliona cocked her head sideways. 'What d'you mean?'

'Well, what are you angry at in particular? Can you name it?'

'My body for being pregnant.'

Marissa started. It didn't seem right to invite Cliona to punch the cushions and pretend she was punching her own body. She had to try a different tack.

'Okay, why don't you feel how strong the anger is that you are feeling right now and then punch the cushions to get it out?'

'Like this?' Cliona punched the cushions on the chair. The first one bounced right out and landed on the floor.

This isn't really working the way I imagined.

'Maybe not like that. Hang on.' Marissa rearranged the cushions in the chair so they were side by side instead of one on top of the other. 'Try again?'

'This is stupid,' said Cliona. 'How is punching a cushion going to help me stop being pregnant?'

'It isn't,' said Marissa, 'but it might tire you out, it might get the anger out of your body, it might help you calm down so you can figure out what to do, instead of feeling angry and trapped.'

'Ah. Yeah, you're right there,' said Cliona, her hands making fists again, 'I fuckin' do feel trapped. Okay, this is for feeling trapped.' She punched the cushion again. 'And this is for you, Brendan, you fucker, for not sleeping with me.' This time the punch was harder. 'And this one is for Andy, for taking advantage of me. Yeah, you bastard!' She punched even harder and the chair teetered backwards on two legs, then righted itself. The tears were drying up now that Cliona was focusing on punching. 'This is for Nan, for her judgemental, righteous attitude towards me!' Punch. Cliona walked around the room, shaking her hands. 'That hurt!' she said to Marissa. 'But I'm beginning to feel a little bit better. Can I do it again?'

Thank God it's working. 'Yes, of course. We have plenty of time left.'

The cushion took blows for Brendan again, then Andy, then Brendan again, then Cliona's father, whom she had never met, then Brendan again, then Ariana's father, for leaving in the first place, and then once more for Andy. By this time Cliona was exhausted.

Marissa took the poor cushions off the chair, shook them out, put one back in her own chair and handed the other one to Cliona.

'Hey, Marissa,' said Cliona as she sat back down, adjusting the cushion behind her, 'that was great. Really. I feel much better now. I'm still fucked, but I feel better.' She blushed. 'Sorry for all the swearing.'

'That's okay. Really, I don't mind it. As long as you feel better. That's the main thing.'

'Yeah. So I won't lose it later on with Ari. Or even with Nan. Hey, I don't have to tell anyone else today, do I?'

'No, of course not,' said Marissa. 'Not until you're ready to.'

Cliona thought about it for a while. 'We have another session next week, don't we? I can wait until then to decide what to do, and then we can talk about it, can't we?'

'It's up to you. You might want to talk about it with someone else in the next few days. You need to do what's right for you.'

'Thanks, Marissa. I know you can't help me deal with this, but in a way you have helped me deal with it already, if you know what I mean.'

Marissa smiled. 'I think so. Do you want a tissue for the road?'

'Honestly, no, I'm good. I'm all cried out now, for now, I think. And I'm not as angry. This was a good session.' Cliona got up and put on her coat. 'You're a good therapist, Marissa. I hope you know that.'

Marissa smiled, but said nothing.

'See you next week.'

Cliona let herself out.

Poor Cliona, what a thing to happen. Oh no, that's a judgement, isn't it? I'm full of judgements tonight. Sigh. I don't feel like a good therapist...

The room felt damp somehow. Marissa felt the need to burn sage to clear it.

Martin next. She felt nerves in her stomach building up again. She hoped perhaps something had happened and he wouldn't come this time. But another part of her wanted to see him, to know if he was okay. She wanted to tell him everything that had happened, but she knew she couldn't, or she would breach the boundary between therapist and client. No, she wouldn't tell him. *Martin, you're a funny fish... I wish I could see Spirit the way you do.* 'But you *can* see Spirit,' said a whisper in her mind. 'Just not with your eyes.'

Not knowing quite what to do with that, she sat down in the chair that had suffered Cliona's beating. She lit a fresh candle and looked into the wick, trying to focus on the different colours of the burning light.

'Have you read *The Wonderful Story of Henry Sugar*?' said a voice from behind the door. 'And can I come in?'

Marissa's heart leapt. 'Martin?'

'Yes.'

The door opened and Martin appeared. His face was soft, vulnerable almost, as if he had been crying. He came in and hung his coat on the back of the door beside hers. *Hmmm, he usually sits down with it still on.* He went to the chair and sat down.

'I saw you staring into the candle. Did you ever read that story?'

'*Henry Sugar*?' asked Marissa. 'No, I've never even heard of it before.'

'*The Wonderful Story of Henry Sugar* – it's wonderful,' Martin said. He smiled, his eyes twinkled and his face lit up the room. 'See, I made a joke!'

He looks well, better than I've ever seen him.

'You look well,' said Marissa with a smile.

'Thanks, Marissa. Yes, I'm feeling well too. I've had the best week I've had in a long time. For as long as I can remember, in fact.' He shifted in his chair. 'Last week's session was very strange for me. For you too, I think.'

Marissa could only nod. She didn't want to put anything into words. *Not just yet, anyway.*

'Can I be candid with you?'

'Of course.' Marissa's breath was quickening, her hand was gripping the arm of her chair, her nails digging into it. She hoped that Martin wouldn't notice.

'I think I was possessed. I know that sounds weird, but I really do think I was. And I believe that since last week, I've not been possessed anymore. Something happened in here, with you. I don't remember what it was. But do I remember I needed to go home and rest afterwards, and I slept for nearly two days straight. And when I woke up, I felt – well, clear. Level-headed. More like myself. Only I don't actually remember being myself. This has been going on for so long.' He shook his head. 'I'm sure it makes no sense to you. Sorry. But I have to get it out. Maybe the words aren't right, though?'

He looked at Marissa, trying to judge her response. She had relaxed her tight grip on the arm of the chair. *He's absolutely right, something very strange did happen last time. It's reassuring that he's aware of it. How aware is he?*

'You don't remember anything?'

'No. All I know is that I don't hear voices in my head now. That I can sleep at night – like, I actually fall asleep! And last night I had a dream. I was back at school, primary school, playing with the headmaster's cat. I loved that cat. She was so beautiful – black, with a streak of silver across her head like she'd been hit by lightning.'

Marissa's hand involuntarily gripped the chair again. This was hitting close to her heart. It felt like too much too soon.

But Martin was smiling. 'I feel happy, Marissa, and I think it's because of something you did. I don't know what it was, but I wanted to say thank you.'

'Oh,' said Marissa, as if waking from a dream. 'Well, there's nothing to thank me for – not that I know of, anyway.'

Martin changed position in his chair. 'Thanks, though. I want to say it now because I won't be coming back to see you. This is our last session.'

Marissa sat up straighter and opened her mouth, then closed it again.

'It isn't you,' Martin continued. 'I just need a break. I need some time away from here, from all of this.' He waved his arm around the room. 'I've been coming for so long and I'd never had any relief before. But now, you – well, it's amazing. I can breathe again. My energy is coming back to me. I want to make plans, I want to sing and dance, and maybe meet a girl.' He blushed.

There was a moment's silence.

'I think I know what you mean,' said Marissa slowly, remembering why she didn't want to talk to Dolores, 'and it's okay with me. We only have one more session left this cycle anyway. I'll tell the office for you, so you don't have to.'

Martin lifted his head. 'Would you? Oh, Marissa, that would be great. Really great. Thank you. That would save me having to explain myself.'

He got up and got his coat.

'There's still lots of time tonight,' said Marissa. 'Do you want to talk some more?'

Martin put his arms into the arms of his coat, hoisted it up onto his shoulders and started buttoning it. 'No, no, thank you. I'm very happy. I just came to say goodbye, really.'

Marissa smiled, feeling it was for the best for her also. 'It was lovely to meet you, Martin.'

'Maybe not a pleasure, but definitely an experience,' he said, chuckling.

As he made his way towards the door, Marissa started to get up from her chair to say goodbye.

Martin turned to her. 'Don't rise up, Marissa, not for me. For Isis maybe, but not for me.'

Marissa started, feeling a white heat flashing in front of her eyes and a hot sweat soaking her body. She blinked several times and then the whiteness was gone. And so was Martin.

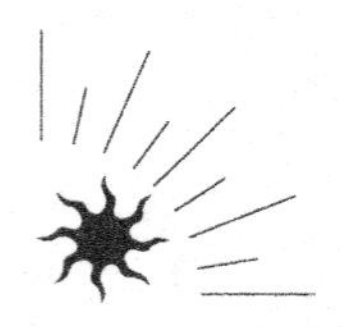

CHAPTER FIVE

How did he know about Isis? What is he going to do now? Will he ever come back to therapy?

Marissa couldn't get last night's session out of her head, but eventually work took over and she became engrossed in a project for Noreen which was due before the end of the day.

Then a text came in from Terry.

I'm in Dublin this weekend, want to meet and do the homework?

Visions of the sofa back in Clifden suddenly appeared in front of Marissa's eyes and her heart started racing. She could see Séamus, his face exaggerated, leering into her face with a toothy grin, saying, 'How are yiz all doing?' The now-familiar feeling of paralysis rippled through her body like a truck, hitting her and knocking her flat. She started shaking. Her breath was shallow and fast, she felt hot sweat dripping down her back. *Another panic attack?* She couldn't focus, she did feel panicked. *I have to get out of here.* She needed to feel the ground beneath her feet, feel her feet in her shoes, feel her legs moving. She got up from her desk and walked out of the office without saying anything to anyone, but Sarah saw her and followed her into the elevator.

'Hey, you okay? You don't look so good.'

As dear as Sarah was becoming to her, Marissa didn't want her there. When she became panicked like this, she wasn't able to speak. She turned her face away. The elevator took forever to reach the ground floor and as soon as the door opened, she shot straight out of it, then out of the main door and onto the concrete surround. She paced in big circles in front of the building, walking briskly and looking straight in front of her, trying to control her breathing.

Sarah followed her, looking genuinely worried. 'You didn't bring your coat – aren't you cold? Do you want me to get your coat for you?'

Marissa stopped for a moment and looked at her, and the compassion in Sarah's eyes was enough to bring tears to her own. Still unable to speak, she just nodded and started walking again.

'I'll be back in a jiff,' Sarah said and ran inside.

Got to calm down. Got to calm down. Marissa repeated the thought over and over as she tried to pull her focus back to the physical sensations she was feeling, but right now the only sensation she could focus on was the feeling of being overwhelmed.

An hour seemed to have passed before Sarah came back and put her coat over her shoulders.

'Marissa, you've really got me worried now. What's happened? What can I do?'

'Walk with me,' whispered Marissa, now looking at the ground. She stopped the circling and together they walked up and down the main street. Sarah pulled her own coat closed and gave Marissa plenty of space, and after ten minutes Marissa felt her body starting to calm down. Her mind was still whirring though. *I thought I was safe, I thought it was over, He's still out there, I know he is, I'm not safe at all, if he wants me he can find me... Oh dear oh dear oh dear...* As she controlled her breathing better her spinning thoughts were still present, just spinning a little bit less quickly. Sarah said nothing and Marissa was grateful for that. She didn't have the energy to explain herself.

After another few minutes Marissa felt her anxiety levels drop a little. *I will be okay, I am protected, I can do this.* Those thoughts really helped her come back to her centre. She slowed her pace, and after another minute or two, she was able to stop walking altogether, although the anxiety still thrummed in the background like a washing machine.

She took a breath before speaking. 'Thanks, Sarah, that really helped.'

Sarah looked pleadingly at Marissa. 'Tell me what's going on.'

'Honestly, Sarah, I'm not able to tell you right now. I'm still trying to make sense of it all and just be able to be here.'

'Is someone hurt? Or sick?'

'Nobody's hurt or sick, and no, Matt hasn't broken up with me.'

Marissa smiled and Sarah took the cue and smiled too. Something inside of her shifted and brought her back more fully to the present moment.

'Okay, then I guess I'll just have to wait until you're ready to talk about it.' said Sarah, unwillingly, with compassion and disappointment in her voice.

'Yes, thank you.' Marissa looked Sarah square in the eye. 'I know how difficult this is for you, and I really appreciate it. I'm using all my reserves right now, I don't have anything left.'

They turned and started walking back towards the office, this time at a much slower pace. Marissa stayed focused on her feet in her shoes, on the ground beneath her feet. *I can do this, I will be okay, I am okay.* It was as if a part of her that was out of control was listening to her reassurance, and wasn't completely buying it. But for now, it would do.

With a little more energy in tow, Marissa could now reassure Sarah, too. 'Sarah, you're a good friend to me. Thank you.'

Sarah took Marissa's hand and squeezed it. 'Hey, I do my best.' She pulled her hand away quickly. 'I meant nothing by that...' she added.

'Yes I know, you're a man's woman, no mistaking it. Don't worry, I won't think you've got a crush on me or anything.' Marissa said, trying to lighten the situation.

'That would never happen,' said Sarah, happy to play along. 'Of course, *you* might have a crush on *me* – but that would be perfectly understandable!' She giggled.

Marissa chuckled. 'No, I don't think so. Not in this lifetime, anyway.'

'Oh? There are other lifetimes?' Sarah seemed genuinely interested.

'I think there might be. I don't know much about this, but I have heard that people can have past lives. Whole other lives as somebody else. Then they die, and get born again, into another body, another family, even another country, language and tradition. It's mad, isn't it? But it might make sense of some of the things that have been happening to me lately. Spiritually. I guess I've been having a spiritual awakening. It's not a pretty thing.'

'Spiritual awakening! Not pretty? But I always thought "spiritual" meant "beautiful and loving". I would have thought a spiritual awakening would be something, well, exhilarating. You do seem upset, though. I wish I could do something to help.'

Marissa looked at her friend. 'Exhilarating is right, for many reasons, not all of them nice ones. And anyway, you're partly to blame for it. It started when I went with you to Peru.'

They were back, standing in front the office building. The compulsion to go back to work was ingrained in them both but they both hesitated, none the less.

'Do you want to go in?' asked Sarah, ignoring the comment about Peru.

'Yeah, I think I'll be okay now. Thanks.'

Sarah looked at her phone to see what time it was. 'There's only a few hours left of the day, and it's Fri-yay, so you could probably skive off a little early, if the manager lets you.' She grinned, knowing full well that Marissa was the manager.

Marissa's eye's twinkled. 'Fri-yay? That's a new one on me.'

'It kind of has a groovy ring to it, don'tcha think?'

Marissa shrugged her shoulders and smiled for real this time, then pushed the door open. The panic was over. Sarah deposited her at her desk.

'So how about a drink, say, in that little place around the corner, in half an hour?'

'Sarah, it's too early, and you know it.'

'You're a tough nut to crack,' she said, half serious and half smiling, 'but it was worth a try.' She winked. 'I'm happy you're feeling better now.'

Marissa *was* feeling better, but it was one of those occasions where time was dragging its heels. Every minute seemed to last an hour, which always happened when she needed to be somewhere else.

She kept looking at the time on her phone. *The earliest I can get out of here is 4:40, I can shut down my computer at 4.30, but it's still ages to wait.* The panic had subsided, but the shock of the experience had not. She was certain she was over it, but to feel her body react as if it was a completely separate part of her was very disconcerting. *If I can't control myself, what* can *I control?* She looked at the work on her computer screen, trying to focus on it gave her a headache. *Coffee, I could make a coffee.* That preoccupied her for about 15 minutes.

Marissa had had panic attacks before, three of them in fact, just after James had left. She remembered every detail of them, well, her body did, anyway. They felt like hell. One of them had been so bad she had gone into convulsions on the floor for an hour, alone in her flat. She actually wanted somebody else to step into her and take control of her body – anything, anything to stop it – she would have let them hit her on the head, tie her down, or strap her to a bed and anesthetise her... It was terrifying, the worst thing that had ever happened to her. Once she recovered from that one she decided she couldn't be left alone, and had moved back with her parents. *I really, really don't want to get that bad again. Not now I've got my life back on track, not now I've almost finished the studying part of my diploma, not now I only need another year or so to become a qualified psychotherapist. Not now, not ever. It's true what they say, the fear of a panic attack can be just as bad as an actual panic attack.* She recalled her client work in Cabra, and then remembered she had promised Martin she'd look after his administration.

She looked at the time again, realising the office in Cabra would be closing soon. *I'll do it now, if I phone today, they might have enough time to organise a new client for me.* 'Yes, I need the hours,' she said to herself, feeling comforted by the sound of her own voice, and by having a purpose. She dialled the number.

'Priory Counselling, Cabra, can I help you?'

'Hi. It's Marissa. I'm one of the volunteers.'

'Oh, hi, Marissa, you caught me just before I closed up for the weekend. What can I do for you?'

'I wanted to let you know that Martin won't be back. He finished his counselling with me, last night.'

'Shall I put him down for a new counsellor?'

Marissa took a moment. Since her listening skills training she'd been seeing signs everywhere of people not listening, and it tended to irritate her.

'Actually, no, he finished with *his* counselling last night. He's taking a break for a while. He doesn't want to see anyone else.'

'Oh! That's unusual for him, he's been coming for six years. Are you sure?'

'Very sure. He asked me if I would pass on the message for him, I'll talk to Mr Blakemore about it in supervision, I just thought if I told you now, you might be able to organise a new client for me in his place, for next week.'

'Oh, yes, I can do that. Certainly. We are very backed-up. I'll have a file ready for you for ... Thursday, is it?'

'Yes. Yes, that would be great. Thank you.'

'Have a lovely weekend.'

She felt more grounded now, and Terry's text still needed answering. Marissa wasn't sure what to do about it. If the memory of the shamanic weekend could set her off like that.... She saw an image of Terry in her mind, throwing his head back and laughing, his eyes twinkling. *Terry...* She really liked him. *Maybe it would be good to see him. But maybe it's too soon for me to do any shamanic work right now – Well, it was his text that triggered a minor panic attack, wasn't it? Yes, it was, but it was minor and I got over it and I am just* fine *now. But maybe I'll give shamanic work a miss for the moment.*

Hi yes would love 2 c u, when u coming 2 Dublin?

The phone beeped a response right away.

I'm on train now, staying with friends in city till Sun. Want 2 meet?

Yes, but no homework. Just coffee?

Oh? Ok. Dinner? Tmrow?

Yes gr8! :-)

Brill ok. Tell u where & when tmrow. Bring ur beau.

Yay!

It was 4:30pm at last. She turned off her computer, and didn't wait for ten minutes after all. She was more than ready to leave. Sarah had already left. Marissa was exhausted, as she went back down in the elevator she realised that her panic attack had taken more out of her than she'd realised. She had planned to visit her parents that night on the way home, but the thought of it weighed her down; her limbs felt heavy imagining herself at their door. No, she needed her own space. She needed to go home to her flat and rest, watch crap TV, and process her emotions. She really needed to sleep.

Marissa picked up a ready meal on her way home and was glad to get in and lock the door behind her. Feeling sticky and dirty from the panic attack, she ran a shower, shed her clothes onto the floor and stepped into the hot spray.

Freshened up and in more comfortable attire, she lay curled up on her bed and reached for her lapis lazuli egg, which was under her pillow. She stayed in the same position for a while, eyes open, mind racing in fits and starts. Then she felt a calmness creeping into her, softly, hesitantly. Like a summer breeze, the sensation of sweetness entered her, softened her, lifted out the tangle of emotions. She felt her body relaxing, felt a pulsing in her hand, the one that held the egg. She felt mute, but relaxed, not like she had been with Sarah earlier. She was more relaxed than before. She couldn't even formulate a thought, there was no language at all, so she couldn't ask her guides what was going on. She didn't even think to ask them, the relief was sublime and she wanted to stay with it. Marissa sighed, and then the wave of love, if that's what it was, came rushing over her again. It was stronger this time, a beautiful, comforting, blissful wave of warmth and love. She imagined a blue cloak being placed around her, with a golden light enclosing her inside it. She slept.

It was 11pm, dark, and Marissa's ready meal was still on the counter top. She got up and padded barefoot around the kitchen, peeling off the lid and putting it in the microwave to heat up. She ate, fed the cat and went back to bed, but now she was awake. She still held the lapis egg, feeling supported by the solid feeling of it in her hand. She turned on her reading light and studied the egg more closely, looking at the depth of the different shades of blues, the streams of white running through it, and the sparkle of the gold in the lamplight. *What a remarkable stone. Is it really natural? My brain feels so muddled, I need to make sense of everything that's going on.*

Grabbing a notebook and pen she got back into bed and opened it. She turned the pages to try and find some white space to write in. Something she had written in a workshop caught her eye, but the words seemed scrambled. She peered at them, as if by looking at them they'd unscramble themselves before her eyes and tell her something other than what was in front of her, as if they held a hidden message within. The urge to write was gone; she closed the book with a snap. *I'm looking for answers where there are none.* She lay back in the bed. *Answers to what, though? What exactly do I want an answer to? Okay. I'll try again. Think, Marissa.* She picked up her pen, opened the book once more, this time from the back cover and wrote on the first blank page that she found:

Martin had a demon inside him. (She shuddered)
That demon saw me and somehow recognised me (?!!)
He left Martin and Martin feels better now.
Where did the demon go?

She took a breath, glad to get this all out on paper. It seemed more real, somehow. She encircled the last question. *Is this what I really want to know? Do I really want to know this?* She thought not. Not just now, anyway. She continued to write.

I met Isis. She called me Tori Scarlett Lightbringer.
My middle name is Tori.
It couldn't be a coincidence. Or could it? Or did I make the whole thing up?

Maybe this is what I want to know. Yes, I think it is, but I'm missing something. What did I do to deserve all of this? What has brought it on? She thought she remembered saying it was all Sarah's fault because of Peru? She knew that had been out of order. *Sarah won't mind. We are good. I was having those dreams long before Peru. Sarah just facilitated something opening. Something I'd rather have kept closed.*

She allowed images from her trip to Peru to float into her mind, the airplane, the market, the smells of food. She suddenly wanted to get her alpaca hat and scarf, but the bed was too warm and cosy. She let that go. Then an image came to her of the mountain, that beautiful, glorious mountain, she felt her heart open. Then she mused on her shamanic guides, and eventually the lessons she had had with Séamus, that weekend in Clifden. Her stomach tightened and a shiver ran down her back. *Okay, I need to pay attention to that.* She picked up her pen again.

> *What was going on with Séamus? What was that??*
> *Do I continue to work with Séamus? Do I keep doing shamanic work?*

Butterflies had taken over her stomach. She had hit on something. But she wanted to pursue this train of thought. She had to keep going to get to the nub. She put a circle around Séamus's name, and visualised his face. It felt horrid, nasty to do this, she pushed the image away as quickly as she could. But she held onto the thoughts.

> *Séamus and shamanic work. Can I have one without the other? Am I in too deep with the apprenticeship?*

She circled 'Séamus' a second time, then 'apprenticeship', then the pen kept drawing circles until she had almost filled the page with circles. She opened a fresh one and wrote a list:

> *Martin*
> *Demon*
> *Isis*
> *Tori*
> *Spiritual awakening*
> *Shamanic work*
> *Séamus*
> *WHAT IS REAL???*

Tobermory jumped on the bed and stepped onto the notebook in her lap, wanting her attention, demanding to be adored. She put down the pen and pet him and kissed him for a minute or two, then gently pushed him aside. He curled around in a circle beside her and started purring, the tip of his tail wagging slightly. She picked up her pen once more.

> *Tobermory and his new silver streak. What happened to Tobermory? And how come he's here now? Does he know when I'm getting upset? Probably. Is he okay?*

She examined the cat once more. As she stroked the soft black fur on his back, his tail continued to wag, yet he continued to purr. *He's okay, he's fine. He's eating and doing cat things, there's nothing that shows me he isn't okay, nothing out of the ordinary. Except for his silver streak...*

Martin's cat at primary school had a sliver streak...

White heat filled Marissa once more. *This is terrifying. The deeper I go with this, the worse it gets. It's been crazy ever since I went to Peru and met the shaman. Maybe I should give it all up.*

She studied what she had written, checking how her body felt to see everything in writing. It was doing okay; holding the egg in her left hand was comforting. Her mind seemed clear. But there was something missing, like a jigsaw puzzle piece that would complete the picture.

So what do I do now? What do I want to know? What do I need to know? A sudden tiredness came upon her; her body didn't want to move anymore, her mind slowed right down, all she wanted to do was sleep. *Perhaps I just need more rest.* She put the notebook and pen on her bedside locker and turned off the light. *I'll think about it some more tomorrow.*

The next morning Marissa fished her phone out of her handbag. She hadn't realised she'd left it there and the battery had died. She plugged it in, and as it came back to life she received several messages: five texts and six missed calls from Matt, two missed calls from her mother and one from Sarah. She left the phone on the table to charge and made some tea. She had enough on her mind and she wasn't ready yet to assure everyone that she was fine. She wasn't fine, not really, not yet anyway.

She put the kettle on, then picked up her notebook and looked at her list from the previous night. She took the pen and crossed everything out except for one thing:

WHAT IS REAL???

Stirring cold milk into hot tea, she went outside to her sanctuary. It had been raining so she put her mug down on the stones and went back into the kitchen to get a cloth to wipe down the deckchair. The sunshine after the rain felt warm on her face. Sparkles twinkled through fresh raindrops on the leaves of her favourite tree. She settled herself on the chair, tea in hand and cloth draped over the side of the wall to dry.

I think I should journey to see my guides. Who is Isis anyway to tell me I'm safe? How can I trust her when I've only just met her this one time? And how did she know that the demon was gone, 'for now'? And if it is only for now, is he going to come back?

Marissa closed her eyes and felt the sun warming her, her fingers wrapped around the steaming mug of tea, the chair beneath her and the ground under her feet. *I'm not panicking again. That's good. Maybe I won't go to them. It feels safe here, the sun on my face is nice. I'll do it later.*

Her phone went off again, but she didn't get up. *I have to rest. I don't want my panic attacks to come back. Looking after myself is the most important thing. I'll do whatever I have to do so that I can keep the flat, keep my life together and keep safe. Even if it means not doing shamanism anymore. Though I do love it so much, and the gang, we are becoming close, like family.* She sipped her tea. *But I have to stay safe. I love the work, but maybe the work doesn't love me.*

CHAPTER SIX

'But I had this whole romantic evening planned for tonight...' Matt's voice tapered off on the phone.

'Really? asked Marissa.

'Well, kind of. I did book a restaurant, but I was going to buy you a rose when we got there. It *is* Valentines weekend.'

Marissa giggled. 'Honestly Matt, you don't have to worry, a rose is a rose is a rose and I really *do* want to see Terry... *Please* can we have dinner with him?'

'I just feel bad – our first Valentine's Day and I didn't see you yesterday, and I didn't get you anything.'

'Hey, it's cool, we are both busy people. And I didn't get you anything either. How about you and I go for a pint first, just us, then we can eat with Terry, then after that I'll come back to your place and we can spend day Sunday together. If you want to? I'll buy your pints all night, Yes?'

'I've my workshop Sunday, and it's in town, closer to you than to me – so that won't work.' Marissa could hear the disappointment in his voice. 'Ok, compromise, I could stay at yours if it's not too late a night. And you still buy the pints. Then you can introduce me to Terry and his friends.'

'Yay!'

After talking roads and weather at the pub that evening, Marissa ordered a Diet Coke and sipped it while Matt waited for his second Guinness to settle. He was still concerned about her. She hadn't told him about the panic attack at work, but she did mention a bad dream that she had woken up with that morning; some kind of animal had bitten off a chunk out of her arm and had run away with it and she was left standing there looking at the chewed, bloody mess. She shivered at the memory of it. Matt's voice brought her back to the moment.

'You're not okay, Marissa, not really. You seem unbalanced. I know you felt good after your vision of Isis, but I still think you should go to Dolores. I know you said you didn't want to, but I really think she could help. You're not out of this just yet.'

Marissa was exhausted from her own thoughts; she didn't want to have to deal with Matt's concerns, and she had only told him about the dream because he had pushed her. She sighed. 'Okay. I will, I'll make an appointment. Promise.'

'No, Marissa, you've said that to me before. Please send her an email from your phone right now.' Matt lifted the pint to his lips, drank deep and when he put the glass back on the table he had a Guinness moustache. He wiped it off on the back of his hand, and the back of his hand on his jeans. 'Go on. I'm watching you do it.'

Marissa pulled her phone out of her handbag. The battery was at 70%, so she had no excuse this time. 'So much for a romantic evening' she muttered while putting together an email.

Hi, it's Marissa. I'm wondering if I could book a Reiki session with you please? Thanks.

'Done.' Marissa made a face, switched off the screen and put the phone back in her bag.

Matt nodded. 'I heard that. Hey, I know I'm annoying you but you live too far away from me for me to just call in on you when I get worried.'

'You worry about me rather a lot these days,' said Marissa.

Matt raised an eyebrow. 'Not without cause.'

'Yes, okay, it has been a little crazy the last couple of weeks.'

Matt sighed. 'Crazy is an understatement.' He took another drink of his pint.

Marissa looked around the bar, it was getting busy. Terry wanted them to meet him and a few of his modelling friends in an Italian restaurant on Parliament Street just up the road from where they were. They still had half an hour.

'Look, I'm really trying to figure this all out,' Marissa said. 'Please, give me some time. Let's talk about something else. Anything that isn't about me. *Please*?'

Matt smiled. 'Okay. You can tell me about Dolores after it's happened. I won't push you any more on that. But I do expect you to go.' He winked. 'Hey, did I tell you that I'm restoring a BMW bike at the shop? It's a classic bike! I've had to order parts from Germany. They don't make them like they used to. Let's get another pint – you're buying!'

They walked into the crowded restaurant about forty-five minutes later. They were a little late. Matt got so involved talking about his restoration project that they had lost track of time. Not that Marissa was listening to him – she had drifted off somewhere else. But she felt more awake when she saw Terry sitting with a group of people at a table at the back of the restaurant. He saw her, jumped up and waved. As they made their way through the crowd, he was literally jumping up and down with excitement.

'Darling! Here you are! It's so great to see you again! God, you'd think it'd been months and months since I'd last seen you. Isn't it incredible when we step out of space and time!' He leaned across the table to give Marissa a hug and whispered into her ear, 'You look dreadful! What happened? Did someone die?'

Marissa pulled back almost immediately, 'No! And thank you for the compliment!'

'Oh no! I didn't mean to upset you – it's my friends, they bring out the worst – ahem, I mean the best – in me... And we've been here a while. I've been drinking on an empty stomach... Come, sit down, join us. This must be Matt.'

Matt offered his hand, Terry scoffed at it and pulled him in for a hug, which Matt received a little nervously, unsure of himself, his body tightened.

'Sit beside me!' Terry said to Marissa. 'You just missed the waitress. We've ordered already, but I've saved a menu for you.'

Marissa sat beside Terry and Matt sat opposite her and beside a tall, dark-skinned young man who was wearing a bright pink T-shirt and had his hair spiked in a mohawk. He also had pink eyeshadow and pink lipstick on. Matt quickly picked up the menu and started to read it.

'This is Joy, Kamil, Vanessa, Ed, Lulu and Bruce,' Terry said, waving his hand around the table. 'Guys, this is my friend Marissa from shaman school.' *Could you say it any louder, Terry?*

Everyone briefly looked over towards Marissa and smiled, and then went back to their conversations. Marissa felt very plain and unkempt all of a sudden. As exotic as shaman school sounded, she didn't look as polished or as beautiful as any of Terry's friends. *That must be Bruce at the end of the table. He looks like a bodybuilder.* She reached her hand up to her hair and scrunched it to try and tame the curls. She had made an effort, but next to Terry's friends she felt dumpy. Everyone except for herself and Matt looked like they had just walked off the catwalk.

'We've just been in a shoot for a magazine,' Terry said loudly, confirming her suspicions. 'Some of the clothes they made me wear today were *divine*. I wanted to rob one of the jackets.'

Ed giggled and leant sideways into the table, pointing at the back of his chair, where a bright pink leather jacket hung. 'Hey, Terry, look!' he shouted over the crowd.

'You didn't!' cried Terry. 'Oh my God! I don't believe you, Ed! What a sneaky fecker you are!'

Terry giggled with delight and Ed sat back in his chair and laughed again, really letting it loose.

'How the hell did you sneak *that* out, man?' Terry gasped. 'It's so pink!'

Ed shrugged his shoulders and continued talking to Kamil.

Turning back to Marissa, Terry said, 'Well, if they paid better, I could afford to buy one. But it's not really my colour, anyway. Shall we get some more wine? What are you drinking, my love?'

Matt had found the bread and was slathering a piece with butter. He was very quiet and his lips were tight. Marissa had a feeling he felt out of his depth. She was feeling the same way a little bit too. *It's not the romantic valentine's evening you were hoping for. Sorry, Matt!*

Terry leaned in. 'So, why don't you want to do the homework with me? Not that I'm in any fit state to do it tonight, and now that I think about it, I probably couldn't make the time to squeeze it in tomorrow... But tell me, girl.' He looked Marissa square in the eye. 'You and Séamus getting all cosy on the last day there, there *is* something going on, isn't there?'

To Marissa's relief, just at that moment the waitress came over. 'Are you ready to order?'

Matt looked up and realised that Marissa hadn't seen the menu yet. He handed it to her and said, 'Yes, actually, could I get the cannelloni?'

Marissa scanned the menu quickly, then said breathlessly, 'I'll have the spinach and ricotta ravioli, please.'

The waitress smiled, wrote it down and took the menu away.

Terry was still looking at Marissa. 'Well?'

She held his gaze. 'Yes. Yes, something is going on. I'm still trying to figure it out.'

Terry took a swig of white wine and sloshed it around his mouth for a moment before swallowing it. 'I *knew* it. That bastard. It *was* Séamus, wasn't it? What did he do to you when he got rid of us all?'

'I don't know, honestly. But that's not it. But then again, it might be it. Jeez, Terry, I really don't know.'

Terry softened. 'I'm sorry I said you looked dreadful. You've been through the wars. I wasn't thinking.'

'That's okay. Let's talk about something else. We can talk again later, yes?'

'Yes. I'm not going anywhere. Now,' Terry turned to Matt and cleared his throat. 'Now, tell me, Matt, what do you do for a living and how did you meet the lovely Marissa?'

After dinner Matt and Marissa walked quietly back to Marissa's flat. It had been an experience. Matt, who was usually at ease with everyone, hadn't found a comfort zone at all with Terry's friends.

Marissa was grateful for the quiet space to clear her head. Matt started talking first.

'I'm sure he's very nice when you get him on his own,' he said. 'I don't have many gay friends. In fact I don't even know if I have one gay friend.'

'Maybe it's the modelling set and nothing to do with being gay?' Marissa suggested, but deep down she was also glad to have left them to it.

They walked quietly for a while, enjoying each other's presence without needing to say anything. As they approached Marissa's flat she realised she wasn't quite ready to be alone yet.

'You said you'd stay over tonight – do you still want to?'

Matt looked at his watch. 'I do have an early start tomorrow, like I said on the phone, I've got a Tai Chi catch-up workshop in the morning.' Then he looked at Marissa whose disappointment was obvious, even to him, in the dark. 'But I can make it if I get up early and go straight there.'

She nodded, relieved once more.

'What are you going to do tomorrow?' Matt asked as they walked towards her flat.

'I'll meet Terry for a quiet coffee and maybe call into my parents'. I've still not managed to get over to see them since their big news.'

'Grand. So I'll stay then. I'll need a toothbrush... I didn't want to assume. Maybe I should leave one at your place just in case, for next time, like?' Matt's big grin lit up his face, which then lit up Marissa's face. Everything was good. They put the dinner behind them and made a detour to Marissa's local shop. Matt bought a toothbrush and some deodorant, and a box of chocolates.

'What's that for?'

'For you, my love,' he said, handing it to her. 'Happy Valentine's Day. I made it with only twenty minutes to spare.'

Marissa grinned. *I could really get used to this.*

It was cold in the flat. Marissa put the heating on. They cuddled up on the sofa under blankets and Matt opened the chocolates. They each took one and Matt clinked his chocolate against Marissa's. 'To celebrate my new toothbrush moving into your place.'

+++

Matt let himself out. Marissa stayed in bed, but noticed she became tense once his warm body had left her side. After a time she became so restless she had to get up. She made tea and took the cup back to bed with her to find Tobermory waiting in the warm spot where she had been. Her notebook was still on the floor where she had left it and her phone was beside her bed. She picked it up and texted Terry.

Thanks for dinner, u didn't have to pay really. My turn today 11am muffins & coffee @ Coffee Mania?

While waiting for his response, she noticed there was an unread email in her inbox. It was from Dolores. Her heart jumped, she took a breath, then opened it up.

I can see you Monday evening at 6pm in Greystones. Please confirm. Dolores

Marissa wrote back:

That's wonderful. Thank you so much. See you then.

As she sent it, the phone buzzed. A return text from Terry:

Sounds gr8, y, c u soon - is that on Georges St?

Yes, c u soon xx

She sent the two kisses before she realised she had done it. *Well, who cares?* She smiled, For all of his eccentricities, she really did like Terry.

Terry's eyes were blotchy and red and he was wearing the same outfit as the night before. He joined Marissa at her table and ordered a large pot of tea. Marissa asked for a couple of muffins. Terry nodded at the waitress, then smiled at Marissa. Sitting there sipping her cappuccino, she felt calm and collected, as if in the eye of a storm. She didn't know what was coming, but right now it was okay. She had a sense that Terry was part of this, and seeing him would help her decide.

'Lookit,' he said, 'I know I can be a right ass when I hang around with those people – they're so competitive and I get caught up in it. I'm a mess today – we ended up drinking tequila shots till 4. But it's still me, I promise.' He smiled. The waitress brought Terry's tea so he kept silent until she had laid out all the things, and then left them.

He leaned in. 'Now, girl, tell me, what's going on?'

Marissa had plenty of experience of talking about a 'problem' without saying anything – she was practically an expert after all the client sessions she had done for her college course. Here, with Terry, she wasn't able to hide herself as well as she usually did. But her state of calmness helped her stay level.

'You mentioned Séamus last night,' she began, 'asking what he did to me when you weren't there. I don't know. Honestly, I have no idea if he actually helped me, or if he hurt me either, but what I do know, is while he was working on me, I felt paralysed.' She took a breath, then continued. 'I couldn't sit up, I couldn't speak, I couldn't even breathe for a few moments. I was scared. And then the moment passed.'

'And there I was thinking he tried to kiss you!' Terry laughed and poured some tea into his cup, made a face and poured it back into the teapot.

'Anyway,' he added flippantly, 'I'm pretty sure he's been sleeping with some of his students. I'd put money on it that he and Brigid had a fling, too.' Seeing Marissa wasn't buying into that line of thought, he changed his tack, and his tone. 'Actually, this is probably worse than a kiss, because you don't *know* what he did.'

'Yeah, I guess so. I really have no idea, but I'm seeing my Reiki teacher tomorrow evening and she's great. She helped me before. If he put something in my energy she'll find it.'

The waitress came back with two muffins, one chocolate and one raspberry. Marissa looked at Terry, who gestured that she should choose, so she chose the raspberry. It looked like it was about to explode, there were so many raspberries in it. She cut it in half and a raspberry jam-like substance oozed out of it onto her plate.

There was a silence before Terry asked 'So Are you gonna quit?' He looked up at Marissa to make sure she had heard him correctly.

Marissa cleared her throat. 'Hey, you do come straight to the point, don't you?'

'No messing around with me!' Terry smiled as he cut his muffin in half and took a bite out of it. 'Mm yummy, and fresh. Odd for a Sunday!'

'Yes they have their own bakery in here, it's great.'

'Well?'

'I don't know. I haven't decided yet. I love the work, and I love our group, but the thought of seeing Séamus right now gives me the shivers. Worse than the shivers.'

'I'd imagine so. Maybe wait until after you see your Reiki teacher. See what she says.'

Terry poured out more tea and shook his head. 'It's still too weak. Particularly for a Corkonian like me.' He poured it back into the teapot then opened the lid and looked inside, pulled out one tea bag with his spoon and asked, 'Why are they so stingy with the tea bags in Dublin?' He put it back in then tried to squeeze more tea out of the bag. Then he looked at Marissa once more. 'Well, lookit, we are friends now no matter what. So if you stay or go, you and I will always be friends. Deal?'

Marissa smiled, some part of her very relieved, another part quite distressed. She sat in the middle of a soup of emotions and brought her attention back to Terry's face.

'Yes, deal. I'd like that. I'd like that very much.'

Terry sighed. 'Good. Mores to the point, do I have to phone Liz now to do my homework?'

'Yes, I'm afraid so. For now, anyway.' Marissa smiled again, feeling a little more relaxed.

'Listen here, missus,' Terry said firmly, 'you'd better look after yourself. And tell me what your Reiki teacher says.'

'I will, promise.'

Later that afternoon Marissa called in to visit her parents. The house was a hive of activity, there were boxes in the hallway and the carpet in the front room was partially pulled up, exposing the underlay and tiles beneath.

'What's going on?' asked Marissa as she narrowly dodged the corner of a painting that had been taken down from the wall which had been resting precariously against one of the boxes.

'We're redecorating!' said her mother. 'Great to see you, dear. Would you like a cup of tea or coffee?'

'No, I'm grand, thanks, Mum,' said Marissa, surveying the damage. Well, it seemed like damage to her; it was her childhood home and it hadn't changed in all the years she'd lived there. She was curious as to what they were going to do with it. *I guess if I came into money, I'd want to redecorate too. At least they're not selling it.*

'We were thinking of selling,' her mother explained, 'but your father rightly said that nobody would buy it in this condition.'

Marissa's heart sank. *I love this house.*

Her mother continued, 'I think a lick of paint, some new furniture and maybe a new kitchen and I'll be happy here for another forty years! Don't worry, love, we wouldn't sell it without telling you and Eli first.'

Marissa decided she'd get that cuppa after all. She deftly made her way to the kitchen, found the kettle and filled it up. Her dad came in, holding a plank of wood and singing. She couldn't remember the last time she'd heard him singing.

'Hi, Dad!'

'Hello, love! Great to see you.'

'Where are you going with that plank?'

'Ha, ha! To RTÉ to audition for *The Late Late Show*!'

'Ha, ha! No really, are you building something?'

'Yes! I'm putting up shelves in the bedroom. Your mother has always wanted shelves in there and I've never gotten around to it. I'll tell you, Marissa, love, it's great to have some money in the bank and no troubles on your shoulders. For all his arsing around in the past, my brother has treated me right, and I'll always be grateful to him for that.'

Arsing around? Dad! 'Go on Dad, tell me, how much did Uncle Lou give you?'

Her dad tapped his nose, 'Enough to pay off all the business loans, clear the mortgage and have some fun. There's about twenty grand left. He said he'd be dropping some to you and Eli, too, now that he has your bank details. He's loaded now! Top 10 Irish rich list, I'd say! So we are unashamedly taking the money, and damnit, we *are* going to have some fun! Starting with the house.'

'I'm really happy for you, Dad.'

At that moment Rose came into the kitchen. 'Stick one on for me too, love.'

'Ahh Mum, this is wonderful news. You must be delighted you've got no debt.'

Rose went over to Bernie and gave him a squeeze as Marissa took another cup down from the cupboard.

'Yes, your poor dad has been so stressed for so long, it's such a pleasure to have him happy. It's like we're a couple of teenagers again!'

Bernie squeezed her back, saluted and went upstairs with the wood.

'Whose car was that in the driveway the other night?'

'It was mine! Can you believe it, a car of my own!'

'Wow, Mum! Dad never said!'

'I've been wanting one for a long time. It's not brand new, but it's new to me. It's getting a service and a valet from your uncle's man right now. Would you believe I actually bought it before Lou showed up with all that money? I was feeling guilty about it, but not any longer. I've got a new sense of freedom. I can go anywhere I want, anytime. Life is good.'

Rose took a closer look at her daughter.

'How are you doing, love? You don't look as bright as you usually do. Is there something wrong?'

Marissa caught her breath, felt her feet in her shoes on the ground, then steadied herself. 'I'm just working a few things out, Mum. There's a lot going on with the degree, with my extra-curricular work, and the promotion. Noreen's putting pressure on me about the managerial position, and I'm feeling a little overwhelmed by the whole thing.' *That isn't a lie, is it? No, it's not a lie.*

'Is there anything I can do for you? Or your dad? Do you want me to talk to Noreen for you?'

Marissa thought about it. 'It might take the pressure off, however I *am* a grown-up now, Mum, I've got to fight my own battles. It's not about Noreen so much as about me, making a decision for my future. I've a few decisions to make at the moment, all at once, and they all feel like big ones. I don't want to take them lightly.'

Bernie came back down to the kitchen, wearing gloves and with sawdust in his hair and on his face. 'What are we discussing? Will you stay for dinner, love?'

'Discussing my life!' said Marissa. 'You know, yes, I'd love to stay for dinner. Maybe you can help me make a decision, especially now that you're not going to focus on the money aspect of it.'

'Well...' said Bernie, washing his hands thoughtfully. Rose tapped him on the face and he threw some water onto his face, then she handed him a tea towel and he dried himself. His hair was thrown out of place and he looked much younger, with a fresh twinkle in his eye.

Marissa always had loved her father deeply, and now she could see what had drawn Rose to him all those years ago.

He continued his train of thought. "You can't stay in college forever, love. You've still got to make a living, and even though you don't need to worry about your mother and me now, you do have to look after yourself. If you don't, then who will?'

CHAPTER SEVEN

What am I worried about? Dolores helped me before. Nothing bad is going to happen. It will be okay. Marissa was nervous. It was only 6pm, but it was already dark. She held her breath, then rang Dolores's doorbell.

She heard bustling behind the garden door then Dolores opened it widely and smiled at her. She was like a bright light, wearing a white dress with large purple polka dots and a chunky necklace made of pink stones, and her long silver hair was up in a bun on top of her head.

'Hello again, Marissa!' She was slightly breathless from whatever she had been doing before she answered the door. 'Come in, it's great to see you.'

Marissa stepped over the threshold and closed the door behind her, following Dolores through the manicured garden path which led up to her healing room. Dolores opened the glass door, gesturing to her to come inside. The room was warm and cosy, lit by candles and a small lamp at the back. It felt like a nice safe space.

'I was wondering when I'd see you again. How are you getting on with your Reiki practice?'

Marissa placed her bag on the floor and hung her coat up on the rack. She blushed and looked down at her feet, then sat down on a small leather chair. 'Actually, I've not been practising as much as I would like.'

Dolores sat in the opposite chair. 'That's life, isn't it – always other, more pressing things getting on top of us. Happens to the best of us. Don't worry, it takes time to develop a daily routine.'

There was incense burning on the window ledge and a faint smell of lavender. A massage table stood in the centre, with blankets and pillows piled up onto it, and a statue of a very happy Buddha looked out at them from the mantlepiece.

Dolores smiled. 'What can I do for you tonight?'

There was a moment when Marissa felt like running out the door. But she looked at Dolores's kind face, her hands cradled in her lap, and she softened. She took a breath. 'I came to you when I was in trouble before and you helped me so much – thank you. I think I need some help again. No, I *know* I need some help.'

Dolores focused on Marissa, her face changing, becoming more serious. Marissa shifted in her chair. She wasn't sure how ridiculous this would sound, or if Dolores would find it ridiculous. She wasn't even sure what *had* happened, not really.

'Start at the beginning, love,' Dolores prompted. 'We have plenty of time, I've nobody coming after you so we won't be in a rush to finish up. I had a feeling we'd need some time together.'

Marissa smiled gratefully. *How did she know? I guess I have nothing to lose, and if Dolores can see something that I can't, well, it would be more than useful to me. I don't know what is real, maybe validation is what I need.* She began. 'I'll begin at the beginning then?'

'Yes please, I think that's the best way to begin.'

'Okay. Well, I'm seeing – I mean I *was* seeing – this client, for psychotherapy. He's bipolar and schizophrenic. There were three occasions where something strange happened in the sessions between us. In the last session, it was as if my client – well, this sounds really strange, Dolores, so I'll just say what it seemed like to me. It was as if he disappeared and some other being stepped into his body and took over. His eyes changed – it wasn't Martin anymore.' Marissa put her hand over her mouth. 'Oh no, I shouldn't have told you his name.' Tears started to glisten in her eyes. *Shit, I broke confidentiality by telling her his name.*

'Don't worry, love,' Dolores said gently, handing her a tissue and pouring some water into a tumbler from a decanter. 'There are plenty of Martins in Dublin, and probably quite a few of them are schizophrenic. I don't know who it is you're referring to, and whatever you say in here is just between us two. Whatever you say stays in this room.'

Marissa nodded, slightly relieved, but still feeling that she had somehow betrayed Martin's trust. *At least she's not looking at me like*

I'm a crazy person – not yet, anyway. She patted at her eyes with the tissue, then looked down at the floor, and continued. 'This being – he was horrible. He terrified me. I could really feel him there, in the room. He didn't feel like my client, like Martin. It really felt like I was there with someone else completely.' She looked at Dolores for approval, and received it, so she continued.

'In one of the sessions, this being, he looked at me directly out of Martin's eyes and then he spoke to me, using Martin's voice. He called me by my name. That really scared me.'

'I imagine it would scare anyone,' agreed Dolores.

'So you don't think I'm crazy?' asked Marissa, hopefully.

'No, dear, of course not. These things do happen, not often, but it *is* possible. It might be better though if we talk about it after you've told me everything. Just to make sure that you don't forget anything important. Keep going for now, get it all out. And take your time.'

Marissa nodded, and blew her nose. 'Okay, yes. Matt, you know Matt, he came to the Reiki workshop – actually that's where I met him.' She blushed and looked at Dolores who acknowledged her without interrupting.

'Matt looked after me when I was very frightened, he's the one actually that told me to contact you now. Anyway. I'm also in training with Séamus O'Driscoll, doing his shamanism apprenticeship, as well as the Reiki with you. Do you know him?'

'I've never met him, but I do know of him.'

'Okay. Well, straight after the thing with Martin, I went to a weekend workshop with Séamus. It was the weekend before last. I felt better there, and it was good to be around my friends and people doing this type of work.' She took a drink of water. 'Séamus was asking us all how we were doing, and one of the students there, she mentioned dark energies, so I mentioned that I'd come across some dark energy too, but I didn't say too much in front of everyone. Séamus took it very seriously and he called me to him privately to ask me more about it.' Marissa shivered. 'I told him about what happened with Martin and he said it was a demon. That kind of freaked me out.' She turned to Dolores. 'It really doesn't bear thinking about. After that, Séamus said he wanted to help me.'

Dolores was nodding. She didn't seem in the slightest way shocked by what was being said. Marissa could have been talking about a trip to the dentist, or taking her cat to the vet. This roused more confidence in Marissa, so she relaxed a little bit. 'So anyway, Séamus did some healing work on me, alone. I thought it would help, but while he was working on me, I felt paralysed. It was really frightening.'

At that Dolores sat up a little straighter. Her expression didn't change, but there was a barely noticeable tremor in her lower lip and a slight tightness in her cheeks.

'He said the work he did he was to empower me,' Marissa said, 'so feeling paralysed didn't make sense. To me, anyway. He also said the ... demon ... was looking for my weakness, but I was stronger than I knew. Stronger than it – he – thought I was.' Marissa looked pleadingly into Dolores's eyes, 'Am I going crazy? Is this for real?'

'Please,' Dolores replied, 'keep going.'

'Okay.' Marissa took a breath. 'Anyway. I don't know what Séamus did to me, or if he did anything to me, I only know that I nearly had a panic attack while he was working on me and he seemed oblivious to that. Oh, then he said I was going to be a great healer and that I wouldn't be given any more than I could handle. The weekend continued, he gave us our homework and I came back home to Dublin.'

Marissa had another drink of water.

'The workshop was in Clifden, I got back home on the Sunday evening and I was so tired I fell asleep almost straight away. I had a vivid dream, where I actually met the... demon.' Her voice quavered on the word. 'He spoke to me directly. Again. He said he couldn't keep away from me.' In barely a whisper she added, 'He said he wanted my soul.'

Dolores shivered. Seeing this, Marissa sank down into her chair.

'I woke up from the dream terrified,' she continued, 'only it got even more terrifying...' Her voice trailed off.

Dolores waited patiently, after a moment she said 'Go on, dear.'

'That feeling that I had, back in Cabra, of being in the room with another person. Not Martin, but someone, something else. I felt it again. Only in my bedroom.'

'He was there with you, wasn't he?'

Marissa nodded, her eyes filling with tears.

'Oh my dear, what a shocking thing to experience. But he didn't stay long, I expect.'

Marissa shook her head, 'As soon as I turned the light on he was gone.'

'Yes, that makes sense. It seems he knew how to cross between the worlds through your client's schizophrenia,' Dolores explained. 'The cracks in Martin's personality, his psyche. *Schizo* means "split", and where there is a split, there's a crack. He must have done this before.'

Marissa took another drink. She didn't really want one, but she wasn't ready to speak. As she held the glass, it seemed as though the water was shivering, but then she realised it was her hand. Feeling the warmth and compassion radiating out from Dolores, she felt validated, but the fear had resurfaced and her body was shaking.

'So it really did happen?' she asked.

'Yes, it seems it really did happen,' Dolores answered compassionately. 'I have known this to happen before. But it's rare, it's something people don't talk about, don't understand. Don't want to understand. And yes, it's real.'

It's real – it isn't something I've made up in my head. Oh thank goodness. That alone was priceless to Marissa. She felt the way she used to feel after crying all afternoon over James – emotionally exhausted, completely spent, but relieved. A great heaviness tumbled in on top of her, she wanted to sleep. Her eyes started drooping, yet her heart felt lighter, even though her body felt so much heavier. She shook herself, like a dog shaking off water. The heavy feeling remained.

'Do you mind if I ask you a little more detail about what happened?' Dolores asked.

Marissa nodded.

'So you had a vivid dream where you met him, then you woke up, you felt his presence in your room... What happened next?'

Marissa brought her focus back. 'I felt paralysed, just as I had with Séamus. Then he spoke to me.'

'He spoke?'

'Yes, I heard his voice. It was strong. So strong it was as if there was an actual person beside me, saying the words out loud, not from inside my mind.'

'He spoke?'

'Yes. I heard him in my head, but it wasn't my voice, it was his. He said: "Yes, Marissa. I'm here. I know where you live. And I can come and get you anytime I want to."'

She shivered as she remembered those words. Saying them out loud felt terrible, it was as if a bomb went off inside her. She separated from herself, the room was spinning around her. Part of her drifted outside her body, the part that was refusing to experience it, to acknowledge it. *It didn't happen. But it did.* And another part of her knew it, knew she had heard those words. Those words were etched onto her soul. And another part... terrified.

Dolores stayed silent.

Marissa's mind was floating. She wasn't present in the room. She floated up and out of her body, up and out of the little healing room, up and into the sky, into the clouds, above the Earth. There she saw the sun shining brightly, even though it was night-time. The sun turned into a golden cross with a loop on top. *I've seen this somewhere before?* She felt soothing energies flowing through her, and the vision and the energies calmed her. She felt herself returning slowly, down through the clouds into the night sky, there was the garden, with the little healing room, in through the celling and there was her body, there was Dolores. It wasn't a crash landing, it was gentle, like a feather drifting back down to the ground. She opened and closed her hands, then looked at Dolores, and smiled.

'I'm still here, though, aren't I?'

'Yes dear, you are here, and safe with me.'

'There's something else - that night, my cat, he's black, well he was completely black before this happened. He came to me in the moments afterward, when the room was, you know, empty again, and he had a lightning strike of silver hair down his face. I only noticed it the next day, but I think he protected me. Dolores, what's the significance of a golden cross? One with a loop on top?'

Dolores didn't reply. Silence fell, but Marissa didn't feel uncomfortable anymore. She sipped her water a couple of times, her had was much steadier now. Dolores had closed her eyes and seemed to be in deep thought. *Perhaps she's consulting with her guides?*

Marissa realised she felt light and free – a little edgy and wild, but happier than she had been since this whole thing had begun. *I told someone everything. And even if Dolores thinks I'm a maniac crazy person, or she tells me to get out and she can't help me, I survived. I really did, and that is a Big Deal.*

Marissa remembered from her psychotherapy training how trauma survivors had a lot of difficulty speaking about the traumatic events they had experienced, but how just talking about what had happened could lead to catharsis and healing. Now she understood what that meant. *Reading about something and living it are totally different things. I'll never take anything for granted again.*

Dolores was coming round, like someone coming out of a faint.

'Thank you, I just need a moment, dear. I admit that that last part, when you heard him speak, I've not heard of anything like that before. But I am not saying that it's not possible. I believe that you believe it, and I believe that it is possible. So put two and two together and yes, it possibly did really happen, although it is all very unusual.'

She looked at Marissa. 'Stand up, dear. Let me take a closer look at you.'

Marissa stood and Dolores walked around her, observing her from all angles.

'I have a friend I must consult with,' she said. 'But I cannot end this session now – we haven't done any energy work.'

'Ah, but I feel much better, Dolores, so much better for having told you.'

Dolores nodded. 'Yes, I imagine so. Gold cross with a loop on top... Like this one?' She opened a drawer and pulled out a small metallic ankh on a chain.

'Yes! Exactly like that!'

'It's an ankh. It's the Egyptian symbol for everlasting life.'

'I just saw one,' said Marissa, 'in my mind, after telling you everything. It made me feel better, calmer.'

'The ankh is very interesting symbol, connected to Isis, signifying fertility and protection. Some call it the knot of Isis.'

'The great goddess Isis! That's wonderful!' Marissa felt a flush of heat rushing up her body. 'I think she's looking after me, Dolores. I had a vision of her shortly after my experience with the, well, you know what I mean. I met her – Isis, I mean!'

'That's a great honour,' Dolores said. 'I'd give you my ankh, but it has great sentimental value for me. Perhaps you should get one for yourself.'

'Now, I do want to put my hands on you,' Dolores continued, 'if only to help you ground and centre yourself a little better. Would that be okay? I can also do a scan while you're lying down to check your energy is clear. I think that would give you peace of mind around whatever happened while you were working with Séamus.'

Marissa brightened. 'Oh, yes please, that would be wonderful.'

'Grand. Please take off your shoes and get up on the table.'

Dolores turned on some gentle music. As soon as Marissa's head hit the pillow and she felt Dolores working on her, she fell into a deep sleep.

When the session was over, Dolores turned the music off and rubbed Marissa's arms and legs to help bring her back into the room. Marissa woke, but found it difficult to focus into the present moment.

'I'll get you some tea,' Dolores said, soothingly. 'Don't get up. I'll be back in a few minutes.'

She quietly closed the door behind her, leaving Marissa alone in the healing room. She lay there trying to focus on the items in front of her, but she was still fading in and out when Dolores came back in with two cups of steaming, hot green tea. Dolores placed the cups on her table then helped Marissa sit up slowly. She sat on the massage table, feet dangling in mid-air, and Dolores stood behind her with her hands on her shoulders to steady her. Dolores started to hum, and the sound of the humming helped Marissa bring more of herself back into her body. She nodded at Dolores, who then released her hands.

Marissa slid off the massage table, went to one of the chairs and sat down into it.

Dolores sat opposite her and pushed one of the mugs towards her. 'Green tea is good for revival.'

'Thank you.' Marissa encircled the mug with her hands. The tea was too hot to drink, but the warmth of the mug on her fingers helped her come back into her body.

As soon as she'd had a few cautious sips of the tea, Dolores told her, 'I didn't find any inclusions, restrictions, bonds or attachments. As far as I can tell, your energy is clear.'

At the word 'clear', Marissa was back in the pyramid, in the bath, being washed by the priestesses.

'The priestesses of Isis bathed me in that vision I had. It felt so real, as if I was actually there.'

'Wonderful. You are protected by Isis, I'm relieved to hear that. Sometimes they work through the dreamscape, and you need an ally there, as well as here.' Dolores winked and Marissa smiled.

She took another sip of the tea. It didn't taste good, but it wasn't nasty either. And it did refresh her and help snap her out of the stupor.

'Do you *really* think it was all real?' *That sounded like such a stupid thing to ask. I'm really not myself at all. Even after the Reiki session.*

'It does seem possible that you have had supernatural help, yes. Whether it was Isis or the angels, I cannot say for certain. Our minds tend to glamorise spiritual experiences, and we can only interpret them based on what we have experienced ourselves.'

'That does make sense alright. Thanks Dolores, it has helped to tell you everything, whether it really happened or not, at least I know that someone knows, and doesn't think I'm a crazy person! Matt was right to make me come.'

Dolores smiled once more. 'You're not a crazy person, you're going through a spiritual awakening, trying to make sense of the energies, of what is waking up in you and what is already awake. It's difficult to talk about these things at the best of times. Thank you for trusting me enough to tell me, and for coming to seek my help. I'm here if you need further support. Are you okay now for going home?'

Thinking of home, Marissa remembered her lapis lazuli, which was by her bed. She hadn't thought to bring it with her, but she felt reassured knowing that she was going home to it.

'Yes, I think so. Thank you for everything.'

Dolores finished her tea and waited for Marissa to drain the last of her cup, then said, 'Don't take anything for granted. Spirit's idea of what we can handle can be very different from our own.'

'Yes, I'd imagine so,' agreed Marissa.

She paid, got her coat, said thanks again and was about to leave when Dolores asked, 'Is there anything else you didn't tell me, just in case it's important?'

'I don't think so... Oh wait, hang on. Isis. In my dream. I met her and she called me by another name.'

'Hmmm, that's interesting. It could be important. Don't tell me what it was. Please keep it to yourself for now. I'll see you again. Remember I'm here if you need me. And give my best to Matt.'

'Thanks. I will! Bye!'

Walking to the DART station in Greystones, Marissa looked at the time. It was 9pm. *Really? I got there at 6 and I only paid for an hour's session. Oh God, I feel awful! And I said so many silly things...* But deep down she knew it was okay, and she felt much more solid and at peace knowing that Dolores took her seriously.

The DART was half-empty when it pulled into the station. Marissa stepped in and sat on a chair facing the coastline. In her carriage there were teenagers with loud music in their headphones, a businessman talking on his phone and an older couple sitting together holding hands. *Ordinary life. Banal and boring. Nothing supernatural to see here. Oh, if only I could have a normal life!*

It was dark outside. The moon was hovering over the sea behind a cloud and the sky was peppered with stars. Marissa brought her awareness back into the carriage and looked at the people sitting there. They seemed content, but Marissa's inner physiotherapist knew that people were great at putting a brave face on things. The teenagers – *They could be on crack, or runaways. One of them could be anorexic or suicidal. One of them could have been beaten by their parents, or a boyfriend.* The businessman – *he could be a gambling addict, desperately trying to make some money before he loses everything.* The old couple – *Perhaps they just put up with each other. They may be too afraid to separate and take the risk of finding true love. Or perhaps they're just teenagers, a businessman and an elderly couple. I don't know anything about any of them. Isn't it easy to come to conclusions about someone just based on what they look like or how old they are?* She glanced to the businessman, who had put his phone down and was reading the paper. *Or by what they're doing?*

The train pulled into Dun Laoghaire and more people got on. The elderly couple got off. Marissa thought of Matt; this was his stop, he only lived a few minutes down the road. But she felt tired, ready to sleep, not able to jump out for a surprise visit. The carriage doors closed and the train pulled out. She got out her phone and texted him.

> You were right. Dolores was gr8. I feel happier now but so tired. She says hi. Goin home 2 sleep. Catch u tmrow

CHAPTER EIGHT

Time went by. Marissa found herself feeling happier as she engaged more with 'real life' and less with the supernatural. Her dreams were becoming quite disturbing though, but she pushed them aside as best as she could. While enjoying her class on Tuesday evening, laughing with Yvonne and Barbara, she caught a part of herself watching herself and she felt relieved that there was life after the ... well, she still didn't want to think about it. It was much easier to focus on what was in front of her instead of thinking about what was in the in-between.

The students were on their final sprint to finish their diploma. They only had two modules left – advanced psychotherapeutic techniques and research, and then their final assessment. The end to all of Marissa's hard work in college was in sight.

Work was busy. Noreen wanted everything ready for a sales conference, so Marissa pulled out all the stops and worked hard to make the best presentation she could. Somewhere halfway through the week, she decided she really didn't want to be working in an office for the rest of her life. Thoughts of being the manager herself and presenting at a conference didn't appeal to her at all. At times in the office she realised that her interest wavered and she'd drift into thinking about her research module, or how to help a client. *I'm a therapist, I guess helping people the way that I can help people is what I'm here to do, I'm not a salesperson or business manager.* Thinking about it, she felt a 'click' in her mind, like the turn of a key, and a tightness in her chest released. *That's it decided then. But I don't want to lose my job just yet, I still like it here, and I need the money.* She knew she'd have to have a sit-down with Noreen soon to let her know. However, that didn't feel as daunting as before. *I have survived worse this year, this will be a doddle compared to what I've just been through.*

On Wednesday evening she went for dinner to Eli and Carol's house. Carol cooked, Eli washed the dishes and Marissa brought cake.

'Aww, go on, Eli, what harm would it do to find out if it's a girl or a boy?' Carol asked playfully.

'Isn't it bad luck or something?' Eli was genuinely concerned. 'I've heard that if you find something out, then you jinx it. Bad energy. I don't know – maybe it's like the Native Americans not wanting you to take their photograph, because then you'd capture a part of their soul on paper.'

'But you wouldn't be capturing anything,' said Carol, 'just finding something out, and what does this have to do with Native Americans?'

Eli shrugged his shoulders.

Marissa came to his rescue. 'I think I know what you're getting at. It's to do with sacredness. I read somewhere that the Native Americans believed the soul was a sacred thing. Maybe the sex of a baby is also a sacred thing, if you put it down on paper, or, in this case, in a scan, then you've taken something away from that sacred beauty.'

Eli pointed to Marissa. 'What she said. Exactly.'

Carol grinned, 'But we know better than that now, don't we? Taking a picture doesn't hurt anyone, and knowing the baby's sex won't take away a part of the baby's soul.' She rubbed her belly, 'Our baby's soul. She, or he, is in good hands with you as the father, Eli. But I would love to know what colour to paint the nursery wall in the meantime...'

Eli relented. 'If it means that much to you, but I'd be happy with yellow or green on the walls. The baby will be its own self, girl or boy, and either way I'll love it just the same.'

Marissa noticed the light behind Eli's eyes was much brighter than it had been for years. She saw his joy at becoming a father, and she was happy for him. *I'm not envious at all. I used to long for a baby, but I think I'm on a different road now. I'm heading in a different direction. But I'm not there yet. I know what I don't want, but what do I actually want?*

On the way home, she tried to work it out. *Okay, I don't want to be an office manager, I want to be a therapist. But I think there's something to this energy work, and I think it would really help people if I could do it. So I should organise myself to do the homework for Séamus and get back to those workshops.* A dark feeling arose in the pit of her stomach as she walked. Each step felt heavier and heavier, until it seemed her shoes were made of lead and she couldn't lift them at all. Her head was heavy too. A blanket of tiredness swept over her. She leaned against a lamppost to rest. *I do need to get my homework done if I'm going to do the next workshop. Then I'll get my qualification and I can offer another type of therapy as well as psychotherapy.* The thought didn't help, and the heaviness, the fogginess, didn't subside. *Okay, I won't tonight then. I'm much too tired, I'll just have an early night and think about it tomorrow.*

The heaviness left her immediately and she began walking once more. Her feet and legs felt freed up, and she felt lighter, back to herself again.

What the heck is that about? Heaviness around doing the work or heaviness around Séamus? I can't tell the difference...

On Thursday afternoon, Marissa got off work early to meet her supervisor, Mr Blakemore, in Cabra. His office was as dusty and musty as always. Light streamed in through dirty windows onto a desk crowded with paperwork, stacks of books, and several mugs and pens.

'Marissa, hello, hello! Great to see you again. It's been about a month, yes?'

'Yes,' said Marissa, moving some paperwork off the armchair where she usually sat and looking in vain for a place to put it.

Mr Blakemore came over and smiled, reaching his hand out for it. He was wearing his usual blazer, camel brown with patches on the elbows, and a cream shirt with the collar up on one side and caught in his jacket on the other side. His hair, as usual, was tousled, not quite making up its mind which side it wanted to part itself on. He placed the sheaf of papers on top of a pile of books on his desk, grabbed an

A4 file and sat in the chair opposite Marissa. As he settled down, his too-short trousers rode up midway to his calves. This had been off-putting at first, but Marissa had gotten used to his eccentricities, so she didn't mind it so much now. He was a 'jolly good fellow', a soft and gentle older man with a good heart, a little scatty, as his office showed, but compassionate, and he certainly knew how to listen, even if he had difficulty remembering people's names.

'So where are we with your client work?' Mr Blakemore opened the file and glanced through it, running his finger down the page to a point halfway through it, which seemed to satisfy his requirements. He turned to Marissa and waited for her to answer.

'Well,' she started, 'Martin has finished up with me. He had one session left on his cycle, which would have been tonight.'

Mr Blakemore put down the papers and looked at her. 'Yes, the office told me. How strange! And did I get it right – he said he was finished altogether?'

Marissa nodded.

'He has been coming here for six years, you know. And to finish, just like that? What did you do, Marissa?'

'What do you mean?' said Marissa, heart leaping into her mouth, wondering if she did something wrong.

'Well, he phoned the office this morning. He explicitly said he didn't finish with *you*, he said if he comes back again, he wants to see you again. I have never heard the like! It's tantamount to a miracle, I would think.'

Marissa eased back in her chair, relief flooding over her. She was certainly not going to be telling Mr Blakemore what really happened... But she could tell him a little, maybe.

She smiled in return. 'I don't know, honestly. We did have a connection. I took him seriously, I listened. Perhaps that's all he needed. And maybe it's just a break for now.'

'Yes, perhaps. But he got results with you that he didn't get from all the other volunteers. And this certainly seems like progress to me, on a case I never thought would ever progress at all. Wonderful work, Marissa. And to have closure with him too – that's uncommon. Well done. Let's move on - now, where are you with your other clients?'

'Cliona only has one session left, but she needs another cycle. Can you put her in for it?'

'Certainly,' said Mr Blakemore, writing a note on the page and ticking a box. 'Is she turning up for her appointments?'

'Oh yes, she is. And she really wants to work too. It's going very well.'

'Good. And Fiachra?'

'He seems to have his life on track now and he said he wants to finish tonight. This is his last session. He doesn't really need it, I think, but it would be good for closure.'

'Wonderful. This could be a rare opportunity for you to ask him what he liked about working with you and what he found most helpful.'

Marissa nodded.

'Don't forget,' said Mr Blakemore, 'this is your work experience placement so it's always good to get feedback, especially directly from a client. That doesn't happen often, not once you're working in practice, anyway. They usually just decide not to come anymore and don't make another appointment.' He stroked his face and drifted away into his thoughts. Then he came back to Marissa and said, 'That's why it was good you got to say goodbye to Martin. It can be difficult not to find out what happened to a client after all the progress you made with them. But that is the plight of the therapist – we get dragged into the crises, the hardships and the trauma, and never hear the good things. It's like jumping into the middle of a story, having to catch up with what happened and then help the direction of it, but you never hear the ending. For some of us, our curiosity gets the better of us and we ask, but it is not in our remit. And sometimes, they do let us know, but we have to stop wanting to know. They never tell you everything, only the things they think they need help with when they are with you, and these aren't necessarily the things they actually need help with in the long term. Remember, Marissa, you're a walk-on character in somebody else's story, not the main character. Not even necessarily a minor character. Play your role well and hopefully their story will be improved. That's all you can do, really.'

He marked the paper once again, then looked up at Marissa and smiled.

'I will organise someone new to begin with you next week,' he said. 'We have someone for you this evening, to take Martin's place. Her name is Joy.' He put the papers down onto the floor beside him and looked at Marissa. 'And now you, a check-in with you. How are you doing? Is everything okay here?'

Marissa smiled. 'Yes, thank you. I'm feeling that I'm making progress with my client hours, and I'm enjoying the sessions. It's good, although I would perhaps like fresh milk in the kitchen sometimes! But otherwise I'm happy.'

Mr Blakemore smiled and nodded. 'Yes, I'll see what I can do about that – a common request. Have you met Dave yet? He seems a little scatty but good at heart.'

Marissa smiled. 'Yes, I've met Dave. He seems nice.'

Mr Blakemore nodded, then looked at his watch. 'I think that's all for now. Do get in touch if you have any problems, or need anything else, and we'll meet again in four weeks or so. I'm hoping to have a few more volunteers working with us over the next month or so, so we'll definitely have to get that kitchen sorted out.'

'Thank you!'

Marissa got tea (black) and took it up to her room, peeking into the room next door on her way. Dave wasn't there, but there was a book on the coffee table that caught her eye. *Success Principles* was the title, and the cover showed a man standing on a mountain-top at sunset with his arms stretched out in victory. *Scott Taylor. How clichéd! Sunset, mountain-tops and success. Isn't Scott Taylor that guy that Emmet likes?* She picked it up and read some of the testimonials on the back.

> *'Scott Taylor is incredibly gifted. He's found a way to explain difficult concepts in such an easy, accessible way. You have got to read this book.'*
> *Kyle Jones II, CEO, Concept Tech*

> *'Scott Taylor saved my life, and he can save yours, too. His work is life-changing, he is a goldmine of information.*

Without him, I would never have written a single book.'
Steve Blanioff, three-time award-winning New York Times bestselling author

'What can I say about this book, and about Scott Taylor? He changed my life. He's helped me discover what I'm really made of and what I can do with my life. Scott is the man.'
Wanda Phillips, Olympic swimming gold medallist, USA

Even more sceptical, Marissa opened the book and looked at the Table of Contents. Just then, Dave appeared. Same jeans, different T-shirt, and he had brushed his hair this time.

'Marissa, right?' he asked with a big grin.

Marissa nodded and smiled back. 'Hi, Dave.'

He chuckled. 'Yep, that's me! Do you like Scott?' He gestured to the book, which was still in Marissa's hands.

'Oh, sorry, I was just taking a look. I've heard of him, but I don't know his work.'

'He's amazing. Seriously, if you want to be a great therapist you need to know his work! He has had some amazing successes with people. I'm saving up, hoping to go to his event this summer in London.'

Marissa closed the book and held it out to Dave, not really impressed with it, despite all the enthusiastic endorsements. He pushed it gently back to her. 'Keep it, have a read. Maybe there's something in there for you.'

'Are you sure?'

'Yes, deffo. I have another copy at home. I've got all of his books. He really is a genius.'

'Okay, I'll take a look. Thank you.' *If a master's student thinks this guy is a genius, maybe I shouldn't be judging a book by its cover.*

'So, lots of clients for you tonight?' Dave asked.

'Hope so! I'm finishing up with one client, starting with another, and I've got someone in between. You?'

'Just the one, again. I'm working with a four session model and they keep missing their appointments, it's very disappointing – I need them to come to all four sessions, as well as needing the client hours, the momentum just isn't there.'

'A four session model, that sounds interesting. But yeah, I've been there, clients not showing up is very frustrating. I hope it gets better.'

'Me too, or I'll really be in trouble. I need to write up the outcomes of at least 6 completed models for my assignment and I've only had two sessions with one person so far. I'm getting worried.'

'Oh dear, that's bad. I wonder if you can offer some sort of incentive.'

'Hmm. Like what, though?'

'I have no idea.' Marissa thought for a moment. 'What could a therapist offer as well as counselling?'

'Washing their car for them?'

'Ha, ha! Well, maybe that's not ethical. You can't bribe someone either. I guess you need to think about that one. Anyway, thanks again for the book. I'll bring it back next week. Got to go – I'd better get ready for my clients.'

'No rush,' Dave said. 'Keep it as long as you want. Like I said, I have another one at home. He encourages this, actually. "Get two, give one away." I like giving them away, and I usually get more than two. Hey, I have the audiobook of this one - he reads it himself. I like to listen first thing in the morning for inspiration. Sets the day off right. Audiobooks are cool, don't you think? So I practically know the whole book by heart now. He does meditations too. You should listen, you'd love them!'

'Thanks, I'll give the book a go anyway. See you next time, hope you have better luck with your clients tonight.'

Marissa took her tea and the book, into her room. She put the book in her handbag, rummaged around inside the bag and pulled out a pink organza pouch with her bundle of dried sage inside. She lit a candle, and once the flame had taken, she placed the sage into it until it glowed and started to smoke. Then she pulled the bundle out of the flame. The glowing subsided, but the sage continued to smoke. Marissa moved around the room, letting the smoke pour into every crevice. It washed over the paintings, over and under the table and over and around the chairs, too.

Once she was satisfied everything had been cleansed, she ground out the bundle on the side of her mug of tea so it didn't burn any further than it needed to. *I'm getting quite good at this now!* She brushed the dust into the candle holder and placed the sage on the table to cool. Then she sat down with her tea in her hands, facing the door, to wait for Fiachra, who didn't turn up.

'Typical,' she groaned, looking at her watch at fifteen minutes past the hour. *I guess he isn't coming then. I did have a feeling... I suppose when things are going well, people just don't want to come. Mr Blakemore is right about not finding out what happens in the end. What a pain.*

She retrieved her phone and the book from her handbag. The first thing she did was text Matt.

Hi how's your day going? My first client didn't show up, just wanted to say hi.

What now? She opened the book to a random page.

You are your own biggest obstacle. You stand in the way of your own success. If you always think small, you will always live a small life. It's time to think bigger.

Nothing new here. Why such a genius then? She put the book back down on the table, took her phone back out, looked at Facebook and played *Crossy Road* until it was ten minutes to the next session.

Nipping out to the bathroom, she caught sight of herself in the mirror. For a moment she thought she saw an older woman hovering behind her. She was wearing a black dress and had long silver hair and many necklaces. Her face seemed wise. She felt very familiar, but from where? She looked again, but the woman had disappeared.

She went back to her room, hid her mug of tea and tucked the book away safely in her bag. She didn't need any talking points to distract Cliona. Cliona needed to set the agenda for the session. The buzzer rang, and Marissa let her in.

Cliona was much more contained than she had been the previous week. She was wearing a tracksuit and her hair was up in a messy bun. She looked exhausted. She sat down and crossed her legs, then uncrossed them, avoiding Marissa's gaze.

'Hi, Marissa,' she said flatly.

'Hi, Cliona. How are you doing this week?'

Cliona eventually looked up. 'I'm doing better, thank you. And thanks for last week. I was in a bit of a state, but I'm alright now. Thank God.' She smiled. 'I got my period. I think it was my period anyway, though I was three weeks late. The test must have been wrong. It hurt like hell, though. Maybe it was me losing the baby. Well, it's not really a baby that early, is it?'

'Are you alright now? Do you need to go to the doctor and get checked out? '

'Well, no, I'm fine now.'

Marisa thought about it. 'It might be a good thing to do. Please consider it. How are you feeling today?'

'Relieved. It's been a hell of a time – seven days of holding all this stuff inside. I'm glad I didn't tell Nan. You were the only one I told. It really helped knowing someone else knew.'

'That's my job.'

'Yeah, I guess it is.'

'How are things with you and your nan?'

Cliona's eyes went up to heaven. 'Nan's a right arse sometimes. She's great with Ari, but she's been damn difficult with me lately.'

'Would you like to talk about it tonight, or is there something else you want us to focus on? Oh, by the way, I talked to the office and they're putting you down for another six-week cycle with me.'

Cliona scratched her head. 'Another six weeks? That's a lot. Have we really done six weeks already?'

'Yes, we have. Tonight is number six.'

'Jeez, that went by fast. Okay, yeah, great, let's keep going then. 'Cos I want to talk to you about Bren. He texted me. Two days ago. He wanted to meet up with me.' She brightened.

'What did you say?'

'Well, duh, I said yeah, of course. It's tomorrow. We're going for a drink down my local. That's what Nan's giving me grief about. She says he's always messing me around, but actually I think it's me that's messing him around. I really want it to work out between us.'

Marissa wanted to ask about Andy, to bring it back to Cliona's body, but she held back. *Curiosity doesn't belong in the session room.* 'So how can I help you this evening?'

'Well, how do I tell Brendan that I'm sorry for how I acted and that I'm working on my anger issues?'

'You said it very well to me just there. Can you say it in the same way to him?'

Cliona smiled, 'Yeah. I guess I worry too much. Maybe we should do more work on my anger issues tonight?'

'It's up to you, of course. Have you been working on relaxing?'

Cliona shrugged her shoulders in a non-committal way.

'If you like,' Marissa continued, 'I can teach you a technique to help you calm down when you feel your anger rising up.'

'Yeah, go on. Sounds good.'

'And you need to relax more, unwind, even when you're not angry, so the anger doesn't build up so much. This one, you have to actually practise it when you're *not* angry, because when you're angry you might totally forget that you can do it, and then it's too late.'

'Naw,' Cliona smiled. 'I'm really good at remembering things. Promise! Let's do it.'

After Cliona left, Marissa got up and stretched. She really wanted some fresh air. She waited another minute to make sure Cliona had truly left the building, as she didn't want to meet her outside. Then she got her key and walked down the corridor, down the stairs and out the front door, into the cold night air.

It was dark and the car park was practically empty. Marissa couldn't understand it – her college mates always said they had difficulty finding placements and getting clients, but she and Dave were the only ones in the building, and before Dave, she'd been the only one there. *Well, Mr Blakemore did say there would be more volunteers coming in the next month. Who knows what's going on behind the scenes here? I guess it's like client work – you can only work with what you know.*

She stretched and took a few deep breaths and noticed a

tightness in her chest, like a knot right on her breastbone. *Maybe I picked up on some of Cliona's anger?* She softened, but it seemed to hurt more now that she'd brought her attention to it. She imagined herself letting go of Cliona's energy, as if it was a rock. She just put it down, but that didn't help. *Hmmm...* She focused on the tightness in her chest, wondering how much energy was hers and how much was Cliona's. *If Cliona's energy was a colour, what colour would it be?* She saw red and orange inside her chest, sharp fragments, like splinters of glass. *No wonder they hurt.* She imagined them dissolving away, but that didn't work either, it actually made it worse. She shook her head in frustration then used her fingers and her imagination, and plucked a bit of the invisible glass out of her chest. She felt immediate relief. *Wow! That worked! Amazing!* She plucked out another and felt another subtle change. *Am I making this up? But I do feel better, so I'll keep going.* She looked once more in her mind's eye to see the orange/red colour of Cliona's energy in her own chest and got an image of something hard and black embedded deep within her heart centre.

Well, I can't get in there myself with my fingers. I know, I'll call on Archangel Michael. Archangel Michael, can you help me? I know it has been a while. I'm sorry I haven't talked to you in so long. Please can you take Cliona's energy out of my heart?

She felt something loosen and lift, then something opened in her chest, around her heart centre. She sighed. It really did feel better. She had a sense that it was more than just Cliona's energy the angel had lifted out of her heart. She had been so stressed, she must have generated some of it herself. *Thank you so much, my lovely angel. I am sorry. I will do better in future.* She felt a tingle in her body, and a lifting, almost similar to when she was lying in the bed with her lapis lazuli, but not as intense. It felt sweet, subtle and reassuring. She smiled.

A car drove into the car park and stopped. *This must be Joy.* The driver got out of the car and walked over towards Marissa. She was wearing a mustard-coloured coat, a cream scarf and long brown boots. She had long dark hair and was wearing tortoiseshell glasses. Marissa waited for her to arrive at the front steps. 'Hi,' she said. 'Are you here for counselling?'

The woman smiled nervously. 'Yes, I'm here to see Marissa.'

'That's me. I needed some air between sessions. It's nice to meet you.'

'Hi. I'm Joy. Nice to meet you, too.'

Marissa led Joy through the building to her therapy room. 'Would you like to hang your coat up?'

Under her coat, Joy wore a patterned dress that reminded Marissa of the Laura Ashley wallpaper she had once had in her bedroom growing up.

Joy stood at the door, not sure what to do. Marissa gestured to the chairs. 'Choose whichever one you like,' she said with a smile.

Joy chose the chair facing the door and sat down. Her body language was tight; Marissa could see how nervous she was. She sat opposite her.

'Hi, Joy, it's lovely to meet you. This is your first of a cycle of six sessions with me here in Cabra. Everything you say in here is completely confidential. I won't tell anyone unless I feel you could harm yourself or someone else, then I am obliged to tell my supervisor. I hope you feel safe enough to tell me anything you like. I will listen and do my best to help you. If we feel you need another cycle of sessions, we will discuss it during our fifth meeting. Do you have any questions?'

'Erm, no, I don't think so.'

'Okay, great. Well, let's take it as it comes. So tell me a little bit about yourself and about what prompted you to come to see a counsellor.'

Joy took a moment to gather her thoughts. 'Where do I start? I suppose I could tell you what I do – I'm a primary school teacher. I've just moved out of my parents' house and into my own place. I'm twenty-nine, a little old maybe for still living with my parents, but I moved out before and it didn't work out. And Dublin's so expensive! It took me ages to get the money together to be able to move out. I'm hoping this time it's more successful for me.'

Marissa nodded and stayed silent to give Joy all the space she needed to get comfortable.

Joy sighed, took off her glasses and cleaned them with a tissue from the box on the coffee table, then put them back on again. She looked at Marissa. 'My boyfriend wants to move in with me, but I'm not ready yet. I didn't feel like I had much space with my parents, I'm enjoying having the time on my own, and I'm only just really getting settled into my flat now. It's chaotic you know, being in a classroom with all the children, I'm teaching Junior Infants right now and they can be very demanding. Don't get me wrong, I love them, each one of them, but it can be very tiring, it feels like I'm juggling, sometimes. So I appreciate my quiet time. I don't think he understands. The reason I'm here though, well, every time he asks me if he can move in I freeze, then I get flashbacks in my mind, and that upsets me. I'm not sure what these flashbacks are about, or how to explain them. I'm probably not explaining myself well here, either.' She stopped then, hesitant to go on, seeming very frustrated.

Marissa took it as a prompt. 'When you say flashbacks, do you mean memories of something that happened to you that was, perhaps, traumatic?'

'Well, actually no, I don't. They're probably not flashbacks at all, really. I call them flashbacks because I don't know what else to call them. They're scenes or pictures in my mind, like stories, or dreams, or memories. But they never actually happened to me. It's so strange. This isn't the first time this has happened to me either. It happened before, when I was doing my Leaving, and again in college for a time. Actually now that I think of it, that was also around exam time.'

'Are the memories, or scenes, always the same?'

'No, not always exactly the same. But when I see them, it feels the same. In here,' she pointed to her heart centre, 'and also here,' pointing to her stomach, 'and here,' pointing to her throat. 'I guess they're like scenes from a movie, but I don't remember seeing a movie like them.'

'Can you tell me more?'

Joy seemed relieved to be taken seriously.

I know what that's like first-hand now. Maybe that's why I had to experience this, so that I can relate better to my clients?

Joy sat back in her chair, making herself more comfortable. 'It's like I'm someone else in the flashback, like I'm having her memories, and not my own. It sounds so strange. I've told my boyfriend about them, but it creeps him out. I thought I should talk to someone who wouldn't judge me. I'm scared, you see, of going to a doctor about this. I don't want to take medication again. I did that before and I think it made me worse. That's really why I had to move back in with my parents. I don't want that to happen again.'

'I don't know if I can help change things,' Marissa said, carefully, 'and I'm not able to decide whether you need medication or not. Maybe you need to visit your doctor?' *Twice in the same night referring people to their doctor... that's unusual.*

'Thanks. No, I'm okay. I don't want to go to the doctor just now. I think talking about it might help.'

'Well, I'm happy to sit and listen to whatever you want to talk about, without judgement. I can reflect it back to you, or we can talk about it together so you can make sense of it.' *Should I have said I was happy to listen? I'm* supposed *to listen, it's not about whether I'm happy or not...*

But Joy seemed satisfied with the answer. 'Yes, please,' she said. 'You're the first person I've told this to who's not made me feel like I'm crazy.'

'I think there are many people labelled crazy who aren't actually crazy at all, we just don't understand them. And I'd like to understand this, with you. Okay, let's go back to the beginning. You said your boyfriend wants to move in with you, and each time you felt pressure from him to do this, you got one of these "flashbacks".'

Joy nodded.

'They're images, like from a movie, or a dream. Are they the same images every time?'

'Nearly the same, but not exactly the same I guess, now that I think of it. And each time it gets a little stronger, more vivid.'

'Can you share one of them with me?'

Joy hesitated. 'Yes, I suppose so. I look at my hands. I can't move them; they are bound together with a thick, heavy rope. I look at my feet; they are also bound. I'm standing on sticks – lots of sticks piled together. And when I look up, there are lots of people, lots and lots of people. They are all angry –angry at me. I don't know why. And then my head goes funny and then I'm back here.'

'When you say "back here", what do you mean?'

'Well, it's almost as if I'm really there, standing on a pile of sticks in front of all of those people. Then I'm not, I'm here.' Joy blushed and added, 'I've read books and seen movies about time travel, but I don't think it's that. That's not real, is it?'

Marissa smiled. 'Not as far as I am aware, no, we can't time travel just yet.'

Joy looked slightly relieved.

Marissa asked, 'Your head "goes funny" – what does that mean?'

'It's like I pass out, or get dizzy.'

And how do you feel when you "come back"?'

'Disoriented.'

'Can you tell me what that's like for you?'

'Yes, I feel blurry, foggy, like I don't know which way is up. It takes me a few minutes to get oriented again.'

'How often does this happen?'

'I've lost count now. I'm beginning to think of it as an episode of something rather than a flashback.' Joy seemed very upset and frustrated. 'I think talking about this is making it worse.'

'Sorry for all the questions. I just want to understand what it feels like to experience this. I'm wondering if these episodes are brought on by stress – you mentioned exams as being a trigger, and now your boyfriend is putting pressure on you. What do you think?'

'Yes, it's possible. Stress related – yes, it makes sense. But they're happening more frequently now.'

Marissa took a minute to think about it and to give Joy some time to compose herself after her barrage of questions.

'I have an idea for you,' she said. 'I don't think we can sort it all out tonight. We need to understand these episodes, or flashbacks, a little better first. And if they really are stress related. It would be good if you could get a small notebook and pen, and when you have one of these episodes, write down the time, place and how you were feeling at the time. And anything else that comes into your mind that might be relevant. You could do it for a week, and then when we meet next week we can see if there's any pattern to it.'

Joy smiled and looked relieved. 'That's a great idea. I don't know why I didn't think of doing that myself before. Thank you!'

'Maybe if you thought of them as episodes, too. That would distance you from them, so you could be better able to document them? Instead of calling them flashbacks and becoming distressed by them. Just for this week, of course, that way you know you're doing something about it, and that might relieve some of your stress, too.'

Joy nodded. 'This does feel better, and I like having a purpose now. Thank you.'

'My pleasure. Is there anything else you think would help you with these episodes?'

'Well, if my boyfriend stopped pressuring me, that would help! But I don't know how to say it to him. He takes everything so personally. If I told him I didn't want him to move in with me, he'd think that I wanted to break up with him. He's stubborn like that. I don't want to break up, but I like things the way they are right now, that's all. I'm enjoying living on my own, for now anyway. And it's great to not have to tell people where I'm going or what I'm doing all the time. My parents treated me like I was a teenager while I was there with them, it wasn't healthy for me.'

'Setting boundaries in relationships can be tricky, alright. Have you brought this up with your boyfriend in conversation? I mean, have you had a level and balanced conversation about it? Or do you just wait until he brings it up, and then it gets emotional and you have an episode?'

'Yes, the last time it happened, he brought it up. And probably the time before that. I avoid talking about it. I'm afraid of the consequences if I say it to him. I don't like it when he gets upset or angry with me.'

'It looks as though you may need to have a conversation with him on your terms, when you're ready to. I know it is going to be difficult, but it will be good for you, too.'

Joy nodded, reluctantly.

'Maybe ask him if you could talk to him about something that's upsetting you?' Marissa suggested. 'In relationship therapy we learned that couples aren't always ready to talk about their relationship issues with each other at the same time. I'm not a relationship counsellor – not yet, anyway – but I do know that I personally need prior warning to be prepared if I am going to talk about something tricky. Like a meeting. So you could ask if you can arrange a meeting with him to talk about something that is upsetting you. Write down what you want to say to him before you meet with him so you won't forget anything. Don't worry, it's just an idea, you've got plenty to do right now as it is.'

Joy shivered. 'Yes, I don't know if I'm ready to do that yet, but it sounds like a good idea. I'll think about it.'

Marissa got home around 9:30pm. She heated up some soup and sat in the courtyard, wrapped in her woollen cardigan. She had a good day. She held her phone in her hand, rereading the goodnight text from Matt. The Scott Taylor book was still in her handbag. It could wait.

CHAPTER NINE

I told Joy last night she should have a conversation with her boyfriend about something that's upsetting her. A conversation about having a conversation... I need a conversation with Noreen but I'm still not ready for it. I guess I can't really ask her if we can have a conversation about having a conversation either. I'll not get impatient with my clients again, now I see that I know what it feels like to want something but not be ready to ask for it. It's Friday, I'll focus on the weekend instead, and maybe I'll be ready to talk on Monday. Monday is a good day for meetings!

More sure of herself, Marissa looked up the TV guide to see what was going to be on that night. Matt was coming over for dinner and they were going to hang out at her place and watch a movie. She was looking forward to that – something simple, no drama, no supernatural excitement. Normal couple stuff. She had seen her parents already that week, and Eli and Carol too, so she was free the rest of the weekend to do whatever she wanted.

A thought slipped past the barrier she was constructing in her mind: *I'm supposed to be doing my shamanic homework this weekend.* She shivered. She felt slightly less anxiety around not doing the homework than she had before, but there was a heavy weight hovering above her when it came to shamanic work. *Okay, I need to face this. Maybe I should give it all up altogether. What will help me decide?* Her heart sank. *I wish it was easier to make a decision...*

'Hey, dreamer, are you here or have you drifted away somewhere else?'

Marissa looked up from her desk to see Noreen standing beside her, smiling. She felt prickles of embarrassment as she quickly snapped back into the room.

'Can you come into my office for a moment please? I want to have a quick word.'

Flashes of nervous anxiety ran through her body as she got up, found her work notebook and a pen and followed Noreen into her office.

'Have a seat.' Noreen gestured to the chair opposite hers.

Marissa sat and waited for either a lecture, or instructions for the week to come, or something that would totally wreck her potential weekend plans. Instead, Noreen sat back in her chair, swivelled it around and sighed. She turned to Marissa.

'I booked a spa weekend in Sligo for myself, but unfortunately I need to go to London to clean up a mess someone made over there. It's too late to get a refund, so there's a hotel room, a massage treatment and a seaweed bath with my name on it going a begging this weekend. Do you fancy it? It's a double room.' She winked.

'Wow, really?'

'Yes. It would be such a pity to have all that luxury go to waste. It's yours, if you want it, as a gift, for stepping up and helping out as my manager.'

Marissa felt her cheeks get hot. She knew Noreen would notice it.

'You've earned it, you work hard, but I know that it's not where your heart is. Look, you're competent and I'm really happy with the quality of your work, but I can see that you're not a company girl, you're here for a job, not a career. So think of this weekend away as a gift from me as your mentor and friend and take it as it's meant – no strings attached.'

Marissa didn't know what to say.

'I'll find someone else to step into the managerial role, don't worry. I know you've just been waiting for an opportunity to tell me this yourself. I beat you to it...' Noreen cocked her head on one side. 'And you haven't hurt my feelings. I want someone who wants to be here.'

Mum! What did you say to her? I told you not to say anything!

Noreen looked at Marissa's shocked face and laughed. 'I know what you must be thinking. Yes, I had lunch with Rose. She wanted to show me her new car and tell me all her news. Of course the conversation included how you were getting on here. I didn't realise you had gotten so far in your studies. Well done! You're going to be qualified soon?'

'Yes,' Marissa nodded, relaxing a little bit. 'I should have my diploma by the end of the summer.'

'So you 'll be a qualified psychotherapist!'

'Well, almost. I still need to finish up on client hours to qualify, then I need 400 client hours to be fully accredited. Only then will I be able to set up my own practice or work for someone else.'

Noreen raised an eyebrow. 'You'll get those hours, I'm sure. I'm happy for you, finding what you love to do. Not many people manage to figure that out so young.' She smiled and Marissa smiled back. 'It's good for me too, as it takes the pressure off both of us – me trying to mould you into a managerial role, and you trying to fit into it. Rose has been a very good friend of mine for many years. We talk to each other probably more than you realise. She's been very worried about you, with the whole James thing... I wanted to take you under my wing and give you some skills for life, for her mainly, but for you also - I feel relieved now. I'm delighted you're on-track with something *you* want, rather than with something someone else wants for you.'

Marissa felt relieved, a huge weight had been lifted from her. 'Thank you. I didn't see it from your point of view, yes, I'm happier now than I've been a long time. But this job, working here, has really helped me get on my feet.'

'I'm glad. And you can stay here as long as you need to, but I might need to shift your responsibilities a little. We can worry about that another time. So, do you fancy Sligo then? You can bring your new man with you.'

Marissa felt a flash of nerves. 'Does Mum know about him?'

'No, don't worry! I overheard you and Sarah chatting about him. And saw all the dreamy looks and the texting, which isn't like you. It's great, though. I'm happy for you. And don't worry, I didn't mention it to Rose, it didn't feel like my place to.'

Marissa felt relieved again. 'Thank you so much. You're right, I've not told them yet... I'm still getting used to it myself. And yes, thank you. If you're sure, I will go to Sligo – tomorrow?'

'Yes, check in at 12, massage at 4 in the hotel spa, seaweed bath at 11am Sunday morning and check out at 2. All yours.'

Marissa's head was spinning. 'Thank you, Noreen, thank you so much. For everything.'

'Hey, you're not quitting on me, and you're still working here. I expect to see you in bright and early Monday morning as usual. I still need you here, doing what you do. And continuing to do it well. Especially when I'm not here, it's good to know you're manning the fort. Is that okay with you? I'll be in London probably until Thursday.'

'Very okay. Thank you. I'm relieved. I was going to tell you all of this, but I didn't know how.'

'Well, don't kill your mum for breaking a confidence – sometimes a nudge is what is needed. You're acting manager until I find your replacement, then I may have to demote you. Okay?'

'Perfect. Thank you so much.'

'Good. Now have fun this weekend and tell me all about it when I come back from London.'

'I've never had a spa treatment. I always thought it was for the ladies!' Matt grinned as he munched on popcorn later that night at Marissa's flat. 'It does sound like fun, and Sligo is great. I wish I could go, but you know I have an intensive Tai Chi workshop tomorrow and Sunday. It's the last one on this current form and there's an assessment at the end of it.'

'One step closer to being a teacher,' noted Marissa.

Matt nodded and smiled, then offered Marissa the bowl. She took a handful of popcorn.

'I never would have thought of mixing Taytos and popcorn – where did you come up with that idea?' said Matt with his mouth full.

'Eli and I would do it all the time growing up. it just made sense to us.'

'I'm happy for you to get the break away – you deserve it. And you should patent the crisps and popcorn idea. It really works!'

'Maybe we will go to a spa sometime the two of us then?'

'Or a weekend away together! That sounds great. Will have to be after my training is finished though. And I'm a bit short of cash, I'll have to save some up specially.'

Marissa felt a flash through her body. *I'm not quite ready to tell him about the money, or for him to meet my family just yet.*

'Sounds good, yes, let's save up, we could get a good deal off-season.'

The next morning Matt let himself out early, as was becoming the pattern. Marissa left food for Tobermory and caught the mid-morning train to Sligo. She had a small overnight bag, a packed lunch, and at the last minute, she grabbed the book that Dave had lent her. The countryside rolled by as the train cut deeper into the landscape.

The further she got from Dublin the more relaxed Marissa found herself becoming. About forty minutes outside Dublin, her lunch eaten, she took the book out of her bag and looked at the cover for a few minutes. *Scott Tayler. Who are you?* She eventually opened it up, skipped the effusive endorsements and looked at the Table of Contents in more detail. *Why am I experiencing such an aversion to this person?* The contents looked reasonable; in fact, the promise they offered to the reader even looked enticing. Marissa turned to Chapter Three and started to read.

> *So, if you have gotten this far then there is no turning back. You are ready to face your fears, leave your old life behind, and climb up the most incredible mountain to follow your dreams. When you believe you can have your dream, you trigger a chain reaction inside your body. The chemicals of regret, shame, injustice, fear - they influence your thoughts. They make you feel flat, apathetic, slovenly. You cannot get momentum. Nothing happens for you, everything happens to you. When you start to feed yourself with hope, inspiration and thoughts of success, when you move your body and exercise, get outside and breathe that fresh air, you change your body chemistry, release endorphins and*

bask in the joy enzymes, it propels you even further up that mountain. Some people say you've got to see it to believe it, I say, start believing and start creating, and you will be seeing it for sure, because you are the one that made it happen.

I guess that makes sense, but what are 'joy enzymes'? Marissa still felt an aversion to the book, but there was something compelling beginning to draw her in. She had read more than half of it by the time the train pulled into Sligo, a few hours later.

Sligo had a lovely feeling to it. Marissa felt safe and happy as she explored the town and found Noreen's hotel. An Italian restaurant caught her eye for later. She was used to being on her own, but this was the first time she had been away for a night in a hotel by herself. It felt very 'grown up', and for some reason she was a little giddy. Perhaps it was the freedom of the burden that was now lifted off of her around her work, from becoming sucked into a job-for-life that she didn't really want. She had liked hearing herself say 'set up my own practice or work for someone else'. Being a therapist full-time was beginning to be something she could really see herself doing. It was one thing getting the qualification; this was another thing altogether, and it excited her.

Tobermory had the flat to himself. It felt much bigger without Marissa. He jumped up onto her bed and sniffed around her pillows, then leapt down and went underneath the bed. He was used to Marissa not being there, but this time it was different... More open? But the door was closed. It felt better – yes, that was it. Nothing under here. It felt much better now. He mewed, leapt back up onto the bed, licked his paws, then curled up on her pillow and slept.

The hotel was clean, modern and welcoming, almost clinical except for little touches such as flowers in the lobby and a display of paintings by local artists. Marissa had no trouble checking in with Noreen's booking. Her room was on the second floor and had a view of the gardens. It was bright and spacious, had a double bed, a bath, small desk, a table and chair, TV and tea and coffee-making facilities. *Really fancy place! I like it here.*

It was already 3:30pm so she left her overnight things in the room and went straight to the hotel spa. She'd never been to a spa before; it was a completely new experience. The receptionist gave her a form to fill out, then took her into a changing room where she was given a white robe and white slippers. She wandered around, taking in the sights and smells, feeling delighted with herself. She poured herself a long drink of distilled water filled with fruit and stretched out on a *chaise longue* in the relaxation room until it was time for her treatment. The massage was glorious. She floated back to the relaxation room and lay down looking at magazines until her stomach reminded her it was dinner time.

Later, in her big double bed, after spaghetti and a silly romance movie on RTÉ, Marissa switched off the TV and settled down to sleep. She was happy. She decided she liked Italian food, silly movies and hotel spa breaks. Even Scott Taylor seemed okay. Life was good, just like this. It was enough. She drifted.

Marissa was standing in the woods, she felt intense pain. She looked down and her arm had been bitten off, chewed fragments of bone protruded out from it, and she was covered in blood. She wanted to scream out, but she couldn't speak. She felt a sense of something large with teeth and claws, hiding in the darkness behind the trees. Was it going to come back and finish her off?

She woke with a jump in the bed, slightly sweaty. She brushed her hair from her forehead and sat up not knowing where she was. *Oh yes, I'm in the hotel.* She was feeling quite anxious so she turned on the light. It was 2am. She caught her breath.

I'm safe, it's okay, it's just me here, there's nothing in here with me.

She lay back down in the bed, with the light still on. *I'm so sick of this now. I was so happy and relaxed earlier, and now I'm a mess. Okay, not as bad a mess as I have been, mind you, but there's something lurking out there, in that forest, and I certainly don't fancy my chances. I want to leave this all behind me. I don't want any more panic, or even the threat of panic. I just want an ordinary life. I don't want to lose control over myself. I'm going to be qualified soon, and I've got Matt now. I don't need anything more.* She reached over to the bedside locker and got hold of the Scott Taylor book. She sat for a few moments unconsciously stroking the cover.

I've got to finish with all of that other stuff. It's not good for me. Magic is just too much trouble. Shamanism and angels – it's crazy dangerous. I don't want to be a crazy person, I'm much happier as I am.

She opened the book and read:

> *Once you have decided your path, you must commit to it 100%. Being interested won't crack it, as there will be obstacles in your way. You will have to try and try again to overcome them. Only committing yourself wholeheartedly will get you to the finish line.*

Reading the words had a calming effect. *Yes, that's it, exactly. I have to make a commitment.* She lay back on the pillows and allowed her body to relax. *I know what I want. My own therapy practice. I can do it, I've got everything I need, I just need to put in those hours. I'm almost there already. I'm finishing with all that other stuff. No more magic, no more shamanism, no more angels.* She stretched out and relaxed, more deeply than she had in a very long time, but some part of her wept at the loss of the beauty of the new connections she had been discovering. She pushed the grief away and brought her mind back to how lovely her massage was. *I can get massages in Dublin if I want them. I can get whatever I want.*

Somewhere deep inside, a crack opened. Just a small one, but for the darkness, that's all it takes. Something that had been waiting very patiently for this opportunity crept in. It was so subtle, Marissa didn't even feel it.

I am giving up magic. There will be no more terror. I can live fine without crazy. There's so much I want to do, I can't have another setback. I need 100% commitment to my new life. She looked at the back cover of the book, then stroked the photo of Scott Taylor, smiling at him as he smiled back at her. *Thanks, Scott. I have decided. It is done.*

Flushed with emotion, she suddenly felt like she wanted to cry. She curled up into a tight ball in the bed, but the pressure of emotion became too much, so she straightened herself out again. The room seemed to be spinning, but after a few minutes, with mindful breathing, she managed to get it to right itself. She wasn't sure if she was feeling relief, or grief. Tears almost broke through the surface, but they stayed beneath, not ready to be birthed just yet.

+++

It was strange to wake up in a hotel room away from home on her own, but Marissa felt strangely peaceful. She made herself a cup of tea and got back into bed, leafing through the Scott Taylor book that had stayed in the bed with her all night. She texted Matt:

> Good luck today, you'll be gr8. I'll tell u about seaweed bath later ;-) xx

As she sat in the warm water, the oils from the seaweed soaking into her body and her long curly hair, Marissa tried to kill off all the reasons why she loved shamanism. But it wasn't as easy as she had expected. *I'm good at it, I loved the work I did with Zaad and Terry, and I think shamanism even helped Cliona a little bit. Maybe I should stick with it.* But she felt heavy in the bath, and as much as she loved the work, she was more terrified of falling apart. *I have to make a decision and commit to it, like Scott says. Okay. I'm not going back to 'shaman school'. I won't ever have to see Séamus again, not ever. Then I won't ever need to know if he actually did hurt me or not. I won't have to worry about any of that stuff again.*

It seemed right. Her brain told her 'Yes!' and she felt some light sense of relief, but somewhere in the pit of her stomach, some sort of hole opened, and some part of her fell away, and it fell and fell and fell... She tried to push the sensation away, disregarding it. She didn't want to go into it. This was her decision, forever.

She sank deeper into the water, closing her eyes, the oils and the warm water nurturing her and relaxing her, the unease in the pit of her stomach easing out with every breath. It still didn't feel right, but she had lived with worse.

She opened her eyes and let the natural buoyancy of her body take over. She floated. Her hair rose in tangles around her face; she ran her fingers through it and it felt smoother and softer than usual. She looked at her legs, covered in gooey fronds of seaweed. and got a flash of a memory of being in a milky bath somewhere, but she couldn't remember where. *I love baths, I should have them more often.*

Once she was dried and dressed again, she checked out of the hotel and went looking for somewhere nice to go for lunch. She had a couple of hours before the train back to Dublin. Sligo had some beautiful shops and she found plenty of interesting nooks and crannies to browse. She saw some rose-scented bath milk and bought some to take back home, and when she had done enough shopping, she found a café, ordered a large cappuccino and a sandwich, and read her Scott Taylor. She was almost finished it.

> *So, what's your vision? Remember, I was homeless, I was pushed to the wall and I had to fight hard to survive and put food on the table for my family. But I had no choice. Somehow, I found the strength to get up every morning and go out and get what I needed. But soon, what I needed became what I wanted, and I discovered that if I fought hard every day for what I wanted, without the need behind it, it happened even more quickly than when I thought I needed it. What do you want? And what do you actually need? Because you can have both, if you want it bad enough.*

What do I want? I want an easy life. And to help people too – yes, I want to help people feel better, so they can have good lives too. I can do that, I'm good at it. And I like doing it.

Marissa put the book down and looked out of the café window. The afternoon sun was obscured by thick, heavy clouds. People were walking past, some looking at their feet, others happily chatting to each other in groups. *They seem content, but it's all on the outside, though. There's no way you'd know what anyone was thinking. Though they all look very sad, look at her in the brown coat – she's got drawn eyes, and him – he does seem like he could be depressed. Maybe they need to see a therapist! So many potential clients, my practice is going to be very busy.*

Marissa realised she had spent the last twenty-four hours not speaking to anyone bar the receptionist and the people at the spa. There was a beautiful stillness within her. She loved the feeling; knowing exactly what she wanted, and seeing that it was in reach. *Yes, I have a lot to look forward to.*

It was time to get the train home.

It was dark when she let herself into her flat. Tobermory immediately came out to greet her, mewing and winding himself around her legs. Suddenly he pulled away, looked at her almost accusingly, then ran out the front door before she had a chance to close it. Marissa shrugged her shoulders in puzzlement, hung up her coat, closed the front door and turned the heating on.

She looked around her flat, feeling like something was indeed out of place. *Maybe that's why Tobermory acted so weird just now? He must just be stir-crazy being locked inside all weekend.* The angel cards and shamanic oracle were still out on the coffee table. *Ahh, that must be it.*

She found a box in her cupboard and put the angel cards and the shamanic oracle cards into it. *There's more to go in...* She looked around the flat and found her sage, the medicine bundle, the drum and her crystals – the quartz and the lapis lazuli, all went into the box. She got her notes from the shamanic workshop and the Reiki workshop and put them into the box too. She felt a pang placing the Reiki notes in, but she knew she had to do it. Then she closed the box and shoved it to the back of a cupboard in the kitchen that she never used. *That's that.*

She got her clothes ready for work the next day, tidied up a little and made a shopping list for food. She did some ironing, called Matt on the phone – his workshop had been great, and she texted her dad just to tell him she loved him. She got into bed and closed her eyes.

But it still didn't feel right. She got up again, went back to the box and retrieved the lapis. *Matt did give it to me...* And the quartz. *Well, it is pretty.* Then she got Sellotape, taped the box shut and put it back into the cupboard.

She put the quartz and the lapis on the mantelpiece where they could catch the light and walked back into her bedroom. Then she changed her mind once more and went back to get the lapis. Placing it on the table beside her bed, she felt better. *Now. That's it. That's better.*

Tobermory was back. As Marissa settled in for her night's sleep, he was on the hunt. His tail twitched, ears were taut, his eyes wide open. He was listening, but there was nothing to hear. He scanned the room, but there was nothing to see. This made no sense at all. There was nothing to pounce on, but something was there, illusive, hiding, all the same. He felt uneasy. It was gone before, wasn't it? He padded into Marissa's bedroom, she was sleeping deeply. He carefully leapt up onto the bed and delicately stepped up onto the pillow beside her, watching her breathing, then he moved down beside her on the duvet. It was warm there, and it was his place to be beside her, even though it didn't seem the same tonight. But he was tired after all the fun outside. He turned into a circle and closed his eyes, tail wagging slightly. He would investigate this more thoroughly tomorrow.

CHAPTER TEN

When she woke up on Monday morning, Marissa felt an inner strength that hadn't been there before, a solidness and calmness, an inner poise. She also had not been woken by a bad dream, which had been happening all too frequently of late. She moved lightly and arrived into work early, which wasn't usually like her. She said hello to everyone, she was in a very good mood (also not like her, not being a morning person). She didn't lose focus when reading her emails, and she managed to keep her cool and find a vital missing file for a frantic and very grateful Noreen. She sent it over to her in London while vetting calls from one of their Australian clients, and sorting the sales schedule for March. At lunch she enjoyed Sarah's chatter, sharing details of her spa visit and seaweed bath in Sligo, but leaving out that Noreen had paid for it.

That night she met Matt for dinner. He came into the city and they went to a small bistro that he liked. They got a table at the back and ordered, and then he turned his full attention to her.

'You look different – more relaxed, brighter in yourself. It's nice.' He blushed.

Marissa smiled. 'I had a good weekend, sorted a lot of stuff out. I feel I've got my head together again. After all that mess.'

Matt smiled. 'That's great to hear. I was concerned, being away for two weekends in a row with the Tai Chi stuff, but I really had to do it, you know. I've got one assignment left, then I have to teach my first class. I'm glad I went, but I *was* worried about you. I had my phone fully charged and nearby the whole time. I kept checking it, just in case you'd texted me. I didn't want to text you to disturb you, but you were on my mind all weekend. You weren't yourself, but you seem so much better now.'

Marissa smiled. The waiter brought a bottle of house wine, opened it and poured a small amount into Matt's glass. Matt tasted it. 'Yes, that's great, thanks.' The waiter poured some into Marissa's glass, then filled Matt's, put the bottle aside and left. The couple waited for him to go before speaking again.

Marissa picked up her glass and looked into it. The red wine had a beautiful velvety sheen and the soft lights of the restaurant gave it an attractive depth. She swirled it in her glass, then lifted the glass up towards Matt.

'A toast. To new beginnings, to the rest of our lives. To fun.'

Matt raised his eyebrow, then lifted his glass, smiling. He winked, then clinked it off hers, 'To us, having some fun for a change. It's about time we had some of that, don't you think?'

Marissa grinned, 'Indeed, yes. Totally!'

They drank deep and smiled at each other. There was silence for a moment. It wasn't an awkward one, but unlike during her client sessions, Marissa felt she needed to fill it with conversation.

'So. I've been reading a book by this guy Scott Taylor. I read the whole book while I was away, actually. Have you heard of him?'

'No? Who is he?'

'Some sort of self-help guru. He seems to have a very big following. Dave is big into him. He lent me the book.'

'Dave ... is he the guy you met in Cabra?'

'Yes, the master's student.'

'Ah, yes. Funny that a master's degree student in psychology is interested in a self-help guru.'

'Yes, I thought the same thing, but his work is different to psychotherapy, or probably psychology too, for that matter. More like popular psychology I guess. It's quite uplifting, really, there are some useful ideas in it. I think there might be something to it. It could be handy to learn a few of his confidence-building techniques. I could share them with my clients.'

'Well, okay, if you like him, that's good. Confidence-building *is* valuable and many people do need a lot of help with that,' said Matt thoughtfully.

The waiter came with the food.

Marissa continued, 'You know he has a whole section on building your own business – it could be useful for you, too, if you wanted to set up a Tai Chi practice...'

She waited for an answer, but Matt was already cutting into his steak. He admired the mashed potatoes and gravy, then scooped some onto his forkful of meat.

'Mmm, delicious,' he said with his mouth full.

Marissa smiled. She had ordered chicken, which also came with mash and gravy. She started eating, still waiting to hear what Matt would say. He chewed and swallowed his food.

'You know, Marissa,' he said slowly, 'I'm not really ready for all that yet. I mean, I love Tai Chi, but I don't think I'll be going into business with it. I don't want a Tai Chi school. Not yet, if at all. I don't even know if I want to teach my first class, I just like learning for learning's sake. It makes me happy. And it makes the garage less of a life sentence, if you know what I mean.' He smiled and piled another heap of food onto his fork.

'Okay. I understand. Well, it's there if you want it – the book, I mean. Dave said I could keep it. Actually, I might give it back to him so I don't owe him one. And get another copy for myself.'

Marissa smiled as she watched him eat, her heart doing little flips as she noticed the boyishness of his cheeky face and the glimmer in his eye. She really was rather fond of this man. He started telling her something funny that happened to him in his class that weekend. *He has lovely hands.* Thinking of the last time he had laid his hands on her, she blushed, looked down at her plate and tried to change the subject matter of her internal dialogue by gathering another forkful of food and focusing on his story, which actually was quite funny.

After dinner, Matt went back to Marissa's and admired the lapis in pride of place by her bed. Then he admired her, and she admired him right back.

+ + +

'Sure, I can do that, and please, don't forget to order the black ones this time,' said Marissa to Tim as she went back to her desk at work the following day. She picked up her phone, there was a text from Saoirse.

Hi can we do journey homework together? Or did u already do it with someone? Let me know! xx

Something rippled through her body, she caught it, hesitated for a moment, then got her breath back. She thought about replying and instead, deleted the message.

'Only eight more evenings before we finish!' said Emmet, rubbing his hands together with delight as he went over to the tea caddy to make himself the traditional before-class cuppa.

Marissa smiled. She had already got her tea and was sitting at the table with Yvonne, not minding as much as usual that she had heard the story about Yvonne's sister's children before.

Yvonne stopped talking mid-sentence and looked sideways at Marissa. 'You seem different tonight. In a good way.'

'Yes. I'm happy!'

'Oh!' said Yvonne, breaking into a smile. 'That's good! Nice to hear it. Long may it continue.'

Kate arrived, carrying a shopping bag from Arnott's. She was also smiling. 'Hello, everyone!' she said gleefully, placing her bag on the floor beside a free chair. She took off her coat and sat down for a moment before getting up again to make herself a cuppa.

'What did you buy?' asked Yvonne, curiously.

'A new dress! I lost four pounds! So it's a "well done" present for myself!'

'Well done, you!' said Emmet, smiling as he sat down opposite Marissa, putting his cup on the table. 'Everyone seems in good spirits tonight.'

'Hi, Ronan,' said Yvonne, nodding to the door as Ronan arrived. 'You still have time for a quick cuppa before class.'

'I'm grand, thanks. Had one before I got here,' said Ronan, a little flustered, taking the last remaining chair. 'Hi, guys. I missed last week's class – what are we doing tonight?'

'Advanced psychotherapeutic techniques,' said Marissa.

'What's that then?'

'I have no idea,' Emmet said. 'It seems to be a mish-mash of person-centred, with deeper listening skills. And it includes some Adlerian and Gestalt psychology. The tutor is nice though, and has lots of experience.'

'Deeper listening skills?' asked Marissa. 'How can you listen any deeper than we are already? If we are focusing on listening to what is not being said, as well as to what is being said, I reckon there's a big chance that we'd be making lots of assumptions.'

'What do you mean?' asked Yvonne.

'Well, I guess I mean if someone only gives us part of the issue, our mind fills in the gaps. Like it does for the movies, or TV. But it only fills in gaps based on who we are and how we think. We could assume we know what the issue is, but we could be totally wrong.'

'There are many different shades of green,' agreed Ronan, raising an eyebrow, trying to look mysterious.

'Exactly!' said Marissa, slapping the table.

'I have no idea what you are talking about,' said Yvonne, looking very puzzled.

'Well, when I say "green" and you think of green, are we seeing the same shade of green in our minds? There's a big difference between spearmint green and mustard green,' said Marissa.

'Or forest green and army green,' agreed Ronan, nodding his head.

'Or muddy green,' chimed in Emmet.

'What if they're colour blind and don't know what green looks like?' suggested Yvonne.

'Yes. Now you've got it. And did you know that some people can't see anything in their minds at all?' Marissa continued, 'For some people, it's very easy to, say, imagine an elephant. But others just have a sense of an elephant, not an image of one.' Marissa was rehashing something that Séamus had said in one of their workshops. She suddenly realised where the idea came from and shivered, then pushed the feeling away. *Well, I learned some useful things from those workshops...*

'Do you know that some people can actually smell colours?' said Ronan. 'It's called synaesthesia. Really interesting condition. My nephew has it.'

Emmet looked at his watch. 'Well, lads, it's time to go in, so we'll find out what deeper listening and the like is all about, one way or another,' he said, rising from his chair and making his way to the sink to wash his cup.

+++

It doesn't rain but it pours. Marissa received texts all through the following day from her shamanic group – Liz, Jenny, Terry, even one from Zaad. It was relentless. When Zaad's came in, she had an urge to text back, but she deleted it unread, as she had done with all the others. Then at 4pm she got a text from Terry that she couldn't ignore.

What's up? Everyone texting asking bout u. U ok?'

Yeh I'm fine. Not coming back. Don't want to reply 2 anyone. Can u tell them 4 me?

There was a moment of nothing, then she saw the bubble on the screen, and Terry replied: Feck feck feck. Yeah. Feck ok. Won't be the same without u.

Sorry. just can't.

Still friends?

Always friends.

Cool. Miss u x

Miss u 2

A shadow fell over Marissa as she pressed 'send' on the last text. She felt sadness well up from deep inside her. She tried to brush it off but she felt heavy and damp, and the feeling remained for the rest of the evening.

On her way home from work she phoned Eli. *He always cheers me up* but he was too excited about his own news to be able to listen to hers. *So much for advanced listening!* He was raving about the baby, how well Carol's check-up went, and their plans for the nursery. It was as if he was speaking in another language. She listened and made the appropriate ooh and ahh sounds, then hung up the phone. She got takeaway and watched a movie, then later that night she took Scott Taylor to bed with her, slept deeply and didn't remember her dreams.

The next morning, Marissa awakened with a splitting headache. *Perhaps I need caffeine? Too much salty takeaway food. That must be it.* She showered, drank a coffee and went into work.

She still had the headache by noon though, so she took an early lunch and went to the coffee shop for barista caffeine, as opposed to the instant they had at work. The texts were still coming in and she was getting very frustrated with it now.

Saoirse: Terry told me OMG u ok? Really not comin back?

Jenny: wot happened? woz it dark nrg like u said in class? (That one got deleted straight away.)

Terry: Tried my best they don't listen will prob text u anyway sorry x

Marissa sighed. She really felt like she had a hangover. *From Diet Coke? No, that's not it. It's more like being scraped out of myself, if that makes any sense at all. I've not felt this way since, well, since James left and I was crying all the time and not eating properly, not sleeping. Strange. I've not been crying, I felt okay yesterday. I'm sure it will pass soon.*

She sipped a cappuccino, her third coffee that day, ate a hot cheese toastie and, finally relenting, took two Paracetamols and a chocolate bar. The food, sugar and pills seemed to help a little bit and by 4pm she was feeling mostly better. She had managed to get all her work done, and some of Sarah's too, and she was looking forward to meeting her new clients that night in Cabra.

Marissa noticed how bright the sky still was when she got to the Priory. The days were beginning to have a stretch in them. She called in the office to get the new client pack - Cedric, male, thirty-five, on depression medication. He was first tonight, taking Fiachra's place. After settling into Room Three she heard the buzzer buzz, so she went down and met him at the front door.

Cedric was a tall thin man with short blond hair, wearing a dark blue sweater. He seemed a little nervous. He had no coat with him so perhaps he was just shivering with the cold. *I'm not going to assume anything.*

'Hi, is this the right place?' he asked. 'I'm supposed to see Marissa, I think that's her name.'

'Yes, that's me, come in. Cedric is it?' Marissa smiled in welcome. He nodded.

She walked him through the long hallway and up the stairs, down the corridor and into her room.

'Here we are, Room Three. This is where we'll have our sessions. Next time I'll just buzz you in and you can find your way up here yourself? Now, please, have a seat,' she said with what she hoped was a reassuring tone, gesturing to the free chair.

'Nice to meet you. This is our first of six sessions. Everything that we say in here is confidential, unless I have cause to believe that you will harm yourself, or someone else, in which case I will need to report it to my supervisor.'

Cedric nodded again.

'How can I help?' asked Marissa.

Cedric shifted in his chair, crossing and uncrossing long spindly legs. Marissa waited patiently, not pushing through the silence. After about five minutes he began to speak in a soft voice.

'My mother died. It was very sudden. About three months ago. I'm still having trouble coming to terms with it. My doctor said I should see a counsellor, so I'm here. I've not got much spare cash. The funeral cost me most of my savings.'

'I'm sorry for your loss,' said Marissa, wondering if it was appropriate to say that.

'Thank you. She wasn't even sick – Mum, I mean. Well we didn't think she was sick anyway. It was a heart attack. Seemed to come out of nowhere.'

Cedric was silent again. Marissa waited for him to continue but this time the silence went on for longer and Marissa felt it would be wrong to interrupt it. Cedric looked down at his feet and Marissa held him in her gaze. She could feel the room getting heavy.

There was a splash – a tear had fallen from Cedric's eye onto his shoe. Marissa reached over for the tissues and handed them to him. He took one gratefully, blew his nose and looked up at her.

'I just don't know when they will come – the tears, I mean.' He blew his nose again.

Marissa waited a moment before replying, 'That's okay, just feel whatever it is that you are feeling. This is your space to talk, or not to talk. Whatever you choose to do is up to you.'

'I wish I could control it better,' Cedric admitted. 'That's really why I'm here. Sometimes at work – I'm back at work now – I just start to cry. For no reason. Well, obviously there *is* a reason, but there doesn't seem to be a reason at the time.'

Marissa waited again before responding. 'I understand,' she said. 'You're saying that there seems to be no particular trigger that sets your tears off.'

'Yes, exactly.' Cedric looked around the room, then put the tissue on the table. 'Is there a bin anywhere?'

Marissa got up and brought the waste paper basket over. Cedric put his used tissue in it and took a new one. 'Thanks.'

Marissa sat down. 'No problem.'

'So, yeah, I'm here because I don't want to cry over nothing.'

Marissa took a breath. 'I don't think it's nothing. You *are* grieving. You must have loved your mother very much.'

Cedric started to cry again, this time more profusely. After a while, he gathered himself and spoke once more. 'I'm a grown man, for God's sake, I shouldn't be crying like this.'

'Who told you that?'

Cedric looked at Marissa. 'What do you mean?'

'Well, who told you that you shouldn't be crying?'

He thought for a moment. 'I don't know exactly. I suppose it's an idea that I have.'

'Take a moment and really think about it.'

Cedric looked off in the distance for a while, then his eyes settled back on Marissa. 'Ok. I think I remember. I was about eight years old. I was playing football and I missed the goal and started crying. My dad told me to stop it. "Boys don't cry," he said. Well, Dad, I'm not a boy now, I'm a man, and I can't stop crying.'

'Yes, you are, you're a sensitive man who has just lost his mother, whom he loved very much. Can you give yourself a break?'

'A break? How?' he said with a sniff, wiping his eyes once more.

'Well, for me, as a therapist, seeing a grown man cry is not an unusual thing.' *Okay I've actually not seen very many, if any, but he doesn't know that.* 'And I think it's much healthier for you to express your grief than to hold it back. It's your body letting go of emotion.'

'Give myself a break.' Cedric shrugged his shoulders and sat back in the chair, relaxing slightly. 'I suppose it's hard enough feeling this sad, let alone trying to control it.'

'Yes, it can be very tiring when you're holding back emotion. Maybe it's too big for you to hold it all back, all the time? Maybe it's during those moments when you're focused on something else, using your energy on something else, that it breaks through. Like a dam bursting.'

Cedric reached for another tissue. 'Yes, okay, it sounds like it could be that.' He wiped his face, crumpled the tissue in his hands and looked a little brighter. 'I thought there was something wrong with me.'

'There's nothing wrong with you. I'm wondering, though, do you give yourself time to cry when you are alone?'

He thought about it. 'No, not really.'

'So, if your grief builds up every day and you're focused on not feeling it, or holding it back, it's still going to build up. What if you allowed yourself to feel it so it didn't build up as much?'

'That sounds awful. I don't really *want* to feel it.'

'Yes, I know, it is difficult, but you don't want the dam to burst. It might be better if you can vent the pressure behind it when you feel safe to do so, instead of waiting for an explosion.'

Cedric thought about this. 'Well, I suppose I could try that. But how do I do it?'

'I suppose you just make a space for yourself and let yourself feel sad.'

'Are you sure that this is normal?'

'Yes, totally sure. Grief happens in different ways to different people. This is how you are experiencing grief right now. It could be different next week, or if something new was to happen, say in a few years' time, you could feel it differently then. I think if you see this as your grief experience for the loss of your mother, it might be easier for you to let yourself feel it. And they do say that if you hold back a feeling it can make you sick.'

'Okay. I'll try it. But what do I have to do, again?'

'Well, you can't push it or force it. But you could take some time every day to sit with the grief, to allow yourself to feel sad. You might cry, and it might be uncomfortable, but you could imagine the pressure inside of you is releasing, so the dam's not liable to burst as often. I mean, it doesn't mean you won't cry when you don't want to be seen to cry, but you might not cry as often. I suppose you'll have to try it to find out if it works.'

Cedric had gone through three more tissues while Marissa was talking. But he seemed in better spirits.

'Thank you so much. It's really helpful to be able to talk about it without having to mind you. I mean, every time I talk about it, the person I talk to gets upset for me, and then I get upset because they're upset. You don't know me; this is your job. You're supposed to listen to me, and you're okay with me being sad. It's strange, isn't it? So many people don't like feeling sad or being around people who are sad.'

'Totally. Sadness is just as valid an emotion as happiness, but people have a problem with it because it isn't pleasant to experience. The first thing most people want to do is turn it off, a little like your dad saying, "Boys don't cry." But they do cry, and if we were allowed to feel our feelings, they wouldn't build up and make us ill. And we all feel sad from time to time, and you're grieving. Grief is a massive sadness. It's not a small thing. If you get to know yourself a little better and learn how you grieve, find out what you need when you're grieving, then you can manage it better.'

'Thanks, Marissa, this has really helped.'

When Cedric left Marissa lit some sage that she found in her handbag and let the smoke fill the room. It seemed to lift some of the sadness that Cedric had left behind him. But then she had a sudden flash of white behind her eyes, realised what she was doing and a tremendous guilt set in. *I said I'd not do this type of thing any more. But it helps lift the room up a bit. I need a good clear room for my next client. Maybe burning sage is okay?*

She smiled and softened, glad that Cedric was feeling better. *I told him to look after himself, and I need to look after myself too. So that I'm at my best for the next client. And I want the room to be at it's best for my next client. So using sage is okay.* Her body still felt a little guilty, but it lessened as she sat down to wait and took a few deep breaths. There were still a few minutes before Cliona was due, so Marissa thought she'd go find Dave and tell him she was enjoying Scott Taylor. She went out into the corridor to find him but his door was closed. The light was on inside the room, though. She could see it pouring out from underneath the closed door. Shadows were moving on the floor from the people inside. *He's with a client. That's good!*

She went back into her room, sat back into one of the chairs, closed her eyes and checked in to see how she was feeling. Cedric's sadness was a damp sort of feeling. She had felt damp the day before, but this was different, more of a stagnant dampness, like moss. She didn't want to feel it, or for Cliona to feel it. Saging the room had lifted some of it, but not all. *It must be in my energy field, not in the room. Maybe Reiki will help?*

For the first time in several weeks, she connected to a source of Reiki. It felt very weak to her, as if she could barely connect to it at all. She breathed and visualised the Reiki light coming down into her body through her crown, down into her heart, up and over her shoulders, down her arms and out of her hands, but she didn't feel anything. She shrugged it off. The buzzer buzzed and she let Cliona in.

'Hi, Marissa.' Cliona stood at the door catching her breath, seeming a little put off by Marissa sitting in the chair that she usually sat in. 'No, don't get up,' she said gruffly.

She hung her coat on the back of the door and sat down in the other chair. She was wearing jeans and a baggy top. Marissa looked at her; she was beginning to be able to tell what kind of mood Cliona was in based on what she was wearing.

'So I have some news.'

'Okay,' said Marissa, focusing on Cliona. She was sitting with her knees together, her elbows on her knees and her head in her hands, as if posing for a portrait.

'So. Two things happened this week. Since I saw you, I mean. First thing is ... Bren and me are proper back together. Proper, like. I told him I was working with you, he said he'd give me extra space to figure out the anger thing, and we said we loved each other to each other. I'm excited about that, actually.'

She took her head out of her hands, looked straight at Marissa and waited for her approval. Marissa started to smile, but Cliona quickly held her hand out in the 'stop' signal, so she held back. Cliona started squirming in her chair.

'Second thing...'

Heat prickles travelled down Marissa's back and agitation crept into her body. *This is just like the last time! Not again, no thank you.* In her mind, she pushed them away from herself and felt them leave. Her body relaxed.

Cliona shivered.

Did I send that back to Cliona? What was that? Marissa stayed silent, allowing it to play out naturally.

Cliona eventually spoke. 'Okay. Well. Second thing is, that wasn't my period I got last week. So I'm still pregnant.'

Marissa almost said, 'Oh shit,' but managed to hold herself back. She hoped that her face hadn't given it away.

'Well, anyway, it's dead early in the pregnancy, and me and Bren had sex... So I'm just gonna tell him it's his.'

Once more Marissa had to hold herself back. *No judgement.* She took a breath and tried to look as though she wasn't struggling with herself.

Cliona was ahead of her. 'Shit, isn't it?' she said, grimacing. 'But I think I've got used to it. And it *could* actually be his ... kind of.'

She brightened. 'Ari will be happy once I tell her she's gonna have a little brother or sister.'

Marissa didn't know what to say, so she kept quiet.

Cliona made an effort at a laugh. 'I guess I'm just going to get shit on by life, hey.'

She was looking at her directly, waiting for some kind of response. Marissa really couldn't get out of it. *Bring it back to the feelings, that's my catch-all.*

'How do you feel about it?'

'I feel fuckin' shite actually. Like a dried shite. Or a boiled one. Not sure what kind of shite. I feel like three different kinds of shite. There you go. What *should* I be feeling about this then, Marissa, hey?'

'I'm not sure there is a particular way you should be feeling, Cliona.'

'Yeah, so there you go.'

Marissa needed to steer it away from the pregnancy thing for a bit while she got her head around it. 'So how is it going with you and Bren?'

Cliona softened and sank back into the chair, her face flushed and her eyes glistening. 'Ah. It's great. He's so, well, dreamy. We're in our honeymoon phase. It always gets like this when we get back together again. Nan called us the lovebirds.' She sat up again. 'But I feel shite from the pregnancy, and from not telling him, and knowing that I'm gonna have to tell him, and Nan, soon. I'm nearly two months gone now.'

Cliona's phone went off; it was a Beyonce tune. She took it out of her bag and looked at it. 'It's Bren. Can I get it?'

Marissa nodded, glad of the distraction.

'Hiya, yeah, good, yeah, yeah, okay, yeah, see you later, yeah, perfect.' Cliona hung up. 'He's comin' over tonight for dinner.' She switched off her phone. 'Sorry 'bout that.'

'It's okay. So your nan knows you're back together?'

'Yeah. Actually, she seems happy about it! Total surprise, there. She's said so many times how she didn't like him. Now she's even gonna cook for us. I don't know what's gotten into her.'

'Have you been sick with the pregnancy?' Marissa finally felt she had an angle.

'Yeah, I have actually. Morning sickness – what a joke, where did they get that name from anyway? I'm sick in the morning, alright. Vomit my guts up at night-time too, and sometimes in the afternoon.'

Wonder if her nan figured out about the pregnancy...

'So how did you find out you were still pregnant? Did you do another test?'

'Yeah. I stopped bleeding after two days – it wasn't the same as a period actually, not as heavy, like. So I kinda started wondering. It did hurt like hell, though. I got three tests, did them one day after another, all positive. So I guess the little blighter is stuck in and gonna stay the distance.'

Marissa was going to ask about Andy, but decided not to.

As if hearing her thoughts, Cliona shook her head. 'Don't mention that fucker's name to me. He's dead to me. You're the only one I've told. I've gotta trust you that you won't say a thing. He doesn't exist.'

Did I say that out loud? 'Of course Cliona, I would never break our confidence. I say it when we start to work together, and I mean it. It's part of the job.'

Cliona sat forward. 'Have you ever broken it? Even, like, if you thought someone was gonna hurt someone else?'

'No. And I hope I never have to, that it never comes to that. Because it can be quite serious if I have to break confidence.'

Cliona sat back again. 'Well, I'm not about to kill myself. It's going too good with Bren. So I decided Mr Fuck Face is dead to me, and this is Bren's baby, and I will tell them I'm pregnant, like soon. Like this week, I guess, if I'm already nearly two months. Fuck, I hope he doesn't go ballistic – Bren, I mean.'

There was silence for a while.

This is really putting me to the test with my non-judgemental confidentiality creed. Heck. This is a difficult one. But she's made up her mind; all I can do is support her, I guess.

'So how can I help you with all this?'

'Can you help me figure out what to say to Bren? That would be great, Marissa, I would really like that. Thanks. Hey, if you weren't my therapist, I would love a friend like you. I don't have anyone else that I can talk to like this.'

Between sessions Marissa got a quick drink of water. She didn't want any caffeine after all the coffee she'd already drunk that day. She walked back into her room. It had seen a lot of emotion that night, but she thought she was doing okay.

I got into a thicket there with Cliona towards the end of that session, though, didn't I? I didn't want to be encouraging her to lie. Oh well. She seemed to be happy enough just getting her thoughts together. Maybe sometimes maybe people just need to talk it out, or feel heard. I have to learn how to hear confidential things in a way that I'm not actually holding onto them. It's none of my business, really, as a person, that is. Marissa the person knows nothing about Cliona, Marissa the therapist... she's different to the person. Maybe. I don't know. This is hard. At least I know I helped Cedric feel better knowing that crying is normal.

She looked at her watch. *What is Joy going to bring me tonight?* Just as she had the thought, the buzzer sounded. She let Joy in and she appeared at her door in her mustard-coloured coat like a breath of fresh air.

'Come in. I love your coat. Where did you get it?'

'Grafton Street, I think. It's last season's colour, so it was in a sale. Thanks!'

Joy hung her coat up on the back of the door next to Marissa's drab grey one, revealing a pretty floral dress beneath. She chose the chair that Marissa had been sitting in for the previous two sessions.

Marissa sat opposite her. *I do need to get some more colourful clothes. New wardrobe for the new season? Joy carries it off so well, I don't know if I could dress like that myself though.* She turned her focus back to the present moment and to the client session.

'So, how have you been this week?'

'Good, thanks. I've actually not had as many episodes since I talked about them with you. And I'm much happier calling them “episodes” – it puts a distance between them and me. “Flashbacks” seemed, well, too personal.’

Ah yes, I remember from last week - bound hands, bound feet, on a pile of sticks, being burned – like a witch perhaps? As she had the thought, Marissa felt her body tense in anticipation of something. *Or was that a full-body ‘yes’? Like we covered in the shamanic workshop?* Marissa’s body tensed, as if awaiting some kind of punishment, but it didn’t happen. *Why do I keep coming back to energy work? I have to stop that.* She relaxed.

Joy was still talking. ‘And I had a dream! I remember everything that happened in it. I saw the same things that I see when I have an episode. I was there, in front of all the people. They were looking at me. But I didn’t *feel* anything this time, so it was easier – maybe because it was a dream? Anyway, they were looking at me and some were shouting. Someone threw a handful of wet mud at me and it hit me in the face, it hurt! I felt that. Well, it hurt like the way you feel hurt in dreams, I suppose. Anyway, I looked down at myself and saw I was wearing a long black dress. It was really old-fashioned. The crowd started chanting and I didn’t understand what they were saying at first. It was like they were talking in a different language. But after a moment, I was able to understand. “Burn the witch!” they said. “Burn the witch!” I think they meant me.’

‘You remember quite a lot from your dream.’

‘Yes, it was very vivid and I wrote it all down after – that notebook was a great idea. I had it by my bed and when I woke up – it was 4am, three nights ago – I wrote it down so I wouldn’t forget. There’s more, hang on.’

Joy reached down to her handbag by her feet and found her notebook, pulled it out, opened it and read something to herself.

‘Yes, they said, “Burn the witch!” Then a man wearing a tall hat made a speech accusing me of witchcraft. He read some kind of proclamation. He showed it to the crowd, but I could see it from where I was standing. There was a symbol on it. I’ve never seen anything like it before. I drew it in my book because it stuck with me. Look.’

She held the notebook out to Marissa with the page open. The drawing took up most of it. The most obvious thing was a triangle in the centre. There were circles and curved lines around it. It was scrawled, like the work of a child, and seemed vaguely familiar to Marissa, but she wasn't sure what it was. Marissa became suddenly very tired, she wanted to close here eyes, but she was in the middle of a client session. She forced the feeling of tiredness away, but it was suffocating.

'That is interesting,' she said, trying not to yawn as Joy put the book face down on her lap.

'I've never seen it anywhere,' Joy said. 'Have you?'

'No, I don't think so. It's most unusual.' The feeling of tiredness started to lift, freeing Marissa to be present to Joy once more.

'Yes, that's what I thought too! Anyway, after his proclamation, the man lit something – I think it was a torch – and he set the sticks on fire at my feet. And then I woke up.'

Marissa pondered, her brain seemed to have just come out of a fog of some sort and it was more difficult to make the connections than it usually was. *Okay, it's possibly a past-life issue. I've not worked with anything like this before, maybe my guides can help? But I don't have guides anymore, and I am only a psychotherapist. And Joy is here for psychotherapy. So why would I even have anything else to offer her? I have to draw a line. I'm drawing a line here and now. Psychotherapy clients come for psychotherapy, not shamanic healing, or Reiki, or anything spiritual. I'm not obliged to do anything but listen. And Joy doesn't know I'm training to be a shamanic practitioner. Was training... I am no longer in training. And Joy doesn't know anything about it. All I asked her to do was to keep a diary.*

'So did you keep the diary?' Marissa asked.

'Yes. Yes, I did.'

'Did you see any pattern to your episodes?'

Joy opened the book again and turned the pages back and forth. 'Actually, yes, I think so. I had four episodes this week, not including the dream. Each one seemed to happen directly after my boyfriend brought up moving in with him.'

Marissa raised an eyebrow. 'So now you know that the episodes seem to be a response to the pressure he's putting on you to move in together.'

'Yes, yes, I think so. But then I caved. I said yes. He's going to move in the week after next.' Joy sighed.

'Wow, okay. How do you feel about that?'

Joy shrugged her shoulders. 'Okay, actually. I might even be looking forward to it. I'm not sure yet.' She closed the diary/notebook and sat back in the chair. 'But it was after I said yes to him that I had the dream... That's interesting.' She smiled. 'Thanks, Marissa, this has really helped me. Maybe now I won't have any more episodes!'

'Fingers crossed,' said Marissa, glad to be of help, even though she knew there was so much more she could have offered. *No, no there absolutely is not.*

'So can I tell you about this thing that happened at work?'

CHAPTER ELEVEN

It was Friday. Marissa left work at 5pm and saw Saoirse waiting for her outside the building. She broke out in a cold sweat. She had had a good day, but she wasn't ready to deal with this type of confrontation. And Saoirse had seen her, so she had no means of escape.

Her heart started racing as Saoirse approached her. *What do I do? What do I say? I can't ignore her.*

Saoirse was smiling, this made Marissa very angry. *How dare she come here? Some cheek she has to show up at my workplace!*

'What are you doing here?' Marissa snarled. 'Why are you following me? How did you find out where I work?'

Anger flowed through her veins. It felt good, she felt alive. She let it take over her body. All of the pent-up emotion, fear and exhaustion she was carrying turned to hot fire veering on rage, and she was going to aim it all, at Saoirse.

Saoirse must have felt it. Her face crumbled and her happy smile was replaced by a look of distress.

'Oh God, I'm so sorry,' she said. 'I didn't mean to upset you. You mentioned the name of your company one time, and I just looked them up, that's all, and figured you'd be finished around now.'

Marissa's fists were curling and uncurling as if they wanted to punch Saoirse all by themselves.

'Some things *are* private, you know,' she said curtly. 'And why do I have to tell you everything? Or anything at all?'

'You don't – of course you don't,' Saoirse replied, taking a step backwards. 'It's just that, well, we were worried about you.'

'*We*? You're not my family, what business is it of yours?'

'Look, I'm so sorry to have upset you. I shouldn't have come.' Saoirse looked genuinely upset.

Marissa started to cool down almost as quickly as she had

heated up.

'Jenny thought it was a good idea,' Saoirse explained. 'I asked her first, but I should have known better.'

'Fuckin' Jenny. Jenny thinks *everything* is a good idea.'

'Yeah, she does,' agreed Saoirse, 'you're right. And I should have asked you first.' She smiled again, albeit a little meekly, then added, 'Fuckin' Jenny!' She looked at Marissa hopefully, and Marissa couldn't help but smile.

She breathed out and her anger level dropped once more. 'Lookit, Saoirse, I'm sorry for losing it just there. I'm not myself. I'm trying to sort myself out. I guess I still need some space.'

'Can we sit down and talk about it? Do you have time now?'

Marissa thought for a moment, she had no plans that evening, she really didn't have any excuse to say 'no' to her. It might even be nice to spend some time together outside the workshops, she did really like Saoirse. But that didn't mean she was going to make it easy for her.

'I don't know,' she answered, scowling. 'I'm not ready to talk about it.'

Saoirse paused for a moment. 'Well, can we talk about something else then? I just really want to know if you're okay, that's all.'

'Okay.'

They walked, and as they walked, Marissa calmed down further. It was a nice evening; the air was crisp and it was still light.

'Do you know a place where we could go?' Saoirse asked. 'Maybe for a coffee or a bite to eat?'

Most of the coffee shops near the office closed at 4pm, so nowhere came to mind. 'Can we keep walking?' Marissa said, finding the movement was helping her stabilise.

'Sure, why not?'

Marissa kept walking, heading towards her flat, which was forty-five minutes' walk away. Saoirse didn't seem to mind where they were going; she just followed Marissa's lead. They talked about the weather, the stretch in the evenings. Saoirse told Marissa about her job, working as a researcher in the Natural History Museum; how it was on a contract basis and she was always worried they wouldn't renew her contract. Saoirse told Marissa that Finn had tried to ask her out, but she had a feeling he had a girlfriend, and when they were doing the homework together, he'd got a phone call from her. 'I knew it!' Saoirse exclaimed. 'It's not right – he can't play the field like that. And I was beginning to really like him too. Sure he could be doing it to me, next.'

Marissa told her about Matt, about how busy he was with his studies, and about her brother and Carol and the baby on the way. By that time they had been walking a half-hour or so, and Marissa was much more relaxed.

Saoirse saw this. 'So,' she said, 'I don't want to ask you what happened if you're not ready to talk about it, but are you really not coming back to class? Terry said you were going to quit.'

'No, I'm really not coming back.' To her surprise, Marissa found her voice wavering. She wasn't feeling the 100 per cent certainty she'd been feeling earlier.

'Shit,' said Saoirse. 'I remember Séamus said right at the beginning that one of us wouldn't finish the course, but I didn't for the life of me think it would be you.'

'Me either. Yes, I remember him saying that too. I thought it was going to be Jenny! But I guess stranger things have happened.'

'Ha ha, yeah Jenny. Nevermind. Stranger things, like what?'

'Seriously!' Marissa glared at Saoirse who jumped back, shocked once more. Marissa was a little shocked too. *What the hell is going on with me?* Saoirse looked stricken. *Feck sake I didn't mean to upset her again.* 'Seriously. Sorry Saoirse, I need to look after myself. I can't go there right now, I said I'm not able to talk about it, not now and maybe not ever. I'm not coming back.'

'Not ever?'

'Ever. So you'll have to tell the others to please leave me alone. About the homework and stuff. Anything to do with the workshops. Or shamanism. Will you? Please?'

They were close to Marissa's flat now. She stopped and looked at Saoirse, with the 'please' still radiating from her eyes.

Saoirse almost had tears in her eyes. She nodded, albeit reluctantly. 'I can see you're upset, and doing this your way. Which is fine. But I like you, Marissa, so that leaves me feeling a little sad that I won't see you in the workshops.'

Marissa looked down and started walking again. A moment passed as they walked in silence.

Then Saoirse asked, 'I'm wondering then, can we be friends? Outside the workshops, I mean.' A wry smile crossed her face. 'It sounds funny saying that as an adult – it sounds like something a child would say.'

Marissa didn't have to think this one through. 'Okay, yes. I would like that too, to be friends with you. We're almost at my flat, do you want to come in? Meet my cat? I'll make you a cup of tea or coffee? Or dinner?'

'Sounds great! Thanks, Marissa.'

Saoirse left just before 10pm. They had had a nice evening together watching one of Marissa's DVDs. *I can't believe Saoirse hadn't seen* Star Wars *before.* And Tobermory took to Saoirse right away, even climbed up into her lap and purred during most of the movie.

Marissa got into bed, then texted Matt, got a text back, and texted him back once more. She switched off the phone. *Not going back, not ever. Yes, this is the way forward for me.* She turned off the light and fell asleep almost straight away.

She was in the forest, it was dark, she got a sense of something large, something with claws and teeth. "I'm not doing this again, not tonight." She changed her direction and walked away until she felt it was far enough behind her.

She walked until she felt crunching beneath her feet, until her feet stopped walking altogether. Her feet were stuck and she couldn't move forward anymore. Was it mud? She pulled at them, there was some give, but her feet kept snapping back into place. It felt like chewing gum or toffee, but could the ground be made of toffee? That made no sense. She noticed there was a hammer beside her and a box of nails. The box was open and the nails were spilling out all over the ground.

She tried to get her bearings. Looking down, she saw she was wearing her old tennis shoes. She managed to pull out one of her feet out from the sticky substance she was caught in. Looking for solid ground to put it down on, she discovered a plank of wood nearby. She laid her foot upon it and put her weight down, yes it would take her weight. She pulled at the other foot, loosening it, wobbling on the plank of wood. Then she saw the other planks around her, now it looked like a box of some sort, and she was inside it, hammer, nails and all.

'Are you finished with wasting time yet?'

She looked up. It was Emelda, watching her from afar, lips tight with disapproval. She had many feathers in her hair, her necklace was a dreamcatcher and her Navajo robes were flowing behind her in the breeze. But there was no breeze.

Marissa didn't know what she was talking about – wasting time? What was she doing here anyway? Marissa turned back to her plight, ignoring her guide, preferring to study the box she found herself in. At that moment it started shrinking, getting smaller and smaller until it started crushing her...

Marissa half woke, turned over and, forgetting the dream, fell back asleep.

She was at the lakeside, her lakeside. The tall, silent mountains surrounded her, the lake was still, bright, with a reflection of the sky above. Marissa tried to walk towards the lake but her feet were stuck. Was it mud? It felt more like chewing gum, or toffee, but how could the ground be made of... Hey, wait, this is familiar. *Looking down, Marissa noticed she was wearing her old tennis shoes.* I've done this before? *She tried to lift one foot, then the other, but both were stuck. With great difficulty, she managed to pull out one of her feet from the toffee-like substance, but where was she going to put it? There on the ground, just behind and to the left of her, was what looked like a page that had been ripped out of a book. She couldn't read the writing on it. Another page appeared beside it, and then another, and another after that. She manoeuvred herself around and placed her free foot onto the first page. Then she pulled out her other foot, swung her leg around and put that foot onto the second page. She was safe now. She got her balance, but she now had her back to the lake.*

In front of her, another page appeared. She stepped onto it. Then another appeared, and she stepped onto that. Like stepping stones, the pages appeared where she needed them, leading her towards a grassy bank.

On top of the bank stood a tall, well-built man, he had been watching her the whole time. He wore a silver suit and looked very smart. He had perfect blonde hair, blue eyes, and was he wearing make-up? He smiled at her and even his teeth seemed to sparkle. When she got closer to him he offered his hand and she took it. He pulled her up effortlessly onto the bank beside him. Keeping hold of her hand, he looked into her eyes and said, 'Hi, I'm Scott Taylor. What's your name?

Marissa woke with a jump. Scott Taylor's voice was loud in her ear, as if he had been speaking right into it. It was around 6am and still dark. She switched on the light and reached for his book, which was beside her bed. Turning to the 'About the Author' page at the back, she studied his photograph, which was now familiar to her. He wasn't wearing a silver suit, but his face *was* almost the same as that of the man she had just dreamed about. *He must have gotten into my subconscious mind. I've never heard his voice, though – I probably made that bit up myself.* She rubbed the ear that was still reverberating and it helped her settle.

It was nice and warm under the duvet, yet she was no longer sleepy. She opened the book and started to read, starting once more from the beginning.

✦✦✦

I have heard from some of the others that you have bailed on me. Is this true? When were you going to tell me? Ah, Marissa, don't leave. You have so much potential. Has this dark energy thing gotten on top of you? Don't let it win. You can't walk away from who you are. Phone me.
Séamus

The email came as a surprise. Marissa had genuinely thought she could just disappear from the course and nobody would notice. *Obviously not. I really don't want to phone him; I suppose I'd better email him back.*

Hi Séamus,
Yes, it's true, Only really decided last week. Wasn't ready to tell you yet, but seeing as you are emailing, I won't be coming back. This isn't for me. I'll stick to the psychotherapy. Thanks for everything.
Bye, Marissa

She pressed 'send'. About ten minutes later, her phone started ringing, caller unknown. She put it on silent and let it go to voicemail. It was 10am on Saturday morning, time for a cuppa. Matt was picking her up in his car at noon and they were going for a drive, then out for lunch.

Wonder where he's taking me? I'm glad I sent that email, and ignored his call. Séamus has some cheek thinking he can change my mind just like that, after all that he did. Not that I know exactly what he did...

She was feeling much stronger now. Reading Scott Taylor seemed to have helped. *You're a fool if you keep doing the same thing and expecting something different to happen.* She wasn't sure if Scott Taylor had said that, but it felt right. The book was becoming quite raggedy-eared from all the reading, but it felt good to hold it in her hands. When her cuppa was made, she got back into bed and opened it at a random page.

> *When you do what you want, when you want, how you want, then you are truly happy, then you are successful.*

Yes, that makes sense. She turned to the chapter on 'Finding your own way by putting one foot in front of the other', took out her pen and underlined several sections on motivation, choice and self-determination. As she drew the lines, sometimes twice under the same sentence, she felt herself solidifying. *One foot in front of the other... sounds like my dream.*

She *wasn't* going back to shamanism and she had told Séamus now, and everyone else in the group knew, so that was the hard part done. It hadn't been so bad really. *It is done now!* She read:

> *Mark the little things as well as the big. You criticise yourself too often and don't often congratulate yourself. It's time to turn that around. When you turn around your thoughts, your life turns around with you.*

Yes! How did he know?! I should mark the little things, like saying goodbye to Séamus. That wasn't really a little thing, I guess. And I did good – well done, me! Marissa nodded her head and continued reading and marking text for another half hour or so, then got showered and ready for her date with Matt.

He rang her doorbell at noon on the dot. When she opened the door, he was smiling at her, his face radiating like the sun. She couldn't help but shine right back. His wild, light brown hair was looking tamer than usual; he must have made an effort to brush it down. He was wearing a brown wax jacket over a grey patterned jumper, black cords and runners.

'Hi! The weather is good today, but bring a raincoat just in case. Are you ready to go now? It will take some time to get there, so I won't come in, if you don't mind.'

'Okay, I'll get my coat. Hang on.'

Marissa ran in and checked the back door was locked, the windows closed and the cooker and immersion off. She got her bag and coat and was about to leave, then ran back to the bedroom, shoved the Scott Taylor book into her handbag. She locked the front door and followed Matt out to his car, bag clutched to her stomach. He was parked on the street, right outside her flat. His hazard lights were on, she scooted around the car and quickly hopped into the passenger seat and he pulled out into the traffic.

Matt drove in a big loop so that they got out of the city quickly. Within a half-hour they were driving down smaller country roads. Marissa rolled down the window, enjoying the fresh air, the bright sunshine and the greenery. As she relaxed, she realised that she had been unconsciously clutching her handbag to her stomach. She thought about putting it down by her feet, but felt strangely uneasy about it.

'Isn't Dublin great?' Matt said, his eyes on the road. 'We've got the sea, then the city, and we can get into the country so fast.'

'Yeah, but it's grown so big, so quickly,' Marissa replied. 'It's taken us thirty minutes to get outside the built-up area and we used to be able to do it in ten.'

'I guess there have been more people coming to live in Dublin lately, that's true,' agreed Matt, 'and so many new houses and apartments being built. They're just flying up.'

'Where are we going?' asked Marissa with a smile, turning to him in anticipation. The breeze from the window threw her hair over her face. She pushed it back with her hand, but the wind was too strong and it came back into her eyes. She put her bag on the floor of the car, laughed and rolled up the window, feeling more like herself again.

'I thought we'd go to Kildare, to the National Stud. I love it there, it's so peaceful, and they have a great restaurant. Have you been before?'

'Is that the place with the Japanese Gardens?' asked Marissa.

'Yes, that's right. We can go there too.'

'I remember Dad taking me when I was small. It's been years since I was anywhere like that. It's a nice day for a walk, alright. Thanks!'

'Well, we haven't really gone on a date yet, just dinner, movies, and of course some firefighting,' Matt said, smiling and winking at her.

'And a Reiki workshop!' reminded Marissa, ignoring the firefighting comment.

'That was where we met, though, it wasn't a date.'

'Funny that. I felt I already knew you when we met. I guess I remember it as a date.'

A few moments passed, then Matt said, 'We could do the Level 2 workshop together, if you want. It's coming up next month.' He paused, then added, 'I'm doing it anyway, and you're welcome to come with me, if you feel ready for it.'

Marissa frowned. 'I'll think about it. I just told Séamus this morning that I'm not going back to his class.'

'Oh! Wow. Okay. How did that go for you?'

'It was fine. He actually emailed me about it today, so I just replied and said I wasn't going back. He phoned straight after I sent it – at least I think it was him. I didn't get the phone – it went to voicemail.'

Matt drove for a little while. 'Are you sure about this, Marissa? It's harder to pick something up midway – if you change your mind, I mean.'

'Yep, I'm totally sure.' She reached down to her bag and pulled out her Scott Taylor book and opened it. 'From the eminently quotable Scott Taylor... Hmm, let's see now. Yes, here, this, "When you make a decision, make it with all of your heart. Stand fast to it, proud and strong. This way you will put all your will power behind it, and make it happen." Perfect, eh?'

'Sounds good, sure, but what if it's not the right decision?'

Marissa twisted round in the car seat to stare at Matt. 'Well, how do you know it's the *wrong* decision? You've got to choose something at some point, haven't you? So why not with all of your heart?'

She waited for a response, impassioned, ready for a fight.

Matt sighed, shook his head and kept driving. 'Nearly there now. I think it's just down this road and past the village on the left.'

Marissa turned back to sit properly in her seat, book still in hand, now wanting to argue her point. She had to prod Matt to get a reaction. 'Do *you* think I'm making a mistake not going back?'

Matt sighed again. 'I honestly don't know. Really, I'm still just getting to know you. That's what today is about, I suppose – spending some time together, having fun, getting to know each other. Ahh, here we are now.' He drove into the car park and found a parking space. Switching off the car, he turned to face her.

'Marissa, I guess you need to decide what's best for you, and whatever you think that is, I'm happy to support you. Maybe we should focus on that, and not on the drama. Let's have a day off of all of this, and just have some fun together. I'd prefer to do that, if that's okay? Can you leave the book behind for now?'

'Yes, okay, Good idea.' Marissa shoved the book under her seat, got her handbag, and they both got out of the car and went inside.

'Do you want to stay?' whispered Marissa as Matt pulled up outside her house. They had had a lovely day and a beautiful meal together.

'I'd like to,' Matt replied, smiling, 'but I think I'll do the gentlemanly thing and just walk you to your door tonight. We kind of got intense I think, starting out together, and now we're settling down, I'd like to do this properly.'

Marissa felt disappointed. She wanted him to come inside.

'Leave you wanting more,' Matt whispered to her with a smile.

Marissa laughed, but felt bereft at the thought of him leaving. She leaned towards him over the gear stick and kissed his face, kissed his cheek and whispered pleadingly, 'Come inside with me.'

Her hot breath on his skin made him shiver. He kept his hands on the wheel and turned towards her, kissing her on the lips.

'Come on, I'll walk you to the door,' he said. 'Have you got your book?'

'Oh yes, thanks, I forgot all about it. Hang on...'

Matt got out of the car and waited for her to do the same. She slung her bag over her shoulder and he linked arms with her as they walked up the path from the gate to the door. She found her keys and then his arm slid out from hers and he pulled away. Her heart sank. *He really means it.*

'I'm tired,' he said. 'I've had a lovely day with you, but I'll say goodnight here. Text me tomorrow?'

Marissa tried to hide her disappointment. 'Okay. Thanks for today, Matt. It was lovely. I really enjoyed the day out.'

Matt smiled, and her heart opened. She realised she was falling in love with him.

'See you,' he said, and went back to his car, got in and drove away.

'Has she left us?'

Emelda was on her knees by the lakeside, pleading with the sky as she prayed over beads that had been made from river stones collected over many generations. They were different colours and sizes, all threaded onto a slim string of braided horsehair. She looked at her reflection in the pool of water beside her. It was fuzzy. The water was uneasy. There was a spatter of water beside her and a splashing further away. She looked out and saw the serpent gazing back at her. He was white under the moon, with grand ears and long delicate antennae, but there was a fuzziness about him, as if he was getting ready to moult. Or he was unclear, too.

'Never in my many lifetimes...' Emelda said, shaking her head and rising to her feet.

The serpent seemed to understand. He spat into the air, then bowed his head and disappeared under a surge of water.

Emelda walked away from the lake and threw her hands over her head in despair. 'Aye! Aye aye aye! It was not supposed to end this quickly. This is not right.'

'Why not visit in her dreamtime?' a mellow voice said.

Emelda turned to see Grandmother Medicine Woman standing beside her. The women nodded their greetings to each other.

'I have tried already,' said Emelda, shaking her head, 'but the girl is stubborn.'

Grandmother laughed, a loud cackle that reverberated off the stones. The mountains echoed it. 'We are always here, she is just not listening.' She looked up at the sky with knowing expectation. 'But if we keep trying, she will hear us eventually.'

'Have you tried? Why is it always up to me?' Emelda hadn't heard what had been said and was becoming emotional. 'This girl, she goes off the track we have set for her. All the work she is supposed to be doing now...'

The grandmother interrupted her, 'Aye, aye, aye, Melda! This girl, she sets her own track. This is part of it. You know it. Where is your faith? Have faith, Emelda. Give her time. She will hear us when she is ready.'

'I do not know, but I am sure of it that there is something wrong. But yes, I will keep trying. I will keep knocking on her door. I will break it down if necessary.' Emelda said, determinedly.

The grandmother laughed again. 'And you think yourself more powerful than she?'

Emelda seemed caught by surprise. 'No, no, of course not!'

'She will come back to us when she's ready. Trust. It is all part of the greater unfoldment.'

The grandmother faded away, leaving Emelda once more on her own.

'I will keep trying,' she whispered into her hands, which were still clutching the beads. 'And I will not rest until she hears me.'

+++

'So let me get this right. You're saying, when your manager criticises your work, you take it personally. You get upset about it, and the upset stays with you to darken the rest of your day?' Marissa was the therapist, and Steve, from her counselling class, was the client.

'Yes, I guess that's what it is. It cuts me deep, whatever he says.' Steve scratched his head as he thought.

Marissa didn't interrupt or prompt, as instructed.

'I do get very upset when he says something negative,' Steve admitted.

It was time for the "Shift of Focus Statement". Marissa thought for a moment, constructed it in her head according to how they had been shown in class, and then offered: 'So how do you feel when he says something positive?'

A moment passed.

'You know,' said Steve, 'now that I think about it, when he tells me I did a good job, it's the same thing – it really affects me. I get happy for a moment, then, because it's good feedback, I kind of let it go.'

Time for "Amplified Reflection".

'You don't hold on to the positive feedback, because you don't believe you're worth investing in.'

I don't like this method. That's a nasty statement. It sounds very judgemental.

Steve shrugged his shoulders. He looked despondent, a little hopeless in fact. Marissa didn't like his reaction either, so she put up her hand to call the lecturer over.

'Sorry, Ms Greene, I know we're supposed to make a statement to amplify the client's thoughts to magnify their negative thought process, but doesn't that reinforce their way of thinking? Especially if they have low self-esteem and a deep need for external validation. I don't like this.'

Steve looked up, interested in the direction this was taking.

Ms Greene responded, 'It is supposed to blow their thought process out of proportion so they can see how ridiculous it is, but you're right, in some cases the client may not see it that way. Just as some people don't recognise sarcasm. It's also good that you know what you don't like, Marissa. You need to learn to find what works for you as the therapist, and sometimes that's by finding out what doesn't work. Tell me, what was the statement?'

Katie, as the observer, had written down both the "Shift of Focus Statement" and the "Amplified Reflection", so she was able to read it out, word for word.

The lecturer nodded and turned to Marissa. 'Your statement is correct for this model. But what would you rather have said? Let's rewind the session a little – Steve, is that okay with you?'

Steve nodded his head.

Katie offered, 'Steve had just said that criticism from his manager upset him more than he felt it should, but he didn't hold onto praise.'

Marissa cleared her throat. 'So, Steve, just to recap, when your manager criticises you, you get very upset, but when he praises you, you get happy for a moment – did I get it right?'

Steve's body language changed; he engaged with Marissa and there was a glistening of emotion behind his eyes. 'Actually, it's more like elated than happy. It's an intense sort of happiness.'

'So either way, your response to his criticism, both negative or positive, is amplified?'

'Yes. I didn't see it like that I suppose, but yes, that's exactly what happens. I do get deeply upset, or elated, but the good feelings disappear so fast, and the bad feelings hang around for hours, even days, sometimes.'

Marissa continued. 'So you don't really register the good stuff, you don't allow yourself to experience it, while you replay the bad stuff over and over again. Your manager, he is an authority figure in your life – would you agree?'

Steve nodded his head.

'And you admire him? What he says to you is important.'

Steve nodded again.

'I'm wondering, then, if you are attaching to your manager the way you might have attached to, say, your father. Did you have a similar response to criticism or praise from him?'

Steve was taken aback. He looked confused for a moment, then his eyes widened. 'You know, I think you're right.' He scratched his head once more. 'Dad did do that to me, now that I think about it. Yeah.' He added, 'But my manager isn't my father. I don't need his approval, I just need to do my job well.'

Marissa looked at Ms Greene, who prompted her to continue.

'Whose approval do you need, Steve?' Marissa asked quietly.

Steve thought about this. 'My own,' he said proudly.

Marissa nodded. 'So what do you think would be helpful for you to remember, for the next time your manager says something that upsets you?'

Steve was silent.

'Can I make a suggestion?' Marissa asked.

'Okay'

'How about you talk to little Steve, the little boy part inside you? You could tell him he's great, that you're proud of him and that maybe you made a mistake and you can fix it, or learn from it, and it doesn't mean that you're a bad person.'

'That sounds amazing. Yes, I could definitely do that. Thanks so much.'

Ms Greene smiled and Katie was watching, spellbound. Steve was delighted.

Ms Greene said, 'In class it can be difficult to emulate the exact conditions required for a client session, however in this case, Marissa, I can see that the Motivational Technique is probably not the right framework for you. That's what these lessons are for, to help you find your own way. And you certainly have, so well done.' She turned to Steve, 'How did you find that, Steve?'

Steve was smiling. 'I think she hit the nail on the head there. I took a workshop on the inner child but I never thought it was affecting me at work. I will definitely look after little Steve while I'm talking to my manager.'

'Good work.' Ms Greene nodded and left to help another group across the room.

Steve turned to Marissa. 'Jeez, Marissa, that was great. That was more productive than the last four sessions with my own psychotherapist! Ten minutes with you and I'm a new man.'

Katie put the notebook down and looked at Marissa as if she was some kind of alien. 'How do you do that?'

'Do what?'

'Know exactly what to say?'

'I don't know exactly what to say,' Marissa answered. 'It just feels right to me to follow a certain path in the conversation. Other paths don't feel as good, so I don't go down them. Honestly, Katie, I think just really listening is the best thing you can do for someone else.'

'Well,' said Steve, 'you've certainly helped me tonight. Thank you so much Marissa.'

'Glad to have been of service.'

+++

You're a medicine woman, there's no avoiding it. You can't run away from yourself, it will only cause you pain.

Marissa woke from her dream covered in sweat, feeling violated, broken into somehow, as if a door that she had closed was being prised open. *Yes, that's it! Something has breached my boundaries.* She became angry. Her first instinct was to bring out her drum and bang heavily upon it again, just to assert herself, but it was packed away in the box, Pandora's box she had nicknamed it, and she didn't want to open that cupboard door.

She got out of bed, found the last piece of sage she had in her handbag and lit a candle. *What am I like? I don't need this stuff anymore, remember?* She put the candle out.

It was only 4am, too early to get up. Getting back into bed in the dark, she turned onto her side and tried to get back to sleep, but that feeling of violation was still there, in her stomach and her chest. Sticky sweat was drying into her pyjamas and she started to feel cold. Wide awake, she turned over. There was a ringing in her ears. It wasn't unpleasant, but it seemed to be getting louder. Then, all of a sudden, it stopped. She reached for the lapis and felt its coolness in her hand. After a moment, a wave of peace washed over her. She closed her eyes again and drifted.

'You think you can run from us, do you, girl?'

Marissa jerked out of some kind of trance and looked at the woman standing in front of her.

'That's right, you can see me. Don't deny it this time, child.'

Marissa felt a chill in her bones. Her fists clenched and unclenched.

' What do you want from me?'

'We only want you to remember who you are. You can't run like this, pretending that everything is plain and simple, simple and plain. You are not plain and you are not simple! Far from it, child.' The woman's voice was assertive and strong.

'I think I can choose what I want to do with my life,' replied Marissa, equally assertively.

'Perhaps you only think that this is the case.'

Finally, Marissa recognised Emelda. She relaxed, releasing her hands. 'I like your feathers. They are very colourful,' she said.

'Thank you,' said Emelda.

'Tell me, what do you want?'

'You need to go back to your studies. You are still awakening, still learning, you can't switch it off and run away from the truth of who you are. You've experienced too many lifetimes where you were doing just that. And we need you. Time is running out. It is now, your time, this time.'

'But I'm not ready,' said Marissa, feeling small, 'and I'm scared.'

The woman made no reply. Marissa started to cry, and as she shrank into her own tears, Emelda disappeared. Marissa found herself back at her lake, in the middle of it, balancing precariously on small stepping stones. Familiar. *She still felt upset – less violated, more like she was a little girl whose mother has just yelled at her. She took a breath, got her bearings and brought herself back into balance. The years of practice were paying off.*

Looking down she saw the next stepping stone was out of reach. She willed it to herself as she had done before, and it moved slowly towards her, as before. But it seemed to take so much more energy than she expected. She eased off for a moment and the stone stopped moving.

'Oh no. But I'm so tired.'

There was a stirring in the waters beside her. She turned towards it, stumbled, lost her balance and fell.

To her amazement, instead of hitting water, she carried on falling. She scrabbled around, flailing her arms and legs, trying to stop, but she just fell ... and fell and fell and fell...

She landed with a bump and jerked herself awake. She was back in her room, in her bed. This time the clock said 5.33am. She sighed. She turned her head and noticed a white feather on her pillowcase, right beside her, exactly level with her eye, perfectly placed so that she would see it. Calmness entered her body. *My angel must be here.* She felt a full-body tingle with a feeling of 'yes', and the sensation startled her. She hadn't felt anything like it for several weeks now. *I thought I'd packed all that away?* Shivering, she visualised herself pushing her angelic connections into a dark room and locking the door. Something inside her clicked and she felt better.

She got out of bed and put her feet into her slippers, then went into the kitchen and put on the kettle. Opening the drawer of the desk in her bedroom, she found a notebook that was half filled with scribbles and notes, one of many such notebooks that she had started and never finished. She thought of each one as a train of thought, some of which had never left the station, while those that did, never arrived at their destination.

Marissa sighed. She made tea, took it, a random notebook and a pen, and curled up on the sofa. She pulled a throw over her legs. Tobermory was sleeping in the armchair. He opened one eye and looked at her, then curled up into an even tighter ball and closed his eye again.

Marissa looked through the notebook as her tea cooled.

> *What if I could fly? Why is life so boring and unimaginably grey? The most exciting thing to happen to me in years was finding out that James actually liked me. But now that we are together, the joy seems, well, gone.*

Strange, I don't remember writing this, yet I remember the feeling it. Hang on, was I bored when I was with James? Maybe a little. Was I just going through the motions with him? She turned to another page.

> *Why do I feel I'm not good enough for James's friends? I try so hard, but I just don't know how to be around them. He laughs with them as if there's some private joke going on, and I'm never let in on it. I hate this. But I love him so much.*

Marissa cast her mind back to her relationship with James. She had never forgotten the happy times, the laughter, but there was more she *had* forgotten – the shouting, the feeling of being deficient, excluded, upset, sad. She remembered James storming out one night after an argument. Then she remembered walking home on her own, to their flat, feeling sad - had she walked out on him that time? She really hadn't been happy for a long time before he left, had she? *I wonder whether he really wanted to marry me? Did I really want to marry him? Or were we just doing what we felt we were supposed to be doing? I realise now*

I never felt elated by it, it just seemed to be the next step in the relationship. Maybe it was good then, that he left me. But he didn't have to say yes in the first place, or leave it so late to leave, or leave the way that he left...

She paused, drank a mouthful of tea, felt it in her mouth and swallowed. She uncrossed her legs and tucked them in underneath her, placing the cup down on the table and rearranging the duvet around herself. *Did I think marrying him would make it better between us? It needed making better. Was I ever actually happy with James? If not, then why was I so devastated when he finally did leave me?*

It felt like a betrayal to think like this, but why? Who was she betraying? Not James... Herself?

Have I ever actually been happy at all? As Marissa considered the question, she had a flashback of the fire ceremony in Clifden, of working with Zaad and how happy she'd felt when she'd brought back the information from her journey for him, how he'd looked at her with grateful eyes. She remembered how good she'd felt when she'd helped Jennifer and Terry, how good she felt in her psychotherapy class when she was able to unlock a door for someone else, even after they'd locked it and thrown away the key. It felt at times that she had the key to everyone's locked door, except for maybe her own. For them, if it wasn't in her hand at the time, she would know where to look, to find it. That made her happy; it gave her a sense of belonging, of purpose, a reason to be in the world.

It's not about men, or timing, or even travelling to other places. I went to Machu Picchu, and even in Peru, I wasn't feeling happy, although it was great. I suppose it's not about that at all. It's not about having stuff. I've got money in the bank now and that isn't making me feel any different from how I was before. So what is life about anyway? And what am I running away from?

She picked up the cup and drank some more tea. It was beginning to lose its heat. She closed her eyes and cleared her mind, allowing herself to drift downwards in her body, to feel into her stomach. *Séamus called this a place of power. I don't feel that powerful, not really. And I'm so tired of this timidity, of being small, of my anxiety. Anxiety is shit. I've had enough of it. I want the magic back. Maybe I should go back to shamanism.*

That white heat, the flash of emotion... It didn't come. She opened her eyes again and looked around the room. Nothing. The Scott Taylor book was peeking out from behind a tea towel on the worktop, but she felt absolutely nothing. She didn't want to get up from the sofa to hold it for reassurance. *No, I have already made up my mind. I'm out. Finished. That's it for me for shamanism. Life is shit and boring, and that's just the way things are.*

+++

Later that day at work, Marissa checked her personal email and found an email from Yvonne.

> *Hi, Marissa, I remember you mentioned over coffee last week that you were short on client hours. I've got to pull back a little bit as my mother is sick, and I've decided to give up my placement. Do you want it? If you let me know, I'll have a word with the admin. It's in St Mary's, the women's refuge centre. It can get a little heavy, but I know you'll be well able for it.*

Marissa thought back to the conversation with Yvonne. *I don't remember saying that specifically, but I'm not going to turn down more client work.*

> *Hi, Yvonne, That sounds great! Thanks for thinking of me – I would love to. Let me know what you need from me. M.*

I guess now that I'm officially not going to do the management role, if this cuts into work hours, I can go part time. And Uncle Lou is still to gift me some more money.

Marissa's body rippled with excitement. The idea of moving into running a therapy practice already, even before she was fully qualified, was thrilling. *Aha! There's my answer. Yes, this work does make me happy. And it would be great to have more time to myself too. I could even ask Dad for a loan, but I don't actually think I need much money once my rent is covered. Life doesn't have to be shit and boring after all.*

Over a late dinner at her place Marissa told Matt what was on her mind. 'I'm not allowed to charge for sessions, though, until I get my diploma.'

'And when will that be?' asked Matt, smiling, pulling her into him and giving her a kiss. He was becoming infected by Marissa's growing excitement.

'Well, it's March now,' she said enthusiastically, 'and we finish the last module at the end of April. There's just one more live assessment; I need to write an assignment, and then it's just the client hours that I need before I get my diploma.'

'So how many more hours do you need?'

'In total, one hundred and fifty client hours plus fifteen hours of supervision to get the diploma. After that, if I go on to accreditation, I need four hundred client hours, but I have lots of time to get them.'

'That sounds like a lot of hours. How many have you done already?'

'Hang on,' said Marissa, jumping up to get her diary. She sat back down on the sofa cross-legged and flicked through the pages, counting on her hands. Deflated, she closed the diary and put it on the table. 'Thirty.'

'Well, it sounds like you should definitely take Yvonne's placement then.'

Marissa shook her head, scowling. 'I was certain I'd done so many more than that.'

Matt got up and took the dishes over to the sink to wash them.

'It's okay, I can do that,' said Marissa, jumping up again.

'Hey, you cooked. I like washing up, and you're a great cook, by the way. I really enjoyed that dinner.'

Marissa glanced at the bin under the sink and surreptitiously pushed the empty M&S boxes deeper into the bag. 'Thanks,' she said, blushing.

'Listen,' said Matt, scrubbing the plates and placing them on the draining board, 'I've a great idea. I've already asked you to do

Reiki Level 2 with me, remember? It's this weekend. Once you've done Level 2, you can have actual clients. You can charge, I mean.'

'Seriously?'

Matt got the tea towel and started to dry the dishes.

'Yes. I'm not planning to see clients myself, but if you did decide to go part time at the office, you could see clients for Reiki for money and clients for psychotherapy, for free.'

Marissa found another tea towel and helped Matt finish the dishes. 'That could be interesting,' she said thoughtfully. She raised an eyebrow, testing the waters, 'It's not shamanism?'

'No, it's not shamanism,' said Matt firmly, looking around. 'Where are the saucepans? From the dinner, I mean. I can do them too if you want?'

'Erm, I did those already. Earlier, I mean. Don't worry about it,' said Marissa sheepishly. 'What's involved in the Reiki workshop?'

'It's two days again, like last time, same hotel, with Dolores. It's more expensive this time, but it will be well worth it, and I'm really looking forward to it. And it would be extra fun if you were there with me.'

Marissa looked at Matt's big open smiling face. He was hiding nothing behind his eyes. She could see how he felt about her and it made her feel extra guilty about fibbing over saucepans. She reached into the bin and surreptitiously pulled out the M&S packages, blushing.

Matt started to laugh. 'Well, you're a great therapist, if not a great cook.'

She laughed too.

'I'm sure Dolores has space for you. Will you come?'

'Yes, okay it's a great idea. I'll come. Dolores is good, nothing bad will happen with her. And I'll go part time with Noreen, and I'll take the extra client hours from Yvonne. Things seem to be moving forward in a good direction now.'

Matt looked as if he was about to say something, then he changed his mind. Then he did said: 'You know what? I'd love a pint. There's still time – let's go to the local down the road.'

'I'll get my coat,' said Marissa.

CHAPTER TWELVE

Marissa knocked at Dave's door. 'Coming!' he said. After a moment he opened it. He wearing his usual outfit of jeans and a T-shirt, and his hair was tousled as if he had just got out of bed. He smiled.

'Hi! Marissa! How's it going? Come in!'

They sat in the counselling chairs.

'I'm good, thanks. You?'

'Very good, actually. Your idea about incentives really worked a treat – I've almost finished my research! I've only got a couple of weeks left, then I can write my thesis. Thanks again for that.'

'What did you decide to go with in the end?'

Dave blushed. 'I, erm, suggested that if they saw me for at least three sessions I'd give them a book voucher for €10.'

Marissa raised an eyebrow. 'Well, I suppose needs must. Fair play for trying. And thanks again for introducing me to Scott Taylor – are you sure you don't want your book back?'

Dave's face lit up, 'Oh no, I'm good, thanks. I just bought his new one. It came with a code to get a discount off his live events. He's going to be in London in six weeks time, I'll be there for sure!'

'You mentioned he did events. Sounds interesting.'

'Yeah. Should be amazing. He usually has a couple of thousand people at these things. Fancy going?'

'A couple of thousand people? That's crazy!'

'Yeah, I know. I've seen a few clips on YouTube. They never give you the whole thing there, just enough to get you wanting more! You should check it out. Anyway, just to be clear,' he cocked his head on one side, looking particularly cheeky, 'I'm not asking you to go with me. I've got a girlfriend, I mean.' He looked embarrassed. 'And I've got a mate living in London, so I thought I'd stay with him.'

Marissa laughed. 'I didn't think you were asking me to go with you. No worries there!'

Dave looked relieved. 'Ah, good, okay. Someone at college got confused when I said the same thing to her, and it got a little messy, so I didn't want that happening again. Anyway, if you did go, we probably wouldn't even bump into each other there unless we planned to. Seriously, these events are massive.' He looked at his watch. 'My last client is due now. Sorry, I'll have to ask you to leave.'

'No problem,' said Marissa, standing up. 'You know, I think I will get his new book, and check him out on YouTube. Perhaps I'll even go to London, too.' *London? Me? No way. Why did I say that?*

'You won't regret it!' Dave opened the door and Marissa smiled again, and left the room.

She went into Room Three and started to prepare for that evening's sessions. *I have no intention of going to London. There's enough going on here, and I'm doing the Reiki 2 workshop this weekend, why do I need another workshop?* She shrugged it off then lit her candle. Without thinking, she got her bottle of St Germain from her handbag, put three drops on her left hand, rubbed both hands together and rubbed them through her energy field. She felt a tension inside her, which she pushed down. *Not tonight.* Almost immediately she felt more contained, grounded and ready for her clients.

She looked at the client sheet for that evening. She was seeing someone new, as Cedric had pulled out of the rest of the sessions in his cycle. *I guess he only needed to feel safe to cry. Fair enough – there's no point coming just for the sake of it.*

The buzzer buzzed and Marissa let her first client in. Running down the stairs, she saw a woman in the corridor. *That must be Margaret.*

'Hello, Margaret, is it?'

The woman nodded, gratefully.

'It's lovely to meet you,' Marissa said, warmly. 'I'm Marissa. Come with me, I'll take you up to our room.'

Margaret was in her mid-fifties with short hair and small, wire-frame glasses. She was wearing a sky-blue coat in a style which Marissa could only describe as something her granny would have worn. She was slow to follow, and seemed to have a little trouble on the stairs. Marissa thought she seemed much older than the age that was written on the client sheet. When they got to the room, Marissa helped her take off her coat. She wore a woollen skirt and a pink cashmere jumper, with a flowery blouse beneath. As she stood there waiting for the next instruction, Marissa noticed that Margaret was hunched over, and looking quite anxious. *Because it's her first session?*

'Come, sit down, make yourself comfortable. Welcome to The priory. I'm Marissa. Lovely to meet you. We have six sessions together. Everything you say to me is completely confidential, unless you are at risk of harming yourself, or someone else. Then I may need to speak to my supervisor about it. But we'll talk about that too, if it should come up as an issue. Now!' Marissa sat in the opposite chair and placed her hands together. She took a breath. 'What would you like to talk about?'

Margaret was wringing her hands together. She looked at Marissa and shrugged apologetically, as if her hands were wringing themselves and there was nothing she could do about it. She looked down at the floor and spoke without making eye contact. 'I worry. A lot. About a lot of things – too many things.'

There was a silence in the room that enveloped them both. Marissa waited for more information, but none was forthcoming, so after a moment, she asked, 'What kind of things?'

'Oh you know, whether my husband will get sick, or my son will die, or I will be in a car crash on my way home from the shops – that kind of thing. Maybe they will never happen. But I worry about them all the time. It doesn't make my life easy, I know that. And I'm not stupid, I know that this is probably irrational. But my thoughts, they take over, and I can't seem to control them.' She sighed. 'They control *me*, more like. I've had enough of it; I thought I'd see someone to get help.' She looked up at Marissa with pleading eyes 'Do you think you can help?'

'I will try to. I think I need to get to know you a little better first, and understand a little bit more about what is going on, and then we can look at the thoughts. Does that sound okay?'

Margaret nodded her head. 'Yes.'

'So let's start with a check-in. How are you feeling?'

'I'm exhausted. I have trouble sleeping. I get restless in the evenings and during the day, and unless I'm doing something else, they creep in on top of me – the thoughts, I mean. It's like they're trying to find a way into my head, and once they're there, it's impossible to get them out.'

As Margaret talked, Marissa felt her own body getting heavier and heavier. She sensed anxiety in the room and kept pressing her feet into the floor, pulling herself back from Margaret in case Margaret's thoughts wanted to find a way into her, too. *That's silly! But I do need to look after myself here. What would work?* She remembered she agreed to go to Dolores's Reiki workshop in a few days time. *Reiki would be good. Yes, I'll try it now.* Marissa visualised the Reiki light above her head and imagined it flowing down and into her body. *It didn't work the last time, oh... wait!* She felt the flow of Reiki spark, then ignite, and for the first time in a very long time Marissa felt Reiki flow through her body. She immediately felt more relaxed. She realised Margaret had stopped talking.

'Shall we look at the actual thoughts themselves now?'

'Okay.'

'Maybe you could pick just the one thought first? To start with.' Marissa suggested. 'It sounds as though you have so many to choose from.'

'Yes, okay, that's a good idea. Which one?'

Marissa thought for a moment. 'Which one is the loudest? Which one appears most frequently? Or should we start with the one that upsets you the most?'

Margaret sat up in her chair and met Marissa's eye for the first time. She seemed calmer now, and when she smiled, her face became more youthful. 'That's a good idea – yes, let's do that. I worry most about dying. Getting sick and dying. That's my biggest fear.'

Marissa had never worked with this specific fear in class. *Strange, as it's probably the most common fear there is. You'd think it would be something we'd have a whole module on, wouldn't you? But no, so, er, how do I approach it?* Something she had read in school, in English class, came into her mind. It was from the play *Julius Caesar*.

'Margaret, this makes me think of a quote from a Shakespeare play I did in school, I don't remember it exactly though. "Cowards die many times before their death. A courageous man never dies but once." '

'Ahh yes. I think that's from *Julius Caesar*. Yes, I loved that play. Studied it at school myself. It's funny how we remember quotes and things that were drummed into us at school.'

'What do you think the quote actually means?'

Margaret was silent for a moment. 'Well, I suppose he's saying that...' She scratched her head. 'Ah, yes. I'm spending so much time being anxious about dying, it's like dying many times before my own death.' She met Marissa's eye. 'I know I am going to die, sometime. But when it happens, it will only happen once. Then I'm dead, I suppose.'

'Me too,' said Marissa. 'But I don't think about it. I don't know if I accept it just yet, but it is something that we all have to face at some point. I suppose you could work with it, think about what it is exactly that you're afraid of, and work through that. I would be happy to help you with it. But worrying about it isn't going to make it happen, or not happen. I don't believe we are that powerful. But worrying constantly about dying will certainly make you stressed, and stress leads to exhaustion, which you've already said you have. And stress can make you very sick, too.'

'Yes, it certainly does stress me, that particular thought. Especially late at night when I'm falling asleep. Sometimes I feel as if I'm drowning and I'm going to die. I wake up gasping for air. Some nights I drown and wake up, then drown again, and wake up again. It goes on and on and I never get to sleep.' She changed position and looked thoughtful for a moment. 'But I'm not particularly afraid of drowning, sometimes it's falling, like I'm falling off a cliff. Or it's... well, you don't want me to share a list of the ways I think I'm going to die, do you?'

'If you think it would help? I don't mind, really, this is your space to talk about anything you want.'

'Thanks. No, I'd rather not. But I am awake most nights, for most of the night. It's a miracle I'm able to get out and about and do the things that I do all day.'

'Is your being awake related to your thoughts, or to your dreams?' asked Marissa, thinking that the two things weren't entirely the same.

'I don't know, actually,' Margaret confessed. 'I guess I don't let myself go to sleep in case I die in my sleep. Yes, that's it. It's not the case every night, or I would never have had a night's sleep in my entire life! Which isn't the case either. No, actually now that I think about it, I believe it happens when I'm more upset than usual.'

Marissa nodded her head. *We are getting there.* 'What if the stress from your daytime thoughts leaks into your subconscious mind, making it difficult for you to relax and sleep well? Maybe it would be good for you to keep a journal for a week, so you could write down all the thoughts you'd been having. Is that something you could do for me? Then we can look at it and see what to do next.'

After Margaret left, Marissa lit some sage and smudged the room to eliminate some of the heavy feeling. She did some stretches to try and lighten the energy. She still was connected to Reiki, it felt good. She touched her toes, then reached up as high as she could, opening her arms out, imagining that the Reiki was flowing out of her and into the room. She heard laughing from the doorway, turned and saw Cliona watching her. She looked different. Her hair wasn't pink anymore.

'Hi Cliona, how long were you standing there for? Oh! You dyed your hair black?' asked Marissa, straightening up and blushing. She gestured to Cliona's usual chair.

Cliona marched in confidently and flicked her newly black (and tidy) hair to one side before sitting down and crossing her legs.

Marissa took her place opposite her, feeling her warm cheeks cooling down. 'It looks good. So, what do you want to talk about this evening?'

Cliona was a little antsy, but no more than usual. 'Thanks. Yeah.' She seemed uncomfortable. 'Lookit,' Cliona said, 'the work we are doing here, it's great an' all, but I don't think it's really helping me. I mean, I've not actually stopped being angry.'

She uncrossed and recrossed her legs, then cleared her throat. Marissa sat still, not wanting to anticipate what was coming next. Anything was possible with Cliona.

'Okay,' Cliona said, looking at Marissa, 'I'm taking a breath now, like you told me.'

They took a breath together.

'Maybe it's not this,' Cliona opened both palms to the sky, 'or you at all. Maybe I'm panicking a little bit and want to blame someone for it.'

Marissa took another breath. 'Has something happened since I saw you last week? Maybe you could start by telling me about your hair?'

Cliona touched her hair. 'Yeah, the hair. It was Nan's idea. She thinks I need to grow up and get a little more serious now.' She put on a voice and changed her poise, pretending to be her nan. 'No more childish messin' about.' She let it go and laughed a little. 'Nan, well, she's talking about me getting a job, but she knows that I can't, not with the baby coming. Look, I'm even starting to show a little bit.'

She stood up, turned to one side and patted her hand on her rather flat stomach.

As she sat back down again, Marissa smiled. 'How's the morning sickness?'

'Ah, rotten. Vomitin' up everything, so I am – breakfast, lunch...' She shivered. 'I can't stand the smell of food. Got to eat, though. Keep the little blighter goin'.'

Marissa nodded, 'And how's Brendan?'

Cliona froze. 'I've not said it yet. To him, I mean. Nan figured it out. Of course she did – you don't vomit your guts up in that house without her knowing about it. She's been real nice, though, tryin' to get me to eat and all. And she's looked after Ari while I've been sleeping it off. Yeah, I guess I need to try to get a job, then I can get maternity payment. That would help a lot with the bills and stuff.'

'Is Brendan working?'

'He has a few gigs comin' up. He plays guitar in a band, did I tell you? They're really good. But yeah, nothin' regular like. If we were to scrape a few beans together for our own place, I would have to work. I want to get Ariana a new dress too, it's her birthday soon. She doesn't know about the baby yet, either. I don't want her knowing first – she'd probably tell Bren before I'd a chance to.'

There was a slightly uncomfortable pause. Then Marissa asked, 'What would you like me to help you with tonight?'

'Okay, okay. The anger thing, check. Still a thing. The Bren thing, check. I've still got to tell him. The work thing, new thing, gotta do it, don't wanna do it, but I don't know how you can help me with that. So. I. Have. No. Idea. What you can help me with tonight. Marissa. It's always me spillin' my guts up – spillin' my guts up in the bathroom, spillin' my guts up here with you. I'm sick of it. Ha, ha, sick of it! I'm funny – I should do stand-up, only there's no money in it. Is there?'

She sighed and sank further into her chair.

'I don't know,' said Marissa. 'You've got to start somewhere, though. You are funny alright, but you're also real. And I want to help you. What did you mean when you said, "The anger thing, check?"'

'Checkin' it off my list, I guess.'

'Where are you with it?'

'I'm still angry at myself for gettin' pregnant. Angry at Nan for being so fuckin' nice to me when I deserve to be punished. I'm angry at Bren for, well, for being nice too. I'm not angry at Ari, she's a sweetheart.'

'Are you angry at your Nan and Bren for being nice to you because you're angry at yourself?'

'Yeah. That's the truth. I'm so angry at myself. Like, I want to claw at myself, hurt myself, I'm that angry... No, don't worry, you know I won't really do it. But I shouldn't have, Marissa. I sure as shit shouldn't have had that night with Shite Face... That's what I call him now, in my mind. 'Cos if I saw him again I'd throw shite in his face... Well, it's my face I see in the mirror – when I see it I want to throw shite at myself.'

They sat in silence while Cliona's anger reverberated in the room. After a few minutes, Marissa could hear Dave in the room next door shutting up for the night. Soon it would be just her in the building. She couldn't leave Cliona like this.

'Let's try something that I learned in college.' She stood up and moved behind Cliona's chair.

Cliona started laughing. 'What you gonna do – make faces at me from behind? Grab me or summat? Ha, ha.'

'No. Hang on, bear with me.' She stood beside her so she could see her. 'See that empty chair, where I just was?'

'Yeah.'

'Imagine you're sitting in it. There's you – right there, in that chair. You're so angry at her, tell her how you feel. Give her hell, go on scream at her, tell her what's on your mind. I'll be a witness to it.'

There wasn't a third chair in the room, and she wasn't about to drag an armchair in from next door so Marissa stayed standing up, making a mental note to suggest to Mr Blakemore that it would be good to get a fold-up chair as a spare for next time.

'Oh. Okay. I'll try it so. It can't be much worse than punchin' pillows... Right,' said Cliona, turning to the empty chair. It took her a moment to begin. 'You. You're a fuckin' eejit! *Look* what you've done to me! And now you're keepin' secrets too. How can you keep all that inside you? You'll not be able to hold it all in. No wonder you're puking up so much. And now you want to get a job and support two babies and a musician with a banjaxed career? You certainly know how to make a life for yourself!' She turned back to Marissa. 'Shall I keep going?'

'Do you have more to say?'

'Yeah, I guess so.' She turned back to the empty chair. 'You left school too young, you're not gonna amount to much of anything. And now you're a mother again, your life is fucked. Like Dad said it would be. Fuck it anyway, Marissa, I don't know how this is gonna help me at all.'

'Okay, stand up now and go and sit in the other chair.'

Cliona shrugged her shoulders, tucked her hair behind her ear, stood up and sat down in the opposite chair. Marissa moved to stand beside her once more, leaving her looking at an empty chair again.

'Now, in that empty chair, that was angry you. Here you are, in this chair, just after being yelled at by angry you. What do you want to say in your defence?'

'My defence? What's that mean?'

'Well, are you just gonna take it from angry you? Or are you gonna stand up for yourself? Explain what happened? What you're feeling after hearing what she said to you?'

'Oh, yeah. Okay.' Cliona turned to the empty chair. 'Listen here, you don't get away with calling me a fuckin' eejit, missus. Look at what you've done to your life – you're some holy fuck-up yourself!'

'No, no, no,' Marissa said quickly, 'you're just being angry you again, only in this chair. Stop a minute. Think about it. Be sad you, upset you, little you.'

'I don't know who that is,' said Cliona twisting round to look up at Marissa. 'I don't think this is working. I mean, I'm not sad, or upset, or little, I'm just angry. I'm fuckin' seriously angry. And I feel angrier now than I did when I got here...'

Marissa sighed, went to the other chair and sat back down in it.

'Okay. Well, we tried. Thanks for playing along for a bit.'

That seemed to placate Cliona. 'Hey, that's cool. You're learning too, right?'

Marissa nodded.

'And I do feel a little bit better,' Cliona admitted. 'Come to think of it, it was good to get that out of my system. I fancy a milkshake now – chocolate, with whipped cream. Mmm. I'll get one on my way home. Nice one! So, what do we talk about now then?'

When Cliona left, Marissa noticed she had a tight feeling in her chest. It was like a stitch, holding her heart tightly. It was uncomfortable. She breathed into it to try to release it, but it wouldn't shift.

The buzzer sounded. She let Joy in, and after a moment she was at the door.

'Marissa? Can I come in?'

'Yes, yes, do come in,' said Marissa, trying to tune into Joy and remember what had happened in their previous sessions, while pushing aside the residual anger from Cliona's session. It felt like sad and small Cliona had stayed behind and was still there in the room. *I guess she got more sympathy from me than she did from Cliona herself. Well, little Cliona, you can here stay for a bit, but you will have to go home, eventually.*

Joy entered the room, hung up her coat, then sat down. She was wearing jeans and a pretty blouse with flowers on it.

'It's nice and warm in here,' she said, sitting back in the chair and crossing her legs.

Nice and warm... Marissa realised she was actually feeling dirty, as if Cliona had spilt something on her. She wanted to take a shower. *I really messed up with her. That technique didn't work at all the way I thought it would.* She pushed the feelings to one side once more, sat up straighter and focused on Joy.

'Well, Joy, what can I do for you tonight?'

'I'm feeling anxious again. My boyfriend is moving in with me in two weeks' time and I think I've changed my mind. I don't want him to move in just yet.'

'Okay, tell me about your anxiety, and your boyfriend, and why you feel this way. Are you having those episodes again?'

Joy brightened, 'Actually, no, I've not had one since I saw you! I'm very pleased about that.'

I got something right after all.

It was dark by the time she stood at the bus stop to go home. Marissa was caught up in a rollercoaster of emotions, not sure which were hers and which were her clients'. She still felt sticky and icky. Thoughts echoed in her mind – fears from her clients, from herself, all blending and merging into a cacophony. *Is this from Margaret, Cliona, or the hidden fears that Joy is carrying? I have to let this go now.*

The bus came and she got on, feeling dizzy, small, not really present. On autopilot, she looked out of the window as the bus sped through the city, taking her home. Her mind was somewhere else, her chest was still tight, and lurking in the background, beneath all the different spirals of energy and emotion, in a dark grey corridor somewhere in her consciousness, sat a small, dark being, waiting patiently for the right time.

CHAPTER THIRTEEN

'Ahh Marissa, its great to see you, I'm delighted you could come today. Of course there's a place for you, come in!'

Marissa sheepishly entered the hotel conference room and took a chair beside Matt in the circle. It was the same room as before, and there were some familiar faces from the previous workshop there too, along with a couple of new ones. There were around twenty people in total, they were one of the last to arrive. Dolores was wearing peach today, she seemed radiant; she obviously loved teaching. There was a Level 2 handbook on each chair, Marissa had a quick look through hers. There were many symbols inside, and the practices seemed much more advanced than those from Level 1. After waiting ten minutes for stragglers, Dolores began.

'It's wonderful to see you all today on this bright and beautiful morning! Today we are going to learn Reiki Level 2. I will give you the attunements shortly, but I want to just check in with you as a group, and set some context for what we are going to do this weekend.'

'Level 1 is for physical healing. Many of you may have noticed your body's have changed, your appetites for food shifting, perhaps addictions have lessoned and aches and pains healing? Good! Level 2 works on the emotional layers of your energy field. So you may experience emotional shifts, which includes feeling difficult emotions. But that's a clearing out, and is good and healthy for us all to do. A spring clean!'

'As most of you are also aware, once you finish Level 2 you can see clients, and you can charge money for the sessions. If you are serious about being a Reiki practitioner, I do recommend you take the Reiki practitioner level workshop as well, as it will cover things like setting up a Reiki business and how to look after your clients, and it's a good grounding in offering duty-of-care. However, it's not necessary, unless you want to be registered with Reiki Federation

Ireland. I do recommend that. As a practitioner, it can be quite lonely out there and with the support of the RFI you can meet other Reiki practitioners and have a community to turn to if and when any issue comes up for you.'

'Now, before we go into what is different in Level 2, I'd like us all to open with a little self-practice. I will come around to each of you and answer any questions you may have about your Reiki practice as it stands up to this moment, to ensure that we are all on the same page before we begin the new material.'

Dolores went over to her portable stereo and pressed 'play'. Warm music filled the room, with flavours of Indian sitar and chanting. It was pleasant, not overpowering.

'Now you can connect to the Reiki light, however you choose to do so. I know some of you didn't take Level 1 with me. I'll be around to speak to you shortly.'

Marissa closed her eyes and visualised a ball of light above her head. She pushed her feet softly into the ground and became aware of her breathing. *Please can I connect to the Reiki light?* Nothing happened. She asked again, and felt herself opening in expectation. A dark thrumming stirred in the pit of her stomach. Her body started to shake and she suddenly felt weak. She looked at Matt, but he was already in the throes of his practice. She brought herself back to herself. *I am going to do this. Reiki is NOT shamanism. So STOP IT right now!* Her system buckled, as if in shock. Then it settled down. It was like a pet that was doing something bold (and knowing it was doing something bold), getting yelled at by its owner and stopping in its tracks.

The Reiki light entered her body. As she relaxed, any dark feelings dissolved away. *Good.* Marissa visualised the Reiki entering her like a fountain of water gently bubbling in over her head, down through her body and into her heart. She felt tingling and warmth and as it filled her, she used her will and intention to gently send it up and over her shoulders, down her arms and out through her hands. As she was doing this, she noticed Matt beside her rubbing his hands together and breathing unnaturally loudly, but she didn't question him. Marissa felt more centred now. She placed one hand on her heart and the other on her stomach and felt the energy flow inside her change, stabilise and flatten out. She started to notice how tight her body was and how much tension she was carrying in her shoulders and neck. After a moment or two, lower back was beginning to ache. *This is a strange feeling?* She moved the hand that was on her heart to her back, but the ache didn't ease.

She looked around the circle in her discomfort. Dolores was talking to one of the women and pointing to her heart. The woman was showing her her hands, but Marissa couldn't hear what was being said. Then she heard a snort. She jumped. It was Matt; he seemed to be dozing off. Marissa chuckled to herself. *Reiki always puts him to sleep. I don't know how he is going to tolerate it when it's stronger!* She caught the eye of the woman who was sitting opposite her. She was nearly laughing, too, at Matt's snort. Marissa smiled back at her. She had a light behind her eyes and Marissa liked her immediately.

Dolores moved on to the next person in the circle. The ache in Marissa's lower back became stronger and somehow moved into the hip that her hand was on. She shifted in her seat to try and get more comfortable but the ache turned into a sharp pain, like a knife digging and grinding deeply into her. She moved her hand from her back to her hip, but it felt worse, so she placed both hands on her stomach instead, bringing her awareness into her body, to investigate what was going on with this pain. *I remember in the classes with Séamus how we did body mapping – mapping someone else's energy onto our own. I wonder if this pain is mine or somebody else's? I never have pain like this – it can't be mine.*

The woman opposite her jumped up from her chair suddenly, and the pain in Marissa's hip lessened, but didn't disappear. Marissa caught the woman's eye again and watched her as she sat back down delicately on her chair. Again, they exchanged smiles, but something had changed between them. Marissa couldn't put her finger on what it was.

Dolores was now chatting to Matt. Marissa leaned towards them to try to hear what was being said.

'I've found it very helpful in combination with my Tai Chi,' Matt was saying, 'but sometimes it's too much to practise both, so I've been doing my Reiki practice at the same time when I practise the slow form. I don't put my hands on myself, but I've discovered when I do them both together it seems to work well.'

'That's interesting, Matt,' said Dolores. 'We'll be looking at "hands-off" Reiki techniques today, it sounds like that's what you're doing. Your Tai Chi could be improving the energy flow in your body and amplifying the effects of your Reiki practice. It will be interesting to see where Level 2 takes you. Good work!'

Marissa wondered what Dolores was going to say to her and started to prepare herself for the conversation, but Dolores simply nodded to her and moved on to the person beside her. *Odd. Is she upset with me? It's true I haven't been practising my Reiki every day, and I wasn't actually planning to do Level 2, but now that I'm here, I really want to.*

Trying to shrug it off, she kept her hands on herself, drawing down Reiki, while Dolores worked her way through the rest of the group. It didn't stop the pain in her body though, but it had flattened out a little. She looked at the woman across the way who seemed to be hiding her face from her now. *What's going on?*

Once Dolores finished her rounds she came back to Marissa. 'I didn't skip you because you'd done something wrong,' she said in a low voice. 'I saw you were working something out, so I wanted to give you the space to do it.' She looked Marissa up and down. 'I see you've still not completely disconnected from Bettina,' she gestured casually across to the woman opposite, 'so see if you can do it now.'

She doesn't miss a thing. 'I only just figured out that's what happened,' Marissa said quietly. 'I really would love to disconnect from her, but I'm not sure how to do it.'

Dolores smiled. 'You're not quite there yet, but you are on the way. You have to learn how to do this for yourself. Think about it. She latched on to you. She's a lovely person, but she does have a tendency to do this to people who are helpers. Like you.'

'I'm trying to disconnect,' said Marissa, not knowing what she was doing, feeling she was not making any progress.

'I'm going to leave you to it for now,' said Dolores. 'If you're going to be a professional healer, you'll have to sort this out or you'll burn out before you even begin.' She smiled encouragingly. 'You're almost there, so keep going. If you haven't done it soon, it could affect your attunement process.'

She walked over to the stereo, turned the music off and sat down in her chair at the top of the room.

Was she giving out to me or helping me? Marissa wasn't sure. She persisted with the complication.

In the meantime, Dolores began to speak to the group once more. 'Now, I've got a good idea of where we all are and I feel able to move forward with you as a group. Thank you for your patience! Let's begin by having the Reiki Level 2 attunements. These are different from the Level 1 attunements as you are bringing more of your body into the Reiki connection. I will be working on your head, heart, spine, hands and feet. You can help me by turning your chairs the other way around, so that you're facing outwards instead of in.'

Everyone got up and turned their chair to face the other way. Marissa sat down in hers, knowing that she would really need to focus on how to disconnect from Bettina and do it quickly. It was somehow easier with her back to her. *Or is that just my mind thinking that?*

'I will come around to you once more,' Dolores announced, 'one by one, and give the Reiki attunement to each of you. Afterwards, you can connect to Reiki and continue your self-practice, noticing how you feel, if you feel any different. When I'm finished, we'll break for tea. I will be doing the attunements in silence. Take the time for quiet contemplation and continue your self-practice while you wait your turn.'

As Dolores worked her way around the group, Marissa closed her eyes and asked Archangel Michael to come and help her disconnect from Bettina. She felt a strong but gentle presence beside her, and her heart softened. *Ahh. There you are, I've missed you so much.* Marissa's eyes brimmed with tears. *Why don't I call on you? I really have missed you, so very much.* She felt a tightness leave her heart, like a whisper, and her heart opened outwards, like a flower opening its innermost petals to the sun. It was beautiful. The pain in her hip and back remained, however. *Can you help me disconnect from Bettina?* Marissa imagined a pair of giant silver scissors cutting through the air, severing any energetic connection that had developed between them, but she thought she saw the angel shaking his head. She felt deflated. *Okay, I'll try something else.* An image of a leech on her hip, sucking her blood, appeared in her mind. *Eww, that's horrible, get it off me!* She put her hand where she thought the leech was and plucked it off. *Eugh.* She shivered. Then she thought she saw the angel nod and smile at her, but it was so hazy in her mind she couldn't imagine his face clearly. But she still felt him there, and the shiver and the sudden feeling of calmness were good indications that she had got it right. And then, just as quickly as it began, the pain in her hip completely disappeared. 'Thank you,' she whispered out loud to the angel.

She felt a hand on her shoulder. 'Well done,' Dolores whispered into her ear. 'Now put it into the violet flame.' She moved away.

I forgot all about the violet flame! 'Saint Germain, Saint Germain of the Violet Flame,' Marissa whispered, 'please take this energy and transmute it for the highest good of all.' *Where did that come from?* She placed the imaginary leech into the imaginary violet flame. Part of her thought this was childlike and ridiculous but another part felt an irritant leaving her system.

It would be so easy to buy into all this stuff, or to dissuade yourself from believing it. I'm on the edge, I think, right now. I could go either way. 'That's just your brain talking,' said a voice in her head. 'Your heart knows the truth.'

Hearing the words, Marissa was overcome by a feeling of pure, intense love. *Oh, how I've missed this feeling!* She surrendered to it. Then Dolores came to her and attuned her to Reiki Level 2.

The hotel staff brought in fresh tea and coffee, biscuits and little teacakes. Marissa stood up and stretched and looked for Matt. He smiled at her, with a sleepy look as if he had just been napping. Marissa wanted to throw her arms around him and kiss him, but they had agreed 'no lovey-dovey stuff' during the workshop. She smiled, and they went over to the table to help themselves.

'I've got to nip to the loo – can you get me a cuppa? See you in a minute,' said Matt, leaving Marissa queueing up for hot water. Bettina saw her and made a beeline for her, Marissa's stomach flipped over.

I've got to stop worrying about this type of thing. Bettina can't hurt me. She is not allowed to suck my energy from me. And now I know how to clean it away!

Bettina introduced herself and started chatting. 'Wasn't that amazing? I felt fire down my spine, and I got so dizzy, I thought I was going to fall off my chair! I just love Reiki, and Dolores is spectacular! What's your name? How long have you been doing Reiki?'

'Erm, hi. I'm Marissa, I've been doing Reiki since just after Christmas,' Marissa said, looking for sugar to put into Matt's tea. He arrived back just in time. 'Here you go, love,' she said, handing him the mug.

'Thanks!' he said, helping himself to several biscuits and a cake. 'Do you want any?'

'I'm good,' said Marissa.

'Hi! I'm Bettina!'

'Hi,' Matt said, through a mouthful of biscuit. 'I'm Matt.'

Bettina looked at Marissa, and then at Matt. 'Are you together?'

'Yes,' answered Marissa.

'We met at Dolores's Level 1 workshop.' said Matt.

Marissa wasn't happy about this disclosure. After the experience with the leech she really didn't want to tell Bettina anything.

'Aww, how sweet, and now you're doing Level 2 together! So romantic!' Bettina smiled.

She still seems nice, though. I want to like her, but my body doesn't want to feel that pain again. One of the other people in the group came over and started chatting to them. She was an older woman who seemed very enthusiastic.

'What did you think of the attunement? Wasn't it powerful? I saw Archangel Michael and Saint Germain in the room with us as Dolores was working on us.'

'Oh you can see angels?' asked Bettina, turning to the new arrival.

'Well, no, I can't actually see them, but I can feel them.'

Marissa thought she'd take the opportunity to ask a question. 'How do you know which one is which? I mean, if you can't see them...'

'I don't know,' the woman answered. 'I guess I can see colours in my mind, I have a picture in my head of Archangel Michael, and when I feel him, I see the picture. I also get a sense of dark purple, or blue, and I feel a very strong and powerful energy.' She filled her cup and added, 'I know he is around me when I feel protected and safe. That's what he feels like for me.'

'And what about Saint Germain?' asked Marissa. Matt was listening with avid interest while consuming his biscuits. Even Bettina stopped talking to hear the woman's answer.

'The energy is different. It's hard to explain. The colour again is purple, but it's more of an amethyst purple – lighter, but still a royal colour. That's the word – royal. Like he's royalty or something. The energy, I mean. Archangel Michael feels like a warrior, while Saint Germain is like a prince, or a king.' She paused. 'It is so difficult to explain this, I'm probably making a mess of it.'

'Yes, it's a little confusing,' said Bettina, dunking her biscuit into her now lukewarm tea and then eating it before it dropped into the cup.

'No, I think I understand,' said Marissa. 'It's kind of the same for me. And I agree, it's very difficult to explain.'

The woman seemed relieved. Tea break was over. Dolores was calling them back.

'You can bring your tea with you if you haven't finished,' she said. 'But please sit back down now. We have a lot to cover today.'

Once they settled back in their chairs, Dolores began. 'In Reiki Level 1 you connect to the Reiki light and draw it down through your body. It's a soft light, like torchlight, very gentle, yet powerful. In Level 2 it's different, more concentrated, like a laser beam. For this reason you can send it over distance to someone who is not in the room with you. You are all now attuned to Level 2, which means that you have this ability activated in your energy field. I want to teach you different ways of working on someone who is not in the room with you.' Dolores pulled a large pink teddy bear out from a big bag that was at her feet. 'Meet Ted.'

Everyone looked excited and keen to learn this new skill. The energy in the room had been chaotic after the Reiki attunements, but after the tea break, and now that they were all focused on the same thing, it felt more grounded again.

'Ted is a surrogate,' Dolores explained. 'When I am working on someone who is not in the same room as me, once I have permission to work on that person, I open a healing space, just like I showed you in Level 1.' She turned to the couple who had not been at her workshops before. 'I will show you again once we start to work on each other.' They nodded. Dolores continued, 'So then I imagine that Ted's head is the head of the person I am working on, his chest is their chest, stomach, their stomach, arms and legs, their arms and legs. You get the idea. It's as if I take a map of their energy field and place it onto Ted.'

Something inside Marissa lit up hearing this. She sat up straighter in her chair and her eyes opened wide. *Mapping the body! But I was mapping someone else's body onto mine before, I didn't know you could map it onto a surrogate! That's fantastic!*

'Once you have done this, you can perform the Reiki session on your surrogate,' Dolores said, 'as if it is the person you're actually working on. Of course for best results you can tell the person you're working on exactly when you're doing it, that way they can lie down somewhere comfortable, wherever they are, at the same time you're working on them. And of course it goes without saying that you must have their permission.'

Marissa put up her hand. 'And can you tell where they are having difficulties in their body when you're working on them using the teddy?'

'Yes, some people can do this intuitively,' answered Dolores, 'just as you feel drawn to move your hands to different parts of the body when you are doing hands-on Reiki, you experience similar feelings in this hands-off practice.'

Marissa nodded, delighted with the answer.

Someone else put up their hand.

'Yes?'

'So you're saying the other person knows you're working on them, gives permission, then lies down. You somehow transfer their energy onto the teddy and work on the teddy, and they feel it?'

'Yes.'

'That's crazy! How does that work, exactly?'

Dolores sat Ted gently down on the floor by her feet. 'We really, honestly, don't know. The closest explanation we have is entanglement theory, from quantum physics. It basically states that if we are energetically connected, we don't need to know where the other person is necessarily, in order to have energy flow between us.'

Someone else put their hand up. 'I see you put Ted on the floor very gently – it reminds me of voodoo! Like a voodoo doll. I mean, if you threw him down hard, or, say, if you stuck a pin into Ted, would the other person feel it?'

Everyone laughed, but there was a tension in it, as if they were entering unnavigable waters.

'I don't know anything about voodoo,' Dolores said, 'but I always treat Ted with respect when I am using him as a surrogate, and even when I am not. The original Reiki tenets still hold. Treat everyone and everything with respect. You see, there is a code of ethics with Reiki. You learned the Reiki principles in Level 1, it's not enough to just know them, you have to live by them, too. So for distance Reiki, I open the space, connect to the person, place them onto Ted, do the session, then disconnect that person from Ted and close the space. And I always give thanks afterwards, it's something that I do personally, because it feels right to me.'

Everyone took a few moments to digest this, some people were scribbling notes in their Reiki 2 handbooks.

'There is one thing that you need to learn before you can do this, however, and that's the Reiki symbol to open up the portal so you can access that person's energy field. It's one of the most difficult symbols that you will have to use with Reiki, but don't worry, you can use the diagram in the handbook to help you with it until you're more familiar with it. Reiki symbols are very powerful, and you can only use them once you have been attuned to Level 2. As you all are now.'

Everyone smiled. It was as if the group took a breath together.

'These symbols are sacred, and they were secret for the longest time. Unfortunately the internet has destroyed this. You can simply look them up on a search engine now and find them. If used incorrectly, they are harmless. However, there are other symbols that are not harmless, and not Reiki. I would stress that you do not look up any type of symbol, or sigil as they're sometimes called, on the internet, because you just don't know what you're looking at. Anything could pop-up in a search, and, if you pay it a little too much attention, it can activate.'

Marissa shivered, remembering Matt's magic book. She felt something push inside her, but she pushed back and kept her focus in the room. *Sigils, symbols... Hang on, didn't we learn a symbol for protection and warding in the workshop with Séamus? Oh no! There is such an overlap here. Mapping bodies onto each other's bodies, and now we can map a body's energy onto a surrogate. I was certain Reiki had nothing to do with shamanism. I wonder...*

'Turn to page thirteen in your workbook, there's a synopsis of all the symbols we're going to work with. I have put in more than we can work with, this weekend. The most important symbol is the Opening Space symbol. That's the one we will look at now. We can try some of the others later, if we have time.'

Marissa kicked Matt and he looked up at her. She leaned in. 'I bet that book you lent me has some bad symbols in it. And you know what, I've never opened it... I'm glad now that I haven't.'

Matt looked concerned, 'Yes, you're probably right. I'll give it back. Don't use it. Let's stick to stuff we know something about. Not that we know much about this just yet.'

Dolores was standing in the centre of the circle, drawing shapes in the air with her fingers. Marissa and Matt watched her along with the rest of the group. It was difficult to follow what she was doing. She drew in a specific pattern, repeating a mantra, 'Once you have drawn the symbol, you activate it, like this.'

That's the same thing we did with the warding symbol, with Séamus. Marissa got a shiver down her spine and felt anxiety threatening in her stomach, but it left her as soon as it started. *I am safe here. Dolores is good, and the angels will protect me. This is okay. I can do this.*

'All of this is in your workbook, but it will take you some time to learn it. This is why we will have a follow-up Level 2 class in about three weeks' time. It will only be for a couple of hours, and we can spend time on some of the other symbols as well as a check-in and a practice. If you can't make it, that's okay, I have them quite regularly. It's good to have a follow up, as the work we are doing is quite complicated.

'I'd like you to take some time now to try drawing this particular symbol. Open your workbook to page fourteen and you'll see the symbol and how to draw it.'

A Japanese symbol. Makes sense, seeing as Usui, the founder of Reiki, was Japanese. I wonder if there's an equivalent in English – it would be much easier! Oh well...

'Say the name,' Dolores pronounced it slowly and they repeated it, 'and then draw the symbol, following the order of strokes just as I have numbered them in the workbook. See how you go. I'll give you about ten minutes.'

That wasn't long enough. When Dolores called them back, the group seemed more confused than they had been before they started. A few of them were looking quite distressed.

Matt was looking disheartened. He had trouble with the Japanese symbology. 'Chinese for Tai Chi is bad enough,' he said quietly to Marissa, 'my poor brain is full!'

'Don't worry,' Dolores told the group. 'You can call on the Reiki Angels and Ascended Masters to help you perfect the symbol as you draw it. That's what I do, sometimes. Even after all these years I can get flustered drawing specific symbols. Let's try it again, and then we can have a look at some of the other symbols after lunch. Some of them are much easier than this one.'

After another fifteen minutes, Dolores called them all to order.

'After lunch I'll split you into two groups – we have use of the room next door. You'll be working on each other over distance, using separate rooms, so you can experience it for yourselves. We'll take an hour's break for lunch, now. You can bring your workbooks with you, but please don't show the symbols in public where someone else can see them. Any questions before we finish up?'

Marissa didn't want to ask about shamanism in front of the group. She didn't want to ask about shamanism at all, but she still wasn't sure about symbols and felt she needed to put her mind at ease. She piped up hesitantly, 'Dolores? What exactly is a symbol? I mean, what's it made of? And how does it work?'

'A symbol is a packet of energy, with a purpose. You invoke it by drawing it; you activate it like I showed you. The intention behind the symbol, plus the Reiki, is what powers it. For example, the symbol for emotional healing. You draw it, empower it with Reiki, and activate it, and the energy in it will help with emotional healing.'

'Yes, but I still don't understand.'

Dolores looked at Marissa. 'You're a psychotherapist, aren't you?'

Marissa nodded.

'Well, say one of your clients is anxious. Before they come to see you, you could draw and activate one of the Reiki symbols for healing. Place it in the room, empower it. Make it really big, so that it attunes the energy of the room for that purpose. I'd imagine if you did that, the session with your client could go much more smoothly than if you didn't do it. It could be worth a try? Play with it and see how you find it.'

'That's certainly an interesting idea. You've given me something to think about. Thanks, Dolores.'

'Anyone else?'

Everyone else's brains were full and their stomachs were empty. Marissa's suddenly growled with hunger at the thought of food.

'Okay then, see you back here in an hour!'

'Same place as last time?' asked Matt.

'Yes! Why not?' agreed Marissa, and they got their coats.

Walking to the pub, Marissa linked arms with Matt and leaned into him once more. 'I don't really want to talk to Bettina. Can we get all lovey-dovey now?'

Matt laughed. 'What's wrong with her? She seems nice.'

'She latched onto me earlier this morning, and it hurt.'

'What do you mean?'

'It was energetic – she hooked into me somehow. I guess it doesn't matter now. I did learn something from it, and Dolores said she didn't do it on purpose.'

'Well, there you go then – sometimes our biggest teachers are the people that upset us.'

'You're very wise today!'

'I was watching Bruce Lee last night,' he said and winked, and they went inside.

Nobody else from the group was there. They got a table at the back and ordered soup and a sandwich.

'Where we had our first date,' said Marissa with a coy smile. 'No pint today?'

Matt smiled back and shook his head 'Not today, no. This seems much more serious than Level 1, I need my head on straight! That symbol for time and space is really difficult. I want to look at it again, but I left my workbook at the hotel – do you mind?'

Marissa got her workbook out of her handbag, They pored over the symbol and discussed Reiki while they ate.

'I'll never learn this!' said Marissa, after trying for the fourth time to draw the symbol without looking at the book. 'It's a totally different language.'

Matt laughed, 'Yes – yes, it is! Totally. Japanese is a different language!'

Marissa couldn't help but laugh too.

Matt added, 'I think we'll be fine – we can just ask the Reiki Angel to draw it for us.'

'It's nice thinking there's a Reiki Angel to rescue our bad drawing skills. Séamus said working with symbols is all in the power of your intention,' Marissa said.

Matt looked at her sideways. 'You know, that's the first time you've mentioned him to me, or said something positive about him, since Christmas.'

'I guess it is. I'm surprised, Matt. There's so much in Reiki Level 2 that is similar to what I've been covering with Séamus. I was convinced that Reiki wasn't shamanism. Maybe I'm wrong.'

'Maybe the principles are the same?' asked Matt, eyeing up the pint that was settling on the countertop for someone else. 'No, I'll stick to the coke and have a pint later on.'

'How was the attunement for you?' Marissa asked him quickly to change the subject.

'Wow, yeah, we didn't get any time really to talk about that, did we? It was weird. I felt hot fire on my spine, then it felt like my feet turned to lead. All the while, I was lightheaded. Maybe I fell asleep too! What about you?'

'I don't know. Maybe because I was focused on disconnecting from Bettina, I didn't feel very much really, at all,' said Marissa thoughtfully. 'Someone else said they felt fire in their spine too. I wonder why that is, and why I didn't feel it.'

'Maybe you should ask Dolores?'

'No, I think I've talked enough for one day. I don't really want to say much more in the class. I hope all we do is practise this afternoon.'

They made their way back to the hotel, grabbing a couple of coffees from a pop-up stand on the way. They met a man and a woman from the group who were standing outside the hotel smoking cigarettes. They nodded hello. They seemed apologetic for smoking; the woman was holding her cigarette behind her, as if to try to hide it.

'It seems strange to be doing Reiki and then to have a cigarette, I know. But I just can't seem to quit. We were just talking about it before you came,' she said, flicking the ash onto the ground.

Marissa sipped her cappuccino. 'Do coffee and Reiki go together? I can't quit this either! I don't think I'd want to.'

'It's not as bad for you as smoking is, though' said the male smoker. 'I'm Colin, by the way.'

'Nice to meet you! I'm Marissa. Do you really want to give up smoking? Could you use Reiki to help?' asked Marissa.

'I thought you weren't going to ask any more questions today,' said Matt with a chuckle, extending his hand to Colin. 'Matt,' he said.

Colin nodded, shaking his hand.

'I'm Jane,' said the woman. 'Nice to meet you both. Yes, I did try, a few times actually. But perhaps I didn't try hard enough,' In a quieter voice, she added, 'Or perhaps I didn't really want to give them up.'

'I like your honesty,' said Colin with a grin. 'I also enjoy smoking. But I do have to give it up soon. My girlfriend is having a baby and I don't want to be smoking around it. How about we do it together? Might be good to have some support. But I don't know how we could use Reiki to help.'

'I suppose you could practise Reiki on yourself every day,' Marissa suggested, 'and then set your intention to give up smoking. Then one day you'll feel ready to do it. And then when you have cravings for cigarettes, you could just do Reiki on yourself until the cravings leave? I don't know, I've never smoked, but this seems like something that could work for anything, really.'

'Now that sounds like a great idea,' said Colin. 'I'm not quite ready to give the cigarettes up just yet, but I know I will soon.'

Jane didn't seem as pleased. She shrugged her shoulders in a non-committal kind of way.

'I can tell you're really *not* ready yet!' said Colin, stubbing his cigarette out on the wall and throwing it into a litter bin beside him.

'Probably not,' said Jane, putting hers out too.

'Let's go in,' suggested Matt, and they all went in together.

Back in the circle, Dolores numbered everyone either a one or a two. 'Ones will be staying in here, twos will go next door. Please separate yourselves out now, make yourselves known to each other then find a partner of the opposite number.

Matt was a two and Marissa a one, but they chose not to work together. Marissa noticed that Bettina was a two as well. Remembering Matt's comment from earlier, she went up to her.

'Would you like to work with me?'

Bettina's face lit up, 'Oh thanks! That would be great.'

'Now,' said Dolores. 'I will be timing it. The ones will work on twos first, for fifteen minutes. Then we will take a five-minute break, then swap around.'

'But we don't have a teddy bear,' said Bettina.

'Turn to page twenty-three of your workbook please.'

Everyone did so. On page twenty-three there was a picture of the human body.

'This picture will be your surrogate. You can use a teddy bear tonight when you do the homework, but for now, the picture will do.'

'I think I'll have to ask my teddy bear's permission first,' whispered Marissa.

Bettina giggled a little bit too enthusiastically.

'Okay, off you go,' said Dolores. 'Find a chair and sit down in your allocated room. When you hear the gong, it's time to start, when you hear it again, you can stop.'

They practised on each other for two rounds, so each of them practised distance Reiki twice and received it twice. Marissa used all of her focus and concentration when opening the space and drawing the symbol, but found her concentration wandering when she was using the image. She didn't know if what she was doing was working, but Bettina was in the throes of delight afterwards while describing how she felt in the room next door with Marissa working on her. When she was working on Marissa, Marissa didn't feel much of anything. She was disappointed again, and focused on her breathing during the two rounds of fifteen minutes. Then everyone was given a new partner for the homework and they took a quick break, then spent the rest of the afternoon working on a few more symbols.

Marissa was feeling quite let down when the day had ended. 'I didn't feel anything during the attunement, and I didn't feel anything during the healing,' she said to Matt as they walked towards the DART station. She was going to spend the night with him, as Dun Laoghaire was only a couple of stops away from Greystones. It was a lovely fresh evening and the sky was perfect blue behind the white clouds. The sun was still out. She turned to him and asked 'Can we walk on the beach for a bit?'

'Absolutely.'

They walked past the DART station until they got to the pedestrian entrance to the public beach. There were a few people out, some with dogs, some with children, some on their own. Marissa liked being there with Matt, with her boyfriend. It felt natural and comfortable being with him.

He had his hands in his pockets as he walked out towards the sea and Marissa followed him. 'I used to come out here with my dad a lot when I was a boy,' he said.

'You did? You don't talk much about your parents.'

'No, I don't really get on with them. I don't visit much. I've not told them about you. I might not tell them about you,' he said wistfully.

'Well, I've not told mine about you, yet, but I don't know how long that will last,' Marissa said with a smile. 'They always have a way of finding things out.'

'I'm happy like this for now,' Matt replied. 'We don't need to rush things.'

Marissa agreed. 'Yes, it's nice like this – no need to call over to family for dinner, no need for difficult conversations. I like the peace we have, just being us for now. Anyway, Eli and Carol are getting all the attention. I wouldn't want to spoil their fun!'

Matt picked up a stone and threw it into the sea. It bounced once, then twice, then a third time.

'Hey, I didn't know you could do that! Do it again!'

Matt picked up another stone and did it again. This time it bounced four times.

'Show off!'

'You do it then!'

'I don't know how to.'

'It's easy. I'll show you.'

After at least fifteen tries, Marissa still couldn't get the stone to bounce once. 'It's not my day today,' she said, disheartened.

'Ah well, some people are good at some things and not so good at other things. Let's go home – there's a pint calling me. And a hot bag of salty, vinegary chips.'

CHAPTER FOURTEEN 

'So then he rang me and we laughed about it! He really did say he felt it. I know I was supposed to send Reiki to Maurice, but I couldn't help it. Dad must have needed it more.'

The next day, Dolores had allocated plenty of time in the morning session for sharing, questions and answers. Marissa zoned out listening to people's stories of last night's homework. She hadn't slept well at all.

Many of the group had remarkable stories about how they felt while Reiki was being sent to them the previous evening as part of their homework. One person said that she saw colours and lights in the room at the same time the Reiki was being sent. Marissa was still feeling despondent; she had had no similar experiences, although the person she was sending the Reiki to said it was wonderful.

Matt, however, was very enthusiastic. He had felt waves of warmth engulfing him at 7pm, which was exactly the time he had agreed to receive the distance healing from Jane. He had slept really well; in fact, his snoring had kept Marissa awake until she did Reiki on herself as she was lying there beside him. She placed one hand on her heart, the other on her stomach, and at one point something seemed to dislodge in her stomach. She felt a shooting sensation through her body, as if something left her system. She then became hyper and agitated. If she had been in her own flat, she would have gotten up, no matter what the hour, and sat on her little deck under the stars. Being at Matt's, with no courtyard as he lived upstairs, and not wanting to wake him, she just lay in the bed awake until she dozed off.

Now, as she sat listening to everyone's stories from the previous day and evening, the tiredness that was still with her caused her to faze out. Everything seemed out of focus, fuzzy.

'Marissa, how did you find it?'

Dolores's voice brought her back to the room, but not fully. She was still hazy, unfocused.

'Em, honestly, I don't know. I didn't feel much during the attunement yesterday. And then during the healings, well, again, I didn't feel very much. But last night something seemed to shift. I became very agitated... I feel quite out of sorts today.'

Dolores listened with compassion. 'This is not necessarily a bad thing – attunements affect everyone differently. And they aren't always instantaneous. Your body will settle in and adjust when it is ready. An attunement is a tuning in, hence the name. But the actual energy transmission causes an initiation, and not everyone is ready for it at the time of the attunement. It is also possible,' she said, turning to the group, 'that an initiation has already taken place, and the attunement is like a small adjustment, as if you can already pick up the radio station and the attunement gives you a clearer signal. We can't see what is going on with our eyes. If we could, spiritual healing work would be so much easier.' She turned back to Marissa. 'Thank you for sharing, Marissa, and for being so honest with the group. Reiki isn't all love and light. It can be difficult and at times and it *can* cause physical discomfort. Sometimes, something has to break before it can be healed.'

I hope I'm not breaking. Marissa smiled at Dolores and looked at the floor.

'We will now do a grounding exercise,' Dolores continued, 'to enable us to hold the energy of Reiki Level 2 in our body. This will help you embody it and come into balance with the changes we have made. As you can see, I've brought the plinths in today, so we will also be doing some hands-on practice with the symbols. As there are twenty of you, I've kept the room next door, and we have ten plinths, five in here, five next door, and we will be working in pairs.'

Plinth. That's it's official name, not a massage table. I guess we're not doing massage, so it makes more sense to call it that. Marissa made a mental note.

Dolores led the group through a grounding meditation exercise which reminded Marissa of the work she had done in psychotherapy when studying focusing. *Another crossover? Maybe healing work is healing work, whether it's psychotherapy, shamanism or Reiki?*

After the tea break Dolores talked a little bit about working with clients and charging money, and again stressed the importance of the Reiki Practitioner course. *Maybe I'll take it, but it does sound a lot like what I've already learned in college. But I could put it down as CBD hours.*

'We are going to focus on three symbols as we do the hands-on sessions,' said Dolores. They were standing up at the plinths and Bettina was the volunteer. She was already lying down on the table in anticipation of receiving Reiki from the Reiki master. 'We will use the power symbol, the symbol for heart healing and the grounding symbol.' Dolores opened a healing space around Bettina, who already seemed to be blissed out.

'Now, to use the symbols while you work hands-on, you draw them in the air, in front of you, like this,' Dolores drew the power symbol, 'you activate it, say the name several times, and then you connect to it. You have a few choices. You can imagine that it's coming out of your hands with the Reiki and into your client's body. Or you can draw it over the client and visualise it sinking into them, doing the healing work to support you. Knowing you can draw big symbols, small symbols – you can have a lot of fun playing with them! Now, feel into it, notice what works for you today. And if it doesn't work today, it might work tomorrow! That's why I'd love you to come to the follow-up evening. It's free. I'll email you with several dates, just in case one doesn't suit.'

Half of the group went into the second room, Marissa wanted to stay where she was because she liked the light coming in from the windows. Matt and Colin chose to work together, Bettina had gravitated towards one of the others in the group and went into the room next door and Jane came over to Marissa. 'Want to work with me?'

'Sure.'

They chose a plinth by the window and both of them brought their workbooks over, as they needed help remembering how to draw the symbols.

'Would you like to work on me first?' asked Jane. 'Or shall I work on you?'

'I don't mind,' said Marissa, smiling, flicking between the pages, trying to decide which symbol to choose. 'Actually, yes, please, I'd like to work on you.'

Jane took her shoes off and climbed up onto the plinth, and Marissa placed a blanket over her legs. 'Tell me if you get cold, or if you're uncomfortable, or if you want me to stop.'

'Why would I want you to stop?' asked Jane.

'I don't know! It just came out... I'm really not myself today.'

'Are you sure you want to work on me first? I can work on you...'

'I'm fine, honestly. I'll open space now. Are you comfortable?'

'Yes, all good,' said Jane, shifting the pillow under her head and closing her eyes.

It had been a while since Marissa had given a formal Reiki session. She took a moment to connect to the Reiki light, then she opened a healing space the way Dolores had shown her in her Level 1 workshop.

Power symbol, to empower the healing. I'll start with that one. She studied the symbol. It reminded her of music. She decided to draw a big power symbol over Jane's whole body. She took a breath, and drew the symbol in the air with her finger, visualising it appearing like a trail of light. She drew it vertically, but Jane was lying down, so she activated it and then imagined it tilting onto its side and floating over Jane's body. *Lucky I have an active imagination!* Then she imagined the symbol slowly sinking into Jane's body, like melting ice. As she visualised it dissolving, Jane's left leg spasmed. But Jane was fine; in fact, she seemed to be even more relaxed than she was before. Marissa went to her head, placed her hands over the top of it and flowed Reiki down her arms into Jane's body. Jane let out a sigh and stretched out. Her toes flexed. *So far, so good.*

After a few moments, Marissa moved down to Jane's shoulders and then to her heart centre. *This would be a good place to put the heart healing symbol.* She kept one hand on Jane and used the other one to turn the page of the workbook. She took her index finger and drew a small heart healing symbol over Jane's heart, then activated it. She then breathed into the heart too. *Oh! That's shamanism... Oh no!* Jane seemed to soften a little bit. *Maybe it's okay. I'll keep going.*

Marissa held her hands over Jane's heart for a few minutes, then moved down to her stomach, but felt pulled to move back to her heart again. She stayed there for quite a time, and then she had a sense to finish there and move to Jane's knees. She walked to the end of the table and placed a hand on each knee, flowing Reiki into Jane's body the whole time.

Jane's eyes were flickering. Her face was softer, fuller, and there was more colour in it than before. She had a half-smile on her lips.

'Are you okay?' whispered Marissa, not sure what to do about the eyes.

'Yes, this is wonderful,' said Jane, opening her eyes. 'My heart feels so much lighter than it did before. It's really wonderful. Thank you. Don't stop!'

'Okay,' said Marissa, relieved. *That really made me uncomfortable. Maybe it's like the leg spasm, it's just her body receiving the Reiki. I've so much to learn.* She moved to Jane's feet and held one foot in each hand. She then decided to draw the grounding symbol on Jane's feet. This was harder – the symbol seemed much more complicated than the others.

At exactly that moment, Dolores came over to see how they were getting on. 'How do you draw this symbol?' asked Marissa.

'This one is three-dimensional,' Dolores said. 'It's different from the others, you can't draw it as you would if you were writing it down. Here, let me show you.' She drew the symbol, explaining how the different parts fit together. Then she let Marissa activate it. 'Good. You're a natural. Come and speak to me after we finish today. I want to see how you've been since we last met.'

'Okay,' said Marissa. 'Thank you.'

After Dolores left, Marissa shut down Jane's session and closed the healing space. She left Jane to absorb the healing and went to the front of the room, poured two glasses of water, one for herself and one for Jane, then brought them back to the plinth. Jane seemed to be sleeping so she put the glasses down and placed her hands firmly on Jane's body – knees, shoulders, arms and hands. She then squeezed Jane's feet, went back to her head and said, 'We're finished now. Would you like some water?'

Jane stirred as if waking from a deep sleep. 'Ooh, yes please. Thank you. That was marvellous.'

'Here, let me help you sit up.'

Marissa offered her arm, and Jane held onto it and pulled herself up. Marissa offered her the water and she drank. She slid her feet onto the floor and stood there for a moment, getting her bearings.

'Thanks that was just lovely. My heart feels different,' she said. 'I didn't realise it had been so heavy. But I have been depressed. I lost my job just before Christmas, and my father is very sick. I've been stressed about money. I guess that's why I haven't been ready to give up smoking, even though I've tried. I could do with saving the money, but I don't know if I can do it. But I do feel so much better now. Hey, it's your turn now. I need to go wash my face or something first – can you wait for me?'

'Yes, take your time, no rush.'

Marissa got up on the plinth, shoes off, and lay down. She heard Matt and Colin laughing. They were swapping places too. Most people were chatting as they prepared to swap around.

Jane came in, looking refreshed. 'Ready?' she asked.

'As I'll ever be.'

'Blanket?'

'Over my legs please. Thanks.'

Jane covered Marissa's legs, then placed her hands on Marissa's knees while Marissa settled herself on the plinth. The firmness of Jane's confident touch helped her feel more at ease. She stretched her legs out and noticed how much tension she had in her shoulders and neck.

'I'll start now,' said Jane.

Marissa closed her eyes. She felt warm waves lapping over her and decided to use this opportunity to release some of that tension in her body that she didn't know she had. She drifted off.

She was in a dark corridor. It seemed familiar. Light from torches flickered and danced on the walls. Ah yes, hieroglyphics. I'm back in the pyramid.

She found herself in a small chamber lit by several oil lamps which were on the floor in various positions. Their light glimmered onto crystals and was magnified in rainbow colours, giving everything a magical quality.

'Come sit by me.' The voice was loving, warm, gentle, yet also commanding and confident. Marissa turned towards it and saw the most beautiful woman she had ever laid eyes on.

'Isis?'

The woman nodded.

'My lady goddess, I am honoured by your presence'

'It is I who am honoured by yours. I know that things have been difficult for you, a little topsy-turvy perhaps?' Isis smiled as she spoke and her loving warmth radiated outwards. Marissa knelt down by her feet, then sank onto her bottom and crossed her legs. The movement felt very natural to her.

'My darling girl,' Isis said, 'I know you feel at a crossroads, but you are not. In actuality, the path turns this way and that, it is never a straight road. At each juncture you must make choices, decisions... You need to go on this journey of self-discovery. You are stronger than you think, but you keep forgetting this. That is the way.'

Marissa couldn't say anything. She just listened, absorbing everything – Isis' presence, the loving energies. She wanted to cry with relief. It was as if she was coming home.

Isis' voice had changed tone as she continued to speak to her. 'Tori, my love, you will awaken in time. Give the girl some space to catch up with you. She is on her way. Trust it. Trust her. Her body is going through the changes, her mind is playing tricks on her, as all human minds do. There will be times when you are out of synchrony during this transformation. It is natural, be patient.'

Marissa felt as if some part of her was listening avidly to every word Isis was saying, yet she also felt that what Isis was saying wasn't for her at all. She couldn't think too deeply about it as the waves of love became stronger, crashing into her, washing away the anxiety and fear, the latent sadness and despair, the lack of purpose. She knew who she was. She knew what she had to do. She had a purpose. She was a healer. Not a healer in the making, a healer right here, right now.

'Yes, that's it,' said Isis. 'You are a healer, you are transforming, coming into your true power. It is bound to be a bumpy road. Call on me.

You always forget this! You keep calling on these little angels, but I am much bigger and more powerful than any angel. Call on me if you feel the need. We are together, you and I. Marissa smiled. She felt incredibly sleepy. The images drifted and her body dissolved away as if it was no longer there...

'We're finished now. Are you okay?' said a very concerned Jane. 'You don't look so good. Shall I get you some water?'

Marissa felt very groggy and for a moment didn't know where she was. She opened her eyes, felt the plinth beneath her and rubbed her face. Something was different, softer yet more consolidated. She sat up, feet dangling, not wanting to stand just yet.

'Yes, please. I'd like some water.'

Jane looked at the two glasses from earlier. 'I'll get some fresh. Give me a moment.'

She went off with the glasses. Marissa slid down off the plinth and walked around it to look out of the bay window. Tulips and daffodils were coming up in the hotel gardens. Spring was in the air. She knew her purpose. She had a direction. And she had felt the Reiki from Jane. She wasn't broken.

'This workshop is moving forward really quickly,' said Matt.

It was lunchtime and they were back in the pub. Jane, Colin and Bettina had joined them this time and the table felt very convivial. Marissa was feeling much better. Whatever funk she had woken up with seemed to have shifted after meeting with Isis. When she saw the menu she realised how hungry she was. The soup of the day was pumpkin, but Marissa wanted something more substantial, so she went for the beef stew. Matt caved and ordered the pint he'd wanted so badly the day before. Jane and Colin started teasing him, asking which was worse, smoking plus Reiki or alcohol plus Reiki. Bettina talked about herself and nobody seemed to mind. It was a pleasant lunch. Matt and Colin exchanged phone numbers and soon they were back once more, sitting in circle for the afternoon session. All the plinths had been removed and the room seemed much emptier than it had done earlier that morning.

'I hope we don't do anything too complicated,' whispered Matt. 'I think my brain is full now.'

'Are you sure it's your brain? Or is it your stomach?' Marissa giggled.

Matt gave her a dig with his elbow.

Dolores began, 'As we learned yesterday, Level 2 Reiki enables us to open a portal beyond space and time. We've already spoken about the portal through space, and we've all sent Reiki to someone who hasn't been present in the same space – that's the distance healing. In some respects we don't actually send the Reiki anywhere – remember, we don't control the energy, we use the power of our intention to will it someplace – but ultimately the energy does the thinking for us. The clearer we are, the less attachment we have to the outcome, the more open we are, the purer the energy. This comes with time and practice. Level 3, the next level, is entitled "Reiki Master" level, but we are never the master of Reiki. Reiki is the master of us.'

She got up and walked around the room as she continued, 'Through our entanglement with the other person, the person receiving the healing, the Reiki seems to travel, but we are already connected, so it's possible that it doesn't actually travel anywhere. It's quite magical, isn't it?

'Now, when we use the symbol to open space and time, we also open time. We haven't looked at this yet. But what this means is you can send Reiki back in time or forward in time.'

This had quite an effect on the group. The possibility of sending Reiki back in time was astonishing.

'Have you ever experienced something that was really terrible, yet while experiencing it, you didn't feel as awful as you thought you would have done?' Dolores looked at the group expectantly. A woman held up her hand. 'Yes?'

'Now that you mention it, yes. My father died two years ago. I thought I would be devastated, but I was able to hold it together. I had to organise the funeral, look after the arrangements and support my mother at the same time. I remember distinctly looking at myself in the mirror and not knowing how I was able to keep myself together.'

'I'm sorry for your loss,' said Dolores. 'It is very possible that you will send Reiki to yourself back then, today, this afternoon, to help yourself through that time. Our minds have difficulty comprehending the implications of time travel. Take a moment, all of you, and think back to a time when you really needed some extra support, and received it. Perhaps you were the one supporting yourself.'

Marissa was straight back to the day that James left. She remembered how devastated she was, but with hindsight, and self-knowledge, she realised that yes, it was possible that she hadn't felt the pain as deeply as she could have done. *Or else I'm making this up.*

Dolores continued. 'You can send Reiki to yourself by opening time and space with the symbol, and connecting to yourself at that time and space in your mind. Use a surrogate to be you and send the healing to yourself. Then disconnect from yourself, and close time and space.'

She sat down and crossed her legs. She pointed to her top knee.

'You can use your own leg as a surrogate too, I find this idea very useful as I always have my leg with me! Map the body you're working on, onto your own leg. You can use your knee as the head, and imagine a small body, like the one in your workbook, all the way down your leg, towards your hip. It's just another way to do it. If you are mapping a body onto your own body, then it's very important to disconnect. Even if you're mapping yourself onto yourself!'

Someone put their hand up, Dolores looked up and nodded.

'It's confusing, but exciting too. Can I ask you - does this mean that you can send Reiki through time, back to yourself, through yourself, as a surrogate for yourself?'

Everyone laughed.

'Yes, actually, it does,' said Dolores, smiling. 'And forward too, into the future. I know – isn't it amazing? I bet you want to try that now!'

'Oh, yes please!' said practically everyone at the same time.

At the tea break Marissa was still getting her head around the idea that she had sent Reiki to herself on the day when she felt she had needed it most.

'Well, maybe you have to do it a few times?' suggested Matt, shrugging his shoulders.

'When did you send it to yourself?' Marissa asked, hoping it wasn't too personal a question.

'I sent it to myself when I was six years old. Our dog had run away. I loved that dog and I was heartbroken. That's the thing, though – I was totally and completely heartbroken. So I sent it to myself, but I wonder if I received it. I was inconsolable at the time, it was the worst thing that had happened in my life so far. Wasn't the worst thing since, but I guess it's a good place to start.'

Marissa looked at him with compassion. *There's so many things about him that I don't know.* 'Maybe because you sent it to yourself today, back then you were able to recover from it quicker?'

'Maybe,' said Matt, with sadness flickering behind his eyes.

'Hey,' said Marissa, 'I guess we'll never really know, but it's a nice idea, isn't it?'

'Yeah, I guess it is.'

'It kind of puts the power back into our own hands, when we thought we were powerless.'

'I suppose,' agreed Matt.

'I think this would be very useful in psychotherapy. Clients could feel they could redeem something of themselves, for themselves, in a traumatic time. I'll need to sit with this and figure it out.'

'You can't mix Reiki with psychotherapy, though,' said Matt as they went back to the circle for the final session.

'Maybe not. But maybe...' said Marissa, still thinking about it.

'It has been quite the weekend, hasn't it?' said Dolores. She was sitting in the circle with the group once more. 'I always love teaching Level 2. Now we have come to our last session together. I want to do something in service to others, to use the power of amplified group intention for the greater good. Is that okay with everyone?'

Everyone nodded.

'Great, thank you. You might have heard the saying "The power of three"? Well, when there are three or more people doing healing work with the same intention at the same time, the power of that healing is amplified. I would like to combine the power of our group intention with the power of Reiki symbols, and your new Level 2 attunements, to send healing to wherever in the world it is most needed. So we can begin by doing a group meditation to clear the debris of emotional energy that I can feel in the room from the work we did before the break, and then send some healing to the world.'

So that's what that was. I was feeling that too.

'Let's start by clearing the room. Then we will create one large Reiki peace symbol in the centre of the circle. So open the workbook to that page so you have it ready for yourself. I want you to visualise this symbol filling the whole room, so we will pull our chairs back to enlarge the circle to make space for it. I will talk you through the room clearing, but let's adjust the circle now.'

Everyone pulled their chairs back so the circle became very spread out, and there was a scrabbling as people got their workbooks out and found the right page.

'We will begin.'

Dolores closed her eyes and seemed to clear her mind, then opened her eyes and looked at the group.

'Connect to the Reiki light everyone, please. Draw it down into your body, as I have shown you. Through your head, down into your heart, up and over your shoulders, down your arms and out through your hands. Down from your heart, down your spine, into your hips and legs, down through your feet and into the earth. This is the Level 2 configuration. Now, you can expand your light, shine it brighter, outwards, as if you're turning the volume up on the stereo or upping the dimmer switch from a low light to a bright one. Good. Now fill the room with light. Don't forget to breathe!'

The group was highly focused on the work. Marissa felt the energies flowing through her; she felt an expansion within her chest, she felt herself opening. She had an image in her mind of a flower that just kept opening, and opening, and opening, its petals blossoming and shifting and making room for more petals, which opened, and bloomed, and made way for even more petals. It was a beautiful sensation. She felt lightheaded.

'Don't forget to flow the energy into the earth, through your feet, so that you don't fall over. Reiki 2 energies are strong – you'll need some time to get used to them.'

Ah, okay. Yes, right. Marissa imagined her feet going into the earth and the energies from the Reiki flowing down into the ground, and something eased, the light-headedness shifted and she felt more balanced. *That's better.*

'Fill the room with light, fill the building with light, the street with light, the city with light.'

Marissa opened her eyes and looked at everyone. They were all connecting and focusing as if this was the most important thing they had ever done. *It's nice to be part of a group like this.*

'Now let go and let's breathe like this for a few moments. We will take seven breaths, seven soft, gentle, deep breaths. They don't need to be filled with vigour, just filled with light.'

Marissa found Dolores's instructions came just when she needed them. She softened her breath and it was easier to breathe lightly, yet deeply. *Breathe in the light, breathe out the light. That felt good. Breathe in the light, breathe out the light. Yes, I can do this. I could do this as a meditation. I think I will. It would be great for settling myself when I get anxious.*

'Three more breaths. Now two. Now one more. Good work. Let go of the breath, stay with the light and open your eyes. We are going to draw and activate the symbol now.'

Everyone opened their eyes. Some of them seemed afraid to move, as if they'd disconnect from the Reiki if they shifted in their chair. A couple of people looked very rigid, as if focusing and concentrating made them tense.

'You're all doing great,' Dolores reassured them. 'Relax – the energies are doing the work, not you. You don't have to do anything. You just have to be. Be the light. Try saying, "I am the light" in your mind. It will help dissolve the tension. Reiki isn't doing. It's being.'

I am the light. Hmm. Maybe. I am the light. I like the breathing one better. But I'll maybe try this one too sometime.

Marissa looked at Matt. Surprisingly, he wasn't sleeping. He seemed very peaceful, though. He smiled at her. She smiled back and felt a wave of love flow through her and into him. He seemed to feel it too – his eyes widened, his smile widened also, and then Marissa felt a wave of love come back to her. It was sublime. *This is so beautiful.*

'Now draw the Reiki symbol for peace, as best as you can. You can make a small one in your lap, then amplify it and send it into the centre of the circle, you can draw a large one in the centre of the circle, or you can imagine small peace symbols flowing out from your hands, and into the large symbol that the group is making. It doesn't matter, it's totally up to you, there is no wrong or right way to do this.'

This is fun! Marissa thought about all three approaches, and decided she liked the idea of making a smaller symbol in her lap the best. She drew it in the air with her finger, activated it, then put more Reiki into it until it seemed to grow and get stronger in her mind, then she pushed it, like launching a row boat on a river, and imagined it floating out towards the centre of the circle.

'Great work!' said Dolores. 'Now stop, and let the symbol solidify. You can put in your intention if you wish, remembering that the energy will go where it's most needed, but it's always good to put in a request. Because this is Reiki 2, we transcend space and time, and you can send your intentions to the past as well as to what is going on now. I like to send healing to all animals who are suffering abuse by human hands, in the present moment. You can choose any cause that you feel drawn to. Let's sit in silence for a moment or two as we gather our intentions and continue to empower the symbol.'

The room felt busy, full of energies moving, yet nobody said a word and nobody was moving about. Marissa felt invigorated. *I'll send it to my family, to myself when I was feeling displaced as a teenager, to the animals that are in pain, to Mum and Dad when they were in difficulties with money, to all the children who are sick... Oh, the possibilities are endless...*

'Now stop sending to the centre. Place your hands on yourselves now, and give yourselves some healing with the intention of bringing your body into balance from the work we did this weekend. In a moment or two I am going to count to three, and on the count of three I will clap my hands very loudly, and the symbol will disappear and the energies within it will go to where they are most needed, following all of our group's intentions.'

Marissa put her hands in her favourite positions, one on her heart and one on her stomach. Matt did the same. She noticed Bettina putting both hands on her lower back. Jane put one hand on her head and one on her heart. *Reiki is fantastic, everyone can do something different and it's still correct. I love this!*

She breathed and felt herself coming down from a high. She felt herself disconnecting from the group energies and coming back to herself again. She knew this, as she felt more grounded and centred again. She visualised a bubble around herself – she didn't want to be pulled back into Bettina's, or anyone else's energy field. She pressed her feet into the carpet and felt the chair beneath her. Then Dolores clapped so loudly it made her jump. It made everybody jump!

Everyone turned to Dolores, who was smiling. 'It is done. And so it is! And now we are finished. Well done, everyone. We covered a lot, possibly more than you are able to process right away. Does anyone have any questions for me? Take a moment, then pull your chairs back in closer so we can have a chat.'

There was some shuffling around as everyone came together again. Bettina put up her hand.

'How does the symbol go to where it is most needed? I mean, how do you send it?'

Dolores smiled. 'I don't have all the answers, as I said earlier, Reiki is the master of us, I am not the master of it. However, with experience and time, and lots of practice, you get to know what is possible. Which is most things! We are limited in this physical reality with our physical bodies, but energy is unlimited.'

'I have a question about clients,' said one of the women. Dolores nodded for her to go ahead. 'If I send distance healing to a client and they get emotional, or upset, I won't know about it because, well, I'm not in the room with them. I won't be able to help them. What do I do?'

'Good question. Remember what Reiki is. It's healing energy. When you bring high-vibrational healing energy into someone's energy field, it soothes them, yes, but it releases low, stuck energies too. Remember in Reiki 1, for physical healing, you can get pains and aches, you can feel ill before you feel well as you release, well, toxins that your body has been holding on to, possibly for years. Reiki Level 2 is accessing the emotional body. So, if someone gets emotional or upset, it's how they are releasing their stuck emotions. It's better they release tham then hold on to them – held emotion can make you sicker than the unpleasant experience of feeling them. If someone gets upset, see it as a sign that they are healing. I prefer to see people in my healing room, but sometimes it's not possible and distance healing is necessary. Either way, I tell people that this could be a side-effect of the healing before we do it. It's very rare that someone becomes so upset that they're not able to function. The pain will pass, and they will feel better for the release. As long as they know it may happen, then they'll be prepared for it if it does.'

Marissa put up her hand. 'I have clients for psychotherapy. They avoid their feelings – they can talk themselves out of feeling them sometimes. I'm wondering if it would be useful to offer them distance healing to help them release their feelings? Or just give them distance Reiki while they are in the room with me, without them knowing? It could accelerate their process. I guess I'm just thinking out loud. I don't know how it would work.'

Dolores thought about it. 'Combining Reiki with psychotherapy is a wonderful idea, Marissa, but I would say from the outset that your clients would need to give their permission for it. Reiki is separate from psychotherapy. So you could say to them, "I also offer Reiki. If you want some energetic help with the emotions that are coming up in this session, I could give you distance healing using Reiki." Or perhaps you could even have a plinth handy and you could offer hands-on Reiki sessions as a second service.'

'I'm wondering then, because in psychotherapy I need to do a number of sessions with clients before I'm qualified, and have supervision sessions where I talk to a supervisor about what I have been doing, is there anything like that for Reiki?'

Dolores thought about this for a while before answering, 'It sounds like you are very supported there, Marissa, but no, there is no supervision requirement for Reiki. However it would be a good idea, particularly for people starting out, so that they feel supported. Especially as lots of weird and wonderful things can happen in a Reiki session, it's always good to check in with someone for support, as the therapist. I do often offer mentoring for my students, so if this is a path you want to go down, I will be here for you for additional support if needed.'

'Thank you.'

Someone else put their hand up. 'When are you teaching Reiki Master Level 3? And what's the difference between Level 2 and Level 3?'

Dolores laughed. 'Don't be in such a rush! You'll need a while to integrate the work of this weekend. Great question, though. I know that some people offer the levels one or two weeks apart, but that's madness. Level 1 is physical healing – it's Reiki as torchlight. Level 2 is emotional healing, and the torch turns into a laser. Level 3 – well, the healing stays like a laser, but it is amplified and penetrates the spiritual layers. Level 3 is for spiritual healing, and really you have your whole life to do this, and you'll never be the master of the energies, so don't be in a rush for a title. If you like collecting badges, you'll want to collect all the titles, I know. I prefer to be with the energy of what is real and in front of me. I hope you do, too. If you're a badge collector, you can get Reiki Level 4, 5, 6 and 7 also. But all you need is within you, and if you don't do your own inner work, it won't matter how many Reiki levels you have, you won't be a powerful channel for light because you are carrying so much heavy spiritual energy.'

'Can we charge people for Reiki now?' asked someone else.

'Yes, you can charge for Reiki. I would prefer it if you took the Practitioner Level first and took some time to acclimatise to your own energies, but you can now ask for an appropriate fee.'

'How much should I charge?'

Dolores was thoughtful. 'This is a very difficult question to answer, and everyone will feel different about it. I'm not at liberty to set a fee for you – you'll have to explore this one for yourselves.'

Nobody else had any questions, and it was getting late. Dolores looked as though she was ready to wrap it up.

'Take your time with the workbook, read it thoroughly and try to do some work with all the symbols. Some of them you will love and connect to right away, some you won't love so much now, but in the future perhaps you will. You can contact me if you need any help with anything, but most of the answers to your questions will be in your workbook – remember to check your Level 1 workbook also. Don't forget to practise using the symbols, and do your self-Reiki every day. It will help you integrate what we have done here. I'll be in touch with dates for a meet-up. Thank you all for coming, and have a wonderful evening.'

It was late. Marissa had to get back to her flat, feed Tobermory and do her laundry. Matt had an early start at the garage, but they didn't want to say goodbye. The waves of love had brought them closer together, and they weren't ready to go their separate ways. They stood together at the DART station, waiting for the train.

'I do have to go, but I can send you Reiki tonight, later on, when you're in bed,' said Marissa.

'And I'll see you on Wednesday, won't I?'

'Don't you have class?' asked Marissa

'Not this week.'

'Wednesday then,' she said with a smile.

The train came and they sat close together holding hands for the few stops between Greystones and Dun Laoghaire. Marissa pressed herself into Matt and laid her head on his shoulder, and she felt that feeling of disappointment again just before the train pulled into his station.

He turned to her, kissed her gently on the lips and whispered, 'Text you later,' then stood up and went out through the open doors of the carriage. It felt like a part of her went out the doors with him. He turned and blew her a kiss as the doors closed, and the train left the station. She waved at him from the window, but he had already gone.

CHAPTER FIFTEEN

Marissa spent the evening doing laundry and thinking about the Reiki workshop. *I sent Reiki back to myself that day when James left the note. I wonder, though, was it enough? Should I send more?* She settled down with a cuppa and the TV, but there was nothing on that kept her attention. She kept changing channels until she switched it off. She picked up her phone and composed a text to Matt:

I had a great weekend, thanks so much for asking me. Reiki 2 was amazing. And so are you xx

She sat wondering if she should send it, or delete the last bit first, when a text came in from Matt.

I had a lovely weekend, I'm glad u came. Do u still want 2 send me Reiki? We could send some 2 each other!

Marissa deleted what she had written and sent back: Oh yes! Gr8 idea. When do u want me 2 send it?

20 mins? I'll send 2 u @ same time? Or should we take turns?

Maybe take turns.... so we can compare notes!

Good idea. I'll text u soon x

Gr8, talk soon so.

She had forgotten about the possibility of sending Reiki to each other. It was a fun idea. The phone buzzed again. *That was quick!* But it wasn't Matt, it was Yvonne, asking her to phone when she could. She wasn't doing anything else, so she pressed the 'call' button.

'Yvonne! Hi, Marissa here. What's up?'

'Hi, Marissa! Sorry to text on a Sunday, but I was able to organise you taking my place in St Mary's Women's Refuge. They want to know if you can come in tomorrow so they can meet you and have a chat. They'll need ID, like a passport or driving licence. They might need a Garda Clearance Cert – do you have one already?'

'Wow, that's amazing! The Priory have a Clearance Cert for me – I wonder if there's a way that they can get a copy of that. I'll phone the office tomorrow and find out. That's brilliant, thanks so much. I'm working tomorrow, though, so I won't be able to do it during the day... Unless I take some time off.'

'Well, I'll text you the number. Bronagh in the main office, she's expecting your call. If you call in the morning, you can figure it out between you. They open at 8. I was doing Wednesday evenings. I can come in for the next two Wednesdays if they can't sort it out quickly, but I really hope you can start soon, as Mum really needs me.'

'That's brill. Thanks, Yvonne, I'll call Bronagh tomorrow first thing. See you Tuesday evening? Is your mum getting better? You're still coming to class, aren't you?'

'Ah, yeah, she's holding on. She's hopeful that the treatment will work. And we're so close. I'll stay to finish the modules and the assignments – no point giving up class at this stage. I'll catch up with client hours once Mum is on the mend. Thanks, Marissa, really I didn't want to leave St Marys in the lurch. We can catch up more in class on Tuesday.'

'Thanks again for thinking of me.'

Marissa hung up the phone and Yvonne texted her almost immediately with Bronagh's name and number.

Exciting. I'll have to speak to Noreen about going part time. No, maybe not quite yet. Maybe I need to talk to Dad first, or Uncle Lou... The next chapter of my life begins!

Marissa decided to get into bed to do the Reiki for Matt. She had a hot shower, put on fresh PJs and found an old teddy that Eli had given her. It wasn't actually a bear; it looked more like a baby turtle, a cartoon baby turtle with exaggerated, oversized eyes. She studied it. It had a head, arms and legs, and a body, but it didn't look anything like Matt. *Although it's big eyes are cute... and he is cute.. Ahem!* She would use it for now, but perhaps she needed to buy a new one, just for surrogate work. *Well, why not? I like teddy bears. Maybe I'll get Matt to buy me one!*

She snuggled up under the duvet but kept her eye on the phone, waiting for Matt to text. After a while she got out of bed and found her Reiki 2 workbook, for the symbols, then got back into bed. She texted him.

Ready?

Still nothing. She opened to the page with the Opening Space and Time symbol. She studied it and drew it on the page with her finger to become familiar with the shapes and lines. Then she closed her eyes and tried to draw it in her mind.

This is so complicated, I'll never get this right. And it's been much longer than 20 minutes now. He's so infuriating!!

She focused back on the symbol and drew it again. She said the symbol's name out loud three times, and was just about to activate it when her phone buzzed.

Ready now! who goes first me or u?

I can work on u, I've the book open to the symbol and a turtle beside me.

Turtle?

Yeah, first teddy I could find.

Ah ok. Had no clue what u meant. And I forgot the symbol, cool. Can u text when ur done?

Yes. I'll send for about 15 minutes? Then ur turn.

Perfect.

Marissa looked at the time. It was 9.30pm. She arranged her pillows so she was sitting up in the bed, then got the turtle and opened a healing space. Drawing the symbol in the air, she activated it and felt a judder down her arms. *That must mean it's working!* She visualised Matt's body, shrank it in her mind and superimposed it on the turtle, which she had lying belly up on the covers in front of her. She felt the Reiki flowing through her; it was definitely stronger than she was used to. *I will have to grow into it, I think.* She placed her hands on the turtle's head and imagined she was sending the Reiki directly into Matt's head, then worked her way down the turtle, taking her time and allowing the Reiki to flow. It seemed to dissolve completely into the turtle, and she enjoyed the connection to him. It felt intimate.

When she had worked her way down the body once, Marissa placed one hand on the turtle's head and the other on the carapace and imagined she was sending Reiki to Matt's head and the base of his spine at the same time. *Top and bottom of the spine – this is great!*

Then she imagined sending the Reiki to Matt's feet and head at the same time. *Oh, I can't do that with hands-on!* She placed both hands over the turtle so they covered it completely and focused on her breath, sending Reiki into his whole body, feeling the Reiki pouring out from her hands and going, well, it didn't seem to be going into the turtle, so it must be going to Matt. She was enjoying imagining him receiving it. She started to feel waves of warmth issuing from her heart, just as she had earlier that day.

She remembered Matt's smile, how the light had played on his face when they had been in the Japanese Gardens, how he had kissed her goodbye on the DART only a few hours before. She felt her body soften and the warm waves of energy flowing down her arms, out of her hands and into the turtle. *Well, going into Matt, not the turtle.*

She looked at the time. *Three more minutes to go.* She felt tension in her face dissolving, she felt her shoulders relaxing, she felt warm and happy. And she felt very connected to Matt. It was lovely.

She looked at the time again. *Time to finish.* She gently pulled her hands away from the turtle, then, looking at the workbook, she drew the 'Open Time and Space' symbol once more to close it down, and picked up the turtle and kissed it gently. Then she disconnected and closed down the session.

She was thirsty, so she got up and got a drink, then got back into bed. Then she texted Matt.

All finished now, I hope u liked it. My turn now? Tell me when you're starting.

She pressed 'send' and waited for his reply. She tucked the turtle up in the bed with her. An hour later, with a heavy heart, she realised that he wasn't going to reply. *Maybe he's fallen asleep? He does have a tendency to fall asleep during Reiki. I'll have to go first next time.*

+++

There was a text from Matt on her phone when her alarm woke her. The time stamp said 3:37am. She felt happier once she saw his name come up on her screen.

OMG Marissa, I fell asleep while u reikied me. I'm sorry
I missed ur turn! It was so powerful, it knocked me out.
I'll call u tomorrow, I mean, today, by the time u get this.
Sorry again! xxMatt

She smiled and turned over in the bed, not quite ready to get up just yet. *I wonder, was it the Reiki, or did he feel the waves of love I sent him too? Oh God, I sent him love. I actually sent him love – people talk about that all the time, sending love, but I actually did it. And it put him to sleep!* She giggled. Then she remembered she was to phone St Mary's Woman's Refuge. It was too early now, though, so she got up and took her time getting ready for work. She ironed her black suit pants and wore a cream blouse and matching jacket.

She called the refuge on her mobile as soon as she got off the bus, just before going to her office.

'St Mary's Women's Refuge, Bronagh speaking.'

'Hi, Bronagh, this is Marissa. Yvonne gave me your name and number. I am hoping to take over her client sessions?'

'Ah yes, hello Marissa, she mentioned you. Can you come in today and meet the supervisor? I can show you around too if you can get here for 3pm?'

'I'm at work today, but I'll see if I can get off early. Can I call you back?'

'Yes, no problem, we are here till 4.30pm in the office. We will need you to bring some identification with you, so we can fill the forms out today for the Garda clearance certificate.'

Shit, I don't have my passport with me – I'll have to go home again to get it.

'Okay, great. I'll just organise things at my end and I'll give you a call later to confirm.'

Shit shit, shit. The refuge is miles away from my house, and further miles away from work... Hang on, I'll take a half-day, and a taxi to get there. Yes! That's what I'll do.

Marissa's taxi pulled up outside of St Mary's at 3:30pm. *Just as well I got a taxi, I would never have found this place myself!* The refuge was at the back of a community medical centre in West Dublin. It seemed relatively new, was surrounded by high fences and had a very different energy from the Priory in Cabra. There were children playing in the playground next door, women standing with babies in pushchairs, chatting and smoking, older women, younger women ... not a man in sight. *Of course, this is a woman's refuge, so men wouldn't be coming here.*

Marissa walked to the front door feeling very conspicuous in her work clothes. She was overdressed and felt very embarrassed. There were two security cameras watching the door and two peepholes at eye level. She rang the bell and waited self-consciously for someone to answer.

'Hello?' a voice with a very strong accent rang out through the speaker.

'Hi, it's Marissa. I have an appointment with Bronagh.'

The door buzzed and Marissa pushed it open. It was much heavier than she expected and she needed to use the full force of her weight against it. She managed to open it wide enough to be able to sidle inside, and as soon as she let go of it, it slammed closed loudly behind her.

A woman in the hallway looked Marissa up and down. She was middle-aged, with very short, practically shaved bleached blonde hair. She had a black tattoo on one of her hands which crept up inside the sleeve of a pink hoodie with 'Superstars of New York' emblazoned across the chest. Her grey tracksuit pants were about two sizes too small for her and her large stomach flopped over the waistband. She had a cigarette in between her index and second finger and a lighter in her other hand.

'Here to see Bronagh?' she asked.

'Yes, thanks,' said Marissa.

The woman pointed down the corridor. 'First door on the left.'

'Thank you.'

As Marissa moved off in the direction of the office, the woman flicked her cigarette lighter and lit her cigarette, then she let herself out of the front door to have her smoke. The door banged shut again.

Marissa shuddered. *I really feel out of place here... I hope I'll be able to work with these women.*

She found a door with a sign saying 'Office' and knocked hesitantly.

'Come in,' a smooth voice said.

Marissa pushed the door open and saw a slim woman with mid-length auburn hair dressed in a plum-coloured skirt with a matching jacket and white blouse standing behind a desk which was chock full of papers, files and books.

'Hi, I'm Marissa. Are you Bronagh?'

'No, I'm Audrey, Audrey Clarke, director of counselling. Nice to meet you.'

Audrey held her hand out to Marissa. Marissa, feeling more at ease in her work clothes, took it and they shook strong hands.

'Glad you could make it,' Audrey continued. 'I'm here to register you in and get your paperwork, and I will also be your supervisor. We tend to multi-task here – they don't have as many resources as they need, I'm afraid, so we all have to pitch in and do as much as we can.'

Marissa didn't see anywhere to sit, so she stayed standing up.

'Did you bring your passport?' asked Audrey.

'Yes, I did.' Marissa reached into her handbag, pulled her passport out and handed it to Audrey. 'Can you get a copy of my Garda Clearance from Cabra?'

"Thanks. No, it doesn't work that way I'm afraid. Lots of administration is always required. Hang on, and I'll take a photocopy of it. I'll be back in a moment.' Audrey squeezed past the desk and past Marissa and out of the door.

Audrey squeezed past the desk and past Marissa and out of the door.

Left alone, Marissa found her curiosity getting the better of her and she looked around the office. She didn't want to look at the papers on the desk, but the walls were far more interesting anyway. There were several photographs of women, some were group photos in black in white, some were in colour. Certificates of all different kinds, shapes and sizes with different names on them were framed on the wall behind the desk. There was a large window with a view of the courtyard between the refuge and the medical centre. Overall, the room, besides seeming disorganised, was much brighter than any room she had been in at the Priory.

She was still looking at the group photographs when Audrey came back.

'Here you go,' she said, handing the passport to Marissa and looking at the photo that she was currently engrossed in. 'These are graduates of our upskill courses. Some of the women that come here dropped out of school, so we offer them training if they want to get work.'

'That's fantastic,' said Marissa, really impressed.

'I am very proud of this place,' said Audrey. 'We have had women who were totally illiterate learning how to read, then taking our secretarial course, and then getting work. It's amazing what someone can do when they're really motivated. Come, let's go somewhere we can both sit down and chat. I'll show you one of the therapy rooms.'

She led Marissa out of the office, up two flights of stairs and into a small room with two chairs and a coffee table, which again, was much brighter than the one in Cabra. There was a small window, the armchairs were relatively new and the painting on the wall was much more hopeful – a field of wild flowers. Audrey gestured to Marissa to choose a chair, and she sat in the other one.

'So Marissa, you're in Yvonne's college. I'm already familiar with the syllabus. She said you'd been working in another placement?'

'Yes, in Cabra, on Thursday evenings. I'll be keeping that on. This will be in addition, as I need to make up the hours.'

Audrey nodded. 'I can offer you Wednesday evenings here, Yvonne's slot – would that work?'

'Yes, that would be great, thank you. What time?'

'It's 6 o'clock, three sessions, finishing at nine. We don't like to keep the centre open past nine – we have a lock-up for the residents so they feel safe knowing that nobody can come in at night-time. It's an actual refuge, so we have women here who have left their boyfriends or husbands. We have childcare facilities that they can leave their babies in before they come to classes, or to counselling. It's rare that the men show up at night, but we have had a few incidents recently, hence the double security camera on the door. I assume you noticed it?'

Marissa nodded her head.

'Nothing for you to worry about,' Audrey smiled. 'We have a library you can use if you like. I'll show it to you. And the more severe cases will be seen by qualified professional therapists, so you don't have to worry about feeling over your head.' Then she added with a grin, 'But I do recommend you wear something a little more casual when you come here next time.' She smiled again.

Marissa looked down and blushed. 'I came straight from the office. I admit I was feeling out of place until I saw you.'

Audrey looked at her own clothes and smiled again. 'No worries. I had a meeting today with the fundraising committee, otherwise I'd be in jeans and a sweatshirt. It makes the women feel more comfortable. Now, there's a café where you can get tea in between sessions, not that there is much time in between sessions. We allow clients to have tea in the sessions too, but not food.'

'Oh, that's unusual!' said Marissa.

'Again, it helps them feel more at their ease,' Audrey explained. 'Babies too, can be a great a distraction, so if they forget, and bring their baby with them, you'll need to remind them to leave them in the creche.'

Marissa nodded, trying to write this into her memory bank.

Audrey continued, 'As I've mentioned, I'll be seeing you for supervision. Unfortunately it won't be after every ten sessions, as I am much too busy, and it could possibly be on a weekend, but we'll make sure we get in the hours that you need to balance your client hours for your qualification. Do you have any questions?'

'Not right now, I don't think,' said Marissa, knowing that she would have lots of questions once she started.

'Oh yes, one more thing,' Audrey said, 'the women who will come to see you, some of them will never have been to counselling before. Many of them will never have talked about their problems with anyone, so they might find it difficult. All they want to do really is have a chat, put words to their feelings, make sense of what happened to them. All you need to do is listen. They might not come back for a second session with you – they might decide that once is enough, although we do encourage it, they will choose this themselves. I would recommend therefore, that you don't go into any framework process with them that you might have covered in your college courses. Unless of course they ask you for it, or seem like they are able for it. We are primarily person centred, so again, please take each session as it comes, as you may have different people every time.'

'Okay, I'll see how it goes with each person on a case-by-case basis,' said Marissa, feeling a little hesitant about the whole thing. *It will be good hours, and if I hate it I don't have to stay.*

'Good. Bronagh will leave a sheet for you in the pigeonhole by reception with the names and phone numbers of your clients for the day. You can text them if they're late.'

'Great! Do I need a key for the door?'

'No, we have security here, and they will be expecting you. There will always be people here, all our counselling slots are full, you'll get to meet some of the other volunteers while you're here, no doubt.' Audrey got up and smoothed down her skirt, then offered Marissa her hand again. They shook hands.

'Come, I'll show you the library and the canteen. We need to apply for the Garda clearance on your behalf, that will take time, but once we have that then you can start.'

Marissa left the centre and walked away from it, not really sure which direction she was going in. She just didn't want to hang around. She felt good about the placement, though. The layout of the centre was a little confusing, but most places were on first visit. As she walked she passed a bus stop, and checked to see where the bus was going. *Into town, great. I'll just get this bus, then figure out how to get home from there.* She waited, and ten minutes later she was on the bus, heading into the city centre. She texted Yvonne.

> What a great setup, it looks fab, thanks so much again.
> Looks like I can start as soon as they get clearance.
> See u in class.

Yvonne texted back: Gud luck so. I'll chat with u tmorw at tea, tell u a few things u might need 2 no.

The bus visited each and every housing estate on the way into town, and it was rush hour, so it was almost an hour and a half before Marissa recognised where she was and was able to hop out. She was exhausted and just wanted to get back to her flat and rest but she was still far from home. An empty taxi approached her. *What the heck.* She flagged it down and hopped inside. The taxi flew down the bus lanes, bypassing the traffic jams and had her home in no time.

She got into her flat and the first thing she did was take off her suit and have a hot shower. When she was in her towel, she looked through her wardrobe for clothes that would be suitable for the centre. She didn't own a sweatshirt or a hoodie, but she did have some old blue jeans. *Penney's here I come!*

Matt phoned her later that evening to catch up with her.

'Do you want me to send you Reiki tonight?' he asked. 'I have a teddy bear ready and waiting...'

'Oooh, yes please! That would be great. Maybe when I'm in bed, so you can put me to sleep!'

'Maybe, indeed. Hey, by the way, I've a stag party with one of the lads from the garage on Friday night, so I won't be able to meet you.'

'Sounds fun.' Marissa tried not to sound too disappointed.

'I'm still meeting you on Wednesday, though, and maybe we could meet Sunday? It's St Patrick's Day! We could go in and see the parade, have a few beers. It'd be fun.'

Marissa hesitated before answering. 'I've a family dinner on Sunday. I know it's Patrick's Day, but it's a family tradition to be at my parents', and Eli and Carol will be there. I know you said you were happy with the way things are, and you didn't want to meet my family and all, but if you wanted to go to the parade with me, I'd have to disappear after for dinner. Or,' on a whim, she added, 'you could come with me and meet them all.' Then she flushed, feeling as if she had violated a boundary. Was it his or her own?

'I'll think about it. I did say I wanted to take it slowly...'

'Okay, I understand. Let me know if you change your mind.'

Marissa felt a cold sweat on her skin. *Well, at least he can't see the state I'm in. I wonder why I asked him... It just slipped out. Probably not a good idea, after all. Damnit.*

'I will. Promise.' *He sounds calm at least.* 'How about 10pm for Reiki tonight? Is that too late? Are you tired? I'll text before I start.'

'No, not too tired. It's perfect. Thanks, Matt, I'll look forward to it.'

CHAPTER SIXTEEN

Marissa slept well after the Reiki that Matt sent to her. Actually, she fell asleep during the Reiki. *And thankfully no dreams, I've not really been able to remember my dreams lately. That's strange. I usually have lots of really colourful ones.*

She brushed her hair and got ready for work. Looking at herself in the mirror, she imagined she had passed some sort of test, but didn't quite know what it was. She was hopeful that the Garda clearance would come through quickly.

Sarah came over to her at work, looking concerned. 'Marissa, can we talk for a minute?'

Marissa was in the middle of resolving a spreadsheet. 'Can you give me a half-hour?'

'Sure. Can we go somewhere private? I'll book the meeting room?'

'Okay. Yes, that's fine. Half an hour in the meeting room, so.'

Marissa couldn't focus on the spreadsheet any longer. *What's going on? Is she okay? Should I talk to her right now? No, as her manager, I can't just change my mind. But she's my friend – we did say, 'Friends first...'*

She sent an email: 'Are you okay? is there something wrong?'

Sarah wrote back: 'I'll tell you when we meet. Finish your spreadsheet!'

When Sarah came into the meeting room she seemed breathless, anxious.

Marissa was waiting for her. 'What's going on, Sarah? Are you okay?'

Sarah flicked her long blonde ponytail and hovered nervously.

'Come, sit down, talk to me. We can figure it out together.'

Sarah sat down.

She looks like one of my clients, about to say something deeply upsetting.

Sarah *was* upset. A tear dripped down her face and she used the back of her hand to brush it away before clearing her throat.

'This is hard for me to say.'

Marissa waited.

'And before you jump in, no, it's not about my love life. It's not about me at all, in fact. It's about you.'

Marissa felt a flash of anxiety. She tried to calm herself as she waited to hear what was coming next.

'That's why I couldn't say it at your desk, or on the email. I needed to say it to your face.'

'Erm, okay. What is it?'

'Are you leaving? Work, I mean? I overheard Noreen talking about them hiring a new manager for your role. But I thought you were up for a promotion, for training... Are you sick? What's going on?'

Relief flooded through Marissa's body and then she realised she hadn't spoken to Sarah about her new plans.

'No, I'm not planning to leave, but I did talk to Noreen about my future here, I told her that I didn't want the manager role anymore, it's not really well suited to me. Well, technically, she guessed it all herself. I've decided that therapy is where my heart is, and its time for me to invest more of my life in that direction. I've started making plans to take on more therapy clients and I think I probably need to go part time here, but I've not asked yet. I'm sorry I never told you. I should have done. I've just been so... Well, there have been a lot of things going on for me. I think I've got it back under control, though. Kind of.'

Sarah sat up straighter in her chair. 'No,' she said reproachfully, 'you never told me, and I was still worried about you from that time a few weeks ago, when you were so upset. You said you'd tell me what it was about when you felt better, but you never told me. So I put two and two together...'

'I'm sorry,' Marissa said again. 'I should have told you. I had a scare, but it wasn't related to the job, it was more of a spiritual crisis.' As she said the words, she felt that that was indeed what it had been. Or still was. 'I don't know if it's over yet, but I do feel much better.'

'Oh.' Sarah looked at her blankly. 'I've never heard of a spiritual crisis... It sounds, well, freaky.'

'It certainly wasn't pleasant. I learned a lot about myself, but I seem to have many more questions now than answers. Anyway, I'm not leaving work, and I won't be leaving you. Friends forever, remember? And do you know what?'

'No, what?'

'I don't want to be *your* manager anymore. I think it's put a tension between us, and our friendship is more important to me than the job. And actually...'

Sarah brightened. 'Actually what?'

'I think *you'd* make a better manager than I would. Honestly, I wouldn't mind working for you as your assistant. Maybe I'll suggest you for the management position! If I have any pull around here...'

Sarah started laughing, 'Pull with Noreen? Good luck with that! But wow, it's really nice of you to say that. And I like being friends with you too. I was really worried they were going to push you out...' She looked Marissa in the eye. 'Seriously, I was really worried about you. Please tell me you're okay. You know you can tell me anything.'

Marissa registered the concern in her voice, and realised she took Sarah's friendship for granted at times. 'Lookit,' Marissa said, 'I'm really sorry. I don't want to make you worry, but I guess I find it difficult to talk about things. Sometimes I just can't get the words out.'

'Ha, ha, the therapist can't talk about herself – bloody typical!' Sarah had a glint in her eye. All was forgiven.

Marissa laughed with relief. 'Yes, it's always been my issue, not being able to talk freely about my own issues. But it's not because I'm hiding anything, it's because I'm still working things out in my own way. I wish it didn't take as long as it does, though. I don't think I've worked this spiritual crisis thing all the way through yet.'

'I'd imagine a spiritual crisis does take a long time to work through,' said Sarah. 'Maybe it won't all get sorted as quickly as you want it to be. But like I said, you can tell me anything.' She stood up and brushed herself down, as if a cat had shed hair all over her, then looked at Marissa. 'Anything at all.'

'No matter how crazy it sounds?'

'No matter how crazy.'

'Even if it's about angels and demons, Reiki, shamanism and psychotherapy?'

Sarah shivered, then made a face and smiled. 'Okay, yeah. Well, I can't help you with all that stuff, but I can listen. And I can help you for sure with relationship stuff.'

Marissa raised an eyebrow. Sarah giggled.

'I promise I won't hide stuff from you anymore, and not tell you when I'm feeling better. And yeah, you're right, maybe some part of me just wanted it all to be over quickly, but it's been going on for a few months now. I can't promise that I won't flip out again. And I may not be able to tell you why, but it's more about not being able to put it into words than not wanting to tell you.'

'Okay, I believe you,' said Sarah.

'I'm glad. Thanks for being so patient with me.'

'I think maybe you need to be more patient with yourself.'

'When did you get so wise?' asked Marissa.

Sarah shrugged her shoulders.

'Hey, off the back of what I said, I'm going to write you the most excellent reference you've ever had and send it to Noreen with a recommendation that she puts you in for the management role. If you want it, that is?'

'*Ooooh*, yes please!' Sarah clasped her hands with delight. 'Thank you!'

During Advanced Psychotherapeutic Techniques that night, Mr Crowley explained the theory behind Gestalt therapy.

'Thought and feeling go together. In Gestalt, the finer details of the felt sense are vital to the therapeutic process. *Gestalt* itself means 'many parts' – you have the whole, then the parts that make up the whole. All of the parts together must be taken into consideration.'

Everyone was writing furiously in their notebooks. Mr Crowley had a way of making anything he spoke about sound incredibly interesting.

'Let's say your client was bitten by a dog when they were eight years old. That event left a lasting impression on them, to the extent that seeing a dog creates feelings of fear. But as an adult they may not be able to associate the fear with the event of the dog bite, all they remember is that they're afraid of dogs. Only through going deeper into the feelings, listening to the body, will the memory surface. Then you and your client can work through it together, to heal it.'

Marissa sat up bolt upright in her chair. *I swear to God that's the first time I've heard the word 'heal' on this course. That can't be right? Really? The second last module of the final year?* She found herself becoming hyper-aware of everything Mr Crowley was saying. She also found the state of hyper-awareness quite exhausting.

'In the two-chair technique last week we looked at working with an aspect of your client's psyche, introducing it to the empty chair for conversation. Today I want to explain to you how you can go even further with this technique, inviting in an aspect of somebody else, someone that isn't even present in the therapy room.'

Oh that's really interesting! Maybe I'll learn something tonight that will help me do this better. It really didn't work so well when I tried this with Cliona last week.

During the break, Yvonne came over to her. 'I want to talk to you about St Mary's. I'm delighted you took me up on it. What did you think of the place?'

They sat at a table together. Marissa pulled the remains of her sandwich from earlier out of her bag. Yvonne had a cup of something she had just made cradled in her hands.

'Well, I was certainly overdressed,' said Marissa, taking a bite of her sandwich.

'Ha, ha. Yes, I should have warned you about that.'

'And I arrived in a taxi...'

'Oh no! Ha, ha! Well, I'm sure they'll have forgotten about that when you go back to start working there. What else? Did you meet Bronagh? Or Audrey?'

'Audrey. She was great. And the building – what a set-up! It's fantastic. They're doing really great work there, upskilling the women, looking after the children and providing a safe space for them all. Impressive. Were there any incidents when you were there? Audrey said something about increasing the security, and I did notice the barbed wire out front, and the heavy door, and the cameras...'

Yvonne sat back in her chair and sighed. 'Yes, that was one of the things I wanted to talk to you about, as well as the dress code. But the women there are lovely, really they are. They're thick-skinned and tough on the outside, but once they relax around you, once they think they can really trust you, they really open up. Actually, they remind me of Jack Russell terriers – they've got a bark, and sometimes a bite, but they're loving and warm once you get to know them. And very loyal, too.'

Marissa had never seen this side of Yvonne before, it was refreshing to see her confident and enthusiastic. 'It sounds as though you enjoyed your time there. Are you sorry you can't stay?'

'Oh, I'll go back. I've already spoken to Audrey about it. This'll just be for the time being, until Mum's chemo is finished. They'll squeeze me in somewhere, but the Wednesday slot is yours now, for as long as you want it.'

'Oh no, I didn't know – about your mum, I mean! You just said she was sick.'

Yvonne looked down at the table. 'Yes, she has cancer. It was in remission for a few years, but it came back. She's seventy-seven now, so the chemo will hit her harder this time around – the side-effects, I mean. I want to be there while she goes through it, and they say the treatment will continue for at least six months this time.'

Marissa nodded sympathetically. She had no experience of illness like that in her family. 'If there's anything I can do to help, let me know.'

'Thanks, you're helping by taking my clients on. I really appreciate it. Mary R. has only just started to talk about what happened to her and I didn't want to leave her in the lurch. I've already told her about you, so she knows that I'm leaving. That's what I wanted to talk to you about.'

'Hello, folks, you look very serious in the corner here,' said Emmet, hovering. 'Can I join you or is it a private party?'

Yvonne gestured to an empty chair, inviting him to sit down. 'I'm just filling Marissa in on my placement. She's taking over from me, as I need to step back a little bit.' She leaned in to Marissa. 'Let Mary tell you about herself in her own time. It's unfortunate she'll have to begin the trust process again from scratch with you, but I have vouched for you, so that's more than she would have gotten from someone else.'

Marissa nodded.

Yvonne pushed her cup away and tucked a stray hair behind her ear. 'You know,' she said, turning to Emmet to include him in the conversation, 'I think I appreciate my hair more now, because Mum will be losing hers. Again. She's taking it very well, she really is. I don't think I'd be that strong if it happened to me.'

Emmet nodded. 'My dad went through it last year. It was tough going, but he's doing great now, the cancer is gone and he's even back walking every day again, though not as much as before.'

On the way back to the classroom, Yvonne added, 'Anyway, Marissa, there's really nothing big or important you need to know, other than every day in St Mary's is an experience! You'll find out yourself soon enough.'

They took their seats back in the classroom and Mr Crowley announced that they were to practise the two-chair technique again.

'Even if you don't like the rest of Gestalt, or ever go further with your studies in it, as I said last time, this technique is incredibly useful, and very adaptable for many situations.' Mr Crowley looked at his watch. 'We have enough time for at least one client/therapist session. I don't want you to rush this – Gestalt isn't about doing things quickly. Find a partner, find a spare chair and see how you get on. If you need me, you can raise your hand.'

Marissa noticed Ronan wasn't paired up, so she went over to him. 'Would you like to work with me?' They hadn't worked together since the first week of the first term, but that experience had stuck with them and there was a trust between them that had deepened over time.

He smiled and nodded. They made some space for the session and set up three chairs in a couples counselling configuration, as Mr Crowley had shown them.

'Would you like to be therapist or client?' asked Marissa.

'Therapist,' said Ronan firmly. Marissa nodded. 'Who do you want to bring into the session? An aspect of yourself, or someone else?'

Marissa thought for a moment. *I'm not really ready to have a discussion with myself right now, and there are so many people I could talk to that that could be safer. Yes, okay, it's safer, but I do need to be patient with myself, so safer could be okay. How about Noreen? It would be useful to have a trial run of the conversation I need to have with her about going part time.*

But then an image of her dad flashed up in her mind. She hesitated. *Noreen or Dad? Why Dad? I don't know why I need to talk to him. Well, seeing as he did just appear out of the blue, maybe I do need to talk to him. And it's Ronan – I don't mind sharing stuff with him.*

'I think Dad.'

'Okay, let's invite your dad into the session then.'

Ronan took the therapist's chair, Marissa sat adjacent to him, and she closed her eyes for a moment. She imagined her father coming into the space with them and sitting down in the chair beside her. He was wearing what he had worn the last time she saw him. She could see his smiling face and it felt as though he was supposed to be there.

'Hello, Marissa,' said Ronan. 'Hello, Marissa's dad.'

'Bernie,' Marissa said with a smile.

'Hello, Bernie,' corrected Ronan. 'You're invited here today to have a conversation with Marissa because she needs to say something to you, with me here as a witness. In your own time, Marissa, let Bernie know what it is you need to say.'

Marissa turned to the chair that her imaginary father was sitting in. 'Hi, Dad, thanks for coming today,' she said and giggled. *This is so weird.* And then the words flowed. 'Erm, I guess I have a bone to pick with you. I don't understand why you don't seem to like or respect Uncle Louis. He's been so good to us. I remember there was a fight a long time ago, and he made an accusation, he said that you gambled away the business. Did that really happen? I'm puzzled, Dad – it's not like you to hold a grudge, and if this is true, shouldn't it be Uncle Lou holding the grudge, not you? If you gambled away my business, I know I'd be upset with you.'

Marissa stopped speaking, rather surprised at herself. She hadn't realised that she had been holding that inside her. It felt good to get it out there, even if her dad wasn't actually hearing it. She was able to put her thoughts in order, to realise that this was something that actually did bother her.

Ronan waited to see if there was more, but there wasn't. 'Would you like to answer now, as your dad?'

'Okay. This is so weird, though.'

Ronan shrugged his shoulders, 'Yeah I guess it is, but let's try it anyway.'

Marissa stood up, walked around the back of the chairs, went to the chair 'her father' had just been sitting in and sat down in it. She turned towards the seat where she had been. She imagined that she was her father, imagined how it would feel to be inside his body. *I could do some body mapping ... yes, why not...?* She imagined she was mapping his body onto hers, so that she could, well, become him. She felt a small shift in her energy field, then she spoke, as him.

'Marissa, love, I've tried to hide this from you, my failings. I'm not a perfect man. And I've been jealous, too, for years in fact, of Louis' success. Our father worked hard; he was a real grafter, as they say. We worked for him. I did everything he asked, I worked hard too. But Louis, he wanted to do things his own way. He was a messer – he'd do everything quickly, and only the things he wanted to do. The chores and mundane stuff, he wouldn't do it at all. And there was no budging him. I was unhappy with the situation, but I kept going regardless, doing what I was told.

'One day after work I stopped by the dog track. I couldn't help it, I put £5 down on a dog to win, and when it did, I was elated. I felt free – it was exciting. Louis started tinkering with computers in the back room, ignoring his other tasks and I got angrier with him – he wasn't helping me at all. And then our father got sick, so we had to manage the whole business ourselves. Louis didn't help – he took on more and more computers, drifting away from the main business and leaving me to deal with all of our father's unfinished business. I hated it, and I began to really dislike him. I was bored selling furniture so I went back to the track for that feeling. I went again and again, and after a time I was going every night. And of course I wasn't winning every time – maybe only once in five or ten times. So the feeling, it was harder to come by. I should have stopped much earlier. Oh, Marissa, there are so many things I should have done instead. Eventually, yes, I lost everything.

'I had to grovel to Louis and tell him. At that stage he had separated himself from Dad's business and set up on his own, but he knew seeing the place destroyed would break our dying father's heart. Marissa, it would have finished him off, seeing his life's work going down the toilet, because of me. So Louis got a loan out, pulled some strings and bailed me out, bailed us all out. Rose – well, she never found out how bad it got. I didn't tell anyone. I gave up the track, trimmed down the excess business and stayed in the shop long after our father died. I supposed I was punishing myself. I resented Louis' success and his interest in what he was doing, and I suppose that resentment became fixed in me over the years. I never let it go. To be honest, I really don't resent his success, but I'm jealous because he found something he loved to do and I never did. I wish I could take it all back. I know that it's all worked out now, but I suppose it's been easier to blame him than to even begin to forgive myself.'

Marissa stopped speaking. She had run out of words, but it had all spilled out of her so easily that the sense of what she had said still hung in the air. She and Ronan sat in silence for a while, both of them speechless.

Then Ronan realised it was his turn to speak. 'Thank you, Marissa's dad – erm, I mean Bernie. Marissa, what do you have to say in response?'

Marissa snapped out of her reverie and stood up. She slowly walked around the back of the two chairs and sat down in her original chair. She looked at Ronan with a 'What the heck was that?' look on her face.

There was no humorous wink this time. He was all business. 'Marissa, can you respond to your father?'

She turned to the empty chair. 'Dad, wow. I didn't know. Any of that. And I believe you. I can see it happening. I'm sorry that I was upset with you, I think if it was me I'd probably have resented him. No, I definitely would have. I almost got stuck in a job out of obligation too, so I have some idea of what that would be like. I forgive you. You're working it out your way, and that's okay with me.' She turned to Ronan. 'Should I go back and be him again? I don't know if I'm able to do that again. What the heck just happened?'

Ronan rubbed his face with both of his big thick hands, then closed and opened both of his eyes as if he was waking up. 'Marissa, did you really not know any of that?'

'No, I swear I didn't know any of it.'

'From the way you spoke, as your father, it didn't seem to me that you were making it up either. It was as if it was true. It felt true to me.'

'Yeah, it was weird. The words, they just tumbled out of me. I was listening to them from outside of myself. If that's even a thing. I was only a baby at the time, and Dad said – I mean I said – I mean he said that he didn't even tell my mum... I don't think I could have made all that up. I don't know what to believe, only that it feels true to me too.'

Ronan said, 'It certainly wasn't what I expected. How do you feel now?'

'I don't know. I think I'm okay.' Marissa took a moment to ground herself. *Feet in shoes on the ground, feel the chair beneath me. Yes, I am here. How do I feel?* 'Ronan, I do actually feel it was real, that we really had that chat, me and Dad.' She took another moment. 'I feel different in here, too,' she said, pointing to her heart, 'as if I actually have forgiven him, or at the very least I understand him better. It's softer now.'

'You got some form of closure from it,' said Ronan, nodding his head, 'so it's a good technique for closing things off.'

‘Yes, I think it is. But he’s not dead. It would be amazing to do this with someone who was dead. However, I don’t think I need to have this conversation with him now in real life. I’m satisfied. Even though I’m really curious now to know if that was the truth, or not. Let’s just say that it was.’ She brightened. ‘Imagine the relief a client would get to be able to really properly say goodbye to someone who had died.’

‘Mr Crowley did suggest it could be used that way. But it’s one thing hearing it in a lecture and another thing experiencing it.’

‘Do we have time for you to be client?’

‘I don’t think so. But I don’t think I could do it just now, I must admit, I got emotional too, listening to you. That’s how I know that it was real, real for both of us, at least. I don’t think I could focus on my own issues right now.’

‘I think it’s nearly time to finish anyway. Hey, thanks for that, Ronan. You know, I don’t really enjoy being a client at all, I tend to hold back a lot in class. But I felt safe with you, I always have. You’re a good therapist.’

Ronan blushed.

Standing at the bus stop after class, Marissa went over the conversation again in her head. Had it really been with her dad? Or just her projection of him? Either way, it felt good. It felt closed.

The bus came. She got on and went home.

CHAPTER SEVENTEEN

Marissa was going to be twenty-eight on the 17th of March, St Patrick's Day. That was the family dinner that she had sheepishly invited Matt to. She didn't really feel like celebrating this year, but she usually didn't feel like celebrating herself any year. It never felt like it was *her* day, she had always shared it with the national holiday, which felt much bigger and more important than her.

She hadn't told Matt it was her birthday yet, either. But after struggling with *Why did I ask him?*, her thoughts shifted to *Maybe we should just get it over with?* Of course, Eli and Carol would be there too. They they would be supportive if something blew up, even though they'd be finding out about him for the first time, too. Marissa felt she needed some support. She needed someone to help her clear her mind and get herself straight on what she actually wanted. *Actually, Sarah had offered...*

'Will you come for a coffee or lunch with me, Sarah?' Marissa emailed. 'I have something I need to figure out and I think you could help me... If you don't mind? It'll be a "friend" conversation, not "management".'

'Sure! Delighted to be of service.'

They got their usual table and Marissa was about to order their usual drinks when Sarah said, 'Actually, can I have a cappuccino instead? It's a more managerial type drink than a Frappuccino!'

Marissa laughed.

Sarah flicked her ponytail as she stirred sugar into her drink and looked Marissa straight in the eye. 'What's going on? How can I help?'

Marissa sighed. She looked at her caramel macchiato, and then at Sarah's cappuccino, and thought she probably should go back to her regular old Americano. *Simple things are best.*

'Come on, tell me,' insisted Sarah.

Marissa started right in the middle, which was where her thinking was at that moment. 'My family like to make drama over religion, even though we are not religious, and of course Matt isn't Jewish. I don't even know what religion he is! And I'm not religious, I never was, really, so I don't care about any of this stuff. But my family think they are, even though they just play along with it and don't really.. Well anyway. Matt's probably either Catholic or Protestant, he's certainly not Jewish, and he certainly isn't religious, either. Mum will decide she doesn't like him without even giving him a chance, Eli will take the piss because he feels nervous about the whole thing, and Carol will probably have a meltdown because she's not Jewish either and the same thing happened to her.'

Sarah's eyes widened as she tried to make sense of it all.

'And then Mum will make some nasty comment, like she did when I brought James home the first time.' Marissa continued, 'Dad will try to calm her down and then he will take her side, I'll get upset and find some reason to be nasty back to them, and the whole thing will end up with me walking out, dragging Matt with me, and we won't talk again for weeks. And on top of that it's my birthday dinner and I've not told Matt that it's my birthday yet, and that will just turn the whole thing into shit.'

Sarah shook her head in disbelief. 'You've got this whole thing figured out, haven't you?' she said. 'Before it even happens...'

Marissa sighed again. 'Well, I've done it already, and Eli has just done it with Carol. I don't understand why they have to make it so difficult for us. It's a nasty mess, Sarah, all because of what? I don't want to do it again, I don't have the energy for it right now either, with my spiritual crisis still not resolved. Can't we just be a family and support each other's choices?'

Sarah put her cup down on the table, sat back and crossed her legs. 'What if it doesn't end up like that? What if your mum actually likes Matt?'

Marissa creased her brows in thought, then frowned. 'She never likes *anyone* when she meets them for the first time.'

'Well, if you're serious about Matt, she'll have to meet him at some point.'

Marissa sighed.

'Maybe you could ask her to be especially nice to him because it's your birthday?'

'I suppose I could...'

'More's to the point, why on earth have you not told Matt it's your birthday? You *can't* not tell him, he'd be very upset. You have to give him time to get you something. Tell him right now. Here, *I'll* tell him. Give me your phone! Never mind the dinner, he needs to know it's your birthday. He'll be upset if he can't get you anything.'

'I never thought of it like that. I was just trying not to make a big deal out of it.'

'It's not always about you, Marissa,' Sarah said sharply.

'Oh!' said Marissa, feeling as if she'd been slapped in the face. 'No, I suppose not. I never thought of it from his point of view.'

'Here, give me your phone,' Sarah insisted.

'No way!' said Marissa.

'Go on! Don't you trust me?' Sarah's face had softened. She had a cheeky look.

'No way, not with that look on your face.'

'You do it then. Text him now. Tell him it's your birthday dinner and you're birthday's on Paddy's Day.'

Reluctantly, Marissa got her phone out of her bag. She turned it on, texted: *Thinking of you* and sent it to Matt, then put the phone down on the table in front of her.

'Did you tell him?'

'Yeah.'

'I don't believe you.'

'I'm feeling shy.'

'It's in four days for goodness' sake, woman, you've got to give him a bit of notice.'

Marissa felt a little bullied, but she knew Sarah was right. Probably. She sighed, opened the phone up again and typed: It's my birthday in 4 days, then pressed 'Send'.

'Okay, I told him.'

Her phone beeped a reply almost straight away.

Sarah was delighted. 'Ooh, what did he say? He must love you!'

Marissa couldn't help but smile. She read the message to herself and blushed.

'Go on, tell me.'

'It's private,' she said, and put the phone back in her bag.

'Spoilsport!' laughed Sarah. 'But at least he knows now.' She finished the last of her coffee. 'That's much more important that taking him to meet your parents. You're in a relationship with each other, not with your parents. Don't forget that.'

'How much for the session?' asked Marissa.

Sarah laughed. 'Yes, I'd make a very good therapist, me!'

When she was alone back at her desk, Marissa pulled out her phone out and read the message from Matt again. It said something about snakes and St Patrick's Day and treating her right and seeing her later that night. She remembered the last time they had been together, last Saturday night, and she saw his smile in her mind's eye. He was a good man, he treated her well, he looked after her. Her heart flipped thinking about seeing him that evening. She was going to miss their midweek get-togethers once she started in St Mary's.

'You know, I think you should consider seeing Reiki clients now,' said Matt over dinner. 'It would give you more confidence to make the break from Noreen, if you start part time, maybe one evening a week.'

'How could I do that? I've got nowhere to take them. I'm not bringing them back to my flat.'

'I know – you need to think about renting a space. My friend Vanessa, she's a therapist, she rents a room with a few others in town. It's not expensive if you rent it for a day, or even for a few hours once a week. There are places that offer rooms like that.'

'Really?' Marissa's interest had been piqued. 'So, I could rent a room for, say, one evening a week, and see Reiki clients there?' She put her knife and fork together and pushed her plate to one side. 'I didn't know you could do that. Would I make enough money if I had to pay for the room?'

'I asked Vanessa for you, as research like, and she said that her rent works out about €10 per hour, so everything she charges above that is money for her. Maybe you'll find a place that's cheaper, if it's not in the city centre. You might even find a place near your flat. It's a good location here, pretty central, with lots of busses...'

Marissa took the plates into the kitchen and put the kettle on for tea.

'Think about it?' Matt asked, with an encouraging tone. He put his yellow sock-clad feet up on the coffee table. 'Maybe have a look online and see what's available? Just to see what's out there. I'd be happy to help you look.'

'Yes, it's a good idea, thanks. I'll have a look and see what's available. I guess I'd need to buy a plinth and blankets and some other things too.'

'Yes, probably. But I've got a few friends who know a few friends, so it won't be a problem. More's to the point, what do you want me to get you for your birthday?' Matt grabbed the remote control and started flicking through the channels for something to watch on TV. 'And why didn't you tell me before? How old you gonna be?'

Marissa flicked him with a tea-towel and snatched the remote, giggling. She turned the TV off and gestured to the feet on the table. 'You're gas,' she said. 'Make yourself at home, why don't you?'

Matt laughed. 'Well, at least I took my shoes off first,' he said with a wink. 'But seriously, what do you want for your birthday?'

'I want to spend time with you. But I can't get out of the dinner. Would you come? To my parents'?' Marissa was hesitant, but she ploughed on, 'I'm thinking it might be good to get this out of the way – I mean, them meeting you. I don't like hiding things from them, and we've been together a while now, I think they already suspect I've got a boyfriend.'

Matt took his feet off the table and sat up on the chair. He didn't reply.

'They may be extra nice to us because it's my birthday...'

'Well, I like spending time with you, too, and it would be silly to spend the day together and then have me waiting in a pub for you while you have your dinner. I'll think about it. But I want to say up-front that I've no plans to introduce you to my parents anytime soon, so as long as you're not expecting me to reciprocate...?'

'No, not at all.'

Matt made a face and stroked his beard, which looked very tidy that night. 'I'm sure it couldn't be any more awkward that when we went out with your friend Terry...'

Marissa shuddered. 'It could be, actually. Awkward, I mean, but in a different way. I didn't know his friends would be like that. I'm sorry.'

Matt smiled. 'I'm only winding you up. Sure that wasn't your fault, couldn't be helped. Okay, I'll go meet your parents, but just know that we've only been together six weeks this week, and I'm not gonna be proposing to you just yet.' He winked.

Marissa smiled and her heart flipped with joy. *Ooh, I suppose that means I want him to meet them! Funny how my body knew this but my brain was so confused over it.*

'So what about your birthday present then?' he asked.

'You could get me another crystal from the Angel Shop?' she suggested, cocking her head on one side, hopefully.

'Great idea. We could go there together, and then go for a walk on the pier, and I'll buy you an ice cream. Wonder if they're open on the Bank Holiday? The parade, then dinner at your parents', then stay with me that night? We could make a weekend out of it. I'll check it out.'

+ + +

Marissa sat in Room Three and waited for Margaret to come. The room seemed strange, somehow, but she couldn't quite put her finger on why. Then she felt a presence move from the back corner of the room to almost right behind her. She felt anxious straight away, a light sweat pooling on her skin, jitters in her stomach. *I'm making this up.* She planted her feet solidly on the ground and heard a voice within her say, 'Don't give in. Stand your ground, claim your space.'

She took out the new bottle of St Germain room spray that she had bought at the Reiki 2 workshop from Dolores and turned around slowly with it in her hand. She didn't see anything with her eyes but she felt the heaviness right in front of her. She imagined herself growing taller, 8 foot tall, 10 foot tall, spreading out like a tree to the sunshine, and she sprayed the mist in front of her, behind her, to the left and to the right.

Then she said out loud, 'Begone, all things here that are not made of pure love.' *Where did that come from? It didn't really sound like I meant it, though.*

Nothing changed in the room, it still felt strange. She visualised her feet going through the floor, through the room below and through the foundation of the building, down into the deep, sweet earth beneath. *That feels better.* She felt energy pulse through her legs and up her body, and she grew bigger in her mind once more. Her heart felt stronger this time. She sent pure light out from it and spoke out loud, but quietly and more confidently this time. 'Begone, all entities that are not made of pure love, pure light. Anything that wishes to do harm, *begone*!'

As she spoke she felt her anxiety leave her and her confidence rise. She was taller again. Her own energy was taking up most of the space in the room now. She extended her senses around the room to check how it was now, and felt nothing.

She waited, clearing her mind, scanning the room with her feelings. *All clear?*

The buzzer rang.

'Margaret, come on up.'

When Margaret knocked on the door after a few minutes later, Marissa was already there to greet her.

'Hello there. Come in, how are you?'

'I'm well, thanks! And how are you?' Margaret came in and hung her sky-blue coat on the back of the door. She wore another wool skirt and blouse ensemble, different colours this time. 'Which seat should I take? It smells nice in here!'

'Either one is fine.'

'This one then,' Margaret said, and plumped herself down in the same chair she had sat in during the previous visit.

Marissa sat opposite her. 'So, how have you been?'

Margaret immediately shrank. After a moment, she shook her head. 'Straight into it then. Okay. Well, I'm not good, not good at all. I tried to keep the journal, like you suggested, but it made me realise just exactly how often I worried, so after a few days I had to stop writing.'

She waited to see what Marissa's reaction would be, but Marissa stayed silent, waiting for more information. None was forthcoming.

'Did you bring it with you? The journal, I mean.'

'Oh yes, I have it here. Just a moment.'

Margaret reached over to her handbag, which was on the floor by her feet. She opened the clasp and rifled through the bag, then took out a battered old copybook with pages that looked as if they were about to fall out of their binding. She closed the handbag and flicked through the notebook to find the page she wanted.

'Shall I read?'

Marissa nodded.

'Erm, okay.' Margaret flicked back and forth through the pages again, as if making up her mind where to start. 'Okay. "Gertrude is going to get hit by a car and die."' She looked up to Marissa. 'Gertrude is my dog. Is this the type of thing you wanted?'

'Yes, perfect, thank you, go ahead,' said Marissa.

Margaret went back to reading. '"Gertrude will eat something poisonous in the garden and die. Gertrude will run out through the hedge in the back garden and never come back. Gertrude will get kidnapped while I'm not looking."' She looked up apologetically at Marissa. 'Are you sure you want to hear all of these?'

'How many do you have?'

'Well, this was a new notebook, so this is just two days' worth.'

'Are all your thoughts about Gertrude?'

'Oh no, I have thoughts about my husband too, and my son, and myself of course. Here – here's some more.' She turned a few pages. '"Thomas will choke at the dinner table and die. Thomas will catch pneumonia and die. Thomas will ride on his friend's motorbike and crash it and die."'

Marissa let out a breath. The room felt heavy again. She closed her eyes to visualise herself, to see if she had shrunk in size, which she had. It seemed as though Margaret's thoughts were filling the room with heaviness, as though each thought was alive and taking energy from her.

Margaret was still reading from her list.

'Margaret?'

'Huh?'

'I'm wondering, did you write these thoughts out as they were happening to you, or did you just make a list of thoughts?'

'Oh, I made lists of thoughts – all the thoughts I had about Gertrude and Thomas, and I've not even started telling you the ones about Kevin. Do you want to hear those?'

Marissa shook her head.

'I want to know what you're doing when these thoughts appear, what you're feeling. As well as the thoughts themselves, of course, which are very important. I mean, writing all these down was a very good exercise.'

Margaret seemed to relax a little.

'But I don't know what we can do with them, in this format I mean,' Marissa confessed.

'Oh, I don't know myself!' Margaret laughed. 'I couldn't believe how many I could come up with, though, and how quickly they all came to me!'

Marissa cocked her head on one side. 'You made them up for me?'

Margaret smiled. 'Oh no, no, I didn't do that, no. These are the thoughts that I would normally have. I just wrote them down as a list as I remembered them.'

Marissa nodded. 'That makes sense. I understand now – you wrote them down, let's say, to get them out of your head, and onto the page.'

'Yes. That's it,' said Margaret.

'Well done,' said Marissa, finally feeling they understood each other. 'That's great. How did it feel to write them all down?'

Margaret shrank back again. 'Overwhelming, to be honest. It wasn't a nice thing to do, and I started to cry at one point. Actually, I cried more than once.'

Marissa let silence come between them for a few moments.

Margaret closed the notebook and put it down on the floor.

'Okay,' Marissa said, 'so now we have lists of what your thoughts are.'

'Oh, this isn't all of them! I have more. I just didn't write them all down.'

Marissa nodded as she took in the information.

'Well done. I know it was tough to do that. Maybe we should change tack and look at your feelings. Would that be okay?'

Margaret thought for a moment. 'I suppose so.'

'Well, what would you like to achieve? There is so much going on in your mind, I don't think we can sort it all out, but we could set ourselves a goal to work on together, and I could help you get there.'

'Okay. Well, this is what I want: to get some control back from my thoughts. They seem to take over my life.'

Marissa had a bright idea.

'You really did a great job writing down all your thoughts. And you want to get control back from your thoughts. But maybe we need to start with you just getting some sense of control over your mind, maybe not necessarily over the thoughts just yet. I think this week I'll give you an exercise to try to get control back of your mind. And as well as that, if you can, you could write down how you feel each day, when you have the thoughts, or even just write down how you are feeling, so you can get more in touch with your emotions. But if that's too much, that's okay. What do you think?'

'Sounds like a lot of things for me to do. What did you have in mind – for the exercise, I mean?'

'Give me a moment.' Marissa took a breath. This was proving to be a challenging session. *If I can pick something useful for her, and it works, we really could break through something here.* She thought back to when she was anxious. What worked best for her in those moments was a mindfulness presence exercise.

'I've got a mindfulness exercise that helps me when I get anxious. I still use it quite a bit. Let's do it together, right here. Then, next time you feel upset or overwhelmed by the thoughts, you can try this exercise yourself, and you will be taking back control.'

Margaret smiled, 'Mind-full-ness? That sounds like your mind is full, why would that help?'

'It's about acknowledging that your mind is full, and changing what it is full of, so to speak. To bring it into the present moment more, and to choose what the thoughts are, that are filling your mind, rather than letting the thoughts choose you.'

'This sounds very good. It's encouraging to hear that you use it too. Yes, I'd like to try it. Thank you, Marissa.'

'Okay. Now I will speak out loud so you can hear what I'm thinking, so you get the idea of how to do it. You don't need to speak out loud when you're doing it, but it can actually help if you do, sometimes, especially if you're feeling very anxious.' Marissa smiled. 'I'm very happy to share this with you. It can really help you bring your awareness back into the present moment. Ready?'

Margaret nodded and brushed a loose strand of hair out of her face.

'Good.' Marissa smiled again then began speaking, saying each sentence slowly, more slowly than her normal speech, and leaving long pauses between the sentences.

'I'm sitting in the chair. I feel my feet on the ground. I press my back into the chair. I can see Margaret. I breathe in, I breathe out. I can hear my breathing.' She stopped and smiled again. 'Do you see what I'm doing here? I'm talking to myself in the present tense about what is going on around me, what I see, what I hear. You try it now.'

Margaret took a moment to register what was needed. 'Okay. I am sitting in a chair. I am looking at Marissa. Is this right?'

Marissa smiled reassuringly. 'Yes, it is. Keep going.'

Margaret smiled in return. 'Okay. I am doing an exercise with Marissa.'

Marissa nodded her head in encouragement.

'I am looking at the table. I can see the candle is burning. It is nearly finished. I can hear people next door moving around.'

'Very good. Keep going.'

'I am speaking out loud. I feel a draught of cold air at my feet.'

'Very well done. You've got it! How do you feel while you're doing this?'

'Actually, much calmer. I feel a little bit more in control. I am doing mindfulness work with Marissa.' She looked up and smiled. 'I like this! I will definitely try it.'

'Great! And I want you to work with the journal again too, but don't make lists this week. Instead, you could write down the thought you are having in the moment you are having it, *and* write down how it makes you feel while you are thinking it.'

Margaret seemed confused.

'Here's an example: "My thought is: 'Gertrude will choke on a bone and die.' This comes up for me because I see a bone in the garden and wonder if she will find it. Thinking about Gertrude dying makes me feel anxious.'

'Ah, now I understand what you mean,' Margaret said, relieved. 'Yes, I can do that too, but I won't be able to do it for every thought I have!'

Marissa smiled. 'Okay, how about you do it for just one or two thoughts every day? The ones that really upset you. Then when we meet next time you can tell me about how you got on, read out your thoughts and we can figure out what to do next.'

'Yes, that's good. It's nice to feel that I'm finally doing something for myself. Thank you.'

Cliona next. Marissa looked back over her notes. *Ten weeks together – wow, that's the longest I've seen anyone. I hope she's finding the work helpful. Maybe I should ask her if she's happy with what we're doing.*

Cliona knocked on the door, walked straight into the room and over to the empty chair. 'Don't get up,' she said, smiling.

Marissa put her notes aside and smiled back, wondering what was going on. She surveyed Cliona for signs of anger or anxiety. Cliona was wearing a denim mini-skirt, fishnet tights, a crop top and a denim jacket. Her hair was still black. She seemed upbeat as she sat back in the chair and crossed her legs.

'How's it goin'?' she asked.

'Good, thanks. Can you believe this is session number ten?'

'Jezuz – no way! Doesn't feel like it.'

'I know,' said Marissa. 'I wanted to ask you if you're feeling that we're making progress together?'

'Shit, yeah! Seriously. I'm happy.' Cliona thought for a moment and then added, 'Do I have to sign up now for another six?'

'Actually, that's a good point. I'll make a note of it. Do you think you want to?'

'Deffo. If I can, I mean? I've had a good week, though. Everything seems to be settling down a bit. And it even looks like I'm gonna get a job. Nan has a friend who can sort me out. I've got an interview tomorrow morning. It's working in a shop.'

What about the skills training that they do in St Mary's... Maybe Cliona would benefit from that? But maybe Cliona can't just show up there, maybe she has to be in a crisis. I need to find out first, before I offer anything.

'How do you feel about working in a shop?'

'Eh, it's better than nothing, I guess. I didn't get my Leaving, so I don't know what else I would be fit for.'

'I'm sure you could get upskills training – if you wanted to, I mean.'

'Girls like me don't go to college,' Cliona said, tucking her legs in closer to her, and looking at the floor.

'I'm going to take you up on that,' said Marissa, defiantly. 'Where did that idea come from? And what is a "girl like you"?'

Cliona shrugged her shoulders. 'It was never an option in my family, college. Once I had Ari I never went back to school, and nobody mentioned that I should.'

'I think you'd be surprised at what you could do now – if you wanted to, that is. There's so many options available. But what *do* you want? If you could wave a magic wand and be anything in the world, what would you be?'

Cliona laughed and relaxed a little. 'Feck, Marissa, right now all I want is to be happy, and have a bit of security. Probably married to Bren, with Ari, and whoever this little blighter is gonna be, and a house of our own. Magic wand stuff. But maybe it *could* happen. Hey, I told Bren. He was made up!'

No wonder all the smiling. 'That must be a relief for you.'

'Yeah, I know,' said Cliona. 'Big one, hey. It's great, innit? He seemed really pleased. He's calling it "Bren junior" already! Ha, ha. I promised him I'd do more anger work with ya. And he knows that I won't be runnin' away anytime soon. I think he needed to feel I needed him... So, yeah, deffo ask for the next cycle. Six more sessions will help me loads. I am determined to make this work.'

Joy was a no-show. *This is the second time this has happened, Fiachra just didn't show up too, when he felt his issue was sorted out. At least Cedric had the decency to tell the office he wasn't coming back. It's really not fair, there are others who would take the session – why can't they just phone and tell the office?*

Disappointed, she packed up her things, blew out the candle and switched off the light. She closed the door behind her and left, feeling a heaviness in the air, a heaviness that seemed to follow her all the way home.

CHAPTER EIGHTEEN

'The last time I saw you was... three weeks ago. You were just about to go on a trip, to Sligo.' Olive put down her notebook and pushed her glasses up her nose, towards her eyes. She was wrapped in a colourful woollen shawl, it was a little cold in her glass room, but the sun was shining and the plants certainly seemed to be enjoying it. 'How was it?'

'Yes, that's right. Sligo was lovely, it seems like a year ago now, so much has happened since then.'

After Marissa filled her in on all the 'things that happened', Olive looked at her and smiled, then asked, 'Yes, but how are you? You've indeed been busy, but you're not telling me much about your internal process. As usual.' Her lips were tight, face serious. She wasn't going to let Marissa get away without answering her to her satisfaction this time.

Marissa, as usual, was feeling put on the spot. She sighed. *Oh, why not tell her how I actually am feeling?*

'Well, okay. I'm disappointed. Anxious, nervous... A little cold...'

Olive reached forward and turned up the heating.

'Feeling that I should be celebrating my birthday, but not really feeling that I have anything to celebrate. Excited to be finishing my course, worried that Matt meeting my family will be a disaster, panicky about finishing my assignments on time and getting them right...'

Olive nodded, still waiting.

'Erm... I'm tired. Fidgety now. I feel that you're wanting me to talk about something else and I don't know what it is.'

'Yes, you do. Come on, get it out. You know me well enough by now.'

Marissa shuddered.

Olive waited for a few moments more, then said, 'You mentioned disappointment. What is that about?'

'Did I? Oh yes, I did. Yes, I'm disappointed ...' For a moment, Marissa wondered why she said that. What am I disappointed about, though? She had a sinking feeling so she tracked it down, following the feeling as if it was an animal travelling deep inside the labyrinth of herself, to find the source of it. But she reached a dead end. A closed door that was not going to budge, and Olive was still waiting for her to reply. So many things, I am still lost, so much to do, it's too much for me. I can't do it all.... Ok I'll try this then - 'I guess, I'm disappointed that I can't do it all?' she offered.

Olive seemed satisfied with that. Marissa was relieved.

'What's the "all"?'

Marissa thought for a moment. 'I suppose work, clients, boyfriend, being happy, studying, family stuff...'

'But you are doing all of that. It just isn't smooth, that's all, dear. That's real life, Marissa, it's never smooth. Well, rarely. We appreciate the smoothness when it is there, and work with the bumps and the dips in our path as they come.'

Marissa nodded, still feeling a little lost, but trying to hide it.

Olive looked at her expectantly. 'What does your heart say about disappointment?'

'It wants to go to the shamanic workshop next weekend.' As the words tumbled out of her mouth, Marissa's body froze. The door inside of her that she had closed so firmly was suddenly kicked wide open. Flashes of images flooded into her mind so strongly she felt them ripple through her body. Laughing in the kitchen with the group, giggling with Terry just the two of them, dancing by the fire, working with Zaad, sitting in circle listening to Séamus teaching in the front room... She got a sense of who she was when she was there, realising that strong feeling of coming home to herself; it felt so strange to her in that moment - as if she was recognising herself for the first time. And then, in technicolour, she saw the sofa and she was lying on it, Séamus was working on her alone in the room, just the two of them, her body paralysed, not being able to speak out... Terror flooded into her and her body stiffened. She got a sense of the cascade of events that happened after that, but thankfully, no images came through. But they were there, somewhere. That energy most definitely was there, lurking at the back of it all, malevolently. Marissa felt so small. She became lightheaded, and dizzy.

'Breathe. You have a large amount of emotion around this stored inside you, still to process... Breathe with me, in and out, in and out.'

Olive's voice was grounding and pulled her awareness back into the room. Marissa breathed and her body loosened slightly, but her eyes were wide and she was trembling. Olive offered her some water, which she took and drank with shaking hands.

Olive wrote something down in her notebook, then turned to Marissa. 'You seem to have PTSD, which, if it goes untreated, can linger for a very long time.'

'PTSD?'

'Yes, post-traumatic stress disorder. I hadn't realised it until now. Your body is holding onto shock and your mind has not processed what happened to you. Which you really haven't told me about. Do you want to talk about it?' Olive's tone changed to concern. 'What happened?'

Tears glistened in the corners of Marissa's eyes at the compassion in Olive's voice. But her heart was still racing, as was her mind, and she began breathing in panting, panicky breaths. The thoughts of having to look into that blackness, let alone voice it to Olive was terrifying. She felt Bear coming to stand beside her; his big, powerful, loving presence wanting to wrap her in his arms to hold her safe. She had not felt him in such a long time and her heart cried out with joy to see him and simultaneously, an intense sadness welled up in her that it had been so long. That shocked her, too. Her heart longed to hold him, be held by him, but he reminded her of what had happened, he was a part of this. It was too much, too too much to deal with. She couldn't do it. She needed peace, stillness, the way it had been only a few moments earlier. She summoned all of her strength and pushed Bear away, shut herself up, locked it all out. Just barely.

Olive noticed everything, she always did. Marissa felt naked in front of her. Probably why I don't like coming here, even though it's always okay. Well, usually it's okay. Not today.

Olive said, 'Your body is so tight, perhaps a massage would help?'

'A massage?' Marissa came back slowly into the room, into the present moment.

'Yes. Some forms of bodywork can be very helpful in releasing the symptoms of PTSD.'

Bodywork.... An image of Dolores doing Reiki on her flashed through Marissa's mind. She realised that she hadn't felt as relaxed as she had after the session with Dolores, since, well, the session with Dolores. It's not bodywork though?

'Okay, maybe I should do something like that,' she said, then suddenly remembered, 'I had a massage in Sligo! I think it helped. I did feel very relaxed afterwards. Do I need another one?'

'Perhaps. You don't seem to be your usual self today, and learning how to take care of yourself is vital for a therapist. You have to make this a higher priority.'

'Okay, I'll organise something. And you could be right about the PTSD. I didn't know it was a thing that I could have.' Marissa rubbed her head, feeling comforted by the feeling of her fingers pressing strongly into her skull. Somehow it revived her a little more fully. 'I thought it was something that only happened to soldiers in a war, or people who had been exposed to violence.'

Olive smiled kindly. 'Oh no, PTSD can happen to anyone, depending on their fragility, their strength of character and the cumulation of events in their life. The symptoms are always different, though – that's why it can be difficult to detect. A person can feel highs and lows, it seems like things are good but they feel disconnected from them. Or PTSD shows up when someone is really relaxed, then suddenly they can become panicked and anxious when there is no apparent threat in front of them. It does sound as if you need to take especially good care of yourself right now.'

Olive talking shop was helpful. While she listened to her, Marissa felt a cloud of heaviness change it's shape around her so it became more manageable. Yes, that's it. I'm okay now. Really, I am.

Olive looked at the clock. 'We are coming up to time. I'm glad we had this discussion. Looking after yourself has to become your first priority until you're feeling stronger. Promise me that you will do something for yourself, to look after yourself, please? Book a massage, take some time to rest.' She opened her diary. 'When will we meet next time? How about after Easter, is that okay?'

PTSD. Marissa held onto that thought for the rest of the afternoon, wondering what it actually meant as far as she was concerned, and what she needed to do about it, if anything. The longer she thought about it in a clinical mindset, distancing herself from it, the more consolidated she became. She felt flickers in the corner of her mind but she pushed them away. She had a flash of Bear again, and she felt another pang in her heart. Tentatively, she continued the line of thought.

I'm terrified of Bear. And I've not seen my guides in the longest time, dearest determined Emelda, and my loving Grandmother Medicine Woman. Is that because of the PTSD? Oh. My. God, I didn't realise! Maybe that's part of the PTSD! Am I doing this myself to keep my mind clear? My guides do seem to complicate things for me.

A moment passed and she still felt level. She tested herself. *I know the workshop's coming up and I'll be missing it.* There was a hollow feeling in the pit of her stomach. She continued. *I haven't done the homework. I won't be progressing with the others. I hate failing, and this feels like failing. But if I* do *go...*

Again, that frozen feeling crept into her body. *I can't do it. I can't go. I'll have another breakdown. I have to look after myself. Even Olive said it, I need to make looking after myself a higher priority. I'll have to keep doing it the way I've been doing it. Maybe I could just focus on looking after myself without having to go back into what happened... But they'll be having so much fun in Clifden without me. Damnit, I can't think about it, I'm torturing myself with this. I'll have to focus on something else.*

Marissa stood in the supermarket aisle and offered herself anything she wanted for dinner, but she didn't want any of it. She bought noodles and steak, with ice cream and cake just because she knew these were things that she usually liked. *Let's get some fancy cat food, too.*

Tobermory was delighted; he was more delighted with his dinner than she was. He devoured it, washed himself clean, wound himself around her legs, mewed three times, and went out of the open kitchen window into the darkening evening.

Marissa despondently sat in front of the TV flicking through the channels, going over her discussion with Olive. I sound like a spoilt child. I have so many things, and nothing is going wrong in my life, not really. So why am I feeling so disappointed? And fragile.

'Yes, fragile,' she said out loud.

Should she really book a massage? Whom should she book it with? Or should she go see Dolores again for Reiki? Reiki. Yes, I should be doing my Reiki practice. Reiki is safe and good, it's good for me. And it's safe. That's something that I can do for myself right now. It feels good to do that.

She switched off the TV and put on some music, lit a candle and sat back down on the sofa. She noticed the Scott Taylor book was on the coffee table beside her. She picked it up and leafed through it, letting it fall open to a random page.

> *In times of upset or frustration, know that whatever it is that seems to be going wrong won't last. It never does! Just like happiness fizzles out, the bad times end and new, good times come. Your next good time could be just around the corner!*

Yes, he's right. It's as if he knew I needed to hear that! The book I mean.

She finally felt the comfort she had been seeking. She held the book to her chest and held it there for a few moments, as if giving it a hug. She felt tingles of electricity as she did this, it felt nice. Then she placed the book on her lap, closed her eyes and focused, then connected to the Reiki light. After a few moments she felt a calmness stirring inside, a warmth and a flow, particularly down her arms.

She put one hand on her heart and one on her stomach, and a few minutes later she started to cry. She went with it. The tears came in floods, growing in intensity. She felt her body opening up, the Reiki energies going in deeper, the sobs becoming stronger, like waves crashing on the shore. Aware of the people upstairs, she tempered her sobbing, but she let it out nonetheless.

And then, just like a storm, it was gone. She sank back into the sofa and lay down. She was pulsing – not just her body, but every part of her.

She stayed there for a while, until she was able to get up. Then she showered and went to bed, dinner uneaten. She brought the Scott Taylor book to bed with her and placed it under her pillow.

I'll keep going. Reiki's okay. Maybe I just need to relax a little bit more.

She slept better that night than she had in a long time.

CHAPTER NINETEEN

Marissa woke early, feeling ravenous. She found eggs and bread, made her favourite breakfast and took it to the chair outside to watch the sun come up. She enjoyed being up early on a Saturday, and as this one was the day before her birthday, it had a special sort of sheen to it. She felt significantly calmer. *I'm looking forward to the parade and dinner with my parents tomorrow. But what will I do today? How will I spend my last day as a twenty-seven-year-old?* Just as she asked the question, her phone beeped a text. She gathered herself and took her plate inside. The text was from Terry.

Hi! U free this afternoon? I'm in Dublin with Saoirse finishin homework. we're goin 2 the nat gallery l8tr, @3, u want 2 come?

Marissa was a little hesitant, but she loved Terry and she had promised she'd be friends with Saoirse. *Sure I've nothing else planned, and if they don't talk about the shamanism stuff, it could be fun to see them outside of that.* She texted back: Gr8, I'm free, c u there!

I'm going, I'm going to have fun, and I'm not going to think about things that upset me.

Entering the gallery, Marissa and found Terry and Saoirse standing beside a William Leech in the Irish artists section. It was one of her favourite paintings: a group of women in a garden with sunlight streaming off their white dresses. *That's a good sign.* She smiled and waved and they saw her and waved back enthusiastically.

Terry's hair was freshly cut and bleached more white than blonde, he was wearing black jeans and a black denim jacket with a white long-sleeved tee-shirt underneath. It set off his blue eyes and pale skin perfectly; he looked like a celebrity. It was a cold day, but

Saoirse looked snug and warm in a blue fleece and blue jeans, with brown calf-length boots.

Seeing them reminded Marissa of how much she liked them and enjoyed their company. 'Hi! You guys look amazing! Thanks for inviting me. Hey, there are so many people here!' Marissa wore her usual black jeans with a black top and black cardigan. The only colour she had on was a green scarf she had bought in a sale the previous week. She shivered and looked enviously at Saoirse's fleece, thinking that she probably should have worn something warmer, and maybe more colourful.

'Hi!' said Terry. 'Yeah, there must be an exhibition on. I didn't realise it would be so busy or I wouldn't have suggested coming here.' He looked at the crowd. 'Do you want to go somewhere else?'

'No, it's grand. It's nice here, I've not been in ages,' said Marissa.

'Me neither,' said Saoirse. 'It's good to see you, Marissa. How's things?'

'Busy!' said Marissa a little too enthusiastically. 'But busy in a good way.'

The three friends started to walk towards the main gallery.

Saoirse and Terry were trying to play down their enthusiasm in front of Marissa, but it was obvious that both of them were a little hyper after doing their homework.

'I want to see the Caravaggio,' said Terry, taking a floor plan out of his pocket. 'But I'm not sure if it's here this month. I think I heard they loaned it out to London.'

'Imagine, it was hanging in the dining hall in that seminary for years and years and nobody knew what it was!' Saoirse said, laughing. 'I wonder if the painting in my parents' front room is worth as much. It has been hanging there for about as long.'

'Yeah, what a story. My dad loves watching *Antiques Roadshow*, but it's very rare that something is worth so much that's staring you plain in the face,' said Marissa.

They stopped to admire a headless male torso. 'He obviously worked out,' said Terry with a nod and a giggle. 'Pity you can't see his face, but with a body like that, what does it matter what the rest of him looks like?'

'Eww, Terry!' the girls said.

'I guess you don't need to feed him, so you *could* keep him upstairs for when you needed him,' Terry added with a wink.

They wondered through the gallery, Terry making lewd comments, and the three of them became more relaxed with one another outside of their usual context. They stopped in front of one of the more colourful paintings.

'What do you think she's saying to him?' asked Saoirse, pointing to woman with a child on her lap and a newspaper in her hand. She was addressing her husband, who wasn't even looking at her. It seemed he would much rather be somewhere else.

'She's giving out to him for being such a layabout!' laughed Terry. 'Hey, I like this painting. It has a nice energy, even though yer man looks like a barrel of laughs, not.' He went to the next painting. 'Hey, this one, it's interesting – what do you think of it?'

The painting depicted three men at a table with a servant behind them. One of them was talking to two children. He had a dog at his feet.

'That man, he's the king, or a prince, and those are his children, and his serving man,' said Terry.

Marissa peered at them in closer detail. The little girl wore a gold and white dress and held a puppy to her chest as if it was a doll. The boy was dressed completely in red and he was reading from a book. His father, the prince if Terry was right, seemed to be encouraging him, but he looked despondent.

'Well, the boy certainly isn't dressed for playing outside,' she said. 'Yes, they do look like royalty.'

'Look, though, doesn't he look sad? The father?' asked Saoirse, studying the painting. 'And the dog, he looks sad too.

'Fed up, more like!' suggested Terry. 'I'll bet that man at the table is their accountant and he's just discovered they have no money left, and the prince has had to cancel the party and find a way to break the news to his wife.' He raised his hand to his brow in feigned distress and put on a very posh English accent. 'Oh dear, we won't be able to hold our ball after all. Lady Marmaduke will be so disappointed!'

Both girls cracked up. Terry really was very funny.

'You should have been a court jester,' said Marissa, giving him a playful slap.

'Maybe I was in a past life,' said Terry with a wink.

Later, they sat with coffee and cake at a corner table in the café. By the time they'd talked about the paintings, Marissa's client work, Terry's modelling job and Saoirse's sister's new puppy, they had run out of things to say that weren't about the shamanic training. *What now?*

'I trained in Reiki!' said Marissa, remembering she hadn't told them yet. 'I'm now Level 2, so I can see clients and get paid.'

'Ooh, that's really cool,' said Terry. 'Are you going to?'

'Yes. I've been looking online and I saw an available therapy room, near my flat. I could rent it. It seems a big step, but I've been thinking about it for a while now.'

'I really think you should do it,' said Saoirse. 'If you do, I'd come and get a treatment from you!'

Marissa smiled. 'Okay! Yes, I'll arrange to see the room. It'll be nice to start earning some money from my trainings, especially as I've spent so much money doing them. I can't earn yet doing psychotherapy, I've got to finish my training hours first. I've quite a few left to do and I feel under pressure to get them all done, but the clients just aren't showing up where I'm volunteering.'

Terry stirred at the dregs of his cappuccino, deep in thought. 'I wonder if we can see clients yet,' he said. 'For shamanic work, I mean. I guess we can't. I don't even know if I want to anyway – have clients, I mean. I'm actually just doing it because I like it.' He swallowed quickly and looked at Marissa. 'Hey, I didn't mean to bring it up,' he added.

Strangely, Marissa didn't seem upset at all by Terry's slip-up. 'Hey, it's okay,' she said. 'I'll be really missing you guys next weekend, but *you're* still doing it. And I'm not an egg, or anything.'

'An egg?' asked Saoirse.

'Yeah, it's something my brother used to say when we were growing up: "I'm not an egg, I don't break so easy."' *Maybe I am broken. I don't know. I feel okay though, and I can stay strong, though, in front of them both.*

'Ah, we were both under the impression that you did break easily, though,' said Saoirse, quickly looking at Terry and then back at Marissa, who flushed bright red.

'Yeah I thought as much. But it wasn't an easy, small thing that upset me, it was a big, awful thing, and I'm still not comfortable talking about it. Actually, my therapist has suggested that I have PTSD. I'm still figuring that out. But we can talk about the classes, and about your work with Séamus, I'm okay with it now.'

I guess that's true. It was a big, awful thing, something I don't understand. I'm allowed to be upset and fragile. Marissa felt a sense of relief at this acknowledgement.

'PTSD – that sounds serious. Wow, Marissa. Can we do anything to help?' asked Terry.

Marissa shrugged her shoulders. 'I don't even know what it means, really. She only said it to me yesterday. She said I need to put myself first, look after myself better, so I'll make an effort to do that. I'll figure it out.' She looked up at them. 'Hey, it's really good to be able to talk about this with you guys.'

'Yeah. Well, we're friends now, always. And it's good to know the boundaries around what we can talk about with you. So we don't upset you...' said Terry.

'Yeah,' said Marissa. 'Lookit, I'm sorry for being such a drama queen. I got a very big scare, and I freaked out. I'm feeling much happier now. Shamanism just isn't for me. Or else it's Séamus, and the way he teaches, or else it's... Oh, I don't know what it is! But it's not for me.' Feeling validated, and much better, she finished the last of her coffee. 'Hey, guys? Thanks for sticking around!'

Saoirse and Terry both smiled. 'So, can we tell you about our homework then?' Terry asked, 'Because this most amazing thing happened and we have to share it with someone...'

'Yeah, go on,' said Marissa, realising that deep down she was craving to hear all about it.

+++

St Patrick's day in Dublin city centre was a riot of colour; decked out with flags, banners and smiles, chock-full of people celebrating loudly. The atmosphere was uplifting and joyful, yet Marissa was conflicted.

'Why are we watching the parade inside a pub when we could be out on the street? It's only just outside.'

Matt was at the bar, fighting through the throngs of people trying to get served. He caught the barman's eye. 'A pint of the black stuff please and,' he turned to Marissa, 'what you having?'

'Diet Coke.'

'And a Diet Coke, ta.'

The relief was tangible on Matt's face as he saw his pint being poured. 'Because cans don't taste as good? Because it's Paddy's Day and pints are called for? I don't know, but this is what I always do. We can go outside and watch the parade after, if you want.'

Marissa's back was turned, she was squinting at a little television hanging from the ceiling in a corner. The pub Matt had chosen was down an alleyway just off the route of the parade and they could hear the crowds, the music and the cheering just outside, but they couldn't see anything. The RTÉ presenter was a celebrity she wasn't familiar with. She was interviewing someone about their float which was shaped like a humpbacked whale, it looked quite lifelike. Marissa had an urge to go and see it in real life, seeing as it *was* just outside, but she didn't want to start her day with Matt off on the wrong foot. So she let go of her need to be outside and tried to settle herself into the room. Then the crowd outside gave a loud cheer and her heart went back outside the door.

Matt reached over a woman who had pushed her way in front of him and took his drinks from the barman with a nod of his head, then he moved away from the crush at the bar. There was nowhere to sit, so they found somewhere to stand. Marissa kept looking at the TV while Matt drank deeply, sighed and wiped the beer moustache off his mouth with the back of his available hand. 'That's better. What time do we meet your parents again?'

'6:30,' replied Marissa, not turning around. The TV was showing a group of small children with painted faces who were talking about how Saint Patrick had put all the snakes in his hatchback and driven them out of the country. Marissa smiled, but she was becoming agitated, and a little claustrophobic too.

'Ah look, there they are! John, Padraig, over here!' Matt was waving. 'Marissa, these are the lads from the garage. Lads, this is the girlfriend!'

Marissa turned to say hello. Both men were tall, taller than Matt, and looked strong, wide-shouldered, both in jeans and T-shirt. They both nodded at her, and smiled at Matt.

'So you're startin' into the black stuff already, eh?' said Padraig, looking enviously at Matt's glass.

'Sure, what else would ya be doing? Can I get you one?'

'Ah sure, why not?'

After another crush at the bar and two pints bought for each of them, they acknowledged Marissa, then the mechanics talked shop, although it was more like shouting with the surrounding noise. Marissa smiled and nodded, but she wasn't really paying attention. She leaned into Matt and whispered, 'I'm going to go out and see the parade. I've got my phone. I can meet you back here in an hour or so, leave you to it?'

Matt looked unsure, then relented. 'Go on so if you're sure! See you later.'

Marissa left the bar and as she walked away from it she felt immediately better. The crowds outside were just as thick as they were inside, but it felt better to be under the sky with the wind on her cheeks and the sun on her face. She found a spot on the main parade route and pushed her way thorough so she could see.

Ah, there's the whale! I've not missed it! It moved gracefully along on wheels borrowed from a tractor, it's tail moving up and down, and an occasional spout of water jetted out hydraulically from its blowhole. The theme for this year's parade was environmentalism; behind the whale was a large orange octopus with a person inside working the many tentacled arms, and beside it, were children dressed up as glittery fish. They were dancing and singing, and cheering with the crowd. Marissa's heart lifted to see them.

After the fish came a drumming band from Texas in tight-knit formation and perfectly synchronised. Marissa's breathing changed as she heard, threaded in between the music, thrumming below the shouting, the heartbeat of the world. She tuned into it, all her senses rushing in, feeling the power emanating from the music. It ran beneath everything, it was the fabric upon which everything was built. All the people in the crowd, in the parade, became actors. Perhaps even she herself was just an actor. The music was the heartbeat, the stage was the world, upon which the actors stood to reveal their many stories.

Everything glistened, the colours were vibrant, Marissa's heart sang. She felt she had come into focus. Something that had been missing had been found, everything was back in its right place once more. Then the song was over, the beat was lost, the spectacle was just a parade once again. Anxiety filled her body, heart flattened, elation dissolving, Marissa stayed until the last float went past to find the feeling again and she didn't notice the time.

'Pass the peas please,' said Eli, taking a second helping of mashed potatoes.

Carol looked tired. She was showing now, six months in and three to go. She smiled at Marissa who was sitting opposite her, and mouthed the words, 'I like him,' referring of course to Matt, who was deep in conversation with Marissa's father at the other end of the table, discussing whether it was worth getting a new timing belt for his old car.

'It does depend if you want to keep her,' he said, following Eli's lead and taking another helping of mash.

'Well, Dad, are you not going to upgrade and get a Merc like mine?' Eli said almost accusingly. 'You've got the money now – why not ride in style?'

'Well, there are benefits to having an older car, isn't that right, Matt?' said Bernie, sounding remarkably upbeat.

'Oh yes, sir,' said Matt, with a gleam in his eye.

Bernie laughed. '"Bernie" is fine, no need for the "sir".'

Marissa felt as if she was watching a movie. This couldn't be real. How easily Matt had slipped in with everyone else. How nice it was, in a strange sort of way. *Sarah was right, I had assumed what would happen, and I got it totally wrong.*

'This food is delicious,' said Matt, putting together another heaped forkful.

Rose smiled at him, then removed the empty serving dishes to make more room on the table and picked up the gravy boat to refill it in the kitchen. She stopped to whisper into her daughter's ear, 'I like this one, Marissa, can we keep him?'

Eli looked astonished, and with wide eyes he mouthed to Marissa, 'What's gotten into Mum?'

Marissa shrugged.

'Things suddenly got a hell of a lot easier around here,' said Eli, a little more loudly than he meant to.

'Why?' said Bernie, pulling away from Matt, 'What did I miss?'

'Oh, Carol has another scan next week,' said Eli, deftly changing the subject. 'We were thinking of getting one of those 3D scans. What do you think, Dad? It's a little more expensive, but you can see the baby's face, and it's more accurate to see the sex of the baby.'

'Oh, you mean you don't know already?' said Rose, coming back with more gravy.

As soon as she put it down on the table, Matt picked it up. Rose smiled at him with approval.

'He likes his food, this one,' she said to Marissa as she sat back down. Marissa smiled in acknowledgement.

'A friend of Noreen's daughter had one of those 3D scans,' said Rose, sitting back down at the table again.

'Did she think it was worth it?' asked Eli.

'Well, she was very happy that they got to see the baby's face, and they had something they could frame in advance of the birth. I don't know if it looked anything like the baby actually looked liked when it was born. They change so quickly.'

'It still might be fun to do, though,' said Eli, hopefully, looking at Carol's reaction.

'You know I wasn't keen to find out the sex, but at this stage, I do feel it's a girl. It might be nice to confirm it before she's born. As far as the 3D thing, it seems a little extravagant for what it is.'

Eli and Matt cleared the table. Marissa wasn't allowed to get up. 'We call her "She who must be waited on hand and foot"' said Eli a little too loudly to Matt. 'Has she told you that yet?'

Matt laughed. 'I kind of figured it out for myself.'

Marissa blushed bright red and Carol playfully slapped Eli. 'Hey, give her a break,' she said.

'I love her, really I do,' said Eli with a laugh and a wink. 'Even though she's a pain in the ass.'

'Thank you very much, dear brother,' said Marissa with a grin.

'Happy birthday, sis,' said Eli, smiling. 'Can we do the presents now?' He walked over to his coat and pulled out a small blue parcel with a pink ribbon and brought it over and put it on the table in front of her.

'I hope you like it. It's from me and Carol.' Carol smiled. 'But I chose it,' Eli added.

'That he did,' agreed Carol.

'Oh, that's a good idea,' said Rose. 'I'll get our present too – just a moment.'

Bernie disappeared into the kitchen with her.

'Can I unwrap it?' Marissa asked Eli.

'Of course you can, silly! What are you waiting for?' he replied.

Marissa ripped open the paper to find a small jewellery box and a folded piece of card. She opened up the box and there was a silver broach shaped like angel with a small green stone inlaid inside it. The card was a book token for €100.

'Jeez, Eli, you shouldn't have,' she said, taking the angel out of the box and holding it up to the light. The green stone glimmered and lit up as if it was alive.

'I didn't want to pick a book for you, I knew I'd get it wrong.'

'Thank you so much. I love it!' She pinned the broach onto her cardigan and folded the token into her pocket.

'Hey, it's from Carol *and* me, and from the baby.' Eli patted Carol's bump, 'We want you to be godmother, by the way...'

'Godmother? Really? Wow, thank you.' She was beaming.

Rose and Bernie came out from the kitchen with a chocolate cake with candles on it, singing, 'Happy Birthday to you.'

Eli and Carol and Matt joined in, 'Happy Birthday, dear Marissa...'

They placed the cake in front of her. 'Happy Birthday to you.'

'Now blow out the candles, dear, and make a wish,' said Rose.

Marissa thought for a moment. *Everything seems so perfect right now.* She looked at everyone looking back at her. *I really want to be happy and free, feel that I have a purpose, know who I am, and be that person. Yes, I want to be completely myself, without being afraid anymore.*

She blew out the candles, and everyone clapped. Somewhere in the background a champagne cork popped and Bernie made a cheering noise.

'Let's have a toast – to our daughter!' said Bernie, pouring sparkling liquid into crystal glasses.

'Those are new, Dad,' said Marissa, thinking back to the tumblers they'd used the last time they drank a toast.

Bernie smiled. 'About time we had some fancy stuff in the house. Happy birthday, love.'

They all clinked glasses and drank.

'Oh yes, and your present from us,' said Rose, handing Marissa an envelope and a small wrapped box.

'Thank you! Which one should I open first?'

'You choose dear!' said Rose.

The box revealed a beautiful tea set for one, with an elegant ceramic teapot covered in pink flowers, and a matching mug.

'I didn't know you had a boyfriend, I would have got the set for two!' said Rose, slightly embarrassed.

'I love it!' said Marissa, 'it's perfect for me.'

Inside the envelope was a voucher for Arnotts for €250.

'To spend on clothes. You said you wanted to get some new ones,' said Rose. 'Of course Arnotts has everything, so you don't *have* to get clothes if there's something else you'd like better.'

'Thanks Mum,' said Marissa, getting up and hugging her parents. 'And Dad!' Bernie hugged her back a moment longer than she expected him to.

'Any ice cream?' asked Eli, 'I'm ready for dessert now!'

'Oooh, ice cream sounds delish,' said Carol, eyeing the chocolate cake.

'Hey, next time we celebrate together, it will be for the birth of the baby,' said Marissa, trying to deflect their attention onto something else.

'Oh yes! June, here we come!'

'Have you all got everything you need?' asked Rose, as she cut the cake and portioned it out, adding a spoonful of ice cream to each dish before handing it out. 'Bernie dear, could you put the kettle on for coffee?'

Marissa looked at Matt. He was chatting with her dad. She liked that. He seemed quite comfortable in the company of her family. It felt good and easy.

I could get used to this.

'I like them,' said Matt as they left Rose and Bernie's house. They were heading back into town to get the DART to Matt's place and thought they'd walk off their St Patrick Day pints and food. Marissa touched the angel broach on her cardigan and linked arms with Matt. They had an hour, plenty of time to get there. She'd pick up the tea set next time she visited.

'They seemed to like you too,' she said, 'which is a totally new thing for me to get my head around.'

'So it would seem,' said Matt thoughtfully. 'Your brother is just like you, you know. It will take me a little while to get to know him, I think.'

'You don't need to make friends with him or anything,' said Marissa, then added defensively. 'What do you mean, he's like me?'

Matt laughed. 'Well, he's funny and clever and a little abrasive at times.'

'Abrasive? *Moi?*'

'He was very generous with his present,' Matt added. 'And the champagne, do they do that every year? It was nice. You did well, your family must have lots of money.'

'Not really - my uncle came into some money with his business and just he paid off my parent's house for them, the champagne is a new thing. It's wonderful actually, to see them so happy. Debt has been a terrible noose around Dad's neck.'

'Yes, it can be that, I always thought that's why they called it a mort-gage, even the word sounds like a noose around your neck. That's fantastic though, about your uncle, your mother's brother?'

'Fathers. They didn't get on for many years, but all seems to be forgiven now.'

Matt laughed. 'Money can do that, it's a powerful thing.'

They walked a little bit in silence. *Glad I told him about the money, well, half told him...*

'I love my angel broach. Eli, isn't usually that thoughtful,' said Marissa. 'But I know why he did it – as a thank-you gift, for helping smooth things over between them and my parents. It's nice to see everyone getting along so well. I think we got a little hyper, the pair of us, when we realised that Mum and Dad actually genuinely liked you.'

Matt shrugged his shoulders and smiled. 'Well, what's not to like?'

Marissa smiled and faced him, then put both of her arms around him and held him tightly, burying her face in his soft coat. It smelled like cigarettes from the bar earlier that day. He put his arms around her in return and squeezed her back. No pressure to do anything more, no rushing to go someplace, they just stood there together and it felt nice, the sense of closeness, how they fit together.

'So are we officially a couple now?' asked Marissa, hesitantly.

'I didn't know that was a thing,' said Matt. 'What's the difference between being official and not?'

'I don't know,' said Marissa, pulling away a little. 'I guess I could change my Facebook status?'

'Well if nothing else is going to change, then that's okay with me.

CHAPTER TWENTY

'Breakfast in bed? Matt! How wonderful!'

Marissa could smell the buttered toast and fresh (instant) coffee. She sat up and Matt placed the tray gently on her lap.

'A rose! For me!' She sat up and plumped the pillows behind her.

Matt blushed. 'Well, it is your birthday weekend, and I want to spoil you today. Especially as we are now official and all. Look, I made boiled eggs!'

'Are you joining me?' said Marissa happily as she organised herself to tuck into it. She enthusiastically tapped the boiled egg with the side of her fork.

'Erm, it seems a little weird to get back into bed now... I'll bring my tea in and sit on the chair here. Hang on...'

He came back and settled into the chair.

'Are you busy this evening?' asked Marissa, enjoying her eggs.

'Can't get enough of me, eh,' smiled Matt.

Marissa giggled. 'Well, actually, I was going to ask you if you'd come with me to check out a room around the corner from my flat, I could rent it to offer Reiki. It's been on my mind to do this since you brought it up and I saw it advertised on the internet. And this room, it looks like it could be good, I think there is a viewing tonight.'

Matt's face brightened, 'That's brilliant! Yes, I'd love to go with you. Tell me more!'

'It's down the road from the shops, one of those Edwardian houses, refurbished. I think they're having a viewing this evening, I'll have to double check.'

'I'm delighted you're going to take a room, but a viewing on a Bank holiday, that's unusual, you should check first.'

Marissa smiled. 'I do want you to see it with me. I will feel better about it if I know you think it's good. I feel I can't decide anything by myself these days! Hang on, you're right about that, I'll check on my phone now, so we can plan the day around it.' She looked it up.

'Yes, they're showing the room tonight, Matt! I've got to see it now, especially after telling you about it. I have a good feeling around it, I don't want someone else to take it.'

'Tonight, okay. But maybe you should phone and check. It's unusual to do that on a Bank Holiday, maybe the date is wrong on the notice.'

Marissa took a breath and called, and arranged to see the room that evening at 6pm. On hanging up the phone, she realised Matt was looking at her, eyes wide and smiling.

'You're really going to do this! Amazing! I'm delighted for you. I'll drive us.'

Marissa instantly relaxed and smiled. 'Yes please!'

'Now. Take your time finishing your eggs, and I'll get showered and dressed. Let's go for a walk on the pier. I want to buy you your birthday present.'

It feels like a second birthday. I could so get used to this!

They had had a lovely day together and Marissa didn't want the day to end, she felt so comfortable around Matt. When he wasn't there she was beginning to feel like she had an empty space in her heart. She was happy they could extend their time together. Matt decided to park the car near the property to see what parking would be like 'for your future clients'. She got out of the car, touching her new rose quartz earrings again, delighted with them.

'Lot's of parking here, that's good' said Matt with approval.

The room was in a tall Edwardian building in Ranelagh which had been partially renovated. The front gates had been painted blue, and a winding path through the garden lead to steep stone stairs and a bright blue door. They were welcomed by the agent and brought inside. The ceilings were tall and the hallway had also been given a fresh coat of paint. There were three therapy rooms on the first floor and four on the second. The third and fourth floors had been converted into flats.

The room Marissa was seeing was on the first floor at the back of the building. At first glance it was a little musty and dark, but once inside it seemed to be hospitable enough. There was a small window at the back of the room that let in a little bit of light. Two medium-sized armchairs took up most of the space, however the room would be big enough to have an open plinth in it too, if the chairs were moved up against the wall.

The agent for the landlord talked the through the details of what was needed and gave Marissa and Matt a few moments alone in the room so they could get the feel of it.

Matt ran his finger up the skirting board around the door and looked up at the main light, which was two fluorescent tubes surrounded by a plastic cover in the centre of the ceiling. The light was almost blue and too bright for a therapy room. The walls, painted magnolia, had slight dampness seeping into the corners, and the green carpet was cheap and had a bleach stain on it. The window was old, hadn't been washed in months, possibly years, and had white iron bars blocking the light coming in. Marissa walked over to see if she could open it, but it was painted shut. She rocked back and forth on her heels and said, 'I don't love it.'

'Hang on,' said Matt, turning the light off. He went to the table beside the counselling chairs and turned on the smaller desk lamp.

'There, that's a bit better, isn't it? Look, I've been in worse. You won't be using the main light anyway, it's totally unsuitable. Get a lamp, a few scented candles, and it will be much better.'

Marissa walked around the room, beginning to imagine what she could do with it, rather than seeing what was wrong with it.

'You could get a wall hanging, burn some incense and play your music. It wouldn't be awful then – in fact, it could be really great. There's a heater, so you won't need to get one. And, it's a good price. You can rent it by the hour, she doesn't mind you leaving your things under the stairs – it's a really good space for you to start in.'

Marissa looked at him. He smiled at her and her heart swelled.

'Yes, I suppose you're right. It won't be forever, it's just my first space. I could add a few things here and there and make it my own. I've not rented a space before – I suppose I'm a little hesitant for many reasons.'

'It's not a big commitment really,' said Matt. 'She only wants a month up front and someone to take it for three months, then it's month to month, so if it doesn't work out – which it will, because I know you, Marissa, you'll make it work.' He cocked his head on one side and winked. 'And look, this room is bigger than even I expected, so you could even see counselling clients on the armchairs when you're ready to do that.' He walked around once more, 'It's in a good area, and close enough to your flat, so I won't be worried about you walking home after dark. Look, let's check out the bathroom, then we can grab something to eat and you can have a proper think about it. But I wouldn't wait too long – it's a good place for you to start up your practice and you're ready to do it now, so it's good timing.'

They stepped out of the room into the corridor. The agent for the landlord was standing there, suited and booted and waiting for them with a hopeful smile on her face.

'Can we see the bathroom?' asked Marissa, touching her new earrings.

'Yes, of course,' said the agent. 'It's just in here.' She opened a door under the main stairway. The toilet was clean and the light was friendlier than the one in the room. There was a small mirror, a washbasin, and a picture was hanging on the wall that said: 'Dreams don't work unless you do.' *Is that a Scott Taylor quote?* Marissa instantly felt more at ease.

The agent said, 'There's a communal vacuum cleaner and tidying things in here.' She leaned past the bathroom door and pressed a wall unit, which opened with a click. Marissa saw there were two vacuum cleaners and space big enough to store a plinth.

'We service the bathroom once a week, but you would need to check it yourself just to be sure, as there are a lot of people working here. We can't guarantee cleanliness based on that, but we have all the cleaning products here if you need them.'

Marissa nodded. Matt looked very enthusiastic.

The agent walked them to the main door.

'And I can burn candles in the room?'

'Yes, as long as they're not unattended.'

'So when do you need to know?' asked Marissa.

The agent looked at her watch, then back at Marissa. 'I have two other people lined up to see the room tonight, and there are two people already booked in. We have Monday, Tuesday and Friday evenings available at the moment, Wednesday and Thursday are already booked. If you book it now, you have more choice over what day you want.'

Marissa looked at Matt once more. He was nodding encouragingly.

'Okay,' Marissa said, reaching into her handbag and pulling out her wallet. She had taken some money out of an ATM earlier, just in case. 'I only really have Mondays available, so I've got to take the Monday slot. Can I give you the deposit now?'

She was shaking, unsure if it was because she was making a big mistake or if it was with excitement.

'Great!' said the agent. 'Let's sign the contracts now, and we can meet during the week and I will give you the keys and go through the alarm codes then.'

'I really did it!' said Marissa, after the waitress had taken their order. It came out as a squeal more than a statement. She blushed and looked down at the table. They were in a nearby bistro; dinner out together felt like a lovely way to end a special weekend and mark the beginning of a new chapter for Marissa.

'I can see you're excited,' said Matt with a smile, pouring water into both of their glasses. 'I think it's a really good move for you. It will open things up for you, especially with those counselling chairs. You can see clients and rack up your experience hours.'

Marissa cocked her head on one side and figured it out. 'I can't charge money for psychotherapy yet, but I could do in six months time when I get my diploma. I wonder if I can see clients for free in the room, just to get my hours up?'

Matt ripped open some bread and helped himself to a generous amount of butter. 'That sounds great' he asked, then bit into it. 'Mmm, fresh bread. I'm starving!'

'You're always hungry, Matt!' exclaimed Marissa. She laughed. She was beginning to feel relief trickling through her body. *Yes, I do need to do this, and it's only a three-month rolling commitment, so if it doesn't work out, it isn't the end of the world.* 'I suppose I would need a supervisor if I was going to see clients there, though. I wonder if the college would help me figure it out. I'll ask them. That would really open it up for me.'

The waitress came back with their soup and Matt's pint. Marissa grinned as she watched him hesitate for a moment, unsure what to put into his mouth next – the soup, more bread, or more of his pint. She relaxed back into her chair and looked down at her bowl of tomato and basil soup with a swirl of cream and a touch of parsley on top. She felt her feet on the ground, she felt present in the moment. She wanted to remember this, as it was the beginning of something new. She felt independent and strong in her commitment to being a therapist. She looked at Matt, who had a Guinness moustache, and laughed again.

'What?' he asked

'I love you,' she said, then blushed and looked down. *That kind of slipped out. Was it okay?* She looked up again. Matt was beaming at her.

'I love you, too,' he said, keeping his eyes on her.

Marissa almost fell through the floor. She caught her breath and was back.

He picked up his Guinness, she shakily picked up her Diet Coke, and they clinked glasses. 'To the next stage of your career and to us, being official and all,' he said, with a cheeky grin.

Marissa's heart flipped. She clinked glasses again, it certainly felt as though they'd reached a milestone.

'We can go shopping together next weekend for things for your room, if you want,' Matt said. 'I'll drive, so you can pack everything into my car, it will be handier for you. You'll need a proper bag to put everything into though, so you can carry it all to your sessions. And a suitcase with a lock that you can keep in that room under the stairs. It's going to be so great!'

Marissa laughed. 'You're really making this so easy for me. I don't have to think about anything myself.' She took some bread and dipped it into her soup. 'Maybe I can get a suitcase off Dad....' She placed the dripping bread into her mouth and ate it. 'Oh! I'll need a plinth – where do I get one of those?'

Matt looked thoughtful. 'Actually, Padraig at work, his girlfriend is an aromatherapist, she must have one. I can find out for you.'

'That's great, yes please.'

'I'm happy to help you where I can, but you'll have to do the work with the clients yourself,' said Matt with a wink. 'You're well able for that, though. I want to help you get started – I'm really excited for you. I guess in a way I'm a bit jealous.'

'Ha, ha, why? You're not going to give up the day job?'

'No, not at all,' said Matt, mopping up the last of his soup with another piece of bread. 'I like the garage, the lads are gas craic. I suppose it's seeing you taking the leap that I'm a little jealous of. I've not done that yet. I've thought about it, but I'm still not ready.'

He put his spoon on the side plate and drained the last of his pint. The waitress immediately whisked both of their plates away.

'There's no rush,' Marissa said. 'You're on a different track to me, I guess. You're doing it for love and I'm doing it for a career.'

'I don't know about that. I just think you're braver than I am. I reckon it's more of a vocation than a job,' said Matt thoughtfully, 'and I like my job security. I've not got family to help me out like you do.'

The waitress brought cake.

'Soup and cake is becoming my favourite meal,' said Matt, his eyes widening with pleasure at the sight of his chocolate torte.

'It was a great idea of yours. You have lots of great ideas,' said Marissa softly, trying to feel in her heart what it might be like not to have a supportive family, to be alone in the world, completely dependent on yourself. *No wonder he noticed how generous everyone was at my birthday dinner. I guess I'm used to it. My family drive me crazy, but they are always there for me if I need them. Emotionally as well as financially.*

She reached across the table and took Matt's hand, looking up at him. She really wanted him to feel that she could support him, now.

'Thanks for today, having you see that room really boosted my confidence. I want to be able to help you, too. You always seem to be helping me out, one way or another.'

As she spoke, she remembered there was something big that he had helped her with, but she wasn't sure when it was or what it was. It was a thing, but it was gone now. She put it out of her mind.

'Hey, it's my pleasure.' Matt was looking directly at her. The honesty in his face gave him a fragility and a vulnerability that Marissa was beginning to appreciate. 'It's scary going out on your own. You're not on your own, though – you've got your family, and you've got me now, too.'

'And you've got me now, too,' Marissa whispered.

They both stayed silent for a moment, then Marissa smiled, and to break the tension, with her other hand she helped herself to a forkful of her own chocolate cake and offered it to Matt, who let her put it into his mouth.

He swallowed it and smiled at her. 'Chocolate cake is the best!'

'Yes, it certainly is,' she agreed.

Later that night back at Marissa's flat, Matt was snoring softly as the streetlight poured through the window, making patterns across the bed. His alarm was set for the crack of dawn so he could tear across town and be in time for work. They had spent nearly two whole days together.

Marissa looked at his face as he slept, this man who was putting his trust in her, who was helping her so openly and generously. This man who knew things that she didn't. He really complemented her. She wanted to remember this moment so she could daydream about it later. She touched her new earrings again. Rose quartz. *Rose for love and compassion, that's what Mairead said.* She lay back and drifted into a dream.

She was pushing a shopping trolley, filling it with pillows and blankets. Each one was nicer than the last. She put a beautiful bright turquoise sparkly blanket into the trolley. It was comforting and vast, and reminded her of the sea. As she put it in, it seemed to grow bigger and bigger. It took a long time to stuff it in, but she managed it.

Then she saw a beautiful red blanket, red like the sands of the desert. She wanted that one too, and pulled it down from the shelf, but like the blue blanket, it grew bigger, expanding quickly until it became almost too large for her to keep hold of. She struggled with it, but somehow managed to stuff it into the trolley on top of the blue one.

Then she saw a navy blue blanket with stars. It was immense, like the sky. She had to have that one too. She pulled it down from the shelf, but the trolley was already overflowing.

And then there was a green blanket, the colour of a meadow. She was getting upset now as she needed that blanket too, and the candles she'd just seen, and there was a statue of a Buddha... Yes, she needed that too.

She noticed that the trolley was changing shape – it was getting bigger. She was able to put in the blankets and the candles, then she added the statue, and then she saw a wall hanging. It was the most beautiful thing she'd ever seen and she knew that it would be so healing to have it in her room that she needed to have that as well.

The trolley was harder to push now; it was made of stone, heavy and ancient, like a Roman cart. The wheels were sticking, and the more she put into the cart, the bigger it got and the smaller she became. She was shrinking, and the cart was getting bigger and bigger and heavier and heavier, but there were still more things to buy, more things that she needed.

There was a sense of urgency within her now – she couldn't leave without all that she needed, but she couldn't move forwards or backwards, so what was she going to do? She was overwhelmed and wanted to cry.

Suddenly the wheels of the cart came unstuck and then it was spinning, spinning as if it was on ice. She was losing control and she couldn't hold on. Panicking, she had to let go and the trolley spun away and the floor opened up underneath her and she was falling, falling through a crack in the world.

She cried out, 'Help! Help me!'

Then she felt a strong presence. Big strong hands were catching her and holding her tightly. She felt safe.

'Bear?' she asked, convinced it was her old friend.

She turned to see his face, and it was Matt.

CHAPTER TWENTY ONE 

Matt left early as planned. Marissa was already awake, and when he said, 'Bye,' and closed the door behind him, she felt bereft. She took her time getting up but she was too early for work so she walked in. She still had the keys from when she was manager, but Sarah was already there, working in her new office. Marissa could see her behind the glass. She had a sleek bob now and she was wearing a very business-like dark blue trouser suit. Flirty Sarah had gone and Manager Sarah had arrived. *It's a new chapter for both of us.*

All morning Marissa felt strangely empty. She couldn't shift the feeling of loss. She wouldn't see Matt until Friday. *I need to snap out of it. I used to get through the week just fine on my own. A natter and a giggle with Sarah might help. And I do want to tell her about the therapy room.*

She sent Sarah an email with 'Coffee?' in the subject line and nothing else, as they used to do. But the immediate response did not come. *I guess she's busier now she's a manager.*

Twenty minutes later the reply came. Sarah had written in the body of the email, which was new:

> *Lunch? I've got a meeting at 11. I'm assuming you want it friend to friend not manager to assistant? Usual place?*

Marissa replied: Yes' and 'Yes, please.' She sighed, overcome by loss again. *Sarah isn't as available as she used to be. Ah well. All things change with time, and it was the right thing for her, and for me too. I'm happy for her.*

At lunchtime they set off together. Sarah's suit set off her blue eyes, and her short bob really suited her face. She was wearing red lipstick, and something about her demeanour had changed too. She walked briskly and Marissa had trouble keeping up with her.

'Hey! Slow down, what's the rush?'

'Oh sorry, I'm still in managerial mode! Give me a minute or two!' Sarah smiled and abruptly slowed down

'You look amazing, by the way,' said Marissa, feeling very frumpy altogether.

'Thank you!'

They went in, got a table and ordered. Sarah started to relax, but she kept looking at her new watch and patting her hair, as if she was reminding herself of her new position.

She leaned in and whispered, 'It feels so strange to have short hair! But managers must be taken seriously, so I needed more serious hair. It was time for a change anyway.' She patted the back of her bob again and flicked her head.

Marissa kind of missed the ponytail, but overall the look really did suit Sarah. 'Well, it looks fab, and you do look very managerial, Ms Boss Lady!'

'Ha, ha, not quite the boss – not yet anyway!' Sarah smiled, pushed her shoulders back and added three sugars to her cappuccino.

'So how is your wild love life?' asked Marissa, wanting to get in there first.

'What a weekend! I cut off my hair, bought the suit and then I dumped them – all three of them! One after the other!' Sarah stirred her drink. 'It was fun, maybe like practising firing someone! Ha, ha! But yeah, I couldn't do it anymore. And they were so annoying. It wasn't that I couldn't juggle them, it was that, well, they weren't worth the effort. It was exciting to have three men on the go, but it was getting distracting. I forgot who knew about who, and who knew about what. I was getting mixed up. And I need to focus on my work now that I'm going to be studying again. It's the best decision.'

'You dumped *all three*?' said Marissa, trying to keep the laughter inside her. 'You didn't even want to keep just one of them?'

'I had thought about it, sure,' Sarah said, 'but when I realised I couldn't choose, I realised that all of them, in their own way, on their own, were so boring!'

'Ha, ha, brilliant!' said Marissa, letting her laughter spill out.

Sarah smiled, then laughed too. She was always a good sport, able to see the lighter side of her behaviour.

'I think you deserve better than boring – you definitely deserve better than boring,' said Marissa.

'I don't know what's gotten into me at all,' Sarah said, sitting back in her chair and crossing her legs. 'I suppose it's time for a new chapter. If I don't get practical and real now, when will I ever do it? I'm "creating the building blocks for the future". I saw that on YouTube somewhere. It sounded good. Anyway, enough about me – what's new with you? How was your birthday with Matt? Ooh, and the dinner with your family? How did that go?'

'It actually went well. I was very surprised. They liked him!'

Sarah shrugged her shoulders and looked puzzled. 'Why wouldn't they?'

'Well, of course they would like him. I mean, he *is* likeable, but ... I didn't think it would be so ... well ... *relaxed* with him there. He seemed to fit right in. Mum even texted me afterwards to tell me not to lose this one...' Marissa's tone changed and her eyes went to heaven. 'As if that's something that I can control. I can't even...' Marissa touched her earrings.

'Ah, that's great, though. It's important. I'm so glad it went well. And Eli, was he...?'

'Yeah, he and Dad were chatting away to Matt like they had known each other for years. It seemed so normal – Matt, Carol, Mum, Dad, like they'd all grown up or something. I had a moment when I thought I was in the wrong house.'

Sarah, still smiling, asked. 'Did Matt give you the earrings? They're beautiful!'

Marissa smiled, 'Yes, he spoilt me. It was like I had my birthday two days in a row. St Patrick's Day always gets in the way, the parade and all, but I had him all to myself yesterday and I felt really special. He brought me breakfast in bed, we went to the pier, got ice cream, and he came with me to see a therapy room. Hey, that's my big news – I've hired a therapy room! I'm going to see clients there from next week.'

'Wow, you hired a therapy room?' Sarah looked impressed.

'Yes, I'm going to start offering Reiki sessions on Monday nights, starting next week.'

'That's fantastic! I might like to try one myself.' Sarah looked at Marissa for a moment. 'You're moving forward with your dreams. I admire that. You have a great work ethic.'

'You're moving forward too.'

'But we can still party, yes?'

'Damn right,' said Marissa with a smile.

Sarah smiled back. 'I mean it, I want to try Reiki with you. It sounds interesting, from what I read on the internet...'

'You looked it up? Really? Who are you again?'

They both laughed.

'Yes, I looked it up. I do care about you, you know. I wanted to know what it was because you were doing it and it seemed important to you. And I would actually like to try it. It sounds as though it would be good for all the stress from being a manager! And I'll pay you for it. You need to pay for the room rental, don't you? Let me pay you.'

It felt strange to Marissa to take money from her friend, but she remembered Dolores saying to in class that an energy exchange was important, even if it was just a cup of coffee. So, after a moment she replied, 'Okay, you can pay me by writing a review for me when I get my web page set up. And a coffee now!'

'It's a deal,' said Sarah, and they shook hands across the table. 'So when can you see me?'

'Oh, I guess I need to start an appointment book! I don't have anyone booked in yet, though, and I still have things to buy, and I don't have a plinth yet, I'm getting one this weekend. So I need some time, but you could come next week as long as you don't expect the room to be perfect just yet.'

'Hey, it's only me.'

'Okay then. You can be my first client – oh wait, second client. Matt wanted to be the first.'

Sarah smiled. She had never seen Marissa so disorganised. It was usually the other way around. 'I can meet Matt if I come early enough then?'

Marissa smiled. 'Yes, of course you can meet Matt – but it will only be quick, so we should arrange an evening out so you can meet him properly.'

'But I've nobody to bring...' Sarah frowned, then shook her head. 'But that's okay. Maybe I need some space without a boyfriend for a while.'

'Wow, you're really serious? But I could ask Matt if he has any single friends...'

'Would you?' said Sarah with a glint in her eye.

They both cracked up laughing.

That evening there was tension in Marissa's college group and it took her attention away from her still-heavy heart. Mr Crowley had given them the brief for their final written assignment and the dates for their final live assessment.

'In fairness, there is a lot of scope in those questions, and we have a month to complete the assignment,' said Emmet at tea break.

They all had the print-out in their hands. There were seven essay titles to choose from.

'But it's five thousand words!' exclaimed Katie. 'I've never written that much, not even for school!'

Marissa couldn't focus on the titles. She folded the paper to read later and put it into her bag. Turning to Katie she said, 'But this is college – I know you can do it, I've got every confidence in you.'

Katie shrugged her shoulders, but seemed to have calmed down a little. 'I had so much trouble with the last assignment, and that was three thousand words...'

'You're so close to the finish line,' said Yvonne reassuringly. 'We'll all help each other get through it. Right, guys?'

'Right,' said Emmet distractedly, looking at his print-out.

'Did you even hear what I said?' asked Yvonne, addressing Emmet directly.

'Yes, yes, we will all help each other,' he said, frustrated. He put his print-out into his blazer pocket, looked at Katie and sighed. 'I know you've got this. I heard you arguing ethics with Jessica from the other group, and ethics is one of the options. You'd be great with that one.'

Marissa leaned into Yvonne and looked at her list. After being at college, where it was a lot more prescriptive, she felt this was a walk up a hill instead of a hike up a mountain, but she wasn't clear as to which one she would do just yet. 'Yes, we will all help each other, if need be,' she said, raising her eyebrows at Emmet and smiling at Katie. 'I know thinking about doing something like this can be worse than actually doing it.'

'And we can form a study group,' said Yvonne. 'If you want to, that is.'

'Yes, please,' said Katie, looking a little more hopeful.

'I don't know if I have time for a study group actually,' said Marissa softly. 'I just hired a room and will be offering Reiki sessions on Monday nights. So with Cabra and St Mary's as well as class, I'm pretty much booked up every evening.'

'Wow, well done!' said Emmet enthusiastically, grabbing a couple of biscuits from the plate on the table. 'That's great! Go, you!'

'Do any of you know if we can charge to see counselling clients yet?' Marissa asked.

'Hello, all, we're on the home straight at last,' said Ronan with a grin, coming over to join them. Emmet shoved up closer towards Yvonne and made space at the table. Ronan pulled a chair over from the table beside them and wedged himself in between Emmet and Marissa. His tea sloshed in his cup as he put it on the table.

'Yes and no,' said Yvonne, answering Marissa. 'We can see private clients, yes, but we can't charge until we get the diploma. They need to know that we are counsellors in training, *and* we need to have insurance to do it. Which is why it's better to do it connected to an institute like St Mary's, as the insurance is arranged through them. So it can be messy. But I see why you're asking – we need one hundred and fifty client hours to get the diploma, and that is a lot of hours. You also need a supervisor for the private hours.'

Marissa's heart sank. 'I knew that,' she said, 'but I keep forgetting. I don't know why it won't stick in my brain – it's as if there's some sort of vortex there and things get sucked into it.'

'Ha, ha,' said Ronan, 'the brain vortex.'

'But I'm the same!' exclaimed Katie. 'I don't understand why, but there are some things that just don't stick with me either, no matter how many times I try to commit them to memory. I think that's why I'm so disconcerted by this assignment.'

'Are you insured for the Reiki sessions?' asked Yvonne quietly.

'Oh no! I don't know! I don't think so,' said Marissa, flushing and making a mental note to look into it.

'So how many client hours have you all done then?' Katie asked the group.

'Jeez, let's not have that conversation now,' said Yvonne. 'We just got our assignment, that's depressing enough.'

'And nobody is worried about the final assessment, are they?' asked Emmet with a glint in his eye and a bright smile.

They all glared at him.

'Well, if looks could kill,' he said, laughing and helped himself to another biscuit.

She was in a forest, moss under her feet, wheeling a normal-sized shopping trolley. Blankets were hanging off the limbs of moss-covered trees and she saw the sky blanket there, waving in the wind. But there was no wind. Was it saying hello to her? She knew it was for her so she went over to it and took it down from the tree. She put it into the trolley, which seemed to be behaving itself better this time. Then she wheeled the trolley further up the path.

There was another blanket there, the red desert blanket. She stopped again and went to take it down from the tree, but she had a strange feeling that something was out of place. It didn't feel good, the blanket. It was as if it didn't want her to touch it. She let go of it, and the trolley, and continued down the path, leaving everything behind.

As she continued to walk, the blankets shrank away, getting smaller and smaller until the trees were just trees again. That felt somewhat better. Gradually, however, instead of leaves and smaller branches, pages and books appeared, looking as if they were growing on the trees. They had writing on them, writing she couldn't read, and pictures and symbols on them that she couldn't see clearly.

The ground became wet and muddy, puddles appeared, and the texture of the scene changed. As she walked, she felt more and more uncomfortable and the trees became pointy and scary, as if the forest was looming in over her, ominous and maleficent. It didn't feel like her dreams usually felt. The sense of familiarity was gone. Maybe this wasn't her dream at all?

She looked at her feet to check her shoes, but she was barefoot, and her feet were covered in mud. This certainly wasn't right, and it was getting darker.

She heard a noise and jumped.

'Bear?' she asked, wanting him to come, but nobody came. 'Not my forest, no shoes, no bear... And where are my shoes? Where is my lake? Where is my serpent? Where are my guides?'

Suddenly, huge grief hit her in the stomach, smashing into her like an ocean and knocking her over. She sank to her knees in the soft mud and started to cry, to wail. She couldn't hold it back, it was too strong, this ocean of tears, sadness and pain. Sobbing overwhelmed her body from her stomach to her throat. Her body couldn't hold it in. She lay on the ground in foetal position crying, crying as if someone had died, as if she was dying... Then, out of the ground around her body grew tendrils, they looked like the roots of trees, but no, they were flatter, like leather thongs. They wound around her shivering grieving body like snakes and started pulling, wrapping around her pulling tighter and tighter, she stopped crying... She couldn't breathe...

Marissa woke up gasping for air. She heard a moan, but didn't know if it was from the dream or whether she had actually moaned... Her face was wet with tears and there were big wet patches on her pillow. She caught herself moaning out loud – yes, it was her, she was crying for real, and trying to catch her breath at the same time. She was disoriented, something wasn't right... She couldn't remember where she was, what was wrong... She needed to get her bearings, she was on the verge of panicking.

At that moment, Tobermory jumped onto the bed and started purring. He walked onto Marissa's body and sat on her legs. That helped. A lot. The weight of the cat helped her anchor herself back into her body and back into her bedroom.

She focused and looked at her clock. It was 4am.

'I'm okay, Tobes, it was just a dream,' she said out loud, trying to reassure herself. But somewhere a part of her was still screaming out in grief. *Something's wrong... I feel so wiped out, emotionally exhausted. I feel bereft – is it because Matt's not here? No, that's not it. I don't know what it is. This is so hard. What the hell is wrong with me?*

She sat up, shook her head and extracted her legs from under Tobermory. Her tears had stopped, but her nose was running, so she grabbed a tissue from the box beside the bed. She blew her nose and swung her legs out of the bed, putting her feet on the floor. That was definitely better. The room seemed to have been spinning a little, but it was coming back to normal.

She stood up, threw her cardigan over her shoulders, walked to the back door and opened it. *Yes, I like to go out here when I'm upset.*

Tobermory followed her outside. It was cold and the sky was filled with a pale orange light from the street lamps. It was frosty, but the Spring flowers were in full swing, the world was alive and awake, even a few birds were singing at this early hour. Marissa dragged her deckchair out with a shiver and saw that it was covered in snails and bird droppings. It had been a while since she had sat outside. She was too tired to clean the chair, though, and it was very cold, so she went back inside and closed the door. She sat cross-legged on her sofa instead and pulled a blanket up over her legs. She looked at the empty table top, just a candle in a holder that she had bought from The Angel Shop.

My angel cards... My oracle cards. Where are they? Why am I not using them? Why did I pack them all away? I can't remember...

And then she thought of her drum. *My drum!* Her hands remembered the feel of it, but she couldn't fathom what she needed a drum for. *I must be going crazy.*

She touched the rose quartz of her earrings, centred herself and thought about Matt. *That's better.* There was a new Scott Taylor book on the sofa beside her. It must have fallen down from the shelf. She looked at it like it was a foreign object, then she remembered that she loved Scott Taylor. *It has been a while since I was reading him, why did I stop?* She felt drawn to pick it up. She held it in her hands and her breathing eased. *Yes, this is what I wanted. That's better now.* She held the book to her chest, feeling herself stabilise. It was still too early to get up, so she took the book back to bed with her, holding it to her chest, and fell into a dreamless sleep.

CHAPTER TWENTY TWO

The email came in from St Mary's – the Garda clearance was through and all was well, they wanted her to start there the following week. And she was meeting the agent after work that night to get the keys for her new Reiki room!

It's all coming together! Maybe I should meet with Noreen and organise to go part time, then I can take the room during the day as well... No, maybe I'll wait a bit and see how this all goes first.

She was still feeling off-centre. She felt a heaviness which was oppressive, as if lead weights were tied to her wrists and ankles. Every movement she made was slow, and grief was clawing at her insides, yet she didn't know what she had lost. *Why grief? What is this about? There's so much to look forward to. Why do I feel a dread hanging over me? I don't understand.*

She replied to Bronagh saying thanks, but once she'd sent the email she felt agitated, so decided to go out for a walk and buy herself a coffee. Being outside calmed her down – she walked familiar streets and found her routine and her breath. She held the hot coffee in her two hands and drank. The taste of it reassured her.

That's all I need. Coffee is like a hug in a cup.

She found her strength again and reorganised something inside of herself. The weight lifted from her, a pressure was released and she felt lighter as she walked back to her desk. She sat and looked at the computer screen, she felt brighter and able to focus on her work.

Matt texted: Hi! I found a plinth 4 sale, do u want it? It should fit in the space behind the stairs. I measured it :-)

He sent two photos, one of the plinth assembled, and one of it folded up. The price was good, too.

Yes please & thank u!

Gr8! I'll buy it 4u and bring it at wkend, still on for shopping?

Yes please! Getting keys tonight :-)

Yay! Call me after x

Out of the corner of her eye, Marissa saw that Noreen was sitting at her desk, which was a rare occasion these days. She hadn't been in the office for the past few weeks and it was possible that this was another flying visit. *I could just tell her I rented a room on a Monday evening without making a big deal about it... so I don't have to ask for part time right now, just hint that I might ask for it at some future date.*

With all the reasons why she wasn't ready to go part-time or tell Noreen turning over in her mind, somehow Marissa still found herself walking over to Noreen's corner office. She knocked on the door. 'Hi, Noreen, do you have a moment to talk?'

Noreen looked up and smiled. 'Of course! Come in.'

Noreen looks stressed – I don't remember those worry lines before. It probably isn't a good time, but it's too late now.

Marissa entered and closed the door behind her.

'Have a seat.' Noreen gestured to the chair across from hers, and Marissa sat down and crossed her legs.

'How are things?' Noreen asked. 'How's Sarah taking to her new managerial role?'

'Oh, everything is great,' said Marissa, delighted at the opportunity to give more praise to her friend. 'Sarah has really stepped up to it, I'm delighted for her.'

Noreen's face softened and her smile was genuine, 'That's wonderful. I love her new rig-out, and the new hairstyle – very serious! I have a feeling that there's a very competent manager just waiting to shine out of our fun-loving Sarah.'

'For sure,' agreed Marissa.

Noreen clasped her hands together. 'So! What can I do for you today?'

Marissa became nervous. *Come on, just sort this out now, get it over with.* 'Noreen, I was wondering if I could go part time? I mean, if I could work a shorter week? Would that be okay? I'd take a pay cut, of course.'

'Part time?'

'Well, you know that I want to be a therapist full time, but I'm not qualified yet, so maybe I could work just four days a week instead of five for now, and then, when I have more clients, I could go to three days a week?' *I sound like a little girl asking for a pony for Christmas.*

'I've been expecting this request from you since we spoke last,' said Noreen. 'In theory, yes, that's fine with me, but practically it will take some time to sort out the administration around it. Which day did you want to take off to begin with?'

'Mondays?' Marissa blurted out.

'You do realise that there are Bank Holidays which fall on Mondays? You would have had those days off with full pay.'

'Oh. I didn't think of that.' She did a quick calculation in her mind. *Monday still feels right, though I don't know why.* 'Mondays are still probably the best day for me to take, for now.'

Noreen nodded and wrote something down in her book.

'I will have to confirm it with you. I'd need you to do an audit as well, so I can see which tasks you can hand over to someone else. But yes, in principle this could work. How about after the Easter break? I'll cover you for Easter Monday, then you're on your own.'

Marissa shivered with delight, relief and trepidation. 'Wow, thank you so much. That's really generous of you.'

'I had lunch with Rose last weekend and she told me you were renting a therapy room. Will you be seeing clients for psychotherapy? I might have somebody for you.' She leaned in and lowered her voice although she had complete privacy in her office and nobody was around. It wasn't usual for people to talk about therapy so Marissa had a sense she wasn't comfortable discussing this. 'My younger sister, she has had a terrible break-up and needs to talk about it. I was thinking of sending her to you, if you were okay with that?'

'Oh yes, that would be wonderful. I mean yes, that's great, I mean ... that's awful, is she okay?'

Noreen laughed.

Marissa tried to cover up her mistake. 'Obviously she isn't okay, right. I'm not supposed to take paying clients for psychotherapy yet, but I could... Although she might actually like Reiki instead of counselling – it's very calming. I've still got to get the room kitted out, and get my insurance sorted… I don't know if I'm ready yet… I suppose you could give her my phone number for now.' *Do I need a new phone number? Oh dear, so much I haven't thought about yet!*

'Take your time. I'm thinking there's a lot more to what you're doing than simply renting a room.' Noreen looked at her watch. 'I've a meeting in ten minutes and I've got a lot to do. But I'll pass your number on to my sister and tell her to give you a shout?'

'Yes, I suppose I've got to figure all this stuff out. Thank you, Noreen, you've always been so supportive.'

'And you've always been very dependable. I'm delighted to be able to help you out in return.'

Later that evening, keys in hand, Marissa stood in her new therapy room. It was hers now, well, for three hours on a Monday evening, anyway. She had a few minutes to get the feel of it before the person who worked Wednesdays would arrive. It was still too dark, even with the desk lamp on, she'd have to get a standing lamp or something.

'I bless this space. I bless all that come into this space. May the healing flow. May my hands be gentle and may there be peace.'

That was lovely. I don't know where the words came from, but they felt right.

She measured the space under the stairs, and Matt was right, the folded plinth would fit in there very nicely. *He's a few steps ahead of me when it comes to thinking about stuff like this.*

Her grief lifted. She walked home past the chipper and bought dinner, and resisted the urge to start into it on the way home.

The evening was bright and clear, cold but not freezing, so she put the food on a plate, washed off the deckchair and sat outside. When she had finished eating, she licked the salt and vinegar off her fingers. She felt much more like herself again. She put the kettle on for tea and dug the print-out from college out of her bag to figure out which assignment she was going to do. Sitting outside with the print-out in her hands, her list and a pen, she felt clearer than she had felt in a while.

> *Discuss the difference between psychotherapy and counselling, and give details and case studies on two prescribed models which could be applied to either.*

That sounds interesting. I already kind of know the answer to the first part. Case studies? I wonder whether they should be documented or from my own experience. And the models... Hmm, I wonder about that. I will have to think about it, but this one would be straightforward enough to do.

Her eye caught another option, about stereotyping and how it impacted on the therapist's capacity for empathy. *I'm not feeling drawn to writing about that... Wonder why? Maybe I should do it because I don't want to do it...*

A third option also looked interesting:

> *Give a brief history of person-centred counselling, covering philosophy, development over time and the self-concept. Give the key principles and practice of the model and make a case for using it as the core driver in the therapeutic relationship.*

This one is pretty standard but oh, I don't know... She felt a headache coming on and she was extremely tired. It was only 7 o'clock. She went inside, put the plates into the sink, lay down on the bed and fell asleep.

Marissa? Marissa, are you there?'

She felt very small, curled up, like a ball. No, that wasn't it... She was small, curled up and in a very small place. It was dark too. She could hear her name being called, but it wasn't actually her name, so no, it wasn't for her. She couldn't reach back out anyway, she had no energy to do that, she was small and wanted to stay small...

She drifted..

She was a small child again, crying for a broken toy. Crying for something lost. She didn't know what it was, crying, crying...

Drifting in the place between sleep and wakefulness, she was lucid enough to know she was dreaming. She pulled herself out; she didn't want to go back into grief. She drifted again...

She was sitting in a room filled with people. They were clapping and laughing. She was clapping and laughing too. This felt better, safer. She let herself pour into this dream. There was a man there, talking. She couldn't see his face, but he had a strong presence. This felt good and safe.

'Marissa? Marissa, are you there?'

She pushed her awareness of the voice away from herself. She didn't want to listen to it. She was here, laughing and clapping. This man was witty! And laughing was good.

'Marissa! Stop that now, come back to us! Marissa!'

She got up from her seat and went to the door, which was ajar. She looked through it and saw clouds, and in the distance... Who was that woman? No. She didn't want to know. She closed the door firmly, and locked it, then went back to her seat. Oh that man was so funny! She clapped and laughed with delight with the rest of the audience.

She rubbed her eyes. It was 9pm she thought it was much later than that. She looked at her phone. *Three missed calls - Mum, Matt and Joanne. Joanne? I wonder what she wanted? Guess she is checking in on me, it has been a while. And I do have news. How does she know? So funny. I'll call her tomorrow.*

She texted Matt: I fell asleep! I'm good. 2 tired 2 talk, will call u tmorw, got keys all is well with room.

She got up and pottered around the kitchen for a while, then put on TV until she was ready to go back to bed and try to sleep again. She was still tired, just as tired as if she hadn't had a sleep earlier that evening. *A salt bath will help me relax. I've not had one of those in ages.*

But it was too late to put on the immersion and her hand on the cold boiler let her know there was no hot water there at all, not even enough to wash her face, let alone have a bath. *Everything feels strange right now. Why? I'm making progress with my plans, but some part of me feels lost. Like I don't have a compass and I can't find my way home... But I* am *home, aren't I?*

She clambered into bed. The Scott Taylor book was by her bedside. She adjusted her pillows, pulled up the blankets, opened the book to a random page and read until she fell into a dreamless sleep.

When she woke up the next morning she was still holding the book in her hand.

CHAPTER TWENTY THREE 

Margaret was very agitated. Sitting in the chair opposite Marissa, she was wringing her hands together. Her hair was dishevelled and she was wearing a pink skirt and a brown cardigan that was buttoned up wrong.

Marissa was getting upset just watching her. She breathed out, pressed her feet into the ground, then looked up at Margaret with unfocused eyes. There was a haze around her, as if her edges of were blurry.

'Are you okay, love?' Margaret asked her.

Marissa refocused immediately. 'Yes, yes, of course! And you? How are you? You seem very agitated...'

'Oh, do I? Sorry about that. Yes. I'm fine. Fine.' She continued wringing her hands. 'But I tried that exercise, and I have to say, Marissa, it really upset me. I'm not happy at all. I'm really not.'

Marissa pushed into the back of her chair, as if trying to make more space between herself and Margaret. 'Yes, I can see that you seem very upset. Has something happened? Can you tell me more?'

'Well, it's obvious!' Margaret exclaimed loudly, then stood up and walked around the room, continuing to wring her hands. 'You asked me to write down how I felt, how each thought made me feel, and I did it, I wrote it all down, and besides there almost not being any time in the day to do anything else but write down all of my thoughts, and how I felt, time and time again I realised that all I was saying was: "This is bad, life is terrible, I'm not happy..."' She stopped, looked up and seemed to realise that she wasn't sitting down. She apologetically came back to her chair and sat back down. 'Sorry, Marissa, I'm very wound up and emotional tonight.'

'That's okay, Margaret. Really, this is your space, you can feel however you feel. I'm not judging you, I just want to help you. Let's get it all out, and then maybe together we can figure something out that will make things easier for you.'

Margaret nodded her head, noticed she was still wringing her hands and deliberately separated them. 'I'll sit on my hands if I have to.'

Marissa tried a different tack. 'One of my tutors at college said that therapy can make things seem worse before they get better. That you're becoming aware of what the problem is, and that can be difficult. So it's probably all part of the healing process, you becoming more upset and agitated. We should keep going – is that okay?'

Margaret nodded, but didn't seem relieved.

'Did you bring your notebook with you?'

'Yes, I'll get it now.' Margaret rummaged around in her big leather handbag which was sitting by her feet. She fished out a very worn, ragged-eared black notebook, opened it and leafed through the pages.

Marissa sat patiently, waiting for her to find her place.

Margaret seemed to get even more upset as she turned page after page. Marissa noticed there were small tears rolling down her cheeks.

'Margaret, it's okay. Really, it's okay. We don't have to do this.'

Margaret looked up abruptly and asked, 'We don't?'

'No, of course we don't. It's making you very upset and I don't want you to be even more upset than usual.'

Margaret snickered. '"More than usual" – yes, I am more upset than usual, and I am upset most of the time. How much is my usual amount and how do you know this is more than that?'

Marissa was stricken.

'Sorry,' Margaret said quickly. 'I'm sorry. I don't mean to upset you, I really don't. I know you're only trying to help me.'

'I wonder if you're actually angry, underneath all the upset?' Marissa suggested.

'Angry?'

'Yes, angry. Would that be possible?'

After a moment Margaret said, 'I suppose so... But what do I have to be angry about?'

'Well, we would need to figure that out. But I think that underneath frustration and upset there lies a hidden anger.'

Thinking about this seemed to settle Margaret down a little bit. Her hands were still and the tears had stopped. She seemed interested in this train of thought, but she didn't say anything.

Marissa sat with her in silence for a while. Then she suggested, 'Would it be okay with you if I looked at your notebook myself? It would save you looking through it.'

'Sure, why not? What do I have to lose?

Margaret held the notebook out towards Marissa, who got up from her chair, took it and sat back down.

'Thank you,' she said, and opened it.

The handwriting was like a child's. The words started off each new line small, tight and scrawny, and as they went across the page the letters got bigger and drifted off the line, so all the lines of writing slanted off the page. The last few lines of each page Marissa read were illegible. *No wonder she had trouble finding her place. Where do I start with this?*

'You can see why I had trouble finding my place,' said Margaret with a sigh. 'Honestly, I don't know what to do with myself at times. I have difficulty living with myself too. Nothing is ever right, things don't go back in their right place, there's always something to put away. Kevin and Thomas have no regard for proper order, I'm always cleaning up after them.'

Something struck Marissa. 'Margaret, have you ever been assessed for OCD?'

'OCD? What's that?'

'Obsessive Compulsive Disorder.'

The words seemed to sit in the room with them, taking up almost as much space as Margaret did.

Margaret broke the ice. 'I wouldn't know, love. I've never been assessed for anything. The doctor just told me that I seemed overly upset and should see a counsellor.'

Marissa wasn't sure how to proceed. Perhaps it was best to move on. She would have to ask Mr Blakemore about this the next time she saw him. She certainly wasn't qualified to diagnose, and the last thing she wanted to do was make Margaret think she had OCD without a proper diagnosis.

'Okay, it might be something for later on.'

'Okay,' Margaret said, her hands moving towards each other once more. 'Is it bad, OCD? Would I need to go to a hospital?'

'Honestly, I don't know. It was just a thought that came into my head. It's probably nothing at all.' *She is upset, and there's only so much I can do for her here.* 'You *can* see, though, how one thought can start another, and another, and another, and that could make the idea of OCD into something really scary, when actually it might even not be that at all.'

'Oh. So I shouldn't worry about that then?'

'No, don't worry about it. It was just me thinking out loud.'

Margaret nodded.

Marissa flicked through the journal, trying to find something they could talk about, something that would help, but where to begin? Then something clicked. Everything Margaret was writing about was negative, yes, but it hadn't happened yet, and might not happen at all.

'Margaret, most of your thoughts are about bad things that might happen, yes?'

'Well, yes, I told you that already.'

'Yes, yes, you did. But what about the *good* things that might happen?'

'Good things?'

'Yes. I've been reading this book, it's by a man called Scott Taylor – have you ever heard of him?'

'No.'

'Well, anyway, he says that what we think about most of the time is what we get. If we think bad things, we get bad things; if we think good things, we get good things. I suppose that's a little simplistic, but I'm only seeing bad things in your book here, you're not thinking any good things at all. And then if one thought leads to another, and another, then you're thinking about negative things all the time. That's very upsetting. Do you see what I mean?'

'No good things at all? That's not good... I'm sure I must think good things some of the time. I just didn't write them down because they don't upset me.'

Marissa closed the book and put it on the table between them. 'It's neither good nor bad, it's just the way it is, for now. But I think I see a way for you to turn it around. If you want to, that is.'

'I *would* like to...'

'Great. So, we were focusing on what you were thinking and how you felt while you were thinking it, but maybe what we actually need to do is create good thoughts, so you can replace the bad thoughts with the good ones and then think more and more good thoughts to change the energy of what you're doing... What do you think?'

'Honestly, love, at this stage I would try anything. But I don't know how to do this.'

'Shall we learn together?'

'Okay, I'll try. Where do we start?'

'What's the most common negative thought that you've been having?'

'Well, that's easy. It's about Thomas, my son. I keep thinking that he is going to get sick and die, or get hit by a car and die, or that someone is going to hurt him, or..'

Marissa held up her hand. Margaret stopped talking.

'So you're creating scenarios where something bad happens to Thomas.'

'Yes.'

'You might not like this question, Margaret, but you're doing really well tonight, so I'm going to ask it.'

Hearing she was doing really well made Margaret sit up straighter in her chair. She looked like a child that had been given a good mark by her teacher. She smiled and prepared herself for whatever Marissa was about to ask her.

'Okay, ask away.'

'Have any of your bad thoughts ever happened? To Thomas, I mean.'

Margaret scratched her head. *It's funny that people actually do this when they are thinking about something. I keep seeing it in these sessions.*

'No, actually. No, they haven't happened,' said Margaret.

'That's good, isn't it?'

'Yes, it's very good.'

'So, if the bad things don't happen, what good things could happen instead? If you need to think about Thomas, couldn't you swap the bad thought for a good one?'

'Like what?'

'Okay, instead of thinking that Thomas was going to get sick, maybe you could think about how healthy he is. Maybe I need to know more about Thomas. What does he do?'

'He's taking his final exams this year. He's going to be a doctor.'

'Oh, that's fabulous! A doctor! So you could think about him doing really well in his exams and becoming a great doctor, treating lots of patients and being very successful in his practice.'

'That would be very nice. It seems strange, though.'

'Well, wouldn't you like him to do well?'

'Oh yes, of course!'

Marissa remembered something she had learned in Cognitive Behavioural Therapy at college. 'Here's the thing – a thought creates a track in your brain. And the more you think it, the deeper the track becomes.' Margaret was looking puzzled, so she tried to make it simpler. 'Imagine a path through a forest that nobody walks on. There'll be a lot of growth around it, won't there, but a path that a lot of people walk along will be clearer, won't it?'

'Okay...'

'So your well-trodden paths in your mind are the bad thoughts – they come easier for you. So now you need to take some energy and make a good thought. It takes more work for you, but you can do it. The more good thoughts you deliberately make, the easier it will become for you to think good thoughts. Over time, by deliberately thinking good thoughts instead of bad ones, you'll find they feel better to you overall, and you'll stop thinking the bad ones.'

Marissa was delighted with herself. She felt she'd explained it really well. Then Margaret said, 'I'm not sure I follow you...'

Marissa sighed. 'Each time your mind gives you a bad thought, why not give it a good thought instead? Your brain says something bad, and you catch it, and say something good instead. You've been great at catching your thoughts,' she patted the notebook, 'so we know you can hear your thoughts better now. But now it's time for you to change your thoughts, to turn the bad ones into good ones.'

Getting through to Margaret this evening felt like a lot of hard work, and Marissa was feeling exhausted, and she had two more sessions to go after this one. But finally Margaret said, 'Ah, okay, I think I understand. Each time I think something bad, I need to think about something good. Like a balance?'

Marissa's relief was palpable. 'Yes, like a balance. You need to balance a bad thought with a good thought.'

Margaret nodded her head.

'But the good thought has to be about the same thing to really balance it – so, if it's a bad thought about Thomas, then you need to think a good thought about Thomas. If it's about your dog – Gertrude, is it?'

'Yes, Gertrude.'

'Then you need to think a good thought about Gertrude, to balance the bad thought.'

'Do I need to write them all down?' Margaret asked, hoping she could give the notebook a break for a week.

'No, no, you don't need to write them down. But it might help to write down a few good thoughts so you have them to hand when you need them.'

Margaret smiled. 'I understand what I am to do this week then. I can do that. Thanks, Marissa, I do appreciate your patience with me. Imagine what it's like to live inside my head!' She laughed.

Marissa didn't laugh. It really wasn't funny at all. 'Don't worry, you don't get to see inside other people's heads, Margaret,' she said, 'and I'm sure there are many people who have the same thing going on inside their heads as you do. I know myself, I think lots of bad things, but I try to think good things to balance them out. It can be difficult to do, but it usually works for me. Maybe this will work for you.'

I don't know if it really does work, or if I really do this, but she needs some encouragement, I hope this helps...

'That's good to hear. So I'm not crazy!'

Best not to address this one at all. 'It's time now, Margaret, so I'll see you next week. Are you okay to go?'

'Yes, thank you.' She put on her coat and Marissa walked her to the door. Before she left she turned around and asked, 'Do you think I need to go to a doctor for a diagnosis? For that OCD disorder you mentioned?'

Marissa was taken aback. She had hoped Margaret had forgotten about that. She wanted to answer honestly, so she said, 'I really don't know. Maybe not for now, if you can learn how to manage this – if the positive thoughts do balance out the negative ones. I will get some advice for you and we can talk about it next time. But please don't worry, a diagnosis won't change who you are. A diagnosis is just a doctor's way of deciding what type of things they need to do to help you – a way to prescribe a course of action, so to speak. And we have done that tonight – we have a course of action for you. And we'll keep working on it together until we find something that works.'

Margaret smiled and left.

Marissa felt drained. She had three nights in a row with nightmares and Margaret's session had been hard going. She looked at her watch, Cliona was coming in five minutes, who knew what she would bring with her this time. She really needed to clear her head.

She went into the bathroom and threw cold water on her face. Counselling could be hard work, and she couldn't take it for granted that she had the answers to help her clients.

My expectations of what I can do seem to be greater than what I actually can do. Maybe I should change my expectations. And Margaret seems to be a strong lady beneath all of her neurosis, but what if she is particularly vulnerable and hiding it? What if she goes home and instead of coming up with positive thoughts, she dwells on the possibility that she has obsessive compulsive disorder? Did I make a mistake by suggesting it? Oh dear, I probably really messed up tonight.

What will I do with Cliona? I'll just sit there and listen tonight, yes. She can say whatever she wants. I won't offer any advice, or try any techniques. I'll just sit there and listen.

Resolute in her decision, she went back to her room, sprayed her St Germain spray to try to wake herself up, and right on time, Cliona knocked on the door.

'Hiya,' she said, coming in and sitting down in the chair that she preferred.

Marissa smiled, trying to ascertain Cliona's mood from her appearance. There was a new, slightly pink streak in her neatly tied back black hair and she wearing a short denim skirt with leggings underneath, sneakers and a denim jacket. Marissa noted that her stomach had indeed grown more noticeable since the week before.

'You checkin' me out?' asked Cliona, cocking her head on one side and grinning. 'You look tired tonight.'

Marissa shifted in her chair to settle in for the session, 'Yes, I'm a little tired. It's been a long day – a long few days, in fact. Anyway, we're here to talk about you. I like the new pink,' she gestured to Cliona's hair. 'How are things going?'

Cliona smiled, put her hands on her belly and shifted to the side. 'Look! It's growing!'

Marissa smiled. 'You're happy about it now?'

'Ah, feck yeah. It's gonna be great. Ari needs a brother or sister. Me and Bren are doing much better, and hey, guess what?'

'What?'

'I got that job! I've already started too! My first day was St Patrick's Day. I know – shit, hey? But it's gotta be done. I get paid tomorrow, it will be so great to get some money. And it isn't in a shop after all, it's in a warehouse. So I don't need to see people much. That's a relief! I answer the phone, take orders, and I get to tell the guy with the forklift what to do. He even let me have a go on it! They don't mind that I'm pregnant! It's bloody brill. I've not had so much fun in ages. Working, I mean. And I'm not as sick as before, and Bren got a gig! Amazeballs hey! He's playing this weekend - he's got tickets for me and there won't be alcohol, so Ari can go too! Nan is even thinking of coming along. Jeez, Marissa, a few weeks ago I thought my life was ending, and now it feels like the whole thing has turned around. It's bloody amazing.'

Marissa smiled. 'I'm so happy for you.'

'Yeah, me too. Thanks. You know, I'm pretty sure you kept me sane the last few weeks. Coming here really helped. Did you put in for the extra cycle?'

'Oh God, I totally forgot.'

'Cool. Maybe I'll take a break for now. Marissa, if I want to come back to see you, though, can I see you, instead of coming back to just anyone?'

'Actually, Cliona, I don't know. But I'm going to be seeing clients privately soon, so it's possible you could come to see me in my new place, if you needed to.'

Cliona smiled. 'Great. Yeah, I think I'd like to stop for now. Things are settling in a good way, so I don't wanna jinx 'em. So I have one more session next week – that makes twelve? That's enough for me for now.'

Marissa was a little deflated. She had come to really connect with Cliona, but she knew that she couldn't hold on to her clients.

'Sure, Cliona, I'm really happy that it's all turned around for you. Let's make the most of the rest of our time together. I'd love to give you another technique that would help you with your anger. Would that be okay?'

'Sounds bloody okay to me!'

And there I was saying I'd just sit and listen. Oh well. I can do this, and it's great to see her so happy. Marissa brightened. 'Excellent. Let's review what we've done, and then I'll give you something new to work with. I won't ask for another cycle for you, I'll tell the office that you're done for now.'

'Thanks, Marissa. Really, thank you.' Cliona blushed as she said it.

'You are very, very welcome.'

Marissa sat in the empty room that seemed even emptier without Margaret and Cliona. Once more, Joy was a no-show. She'd had a feeling that would be the case. She waited fifteen minutes anyway, just in case.

'One less client hour for my diploma,' she said out loud to herself, shaking her head and putting on her coat. She turned off the light and closed the therapy room door. *I guess people don't come if they think that everything is working well for them. Which is a pity. Like they said in college, when everything is good, that's when you actually get into the real work. But I am so tired, maybe it's just as well.*

She walked down the corridor. There were a couple of other volunteers working that night, so she didn't need to lock up. It was getting busier in Cabra as the terms were coming to a close and everyone wanted to get their hours in.

She stopped by the office before she left and used their new communication system to write a note asking for a replacement client for Joy for next week, and to let them know Cliona didn't need another 6 sessions. She placed it in the designated envelope and dropped it into the new letterbox.

As she walked to the bus stop she mulled her thoughts over in her head. *I guess low-cost counselling is there for people who are in trouble, and when they aren't in trouble anymore, they stop. Like firefighting – put the fire out and move on to the next thing. Does that mean that the deeper work is only done by people who pay? Or maybe there aren't as many people out there who want to do the deeper work...*

Back in her flat later that night, she stood in her pyjamas at the end of her bed, hesitant to get into it. She didn't want another nightmare. *Why am I having so many of them? All in a row? What is going on? And why can't I seem to remember them afterwards?* She thought of Margaret and possible OCD and her heart sank, so she pushed the thought away. She decided to write in her own notebook. She took it from a drawer in her desk, grabbed her pen and climbed into bed, opening the book to a fresh new page. She focused on her own situation.

> *Why am I having so many nightmares? Where did all this grief come from?*
> *Why do I feel that a part of myself is missing? What am I forgetting?*

She sat looking at her questions, but no answers were forthcoming. She put the notebook down on her bedside locker and noticed the Scott Taylor book sitting there. She picked it up, then put it down again. *What is the story with this book? Why am I bringing it to bed with me? Maybe I need to ask about that in my notebook too...*
She turned out the light.

CHAPTER TWENTY FOUR 

Marissa woke up feeling anxious. This was more extreme than her usual form of anxiety: she felt as though she'd done something wrong, or forgotten to do something really important, but she couldn't recall what it was. Like leaving the gas on and going away for a weekend. But she wasn't going away for the weekend, she was at home, and the gas was most certainly off. She had checked. Twice. She could only put her feelings down to the session with Margaret. *I hope she doesn't dwell on the possibility she may have OCD... She may have OCD, but I really shouldn't have said anything to her.*

She got ready for work but the severity of the fluttering in her stomach slowed her down. Everything seemed to take twice as long as usual. *Could I have picked up Margaret's anxiety?* The thought struck her as she walked to the bus stop. *I'm not doing any more energy stuff ... except for Reiki ... but I've not done any Reiki in ages. Oh dear, maybe it would have helped me sleep better. I could have tried distance Reiki on myself as a surrogate. I must remember to do that sometime.*

The bus came and she showed her travel card to the driver, went upstairs and got a seat. She tried to connect to Reiki, but it agitated her further, so she stopped.

The anxiety seemed to get worse as she got closer to work. *This is really shitty. I just wish this anxiety would leave me alone.*

Suddenly, it was gone. Marissa cocked her head on one side, checking with her senses. *Has it really gone? Yes! Was it from Margaret then? Oh, I don't know anymore. I'm happy it's gone, though.*

Thankfully she had had a dreamless sleep and was feeling somewhat awake, and it was Friday. *I'm going shopping with Matt tomorrow for things for the new room, and he's bringing me my new plinth and is going to show me how to set it up. He really is a godsend.*

She had just settled at her desk, switched her computer on and made a cup of fresh tea when her phone buzzed. *It must be Matt!* she got it out of her handbag and saw that it was Terry. *Wonder what he wants?*

Missing u this weekend, wish u were here xx

Why? What's this weekend? Oh, the workshop with Séamus ... and I'm not there.

The room started spinning around her and she felt dizzy and nauseous. She folded her arms on the desk and put her head down and cradled it, but that made everything worse. She started to sweat, and then the anxiety came back twofold, seeming to hit her in the stomach. She needed to vomit. She ran to the bathroom and into a stall. Holding onto the toilet, she retched, but nothing came up. She sank down onto the floor, sweating. *What is this about? Missing the workshop? I decided ages ago I wasn't going.*

She remembered something from one of her classes in college, and started reciting the times tables in her mind. *Two times two is four. Four times four is sixteen...* It seemed to calm her somewhat. She pulled her mind away and started visualising the numbers as she did her tables. *Seven sixes is forty two. I see a door, a wall, this really isn't a nice place. Being on the floor so close to the toilet bowl makes me want to vomit again.*

She pulled herself up from the floor and dragged herself out of the cubicle to the sink and stayed there for a moment, leaning into it. Then she fixed her hair. Looking at her reflection, she could see there was an improvement, but she wasn't herself at all. She needed some air. She stood on her feet and held her own weight. *Good.* Then she walked very slowly back to her desk, got her coat and sent Sarah a quick email.

Just having a bout of anxiety. I'm okay, but I need some air.
I'll be back in fifteen minutes.

She didn't wait for Sarah's reply, but got the lift downstairs and went straight outside.

The cold air against her face helped, as did the walking. With each step she got a little stronger. She found herself down a side street where a new bookshop had just opened. *A distraction is good.*

She went in. There was a display of self-help books towards the back of the store, and stacked up right at the front was a brand-new Scott Taylor book. His smiling face was emblazoned on the back cover. It was called *Be the Best You Can Be*.

Marissa picked it up and opened it. There was a promotional flyer inside with a discount code for Scott's London event. *Oh, it's in four weeks. I could go to that!* She tucked it back into the back of the book, deciding she had to buy a copy. She did and felt better almost immediately.

She walked back to work clutching the book in the shop bag to her chest. When she got back to her desk, she took the book out of the paper bag and put it face-down beside her monitor screen so she could see Scott's face on the back cover smiling up at her.

Sarah saw her and ran over straight away. 'Are you okay? You were gone longer than fifteen minutes...'

'Yes, I'm better now, thanks. I found the new bookshop, that's why I was a little longer than I had planned. But I think browsing in there for a while really helped me calm down. I even bought a book! I will work through lunch, if that's okay, to make up for it.'

Sarah's relief was palpable. 'Yes, that's okay. Don't worry about that – I'm just glad you're feeling better.'

'I'm not myself today,' Marissa admitted. 'I've been having nightmares the last few nights, but I feel much better now after the walk, and now I have something new to read.'

She showed the book to Sarah.

'He looks a bit of alright!' Sarah said, noticing that Marissa didn't offer her the book to look through, but kept it in her hands, stroking it as if it was a cat.

'He's brilliant. I love his way of thinking. I can read the book, and I'll be completely back to myself in no time.' She was smiling up at Sarah, as if asking for her approval.

Sarah looked directly into Marissa's eyes. 'You do look tired. Do you want to go home?'

'No, I'll be fine. Sure it's Fri-yay today, isn't it? I'll be fine.'

'Please, look after yourself, yes?'

Marissa smiled. 'Yes, I will. I promise.' She put the book on her lap, turned back to her computer and opened the first of many emails.

That evening Marissa made sure she put the immersion on and gave it plenty of time to heat the water for a long soak in an Epsom salt bath. As she sank down into the hot water, she felt herself relax for the first time in several days.

Tobermory came in through the kitchen window while she was in the bath and leapt up onto his favourite spot on the armchair. He couldn't get comfortable. Something felt strange to him, something wasn't right in his territory. Was there a mouse in the flat? There hadn't been a mouse there in ... well, not since he'd moved in, that was for sure. He couldn't smell anything; maybe it wasn't a mouse. He walked around the chair, looked under it, then under the sofa, but no, nothing. He sat on the arm of the sofa, the end of his tail twitching, as he tried to figure it out.

She felt love all around her. She was laughing, sitting cross-legged on the ground in front of a fire. There were lots of friends there, all laughing and singing. It felt warm and beautiful. Someone had a drum. She could see the faces across the fire; they felt familiar to her, like family, but she didn't know their names. She was happy. She felt safe.

Then she felt a twisting in her stomach, as if someone had dug something into it. A knife? No, it was like some sort of pitchfork for stacking hay. And it was twisting her stomach, wrenching her. It was so painful, was she dying? She screamed out in pain. The images disappeared...

She was at the lake, rolling on the ground. She felt huge relief at being there; she hadn't seen her mountains and lake for so long. The fork, or whatever it was, wasn't there anymore. She stopped rolling, held her stomach and grimaced, looking down in fear of finding her stomach ripped open, but it wasn't.

She turned to her left and saw two old women in ceremonial dresses. They were looking pleadingly at her. One of them had her hands open, as if asking her to come to them. They looked nice. She wondered who they were.

She looked at the water. It was quite rough out there – a storm brewing perhaps? Something was rising out of the water. Was it a seal? she couldn't tell from where she was.

She felt a presence beside her. Looking up, she saw it was a man in a white suit. He smiled at her and offered her his hand. She smiled back, reached up to him and took his hand. He pulled her to her feet and looked into her eyes. As she stared back into his, everything around her faded away. His arm was around her waist, they were dancing, it felt nice, warm, safe, she felt beautiful and he was beautiful...

'Oh Scott,' Marissa said. 'Yes...'

She woke up, not remembering exactly what she was dreaming about, only that it had started out nice, then got awful, and then been nice again. But she couldn't settle, so she found the playlist she was working on for her Reiki client sessions and turned it on.

She drifted away to it. 'Lub dub, lub dub, lub dub, the heartbeat of the world' was a line from one of the songs, but she was so deeply asleep she didn't hear it.

✦ ✦ ✦

The doorbell rang just after lunchtime. It was Matt with the plinth.

'Hiya! How's it going?' he said with a smile and a grimace as he lifted the plinth a little higher.

'Great, thanks,' said Marissa with a smile and a squeal at seeing the plinth.

'Well, are you gonna let me in then? This thing is heavy!'

'Yes, of course!' Marissa got out of the way and Matt came in, hefting the massage table through the door and placing it up against the wall.

'Is there any tea going spare?'

Marissa went to put the kettle on.

'It's quite straightforward to set this up,' said Matt, taking off his coat.

Tobermory came over and rubbed his body against Matt's leg, curling his tail around it.

'Hello, cat,' said Matt, bending down to give him a scratch behind the ears. 'Tobes seems happy to see me,' he said, delighted with himself.

'He doesn't usually greet people at the door,' said Marissa, coming over to greet Matt properly. They kissed.

'Mmm, that was nice,' he said. 'Tea first? Then I'll show you how to set this up – if I can remember, that is!'

'Great! Where are you taking me shopping?'

Matt sat down on the sofa and Marissa brought the tea things over.

'I thought we could go to *Dunnes*, or maybe *HomeStore and More*,' she suggested.

'How about taking a trip out to IKEA? I've not been before, it could be fun. Did you make a list?'

'IKEA? That's miles away! Are you sure?'

'Yes! We could make a day of it.'

Marissa smiled 'I've never been before, too. I've heard that it's a treasure trove...'

Matt looked at her with a smile 'Then I hope you made a list, so that we will only buy the things on your list.'

'Of course I made a list. IKEA sounds great!'

She poured out the tea.

'Do you have any sugar?' Matt asked.

'Oh, yes. Sorry, I forgot, again. Hang on.' Marissa hopped up to get the sugar and Tobermory leapt up onto the sofa where she had been sitting and pushed his head into Matt's body, rubbing himself up against him once more. Matt stroked him.

Marissa came back and saw her place had been taken. 'He's acting very strange since last night,' she said, noticing how loudly he was purring. 'He must like you a lot.' She sat down on the armchair where Tobermory usually resided.

Matt continued to stroke the cat with one hand while he put sugar into his tea with the other. 'So, pillows, blankets, pillow cases and what else?'

Marissa had a glimmer of a flashback of her shopping dream. She pushed it out of her mind. 'I guess so. Yes, three blankets, a cover for the plinth and a free-standing lamp.'

'I've got three plinth covers here. They came with it, as they need to fit it specifically. They can be washed in the machine.'

'I've got to give you the money for it, don't let me forget.'

They finished their tea and Matt set up the plinth, explaining how it worked, then he took it apart and got Marissa to do it. After doing it twice on her own, she felt she had the knack of it.

'Do you have your keys to the room?' Matt asked. 'I'll put this back in the car and we can store it under the stairs on the way to the shop, to save you dragging it there yourself.'

'Matt, you are a godsend. Thank you. You really go the extra mile to look after me. I'm so lucky to have you.'

Later that evening, after a very exciting shopping trip (even Matt bought a few things for his own place), they settled into Marissa's flat for the night with takeaway and a bottle of wine. After they had eaten, Marissa suggested they listen to music and read instead of watching a movie, as she wanted to finish her new Scott Taylor book.

'Is that for your assignment for college?' asked Matt.

'Oh! No, I've not even started that. I haven't even picked which essay I want to do yet.'

'That book must be riveting to take you away from your college work! Can I see it?'

Marissa reluctantly handed it to him. Matt leafed through the pages, noticing that she'd been writing on them and underlining things. Marissa became more agitated the longer he held it in his hands.

'This is the guy that Dave liked, isn't it?' he asked. 'How is Dave? You've not mentioned him in a while.'

'I've not seen him in a while. I think he's been very busy with client work. But he did say he'd booked his ticket to London – to see Scott Taylor, I mean. I think I'd like to go too.'

'To London? When?'

Marissa held her hand out for the book. Matt gave it back to her, and Tobermory, who was back in his usual spot on the armchair, twitched his tail in agitation.

Marissa turned to the back of the book, pulled out the flyer and read out the dates: '19th–21st April.' She looked at Matt. 'I've got the money. Do you want to come with me?'

It felt strange asking him, and it was more out of obligation than actually wanting him there. *Strange. I would love a weekend away with Matt, wouldn't I?*

It seemed it wasn't to be, anyway. 'Can't that weekend,' Matt said. 'I've got my teacher training then. It's residential in Clare, my last training weekend. I'll be qualified afterwards.' He smiled, his sense of achievement showing on his face.

'Wow, brilliant. Well done, you!' Marissa said, feeling relieved and puzzled as to why.

'I'm a little nervous about it,' Matt confessed, 'but I know it'll be fine. You were right about the demo class, that wasn't as bad as I thought it was going to be. And, like you said, I don't have to start teaching right away, just because I can. Hey, you should go to London on your own, It'll be great – a big adventure!'

'Yes, I think I just might do that.'

A few moments passed and guilt seeped into Marissa. She felt she had to say something nice to Matt to make up for it.

'You know, James wouldn't have been happy with me going away for a weekend on my own...'

'But you've done that already. You went to Sligo, didn't you?'

'Oh yes, I did! I'd forgotten about that. It feels like two years ago. I honestly don't know what is going on with my mind, Matt, I keep forgetting things, it's as if my brain is in a fog. And I had a panic attack yesterday at work.'

'Oh no – why didn't you tell me? What happened?'

'I don't know. Oh yes, I remember now. Terry sent me a text.'

'What did he say?'

'He said he missed me and wished I was there.'

Matt cocked his head on one side, puzzled. 'Wished you were where?'

Marissa looked down at the floor. 'Clifden,' she said, getting a little jittery.

'Oh, yes. Of course,' said Matt.

Marissa felt very small all of a sudden.

'That's this weekend?' Matt asked.

Marissa nodded.

'Well, you've moved on from all that now,' said Matt encouragingly. 'You've got your new room, and more stuff than you need to put into it, you're planning to go to London and you're going part time at work. You're doing brilliant!'

'Yes, yes, I am doing just fine. Thank you,' Marissa said.

The weight of the moment slowly passed.

Matt went home around lunchtime the next day, and Marissa's flat felt empty without him. Tobermory was looking very suspiciously at her so she went over to pet him, but he avoided her touch.

'What's up, Tobermory? You like Matt better than me, now?'

She did some light tidying. The sun was out and it was a clear day, so when she was happy with her straightened-out flat, she took a cup of tea and the new Scott Taylor book out into her garden and sat in the deckchair, reading. She had marked some of the passages in it with a biro and made a few notes in the margins. She got to the last page, closed the book and felt a sense of satisfaction. There was a small tremor of anxiety in the pit of her stomach, but she pushed it aside.

She put the book down by her feet and the flyer fell out of it. Picking it up, she read and reread it, then went inside, got her laptop and her wallet, and sat back down again. With the flyer in hand, she typed the website address for the tickets, used the discount code and made her purchase. She was going to London. She just had to get flights and a hotel organised now.

She was about to text Matt to tell him, when she saw Terry's name in her messages list. She opened the message and read it again, wondering why it had affected her so badly. *He's going to his workshop, and I'm going to mine!*

She texted him back: Oh yes, of course - hope u had a blast. Tell me all about it when u come back.

She reread the last part of her message. *I don't want to know all about it.* She changed it to: chat soon x, and pressed 'Send'.

She went inside and put the Scott Taylor book into her handbag for work the next day, to read while she was at lunch. She had truly moved on. For sure. This time. *Yes. Truly. And I am going to London!*

CHAPTER TWENTY FIVE

Marissa had her credit card in her hand and was looking at flights on the Aer Lingus website when she saw Sarah approaching. She quickly flicked over to an Excel worksheet.

'Hey, it's your last Monday here,' said Sarah with a wink and a smile. She was still in deep blue, but she was wearing a skirt today, The ends of her bob were flicked out, her hair was growing and it wasn't as sleek as before. Her lipstick was still 'serious manager' red.

'Hi, Sarah. Yeah, so it is!' Marissa flicked her own hair out of her eyes. 'Did you have a good weekend?'

'Yes, I was studying! Quite enjoying it too. You?'

'I was buying things for my new room – blankets and stuff. IKEA is a mad place. Next time I go there I'll have to rent a van! I also got a plinth for my Reiki room. I'll be seeing Matt there tonight for my first Reiki session – do you still want a session?'

'Oh! Tonight?'

'If you wanted to come tonight, yes, I'm sure I could fit you in.'

'I'm free after work, so yes please! What time?'

'I've the room from 6pm and Matt is coming for 6:30, so I guess around 7:30?'

After a moment's hesitation Sarah said, 'Yes, actually, I could make that work. What's the address?'

Once Sarah had gone, Marissa flicked back to the airline's website, chose her flights and booked them. *Just like that.* An immense sense of satisfaction filled her body. She could take her time and find a hotel later. *London has plenty of hotels – that's the easy bit.* The confirmation email came in, along with an email from Dolores inviting her to the Reiki 2 follow-up evening. She offered three dates: two hours on Good Friday afternoon *I'm working*, the following Wednesday evening, *I can't do the Wednesday either, I'll be in St Marys.*

Or the Thursday evening. *Cabra. All my evenings are busy. Should I take a day off on Good Friday and go? I'll see what Matt wants to do. It would be good to see her, but it's really difficult to fit everything in.*

She wasn't feeling the slightest bit sentimental as she packed up her things at the end of the day, In fact it was quite the opposite – the excitement was mounting. *Sure I'll be back in tomorrow. Monday is like any other day, and now I'll have my Mondays to myself!*

She practically skipped to the bus stop and the bus driver couldn't drive fast enough. She burst through the door of her flat, flung her work bag down, ate some leftovers she found in the kitchen without even bothering to heat them up and found the old suitcase her dad had dropped off for her the night before. He had stayed for a cuppa and a chat.

'I'm really happy for you,' he said, 'and relieved that you aren't just quitting her day job altogether. A phased approach is best. It gives you time to settle into the new routine whilst still having security.'

Marissa loved her dad, each time she saw him he looked a little older. She needed to spend more time with him – no, she *wanted* to. But life was moving so fast. She gave him a strong hug before he left, thanking him for the suitcase. He had furnished it with a brand new combination lock.

'I needed to get rid of this old thing anyway,' he said. 'Your mother is talking about converting the attic, so we've started to clear stuff out. You'll have to come over and go through some of your old things that we've kept for you.'

Now Marissa opened the suitcase on the sofa. Its musty smell captured the essence of her parents' house, with undertones of the unmistakable scents of pea soup, roast beef and her mother's perfume. Folding her new blankets and pillows while juggling her food, she placed them into the suitcase, just managing to fit them all in. Matt was driving over with her new lamp; it was all coming together. She remembered to put out food for Tobermory before she left.

The suitcase bumped behind her on the path the whole way to her new room. It was only a brisk fifteen-minute walk, not too far away at all, but Marissa was glad she wouldn't have to drag all of her things there each week.

She let herself in the main hall door, closed it quietly behind her and walked down the corridor to stand outside her new room. The door was shut. She leaned in. Was somebody in there? She could hear talking.

There were two chairs and a small table in the corridor for clients who were early. She sat down in one of the chairs and waited, looking at her watch. It was ten minutes to six. *If I have a client booked in for six and this person isn't finished, then I'll be flustered, won't I, if the client comes on time or is early. I guess I can't book people in for 6pm on the dot, as I'll need time to set up the room. Or maybe now that I'm free, I could book the whole day. I wonder if it's available. Well, obviously not this particular time-slot.*

She still had to take the plinth out from under the stairs and remember how to set that up, but it would be too noisy to do it outside the room and she didn't want to disturb whoever was in there.

Five minutes to six and the people inside the room were still there. Marissa was getting antsy. She decided to check the bathroom was clean and take her plinth quietly out from under the stairs so that she had it ready.

At 6pm, she was still waiting to get inside the room.

At seven minutes past six, she was beginning to get distressed, but the door handle eventually moved and the voices were coming closer. *Thank God they're finished.*

The door opened and two men stood there, continuing their conversation. Marissa stood up, waiting patiently to gain access, but they didn't seem to be finishing up any time soon. She looked at the time on her phone, then looked at the people.

I have to say something.

'Ahem, sorry, but I'm waiting for the room, I have it booked for 6pm.'

'Oh, excuse us, we're just finishing up,' said one of the men. He was in his forties and wore a cashmere v-neck jumper with a white shirt underneath and a pair of blue trousers. He and the other man said their goodbyes and the other man, presumably the client, left. The man then he turned to Marissa, holding out his hand.

'Sam is my name. Sorry for keeping you. Nobody usually has the room after me.'

Marissa took his hand; it rested limply in hers. She smiled, still irritated and wanting to get into the room.

'I'll just get my things,' said Sam. 'Won't be a moment.'

He went back inside. Marissa felt she couldn't intrude, so she waited outside, counting her breaths until he came back out again. He had his coat on.

'It's all yours,' he said with a smile, and then he left.

It was nearly 6:15. *Only fifteen minutes to set up the room for Matt! Well, maybe that will be enough. This just won't do for the future. I will have to tell the Agent.*

With a sigh, Marissa dragged the heavy plinth into the room, then went out and brought the suitcase in. She closed the door behind her. The room was smelly and Sam had been using the big fluorescent light. Marissa shuddered and opened the door once more for air, then switched off the main light. The room became significantly darker; the waning sunlight from the dirty window didn't bring in much light at all. Marissa switched on the desk lamp on the counselling table, and it helped somewhat, but the lampshade was very dusty and needed cleaning. She turned the big light on again so she could see what she was doing while setting up the plinth.

She struggled with the legs of the plinth and then realised what else she had forgotten to bring. *Oh shit! I forgot the incense, and I didn't bring music or a candle, either. And Sarah's coming! Oh no! I'll have to run home to get it all.*

She started shaking, wanting to have it all perfect for her friends and realising that it wasn't going to be that way. *Breathe, relax, it's only Matt and Sarah, and it's my first time, I won't get it right the first time. It's all learning.* She remembered something from the Scott Taylor book: 'First steps are better when they are small steps. By taking small steps, you're always moving forward.' *Moving forward, small steps. Yes, that feels better.*

She calmed down, slowed down, and started making up the plinth again. Then the sharp sound of the buzzer rang right by her ear, making her jump. The buzzer had a speaker on it. She dropped the plinth and went to it, pushing it to speak.

'Hello?'

'Hi, it's Matt.'

'Oh, hi. I'll be right there.'

Marissa left the plinth as it was and went to the front door to let Matt inside.

'Hi! You look flustered. Are you okay?'

'Yes, yes, I just didn't get into the room until a few minutes ago. I know, but there was someone else in there. He wasn't expecting me. Come in!'

They both went into Marissa's little space.

'I'm your first client, remember?' said Matt, putting the free-standing lamp down in the far corner of the room, opposite the desk light.

'Oh yes, I remember!' said Marissa shaking her head, 'But I forgot the music, the incense and the candles.'

Matt started to laugh, which irritated her further.

'I'll have to run home and get them, do you mind? Sarah's coming at 7:30, so I really do need to get them.'

Matt nodded. 'It's okay, don't fret. We'll sort it all out. I'll come with you for the walk.'

'I'll set the room up first. Do have a seat while you wait,' said Marissa in her therapist's voice, gesturing to the counselling chairs.

'Let me just sort out the lighting first.'

Matt plugged in the new light, turned it on, then turned off the main fluorescent light. He went to the chairs and sat down, switching on the desk lamp. It was a big improvement. The soft light was just right for a Reiki session.

Marissa smiled. Something was going right after all. 'That's so much better. It's a relief to have that big light off, it's horrible.'

'Yes, a fluorescent bulb isn't ideal for a therapy room,' agreed Matt.

'There. Done.' Marissa looked proudly at her handiwork. The plinth seemed to take up much of the rest of the space.

'You will need to be able to walk around the plinth easily,' Matt reminded her.

'I can't really do it easily with the chairs like that. I'll move those now.' Marissa nudged Matt to stand up and they both pushed the heavy chairs closer to the wall so she could reposition the plinth.

'Now it's too close to the door. Hang on...'

She moved the plinth again. She opened and closed the door, making sure that there was room to come inside, then walked around the plinth. It was a little tricky, but she managed to do it. It seemed okay.

'Can we go back to my place and get the stuff now?' she asked.

'Sure,' said Matt.

The exciting day had turned into a downer. As they walked to the flat, Marissa felt as though someone had hosed her with cold water. She almost wanted to cry.

'Did you get the email from Dolores?' he asked.

'Yes, I was going to ask you – did you want to go?'

'I did, looks like Good Friday works best for me. You?'

'I'm working that day, and am in session the other evenings... I could take Good Friday off work though.'

'We could spend the day together?'

'It's a date!'

Matt kissed her inside the door of her flat, she softened to him, surrendered, and then started to feel better. Needless to say, they were delayed somewhat. They got back to the therapy room with the rest of her things rather later than she would have liked, but she smiled at Matt, set the incense burner on the table with a candle and hooked her mini-speakers up to her iPhone for the music. Matt sat down once more while she organised the blankets and pillows on the plinth. It was 7:15.

'Oh shit, Matt, Sarah is coming for 7:30.'

Matt looked crestfallen. But then he smiled. 'That's okay. She can be your first client then.'

'No, it's *not* okay – *you're* to be my first client. I can't give you a whole hour, but I'll text Sarah and ask her to come a little later. I want you to be my first.'

She giggled, and Matt looked a little brighter then. She texted Sarah, asking if she could wait for fifteen minutes, put on the music, and lit the candle.

'Now, sir, would you like to take off your coat and shoes?' Marissa heard her voice change as she spoke. She wondered why she felt the need to do that.

Matt did what he was told and got up on the plinth.

'What's it like up there?' Marissa asked, her normal voice returning.

'Nice. It's comfortable.'

'Are you warm enough? Would you like a blanket?'

'Actually yes, a blanket would be lovely over my legs, thank you.'

Marissa covered his legs with one of the new blankets. 'I'll begin then.'

Matt smiled.

Marissa realised she hadn't brought her little clock with her to keep the time for the session. *So many things to remember. I can use my phone for now, I'll remember next time.*

She took a moment to connect to the Reiki light. She breathed and felt herself slowing down and becoming more peaceful, felt herself coming more into the room. The flow of energy felt strong as it poured through the crown of her head, her whole body softened and she was ready to put her hands on Matt. She began the treatment.

She was only a few minutes into it when a text came through her phone, and through the speakers of her phone. It was very loud and gave her a shock. She felt her heart jump into her mouth with the intensity of it. It gave Matt a shock too; he jumped on the table.

'Shit, Matt, I'm sorry. I didn't turn off the ringer!'

Matt started laughing. 'It's not your night tonight. First night teething problems. Don't worry, you'll figure it all out.'

Marissa went to the phone. It was Sarah. I'm outside :-(

She texted back: Sorry, I'm not ready, can u wait 10 mins? Go for a walk around the block?

Ok

Sorry!

She came back to Matt. 'It will be a short session. I hope you don't mind.'

'The things we do for love,' he said with a grin.

'Thank you. I'll make it up to you, promise,' Marissa whispered, and leaned down to kiss him.

Back in Marissa's flat, Tobermory was on the hunt, determined to find the source of the thing that was upsetting him. He padded into the bedroom and stopped, arched his back then lay low, spreading his senses outwards into the room. Was it in here? No. Nothing. He waited for a moment just to be sure, then crept into the living room in hunting stance, determined to catch this thing in action. No. Not here either. There was nothing out of place – had it gone?

Then he spotted a tiny bit of leftover fish in his bowl. That would suffice for now.

Matt was sitting up and putting on his shoes when Sarah rang the bell. 'I'll head home now. See you on Wednesday evening then?' he said, cocking his head on one side hopefully.

'Yes, lovely. See you Wednesday,' said Marissa as she shook out the blankets and prepared the room for Sarah. The last few minutes of the session had gone well, but it was much too short. *I'll do it right the next time and it will all be fine.* Then she remembered. 'Can you wait a few minutes to meet Sarah?'

'That's the plan,' he said with a smile.

Then Marissa remembered something else. 'Oh shit, Matt, I start at St Mary's on Wednesday evening... But we will have the day together on Friday, I'll sort the day off and we can make a plan. Go to Dolores and then maybe a movie?'

'A movie sounds great. I'll text you and we can figure it out.'

Marissa went to let Sarah in.

'Ooh, this is lovey!' Sarah said, walking into the main corridor and looking up and down at the inside of the Edwardian building. She was holding a bunch of flowers in her hand.

'Come in!' smiled Marissa, happy to see her friend, but sad her time with Matt was so short.

'These are for you,' Sarah said, handing the flowers to Marissa.

'Oh! Thank you! I totally didn't expect you to do that.'

'They're for luck, for your new business!'

'Thank you so much! Wow, they're beautiful. The room is down here.'

Sarah followed Marissa down the hallway. When they came into the room, Matt already had his coat on. He smiled and offered his hand. 'You must be Sarah.'

'And you must be Matt!'

They shook hands and Sarah giggled.

'It's lovely to meet you. Those are pretty flowers,' said Matt approvingly.

Marissa had a big smile on her face. Her two closest friends were meeting for the first time – this was an important moment. Overwhelmed with emotion, she put the flowers down on the table. She wanted to hug them both, but she couldn't move from her spot. They were chatting away to each other with no problem at all. Marissa smiled. *I've picked good people to be my friends.*

'Okay, love, I'll leave you to it. I'll call you tomorrow.' Matt gave her a peck on the cheek and turned to Sarah 'Lovely to meet you, Sarah. I hope we can do this again, maybe the three of us over a pint sometime?'

'You're on!' said Sarah enthusiastically with a big grin on her face.

Matt let himself out, waved to Marissa and saluted Sarah.

'He *is* lovely!' said Sarah delightedly, turning to Marissa. 'You did well with him. I like him already!'

Marissa smiled. 'Yes, I like him too! Shall we get started?'

'Tell me about Reiki first. I want to know what it is.'

Marissa smiled. 'I think you'll find out once you experience it. Come on, shoes and coat off, and up on the table please.'

Sarah smiled. 'I trust you.'

'I should hope so!' said Marissa with a giggle.

Sarah settled herself on the plinth and Marissa covered her with blankets. She lit an incense stick from the candle and changed the music, making sure her ringer was off and taking a note of the time. She had to be out of the room before 9pm.

'I will begin now. You'll feel my hands on you, or sense them over your body. All you need to do is relax, focus on your breath and listen to the music, and I'll let you know when we're finished.' *That was kind of a therapist voice and kind of my voice. Interesting.*

Sarah closed her eyes and Marissa reconnected to the Reiki light, then began the treatment. She started at Sarah's head and worked her way down to her feet. She noticed as she got to Sarah's stomach that she had a small pain in her back as she worked. By the time she got to Sarah's feet, it had gotten stronger. She stretched out to try and release it, but that only seemed to make it worse. Sarah on the plinth was looking very peaceful. Marissa touched the button on her phone and looked at the time. It had only been ten minutes. She went back to Sarah and pushed through the pain, working her way back up to Sarah's head again. Then she checked the time. Another ten minutes had passed and there were still forty to go. *What do I do now?*

She started once more, working from the head to the feet, and back up to the head, but the pain in her back was becoming unbearable. She really needed to sit down. When she had reached Sarah's head again, she sat on one of the counselling chairs, just for a moment.

Sarah must have realised this, as she opened her eyes. 'Are you okay? This is lovely. I feel much calmer now. Thank you so much.'

'I've got a pain in my back, but yes, I'm okay. We're not finished yet, there are still another twenty minutes in your session.' Marissa rubbed her back where it hurt.

'Oh, if you have a sore back then we can finish now,' said Sarah. 'It's fine with me.'

'Are you sure? It has been a long day...'

'Yes, I'm sure. I do feel so much more relaxed now. And I know what you meant – you do have to experience this to understand it. I felt waves flowing through me, I felt warm and cold at the same time, and at one point it was as if there were three people working on my body. I thought you were standing at my feet and I opened my eyes and you were at my head! It is amazing. I've not felt this calm in a very long time. Reiki – I like it! Everyone should be made to have a Reiki session! Maybe I'll introduce it to the guys at work for stress management!'

Marissa laughed. 'I'm so glad you enjoyed it. I'm still settling in with this and I guess I have a lot of things to work out. I think I set the plinth at the wrong height for my arms – that's probably why my back is sore. Don't get up – I want to see if I need to make it higher or lower.'

She stood up and placed her hands on Sarah's legs, realising that her arms were hunched over at the shoulder. 'I reckon if I make the plinth a little higher that might help me. You can get up now. Thanks, Sarah, I'm really glad you liked it. And thanks again for the flowers! It was a long way for you to travel for three-quarters of a session...'

'That's okay. We can grab a drink if you like?'

'Tea at my place? You're not really supposed to have alcohol after Reiki... And if it's okay with you, I'll fix the plinth first, so it's done for next time. Then I need to pack away my things.'

Sarah hopped down and Marissa folded the blankets and piled them on the chair. She put the plinth down on the floor on its side, and she and Sarah unscrewed the legs and figured out how to make the plinth higher. They turned it around and did the other side, then stood it up again.

'I'll hop up on it again if you like, so you can judge it,' said Sarah.

'Oh, great idea, thank you.'

Marissa tested the height with Sarah lying on it. It was too high now.

'Oh dear, everything seems to be a muddle tonight.'

They tried again, this time making the plinth a little lower, and Sarah got on top of it once more.

'It's almost right,' Marissa said thoughtfully. 'It's not exactly the right height for me, but it will have to do. It's better than it was.'

She folded the plinth closed and Sarah helped by stuffing the pillows and blankets into the suitcase, closed it and set the lock. There was no room for the candle or the incense, or the speakers.

'I can just bring those with me every time,' Marissa said. 'That's okay, no problem there.'

They put everything under the stairs, managing to find enough space to pack it all away.

'Well, at least that worked!' said Marissa with a sigh.

'It will take some time to get used to all of this,' she confided to Sarah on their way to her flat. 'I thought it would be easy and straightforward, but there are so many things I didn't think about.'

'I know, but there are so many things you did,' Sarah reassured her. 'You'll get into your stride and it will all become second nature.'

'I like that. Yes, I'll get into my stride and it will all become second nature!'

'Noreen said that to me, about the management role, when I started,' Sarah said. 'She was right too – it's beginning to become more natural to me now. I think new routines, new practices, they take time to get used to, and to figure out. You'll sort everything out, iron out the lumps and bumps, and you'll be flying in no time.'

CHAPTER TWENTY SIX

'I'll put the tea on, so. Thanks for letting me stay over last night.' Sarah filled the kettle and switched it on as Marissa rooted around the kitchen for breakfast cereal. Everything seemed to have moved around in the cupboard. *Was Tobermory in here?*

The girls had been talking and laughing and it had gotten late. Sarah had missed the last bus, so she had slept on Marissa's sofa. She had happened to have a toothbrush in her bag ('For emergencies!') and had borrowed a pair of pyjamas for the night.

'You don't have much food in the kitchen, do you?' she commented. 'I have heaps more at my place. I suppose it's a family thing – we always have too much food, just in case!'

'I usually have much more than I need, I guess I haven't been eating as much lately. Sorry I don't have any eggs, Sarah. I hope Coco-Pops will be okay?'

Sarah laughed. 'I've not had those since I was a kid! I must get myself a box.'

'Oh dear, the milk is off. Toast? I've got butter and jam.'

'Looks like you need to do a big shop. Sorry, Marissa, I can't drink black tea. Shall we get breakfast out on the way to the office? I'm dying for a cappuccino, and they have those big juicy muffins.'

They got the bus to work, Sarah chatting away about what she liked to eat when she was little, Marissa enjoying her bright, enthusiastic energy. *It would be fun to have a sister.* Sarah had three sisters; she was in the middle. *That explains her easy-going independent nature – according to my psychotherapy book, that is. Oh shit, I've class tonight... I forgot my notebooks... Never mind.*

Tobermory still wasn't happy. He prowled the flat looking for the source of his worry, but he still couldn't find the culprit. It definitely wasn't a mouse – he'd been through the entire flat and hadn't found a scrap of anything mouse. He didn't think it was bigger than a mouse, but it was elusive, this thing, it was there but it wasn't there. He didn't like it, not one bit.

He leapt back onto his favourite armchair and licked his paws. He liked Marissa, she was kind to him, she was kin. Pack. Family. As close to family as a cat can get. But there was that niggle again. Yes it was here for sure. Something wrong, something not right. It had been sleeping, but now it was awake... Ah... What is it? Something bad, smelled bad, tasted bad, but was invisible. Not a mouse. It was a wrong-thing. That's what it was. He was determined to find it, to hunt it down, and to kill it. Kill it and remove it from his flat. Or give it to Marissa as a gift. Yes, she would like that. She seemed to be attached to it, she was different when it was awake. It was different, too.

Marissa still hadn't settled on an assignment. *I have to focus. I want to finish my diploma.* It seemed difficult for her to focus lately and she was forgetting stuff quite frequently. Noreen had asked her for tea and she had brought her coffee, she had forgot to pick up the printing from the printers... The list was adding up. She sat in class drifting, thinking about her trip to London as Mr Crowley outlined on the board how to handle trauma if it came up in a session.

'You need to realise that you're still not qualified to go deeply into trauma with the client. Trauma, if it comes up in one of your sessions, can "hang around" with a client for days. It does happen, so if this happens to you, it's more a case of being practical, finding out how to help your client manage day-to-day life, until you feel they are stable enough to unpack bits and pieces of what happened. Of course, if it's too much, you could refer them on to a more qualified specialist. That's what your supervisors are there to help you with.'

Yvonne put her hand up, 'Do you think that you need to take a person back through a trauma in order to heal it?'

'That is a loaded question,' said Mr Crowley with a smile, 'and it depends on how you want to approach it. Having a conversation with your client about trauma can be valuable if you tread carefully. Together, you can agree on a process, but often it's something that you cannot do because when trauma comes up, it's usually unexpected. Also, some clients just want to manage their lives as they are and aren't ready to, or don't want to exhume deep trauma. They just want you to help them plaster over the cracks and fissures that have developed in their daily lives, so to speak. In these cases, coping mechanisms are more important. However in other cases, which are rarer, it might be necessary to relive the trauma so the client can better understand it.'

Marissa snapped back to attention and put up her hand.

'Yes, Marissa?'

'How can the client better understand their trauma if they're only seeing their side of things? They are still only coming at it with limited knowledge. That's why I don't think reliving a trauma is useful.'

'Yes, that's true, especially if the client was a child during the traumatic period. However, what we are reframing in counselling is how the client sees what happened to them, rather than what actually happened to them.'

'So why then do we need to walk them through it, go back in time and relive it, if we can just ask them how they're feeling about it now?'

'This is why there are many pathways to work with trauma, choosing which path would depend on the resilience of the client. It would be on a case-by-case basis.' Mr Crowley turned back to the class. 'There are certifications you can obtain after you get your diploma that specialise in certain forms of psychotherapy, such as addictions and couples counselling, and there are many that work with trauma. I would recommend you get specialist training before you knowingly take on a client that suffers from trauma.'

Katie put up her hand. 'But surely trauma is in the eye of the beholder? I mean, some things may not be traumatic to some and may be to others.'

'True, but as a counsellor in training you can let them know in advance what your limitations are, so if you feel out of your depth, it won't come as a surprise to your clients.'

'Is it wrong to bring them back to the trauma? I mean, if they want to go?' asked Yvonne, looking concerned.

'The one thing we do know for sure about counselling is that there is no right or wrong way to do it. That's why staying person centred is so important. Keep the five tenets and stay easy with the client. Go where they want to go. Listen and reflect. Offer a compassionate heart-centred space. And stop if they want to stop. I hope this helps, and you can always continue after the diploma course to get more specialised skills to offer.'

Marissa thought about Margaret. *Was there a trauma there? She certainly seemed traumatised, but there didn't seem to be any one thing that might have caused it. Of course I've only had three sessions with her so far, and I really didn't know much about her background or history. Shit, I should have asked her more about that.. I hope she's doing okay. I certainly didn't want to traumatise her further by suggesting she had OCD. Being a psychotherapist has a lot of responsibility attached to it.*

Ronan had his hand up. 'I read somewhere that meditation can bring on a trauma response. What are your thoughts on that?'

Mr Crowley thought for a moment. 'Hmm, interesting. I could imagine so, yes. Trauma can be many-layered as we experience it on many different levels. As well as having traumatic memories in your mind, your body can store trauma. In that case, the memory of it would come from body memory. If someone is learning how to be still, then trauma could well up inside them, just waiting to express itself. Or, if a person's been holding back from it and they're still, the experience of trapped trauma release could overwhelm them. Yes, it's probably best to avoid meditation in that case.'

'But how do you know? And how can you heal it if you are avoiding it?' asked Marissa, without putting her hand up, 'Surely the point of psychotherapy isn't to add a band-aid, but to transform emotional pain?'

Mr Crowley looked straight at her. He seemed frustrated with her. 'Yes, it would be ideal if that were the case, however most people just want to get on with their lives. It can be too difficult to open the trauma and work through it. We cannot make someone go where they do not wish to go.'

Maybe psychotherapy isn't about healing after all. Marissa took a step back and didn't ask any more questions that evening, but when the class was finished, she went up to Mr Crowley.

'Sorry, Mr Crowley, can I ask you something?'

He turned to her. 'Marissa, I know what I said wasn't to your liking, but person centred means exactly that – the client is the centre, and if they don't want to go somewhere, we need to respect that. Even if we feel they could go deeper, we cannot push them beyond what they agree to.'

Marissa nodded.

'Was that what you wanted to ask me?'

'No, actually, I wanted some advice on a client of mine, if that's okay.'

'Okay.'

'I think she might have OCD – she displays severe frustration and she has repetitive thought patterns that spiral into panic over things that are, well, honestly too ridiculous to ever be real. Like she worries about her dog getting hit by a car, when the dog is never outside the front door. What should I do? Do I tell her to go to her doctor and get a referral to a psychiatrist?'

Mr Crowley seemed to relax a little bit. 'It is difficult when you're starting out. Ironically, you are being thrown in at the deep end as a volunteer also. Have you asked your supervisor about this?'

'I've not seen him since this came up, but I'm seeing him on Thursday. I just thought you may have something for me that would help.'

'Yes, the timing is not always ideal. And the people that need counselling the most are the very ones that you are not ready for, or experienced enough to handle. You can only do what you can do – we are back to bandage thinking. Little things that will make her day better will help more than you realise. Or just listening to her is also very helpful. Don't jump in with both feet and try to fix things. Because you won't be able to. Not just for her, but for most people.'

He scratched his head and continued. 'Just give your client the space to talk, to be heard, to be taken seriously. Believe me, many people don't get that at home, and it could be exactly what she needs to keep her going for now. You have a higher expectation of what you're capable of delivering at this stage.' He smiled at her. 'Don't be so serious. Just being heard helps people more than you know.'

'Thank you.'

'Just being heard helps more than you know,' thought Marissa on the bus back home. *Well, that could be good advice for St Mary's tomorrow, as well as for Margaret. I'm a little nervous.* She put her hands on her stomach and thought about going to St Mary's. Yes, she felt the anxiety. She also felt very, very tired. *But at least I've made a decision about my assignment tonight. 'The role of person-centred counselling and cognitive-based therapy when working with traumatised clients.'*

+++

Marissa left work half an hour early and took two buses to get to St Mary's. She had deliberately dressed down that day, black jeans and a black top, and her usual black cardigan, with a coat thrown over as it was still cold. Bronagh buzzed her in and walked her up to her new counselling room. She was handed the client list for the evening.

Three clients, with five minutes between each one. I can do this!

She was a little early so she took some time to get her bearings. The room was clean and simple; two chairs, a table with a clock and a candle on it, a window and a painting of flowers in a jug. She sprayed St Germain from the bottle she always carried in her handbag, lit the candle, chose the chair facing the door and sat down. The clock ticked loudly. She adjusted it so that it was at her eye level, and it wouldn't be obvious to her client that she was looking at it.

Right on time, there was a loud knock on the door. Marissa stood to attention.

'Come in.'

The door opened. Peering out from behind it was a woman with long straight black hair. Her skin was so pale it was almost translucent. She was the same height as Marissa and was wearing a dirty white tracksuit. She came inside, but rolled on her feet, as if deciding whether to stay or go.

'Are you the counsellor?'

The woman's voice didn't seem to belong to her body; it was in a strong thick accent, the voice of someone who was looking for a fight.

'Yes. I'm Marissa. You must be Miriam?'

The woman nodded. Marissa gestured for her to sit in any of the seats, she chose one and sat down. Marissa closed the door and sat down opposite her. There was a chill in the air.

'Hello, Miriam, it's nice to meet you. We have as many counselling sessions together as you need. You can tell me anything, and it will be kept between us, confidential. But if I feel that you're a danger to yourself or to somebody else, I will have to inform my supervisor. So, what would you like to talk about with me this evening?'

'What do you want to know?' Miriam asked, rocking forward in her chair, looking Marissa straight in the eye in an accusatory way. She crossed her arms and legs, all the while keeping eye contact with Marissa.

Marissa was a little shocked. *I've fallen straight into the deep end here.* 'Erm, well, this is for you – these sessions are a safe space where you can talk about anything you want to talk about. So it's not actually about what *I* want to know, more about what *you* want to tell me. To get off your chest, so to speak.'

'Like a confession?'

'I suppose, if that's what you feel you need right now.'

'Okay,' said Miriam, rocking back in the chair, unfolding her arms and legs and crossing them again the opposite way. She looked very defensive.

There was silence.

Marissa could hear people walking around in the corridor and children playing in the playground outside as the evening sun began to fade. She remembered her strategy of just listening, and decided she would wait it out.

Miriam scratched her chin and twirled her hair around in her fingers and her face went glassy, as if she had left the room.

They sat like this for several minutes, which felt like hours to Marissa. A question formed in her mind. She checked in with herself to decide if it was appropriate. The silence was beginning to get to her, so she thought she'd ask it to break the ice.

'How long have you been in St Mary's?'

Miriam jumped; the sound of Marissa's voice seemed to take her by surprise. She looked straight at her and replied, 'Almost two years.'

'Have you been to a counsellor before?'

'Yeah. Didn't much see the point of it.'

'So how come you're here today?'

'It's for the skillsbridge programme. They want me to do five sessions. I've done two already.'

'Okay. What did you talk about in the other sessions?'

'Not much. The weather. My dog, the one I had when I was growing up. Mam and Dad – a little bit about them.'

Marissa thought she'd try another tack, to try to build some momentum in the conversation. 'You mentioned making a confession – are you religious?'

'Mam and Dad were, yeah. They took me to church with them when I was little, but I stopped going as soon as I was old enough to run away.' She shifted in her chair. 'I ran away. Left home, lived in a shared house with some other people. Anyway, that was ages ago. I'm here now. Like I said, I'm here for the skillsbridge.'

Marissa waited to see if she'd say anything more, but nothing was forthcoming. *This is going to be a long session.*

After Miriam left, Marissa reassured herself that she had done her best with what she had been given. *It's a little like pulling teeth, but I can't force it. I guess each session is going to be different, hit or miss, depending on who I am seeing. Maybe the next person will be a little more talkative.*

She had just enough time to run to the bathroom before the next session. The bathroom reminded her of the ones at school: big mirrors and small cubicles. There was graffiti on the mirror written in lipstick and marker, there was a poem scrawled on the inside of the cubical door:

If you're sad, remember life isn't so bad,
you're here and safe, it's better than living with your dad.'

Marissa washed and dried her hands and went back to the counselling room.

There was a woman waiting for her, already sitting in the chair. She was stocky, in her thirties, Marissa thought, with very short, tightly shaved hair, which was a little longer on top, khaki pants and a dirty white T-shirt.

'You're Marissa?' she asked.

'Yes, hello. Nice to meet you.' Marissa sat down in the free chair opposite her. You're Mary R.?'

The woman nodded.

'Are there a few other Marys here?'

'Yeah, and we're in St Mary's, but I'm no saint.'

Marissa smiled, then let go of her smile in case it offended Mary. She wasn't sure how to play it here. She felt completely out of her depth. *Yvonne was right, Jack Russell terriers... I hope she's right about them being all bark and no bite...*

Mary crossed her legs and folded her arms. 'Yvonne told me about you. She said you were great.'

'That was nice of her. She told me she hoped that you could continue your work with me, but she didn't tell me anything about you. It's all confidential, what you said to her.'

'Yeah, she said so. Same with you?'

'Yes, it's just between us. I'm very glad to meet you, Mary.'

'Why did she leave, Yvonne?'

'Her mother's sick, She'll only be away for a short while to mind her. When she's better, I'm sure she'll come back.'

Mary nodded. 'Yeah. Okay. I had to look after my ma too, when I was a little girl.'

'Is that what you'd like to talk about with me? Or is there something else?'

'Dunno. I guess I can talk about what I was telling Yvonne, but I don't know, I'd have to start again, wouldn't I?'

Marissa thought about it. 'Maybe not. You could continue where you left off with Yvonne, and if I have any questions, I'll ask you. Would that work?'

'Yeah, okay. Yeah, it could work. But I don't feel like it tonight.'

'Okay. Do you want to talk about something else?'

There was that silence again, creeping into the space between them and sitting there ominously, a space for a horror story, or for mundane, boring, day-to-day activities.

'No, not really. Just wanted to meet you.'

Marissa didn't know if she should reply to that.

Mary R. stood up and brushed down her trousers. 'Well then, Miss Marissa, nice to meet you. Same time next week?'

'We've still got forty-five minutes...'

'I don't feel like talking tonight, to be honest. So I'll go to the canteen. See you next week, so.'

Mary walked out of the room.

Marissa was left feeling slightly bereft and very puzzled. This certainly wasn't the protocol she'd been expecting. She looked at the client sheet. Vanessa was due in forty-five minutes. *Does this count as a full hour? I'm putting it down as a full hour. Unbelievable! How rude.*

After a few moments Marissa settled down, took out her notebook and started to jot down some ideas for her college assignment.

Vanessa was a no-show.

On the bus home Marissa was feeling deflated. *One hour spent sitting around. I've only just started; I have to give it a chance. But this is hard work. Is it supposed to be so hard?*

She texted Yvonne: These women don't really want 2 talk - was it this difficult 4 u?

Yvonne replied about a half hour later when Marissa was waiting at the bus stop for the second bus. Hang on in there. Yeah, it's a tough placement, but there will b 1 or 2 that really want it. Have you met Mary R yet?

Marissa wrote: Yes, she came to meet me, stayed 10 mins then said nice 2 meet u and left. Strange.

> Ha, ha, yeah they're funny fish. She's ok, Mary, give her a chance. I thought we were getting somewhere, she may just need some time 2 get used 2u. See you in class next week xY

Marissa sat outside in her favourite spot in the garden with a warm cup of camomile tea before bed. It had been a really long day. Staying up late with Sarah, getting in early to work, the long trek across to St Mary's and the two buses home had taken it out of her. She was still upset. *Five and a half hours spent travelling and waiting around, to just get 2 client hours. It's not worth it.* Her head felt like a filing cabinet that someone had emptied out onto the floor. Her eye was twitching from tiredness. She put the tea down on the ground beside her feet and closed her eyes.

The twitching in her eye got worse, even when it was closed, and it was accompanied by a banging sensation in her head, as if someone was knocking on a door, trying to break in. *Ah, what is this? I'm just tired, I guess, and I only ate a sandwich on the run for dinner.* She breathed and pushed the banging sensation away, but it was getting louder and it was taking more effort to block it out. She rubbed her face, opened her eyes and got a sense of a woman shouting at her, very upset.

Not now. Please. I'm not doing this now.

She imagined the woman shrinking and becoming very squeaky, like a mouse, getting smaller and smaller until, with a 'Pop!', she dissolved.

Marissa's eye stopped twitching and her body relaxed. *That's better. Now I need to get my assignment started, start advertising for Reiki clients and find a hotel for the London trip ... but I think I'll just climb into bed.*

CHAPTER TWENTY SEVEN 

No matter how much time passed, Mr Blakemore's room always seemed the same. And so did Mr Blakemore. *Has he even changed his clothes since I saw him last?*

Marissa reported to him about Cliona finishing up, and he made a note of that. She told him about Margaret too, and he reassured her that she was doing fine, that she was a psychotherapist in training and hiccups were to be expected.

'It's all part of the learning process. Some of our clients are in dire need, it's true, but I have every faith you are doing the right thing for all.'

He informed her that she would be seeing someone new tonight in place of Joy.

'Please check your client schedule – there will be a file there for her. As for the no-shows, it's springtime now, the weather is getting better, so we have a slight falling off of clients, and people who are always coping tend to feel that asking for help is a failure. But we are here for them regardless. In the summer it can be much worse – a sunny evening and you're almost guaranteed that nobody will show up. Unless, of course, they're dedicated, which can be rare. It's a pity these empty hours can't be part of your degree, but you could put them to use, fill them up with contemplation or doing some study of your own.'

Marissa nodded, but her patience was wearing thin. She was putting in the time, but not clocking up the hours. *At least I have my room for Reiki now.* She thought she'd chance asking Mr Blakemore about it.

'I've rented a therapy room for Reiki sessions and I could also see counselling clients there. Would you be able to supervise my sessions for me?'

'Ah, no, no, I'm afraid, I can't do that. My hands are full here, and there would be insurance implications for me. You'll get there, don't fret. You'll get there.'

Room Three seemed much more welcoming to Marissa after St Mary's. It also felt more like home than, she reluctantly admitted, her Reiki room, which was what she was beginning to label it. She looked around the little room. *What is it about this room that makes me feel more comfortable here than in the others?* She took a moment to breathe, bring her awareness into the present moment and let go of the disappointment she was carrying around her slow progress. *I will get there. It's not just me that goes through this, I guess. All good things take time.* She sighed, lit the candle and sat down to wait for Margaret.

I'll give her plenty of space this week to talk. I won't jump in and I won't come to any conclusions. I won't give her anything to worry about on top of what she is already worrying about. She looked at her clock. It was almost time for the session. *She's usually here by now. Oh, I do hope she comes... What if she is a no-show too? What if she got even more upset by what I said to her? What if something happened to her? What if...*

The buzzer rang. Marissa's heart jumped. She had been so engrossed in her 'what ifs', she hadn't expected it. She buzzed Margaret in, and a few moments later the door opened and Margaret popped her head around it.

'Hello, dear. I have to go to the bathroom, is that okay? I'll be back in a jiffy.'

'Sure, no problem, see you in a minute.'

While she waited, Marissa realised she had just been caught up in 'what ifs', which wasn't her usual pattern of thinking. *What if I was connecting into Margaret's thoughts? What if this is what goes on inside her head all the time?*

Margaret came back, hung up her coat and sat down. She was more presentable this week, her hair was much tidier and she looked more contained in herself. She had her trusty handbag with her, which she left on the floor by her feet.

'Hello, Margaret, how are you this evening?'

'Hello, dear. I am well. I had a lovely walk at lunchtime and I saw a squirrel, which I don't usually see.'

Marissa nodded, waiting for the conversation to unfold naturally.

After a moment Margaret added, 'It seems like a long time since I was in this room with you.'

For Marissa it was quite the opposite, but she nodded her head.

Margaret seemed less distracted than usual. 'It's a lovely evening isn't it?' she said.

'Yes, beautiful weather the last few days,' said Marissa. *Well, roads and weather might be helpful to ground the session in.* 'Where did you go on your walk?'

'Oh, I went to the Botanic Gardens. I can walk there from my house. The flowers are beginning to bloom now. There were even some tulips opening up. It always calms my heart when I can spend time in the Gardens. I love the orchid house – the little orchids are like jewels! Fascinating. Do you know that they breathe through their roots?'

'No, I didn't know that,' said Marissa, genuinely interested. Margaret was very different to how she had been the previous week.

'Oh yes, dear, they breathe through their roots, so you can't really bury them, if you have one. That's why they come in transparent pots, so the sunlight can come in.'

'That's very interesting.'

'I love gardening. It calms me down.'

Ah, that's it, she's spent time in a garden. She is certainly much calmer.

'Now, dear, what were we supposed to talk about tonight? Oh yes, I have my notebook here.' Margaret rummaged in her bag and found her notebook. She placed it on her lap and folded her hands on top of it. She was so much calmer than before, it was like seeing a different person.

Marissa smiled and asked the inevitable question: 'How did you get on this week with your homework?'

'Ah, yes. I don't know. You asked me to find positive thoughts, so I made a list, but it isn't very long. It still took me three days. But that was all I had to do, wasn't it?'

'Balancing thoughts,' said Marissa, reminding herself, too. 'Yes, you were to list some positive thoughts to balance the negative ones, and then use them instead of the thoughts you were thinking. If they were negative thoughts, that is.'

Margaret nodded. 'Yes, yes, I remember now. I couldn't quite remember what to do with them! But I had a better week, regardless. I think just coming to see you really helped me. You said something that made quite a difference, you know.'

'I did?' said Marissa, her heart in her mouth, still expecting to be attacked for the OCD thing...

'Yes, you did,' said Margaret. 'You told me that we didn't get to see inside other people's heads and that you were sure there were many people who had the same type of thing going on as me. So I spent some time looking at people, at their heads. I know – it sounds funny, doesn't it?!' She blushed and clasped her hands together, rocking a little bit in her chair. 'But I looked at their heads, I really did, and I wondered what was going on inside them. I looked at people on the street outside my house, people on the television. I saw people everywhere, all around me, so many people! I kept asking myself, "And what is that person thinking? And what is this person thinking?" I'd never thought about it before. And I realised that I didn't know, that I couldn't possibly know, what any of them were thinking! It could be anything. Like you said, we don't get to see inside someone else's head, we only know what is inside our own.'

'Yes, it's very true.'

'Well, with all the number of people out there, I realised that they might be having problems with thinking too, just like me. I was looking at their faces to try to see if they were happy, thinking happy thoughts. Most of them weren't. Most of them looked sad or troubled.'

'Yes, I've noticed that myself.'

'So I told Kevin about it. He's my husband. And do you know what he said?'

Marissa smiled.

'He said that if everyone thought as many terrible things as I did, and if they all came true, that the world would be a truly horrible place, much more horrible than it is already, and everyone in it would probably be already dead!'

Marissa didn't know what to say, so she held her tongue.

'Isn't that so funny?' Margaret asked, seeming delighted. 'I laughed at that! Imagine everyone having horrible things happening to them all the time! It's just impossible really, isn't it? Well, we laughed together, me and Kevin. We haven't done that in a long time. Then he gave me a hug. He hasn't done that in a long time either. He said, "There you are, love. I've not seen you in a long time. It's nice to see you again." I wasn't sure what he meant by that – he sees me every day. But then I realised it was like the bad thoughts had taken me away to a different place. And when we laughed together, I came back.'

Margaret was looking at Marissa expectantly, waiting for her to say something. Marissa was quiet for a few moments, processing what she had said. Then she exclaimed, 'This is a real breakthrough for you, Margaret. Well done!'

Margaret was beaming. 'So you think I'm making progress?'

'Oh yes, very much so.' Marissa felt very relieved. 'Shall we keep working on it then?'

'Yes, please. It was lovely to get that hug from Kevin, and I really enjoyed the Botanic Gardens today. Life might not be so terrible, not really.'

'I'm so happy for you. You seem much more relaxed this evening too. I don't think I've seen you looking so well.'

Margaret left feeling very happy, and Marissa was reassured about her skills as therapist. *It's interesting how Margaret went away from last week's session thinking about something totally different from what I expected her to be thinking about. I guess I can't have any expectations at all. Every little thing that I say can make a difference, either good or bad. Or maybe it's not what I say, at all. Maybe it's how ready the person is to hear it, or what they think they hear in that moment.*

It was time for Cliona's last session. Marissa was slightly concerned that in pattern with most of her other clients so far, she wouldn't show up, and she really wanted to close off the sessions with her.

But at three minutes to the hour, the buzzer rang and a moment later there was a knock on the door, and a bright, shiny and pregnant Cliona bounced into the room like a Tigger.

'Hi, Marissa!'

'Hello, Cliona, you've brought the sunshine in with you tonight!'

Cliona was beaming. She walked across the room, threw her coat on the floor and sat down.

'I'm very happy to see you so happy this evening!' said Marissa.

'Me too! I love my job! I got paid – and I bought this,' she displayed the colourful fluffy jumper she was wearing, 'And I got new shoes for Ari. She really needed new shoes and it was so good to buy them with my own money, to not have to ask Nan for a lend.' She shifted in her chair. 'We will need new things for the baby, so I will save up some money for that too. Nan said I still don't need to pay rent, even though I offered. She said I'd need money for the baby, and she's right. And ... guess what?'

'What?' said Marissa, caught up in Cliona's happy mood.

'Mam got in touch with me. Nan must have told her that I was pregnant. She wants to meet me, and see Ari too.'

Cliona hadn't really talked about her mother before, only said that she'd kicked her out of the house when she'd found out she was pregnant with Ariana, who was now four.

'How are you feeling about that?'

'Well, I was angry at first, then I did that exercise you taught me, remember? Right back at the beginning, with the coyote. I went to visit him and we blew up a lot of stuff I was carrying inside me about Mam.'

Casting her mind back, Marissa did remember the coyote. The images from that journey with Cliona came back to her in full colour. *Why don't I work that way anymore? It was so effective, and obviously Cliona is still getting value from it. I've not done visualisations with any of my clients for a long, long time.* She suddenly felt bereft. She didn't even know if she could work that way again. It was as if that part of her was, well, closed off to her. An image of a green door welded shut to a wall came into her mind. *No, it isn't a wall, it's a tree. A tree?!*

'Yeah, I felt much better after blowing up rocks with my pal coyote,' continued Cliona.

Marissa dragged her attention back to the conversation, which, to all intents and purposes, was very easy to do.

'Ah good, that's great. I'm glad that he can still help you!'

Cliona smiled. 'So I think I'll meet her, because, well, you know, life is too short, and Ari would love to meet her granny. I think she thinks Nan is her gran. Nan doesn't mind that of course, but Mam is really missing out on seeing Ari growing up. She told me she was sorry and wanted me to give her another chance. That she didn't want to miss this new baby the way she missed Ari as a baby.'

Cliona crossed her legs and sat back in the chair. Her yellow tights were softer than the fishnets she had worn when she had started seeing Marissa. She looked radiant and happy.

'You've come so far since we started together,' said Marissa. 'I'm very proud of you. I don't know if I'm allowed to say that, but I'm still in training, so I'll take the risk. When you came to see me twelve weeks ago, your life was falling apart, and now you've got a job and a boyfriend, you can manage your anger better and you are making space for your mother to come back into your life. You didn't give up on yourself.'

Cliona blushed. If she had been a light, she would have been shining even brighter with the praise. 'But you, you didn't give up on me,' she said. 'You listened to everything I said and didn't make me feel that I was the complete idiot I felt I was. There were a few really dodgy weeks there, Marissa, really difficult for me, and the only thing that kept me going was knowing that I could talk to you about it, that you would help me, you wouldn't give up on me. And I always felt better when I left this room, even if sometimes it was shit while I was in here, it lifted afterwards, or even a few days after. Coming to you was like a rest stop on a long-haul flight – I could catch my breath again before going on. It's been bloody amazing coming here. Thank you so much. The best thing I've ever done for myself has been coming here.'

Marissa blushed. 'I think it's counselling that has provided that space for you, Cliona. It's not about me at all.'

Cliona cocked her head on one side and grinned. 'Ah, but there are so many crap counsellors out there. Even I've heard stories. You don't know what or who you're gonna get. But you're good at this. Keep going! You helped me, so you can help so many more people too.'

She looked around, as if there might be someone watching her. Then she reached into her handbag and pulled out a small box of chocolates.

'Here, I got these for you, to say thanks. It's only small, but I wanted to give you something.'

Marissa accepted the present with a smile, though feeling a little awkward. 'Thank you. That's really thoughtful of you. I do intend to keep going and I'm really happy I was able to help you.'

'Cool. Now, you told me you'd do one more technique with me tonight, so what's the story? Let's do this thing!'

The room seemed significantly emptier when Cliona left. Marissa became emotional saying goodbye. She truly hoped that everything in Cliona's life would be amazing, just like she was. *Working with someone who really wants to work is fantastic. It's why I'm here, doing this. Helping people who help themselves. I know I can't make anyone work hard, they have to want to do it. Maybe that's why so many people give up, or stop coming, or don't come at all.*

The buzzer rang. The third client of the evening had arrived for their first session. Aisling. Marissa cleared her throat, brushed down her clothes and went down to meet her.

CHAPTER TWENTY EIGHT 

There were six of them crammed into Dolores's healing room in Greystones, which seemed much smaller than usual. She had packed away her plinth and desk and they sat on fold-out chairs in a circle. Coats were piled on the floor in the corner, incense was burning in the background and the Buddha on the shelf was smiling with pride. It didn't feel claustrophobic, and there was a nice breeze coming in from the open window.

They had just been working with the 'Open Time and Space' symbol, many of them still found it difficult to draw. Marissa and Matt were still using the diagrams from their notebooks. There was one hour left of the Reiki workshop follow-up session.

'Does anybody have any other questions, or want to share any of their experiences before we do the self-practice?' asked Dolores with a smile.

Marissa and Matt recognised two of the other people in the room from their workshop, everyone else was new to them, besides Dolores. One of the men raised his hand, and Dolores nodded for him to speak.

'I'm still not sure about the symbols – what happens when you're finished working with it? Does it stay hanging there, where you left it? Or do you need to somehow, switch it off?'

'Great question. When you activate a symbol you empower it. As symbols are packets of energy, the energy will, so to speak, run dry after a time. So I've not spoken about disempowering a symbol, but there is a way to do this, if you wanted to. I've not had a situation myself where I've found this to be necessary, however.'

Marissa chimed in, 'So, say, if you were to activate the wrong symbol, you could disempower it?'

'Well, I'm not sure if it would dissolve it away completely, and Reiki symbols are for healing, so even if it was, as you call it, the 'wrong' symbol, then it wouldn't be a bad thing to leave it to drain its power out by itself. For example, if you needed the symbol for peace and you drew the symbol for grounding by mistake, it could actually be that you needed to be grounded first, before peace would come along. Sometimes these mistakes are not mistakes after all. But I suppose if you wanted to, you could visualise the power leaving the symbol and dissolving into the violet flame... Yes, that could work. I really don't see why you'd need to do that, though.' Dolores thought for a moment. 'I think the violet flame would work, or indeed you could just will the energy back to the Universe to be recycled into something else.'

The man seemed satisfied.

'Why do you ask? Just out of curiosity,' Dolores said to him.

'I like to have order, when I open something, I tend to close it again. It just felt to me that the symbols were being left open and I wasn't feeling comfortable with that. But as you say, they would dissolve away themselves, a bit like a fizzy tablet, then I am happy enough with that.'

'Anyone else?'

One of the women put up her hand. 'I'd like to share something that happened to me. I had arranged to send distance Reiki to a friend of mine, we choose a specific time to do it. She was in her house and I was in mine. Just after I got started, there was an accident outside of her house. A car crash, actually, a woman in a car swerved to avoid a child on a bicycle and hit a lamppost. My friend, she ran outside to help. The child was fine, but the car was totalled and the woman in the car, she was quite badly hurt, it was a head injury. Of course I didn't know about this and I kept sending Reiki to my friend. They had to phone an ambulance, they were afraid to move her. And when the paramedics got there, they were surprised she hadn't been killed. They said the injuries were life-threatening. My friend, she described how calm she felt while she stepped in to help support the woman while they waited for the ambulance to come. She held her hand and spoke calmly to her, and the woman didn't pass out, which was important, apparently. She's doing well now, in hospital, recovering.

The woman I mean. My friend told me she thought that my sending Reiki to her may have something to do with it.'

Everyone was enthralled by this story, Dolores included.

'You just never know where the energy is going to go,' Dolores said. 'There is always a greater plan, a bigger picture. We have to trust and believe that the Reiki knows what to do. As I say over and over again, we are not the master of Reiki, Reiki is the master of us. It must not have been that woman's time to die. What a beautiful story.'

Nobody could follow that sharing. Dolores put on some gentle music and they had a Reiki self-practice where they used three different symbols. When it was over, it was time to go.

'You can join me at a Reiki share anytime, for a refresher,' Dolores reminded them as they got their coats. 'You're on my email list, so I will email everyone with the next dates. No obligation. I hope to see you all again soon.'

Matt and Marissa caught the DART to Dun Laoghaire. Marissa was delighted to finally have him all to herself at last. She snuggled into him until the train pulled into the station, then they both hopped out, holding hands. Matt was grinning as they walked up Marine Road towards Georges Street, they swung their arms as they walked, fingers clasped tightly.

'All the pubs are shut!' said Marissa, 'It's a Good Friday, indeed!' She gave him a playful dig with her shoulder.

'Yeah,' said Matt, shouldering her back. 'Mores the pity. If you want a drink, you need to have bought a few cans for home, which I didn't do. Don't worry, I'm good with the Reiki. Let's rent a movie and get a takeaway, and settle in for the evening at mine.'

'Sounds good to me.'

+ + +

The following morning was Easter Saturday. Marissa found herself rearranging Matt's furniture and sorting through his wardrobe. She caught herself, and stopped. She had to get back home before noon, as she had been invited to lunch with her parents. Matt had been invited but he preferred to skip it and spend the day studying for his Tai Chi teacher training certification.

Uncle Lou and Aunty Naomi were at her parents' house, with Amanda and Marcus in tow. Helena and Leo were in Paris for the long weekend. Amanda was delighted to hear about Marissa's new Reiki room and wanted to try Reiki right away, so Marissa placed her Reiki hands on her head right there at the dinner table.

'Oooh, that's lovely! I like it!' Amanda exclaimed.

Marcus was running around the table in circles, making everyone dizzy.

'I don't know how Helena does it,' Naomi confided to Rose. 'He is so high energy, we're exhausted already, and they're not coming back till Monday night!'

Rose served a cold platter of smoked salmon, fresh bread and salads, and promised chocolate cake for dessert. Bernie was in high spirits. He laughed as he watched Marcus, but he was also watching Marissa and Amanda out of the corner of his eye.

'What are you doing, love?' he asked. 'Is that the Reiki?'

Marissa grinned. 'Yes, Dad, it is. And thank you again for your suitcase – it's now living in my room in Rathmines, under the stairs. It will save me having to take blankets over every time.'

'Have you seen many clients, dear?' asked Naomi, sounding genuinely interested.

'I've just started. Last Monday was my first night, actually. I'll be there every Monday evening from now on.'

'Congratulations! Starting your own business! About time. I hope that my gifts have been helping you get up and running.' Uncle Louis lifted his glass in a mock toast to Marissa.

She beamed back. 'Yes, thank you, Uncle Lou, you really have taken the pressure off me. I've just gone part time at work, and will really try to make a go of it. Ideally, I want to see clients for psychotherapy too, but I still have to figure that part out.'

Amanda was squirming under Marissa's hands, so she pulled them away.

'That was nice, Aunty M., but I think I've had enough now,' Amanda said, reaching across the table for a slice of smoked salmon and popping it straight into her mouth.

'Can I try?' asked Bernie, curiously.

'Yes! I'd love to do Reiki on you, Dad!'

Marissa went over and stood behind her father. She put one hand on each of his shoulders and opened herself to the Reiki flow. Bernie was still chatting away at the table as she stood there, so she whispered, 'Dad, just stop for a moment and feel it.'

'Okay love,' he said quietly, and closed his eyes and stopped talking.

The others just ignored them and the noise levels around the table didn't subside in the slightest. Marcus was now jumping up and down and demanding chocolate cake, even though the lunch things had not yet been put away.

Marissa could feel her father relaxing under her hands. She moved them to the crown of his head and he gave a shiver.

'Ooh, that's strange, but very calming. Thank you, love!'

'You're welcome, Dad. Hang on, I'll stay another minute.'

Marissa had a thought. She had nobody booked in for Reiki that Monday, it was still Easter, and she really hadn't organised herself to get clients yet. She had been going to ask Matt if he wanted to try another session with her, but why not ask her dad?

'Would you like to come see the room? On Monday evening? I'll give you a Reiki session, just the way I would for a client.'

'Well, love, how could I refuse? You could ask your brother too, maybe?'

Rose chimed in, 'Yes, that would be great. You should ask Eli, he's getting stressed over the baby and it might be good for him to relax.'

Marissa nodded and stepped away from her father. 'Okay, great, come on Monday then – 6:15? I'll phone Eli later and ask him too.'

'Wonderful!' said Bernie, slapping his hands down on the table. 'Now, who wants cake and coffee?'

'Me! Me! Me!' said Marcus. 'Cake and coffee for me!'

'No coffee for him!' said Naomi and Louis at the same time.

Dad and maybe Eli on Monday. I need Matt to come back too, okay I want Matt to come back. I guess the following week I could ask Naomi and Helena. But I do want to get in some proper paying clients. What about Noreen's sister? She never called me. I suppose I'll need to advertise somewhere that I'm open.

Marissa shivered at the thought of it. She stopped on her way home in her local shop to get some milk and cat food and saw there was a noticeboard behind a glass screen on the wall by the main door. *Well, that could be a good start, keep it local.* When she went to pay, she asked for a card so she could put a notice up.

'That will be €5 per week.'

'Oh, okay, sure. Why not?' She handed over the €5 and got a blank index card in return. Her mind went as blank as the card. 'Can I write this at home and bring it back later?'

'No problem,' said the man behind the counter.

Back at her flat, Marissa tried to construct her Reiki advert. She wrote it out in rough in her notebook:

> *Reiki sessions with Marissa, relax unwind and enjoy – just €25 for an hour, call me.*

That looks awfully sleazy. And what if they start phoning me during the night, or just phoning me for fun? Maybe I shouldn't give my phone number and just give my email address instead? What does Dolores do?

She went to her laptop and switched it on, and made a cuppa while she waited for it to load up. She looked up Dolores's website not only to see what contact she gave, but how she described Reiki. Then she fell down the internet rabbit-hole, spending several hours looking at various Reiki websites. *There are so many different descriptions and they're all ... well ... confusing! I need to clear my head, do something else and come back to it later.*

She reached for her new Scott Taylor – well, not so new at this stage, she'd already read it twice and was working her way through it for a third time. *There's so much in here. I just need to remember everything he says. It's all important and so useful.*

As well as making notes, she had started underlining paragraphs and learning things off by heart, saying them out loud. There were plenty of scribbles in between the sections too, circles and triangles, she probably did that while she was reading. She lay down on her sofa, took a sip of her now cold tea, and opened the book.

After a few minutes, she fell asleep with the book open on her chest.

Tobermory had come in through a crack in the open window. As soon as he entered the room he sensed the wrong-thing. It was a thing, it was wrong, and it was right there! How dare it come back!! It was an invader and this is his territory. It had to go. He would catch it and kill it and dismember it and... But first he had to catch it.

He approached it cautiously and found himself standing in front of the sofa where Marissa lay napping. She was snoring slightly. He knew it was here, somewhere. He was very still, every sense open wide, but nothing moved, it was not a mouse, then. No mouse-like scent. He knew it wasn't a mouse. He's a clever cat. But it *was* still here. And that was not allowed. He waited for the chase, wanting to flush it out. But nothing stirred, just the rise and fall of Marissa's breath. He mewed a little bit, to warn it of his presence, but again, nothing. He didn't like this, he didn't like it one bit.

He leapt up onto Marissa's legs. Definitely closer now. It is up here, somewhere. She stirred in her sleep, but didn't wake. One of her hands dropped to her side and he jumped, arched his back, then settled again. Where is it? So confusing.

After a moment or two, Tobermory walked carefully along Marissa's legs towards her stomach. He knew he was getting closer because the fur on the back of his neck started to prickle. His tail was twitching now - how could something have the nerve to come into his house without his permission? And elude him like this? He thought he heard it, he hesitated, arched his back, but nothing. He stepped up onto her stomach. She didn't stir this time.

Tobermory leaned his weight into his back paws and pawed at the book on her chest because it was in the way, it was annoying him. And, just because he wanted to. Nothing happened. He pawed at it again and felt a shiver of something ice-cold go down his paw, through his body and out through the tip of his tail. OUCH! But he could take it. He was on the prowl, on the hunt. He was going to kill this thing. His hackles up again, he knew it was right here. RIGHT HERE! But still he couldn't see where it was, couldn't touch it, and even worse, he couldn't smell it. Something without a smell, that was BAD NEWS. He cautiously stuck out one of his paws to slap at the book again, but actually, it *had* hurt the last time, maybe more than he wanted to admit. He changed his mind and pulled his paw back in. Tail twitching furiously now, he sat down on Marissa's tummy, thinking about what to do next.

Marissa stirred in her sleep, responding to the weight of the cat on her stomach. She shifted onto her side and the book slid off her chest, fell and hit the leg of the coffee table. Tobermory jumped, hissed then vaulted off the couch, leapt up onto the worktop and flew out the window.

Tobermory felt a little better once he was outside. The evening sun came out from behind a cloud and it was warm. He needed to clean himself, it had been at least twenty minutes since he last had a bath. He reached out his paw and began to lick it. A bird hopped over to him and watched. He swiped at it and it flew away. I am the boss. I am in charge. He was sleepy now. He lay back into the wall in the sun and closed his eyes.

✦✦✦

Sunday and Monday were free days for Marissa. She slept late on Saturday and had breakfast in bed, worked on her assignment and continued working on her Reiki advert until she felt happier with it.

I think I'll have to get a new phone for work, or just stick to email. It would be easier than turning the phone off at night, and if something happened to the family I wouldn't know about it – no, a new phone is the best idea. She got out some markers and drew circles and spirals around the perimeter of the advert card so it would stand out on the board. *Yes, that's good. I'm happy with that.*

When she dropped the card into the shop Sunday evening the shopkeeper assured her that he would put it up behind the glass for her. She waited and watched him, but he didn't make a move. She decided to treat herself to an early fish and chips dinner and ate it in the park (so the smell of chips wouldn't take over her flat) while a fresh breeze played with her hair. She popped back into the shop on her way home and the card still wasn't up.

She had called Eli. He wasn't able to come for a Reiki session and actually didn't sound interested in coming at all, but that was okay. He didn't have to like the same things that she liked. *Just Dad then and hopefully by next week I'll have some people responding to the ad. It will all work out great. What have I forgotten? Ah yes, a hotel for my London trip.* Her heart jumped. *Yes, I need to book a hotel. Where will I stay? It's going to be so exciting going to London. I should book somewhere near the venue. Yes, I'm going to see Scott Taylor live! I can't wait! It's going to be an amazing adventure. Maybe I'll even get to meet him! Wonder where my book is... I'll have a look for it when I get home.*

She spent the evening looking through hotels, mapping the venue, airport and train station. But before that, she tore her flat apart looking for her book, and was very puzzled to have found it shoved behind the bin in the kitchen. She shrugged her shoulders, shook it out and opened up her laptop and sat in bed with the laptop on her lap. Tobermory was nowhere to be seen. After two hours of exploring the internet she settled on a hotel, and had to get up to find her visa card to put a deposit down.

She went into the living room to look for her handbag and found Tobermory curled up in a tight circle on the cold hearth.

'Baby! This isn't like you, when you're cosy armchair is free? Are you okay?'

She went over to him and he opened one eye, saw it was her and stretched, then stood to attention, arched his back and stared her down.

'What's that on your paw? Soot? No, it can't be soot, it's white.'

He stood there, eyeing her. Marissa looked at his bowl, and back to the cat.

'You've eaten your food, so your tummy *is* working, maybe you're just having an off day?'

Tobermory, of course, didn't answer her. She felt the bank card in her hand and remembered she was about to book a hotel.

'Okay, well, your chair is just there, you know, if you wanted to sit on it... See you later baby.'

Marissa went back into her bedroom, clambered into the bed and pulled up the covers, grabbed her laptop and finalised the booking.

Sorted! That's the hotel booked, and it's not too far away from the conference centre. I won't have too much trouble finding it. Woohoo! London, here I come!

+++

On Monday evening her father was coming for his Reiki session, this time Marissa was determined to remember to bring everything she needed. She went out of her way to check at the shop once more and that proved successful, her small advert was finally on display. *Great! The clients will come rolling in now!*

She sat in the chair outside her Reiki room, waiting for Sam to finish. At five minutes past six he still hadn't come out. She leaned into the door, but couldn't hear anything. She knocked, then opened the door. The room was empty. *Of course, it's Easter Monday, he isn't working today.*

Feeling a little silly, she went inside and switched on the desk lamp. Her free-standing lamp had been moved, so she moved it back to where Matt had put it, plugged it in and turned it on. She pushed the chairs up against the wall and went to get her plinth and the suitcase. She quickly realised she couldn't carry them both together.

Ten minutes later, the incense and candle were lit, the plinth was set up and soft music was coming out from the speakers attached to the iPhone. She even remembered to switch off the ringer! Marissa felt a sense of satisfaction. The room was good now. She was ready, and right on time, the buzzer rang.

'Marissa? It's Dad.'

'Coming!'

Marissa pressed the button under the speaker and could hear the door opening at the front of the building. She stepped out into the hallway and saw her father enter through the main door.

'This is very nice!' he said, smiling and looking around as he walked towards her.

'Hi, Dad, welcome to my Reiki room!'

'Ooh, that smells nice,' he said as he stepped inside.

'You can hang your coat up on the back of the door if you like.'

'Thank you. What do I need to do now?'

'Come in, take your shoes off, get up on the plinth here and lie down. I'll help you get up. All you need to do is relax, and I'll do the rest.'

'Okay then.' He clambered up onto the plinth, stretched out and Marissa put a pillow under his head and another one under his knees. He closed his eyes, and she began the session.

As she worked on her father she was overcome with love for him. This man had been in her life, well, for as long as she was alive. He was always there for her, and it was wonderful to be able to do something for him, for a change. She didn't notice the time passing, the new height of the plinth was a big improvement, as her back didn't start to hurt until forty-five minutes into the session. She stopped to rub it and stretch a little bit. Her father had fallen asleep in the first ten minutes. She decided to leave him sleeping and closed the session ten minutes before the hour was up.

I should offer him some water... Oh no, I've no glasses, or tumbler, and I thought I had everything! Oh well, I'll have to figure that one out for the next time.

She watched him from the chair for another five minutes then decided to wake him gently the way Dolores did, by placing strong hands on his feet, arms and hands. She turned down the music first.

'Hi, Dad, I'm finished now. How are you doing?'

Bernie rubbed then opened his eyes. 'Hi, love. That was lovely, better than a night's sleep! Was I snoring?'

Marissa nodded her head and grinned.

'Oh, no!'

'Here, let me help you up.' Marissa offered her arm and her father took hold of it and sat up on the plinth, then he swung his feet over to the side.

'Wait for a minute or two, then you can stand up.'

Marissa helped her dad get to his feet and sit down on the chair. He took a moment or two before putting on his shoes.

'I don't know what you did, but I feel I need to go home to bed!'

'Sorry, Dad, I'd offer you a drink of water, but I forgot to organise that.'

'Ah, that's grand. Sure I'll get one shortly, when I get back home to Rose. Did you have a good rest of your weekend?'

'Yes, I've been working on my assignment. It's coming together. Do you know I finish college in three weeks? I can hardly believe it!'

'That went so quickly! Well, love, I'm very proud of you, and I'm delighted to have seen your new room. Well done and *Mazel tov* on your new endeavour. I'm rooting for you, as always, and I'm always here if you need me.'

Marissa gave him a hug. 'Thanks, Dad.'

'Shall I help you pack up your things?'

'No, Dad, you go on home now. I'll do it. I need to practise setting it all up and taking it all down. It was great to see you and I hope you have a lovely sleep tonight!'

CHAPTER TWENTY NINE

College seemed much more organised around the final assessments than they had been with the mid-terms. This time they had designated time slots with designated clients and counsellors, so everyone could make a note of when they were 'on'. They even had a week to mentally prepare.

'Of course we can't really study for this,' said Katie over tea. 'It would be really bad if we stopped our client in mid-stream and said, "Can you wait a moment? I need to check in the book what to do next!"'

Everyone laughed, but the laughter was tinged with nervousness and anticipation.

'A whole week to wait. I wish we could do them tonight,' said Marissa, helping herself to a biscuit.

'Will you miss us at all, Marissa?' asked Yvonne, stirring sugar into her tea.

'Ah, what a thing to ask! Sure we have one another's phone numbers, we can always meet up after the class is over.'

'Shall we have a party?' suggested Emmet. 'I think the other group is talking about having a party. We could book a room somewhere together – that could be fun!'

'Well, we *have* worked very hard, we deserve a bit of *craic*,' Katie said, joining them at the table.

There were significantly fewer people in the class than there had been when they'd started two years before. There had originally been sixty-two in their year group, split into three classes. Now there were only two classes of around twenty people in each. That was usually what happened – real life got in the way, people changed their minds, and the counselling study did bring up things that sometimes people weren't ready to deal with, so they dropped out.

'I'll come to the party, if you'd let me,' said Barbara with a grin. She'd been missing for several weeks and had just re-joined the class. She was going to take a summer catch-up module.

'It's brilliant there's so much flexibility with the college, you won't be that far behind us after the summer,' said Katie, leaning into her friend with a smile. 'And I'm really glad you've not given up, Barbara. There's plenty of time for you to finish everything. It's not a race.'

'Is anyone going to stay on another year for the degree?' asked Marissa, surveying the group and wondering if she would stay on, too.

'Sure thing!' said Emmet. 'Hey, I didn't do this much work and put up with you all for this long to give up now!'

'Oooh, nasty,' giggled Barbara. 'I've missed the banter, whatever about the classwork!'

'I might do it,' said Katie. 'I've not decided yet.'

'Well, we should make sure we have everyone's number and stay in touch regardless,' said Yvonne. 'If Mum gets better after this round, I'd also like to come back. One more year for another degree, be a shame to waste the opportunity.'

'It *would* be nice to stay together as a group, too,' said Barbara. 'My plan is to work through the summer and keep going then. It gives me another year to get my client hours sorted out.'

'It's time to go in,' said Emmet, standing up from the table and brushing the biscuit crumbs off his jumper. 'Last class of the term. Who would have thought!'

Everyone trickled into the classroom. Marissa sat down at her usual desk, behind Ronan and beside Yvonne. Barbara was on the other side. It *was* great to have her back, it felt like proper closure.

Marissa leaned in to whisper to her, 'Are you going to do the assignment too? Do you need help catching up?'

'I'm good, thanks,' Barbara answered. 'I don't have to hand it in until the end of the summer, so I've plenty of time, but I would like to borrow some of your textbooks when you're finished with them, if that's okay?'

'Yes, sure, no problem!'

Mr Crowley cleared his throat. 'Hello everyone, this could be the last time you all sit together in this particular ensemble. I've been honoured to teach you all, and you're a great group, really keen and bright and interested. You've all come on a long journey, but there's still a ways to go. Remember, once you qualify for your diploma, you can go on and continue to get a degree, and you'll still need four hundred client hours to become accredited with the Irish Association of Counselling and Psychotherapy. But there's no rush to do that. Some people take months, some people years. It's up to you what your intentions are. Aptly, tonight we'll be talking about counsellor burnout. It's important that you look after yourselves as well as your clients. You don't want to have invested so much time in the degree, and the client work, only to burn out and stop doing counselling after only two or three years.'

He sat down at his desk. 'Many of you claim you understand and practise self-care, but in reality, do you really? Not only does it impact your psychological health, it also impacts your physical health, and your client work. An important point – if you're not in good shape, your clients will know it. Just imagine the scenario – someone in great distress comes to see you, but you're exhausted, your energy is low and you're having trouble focusing. Your client may still be in flight, freeze or fight mode, and they'll be judging you, even though you won't be judging them. Their primary judgement will be: "Can my counsellor hear what I have to say without getting upset by it?" This is vital and I cannot stress it enough. If your client feels you will be upset by them telling you something that upset them, then they won't want to upset you. And that changes the whole relationship, not just the relationship in that particular session. There's a fine line between sympathy and empathy. And when we are tired and run down, we are more likely to cross into sympathy, which, again as you already know, ruins the therapeutic relationship. And worse, if you yawn or have trouble staying present, they will think you don't care about them, or that they're not worth caring about.'

'The secondary judgement will be: "Are they practising what they preach?" You can't advocate for healthy living if you aren't living a healthy life yourself. This one is overlooked so often. Your client will know if you're stressed, anxious or unwell. And they'll be less likely to trust you if you are. So let's really look at self-care tonight. And be real with yourself. Are you doing it? Take ten minutes and talk to the person beside you about your current self-care routine.'

Barbara turned to Marissa, who smiled back her. 'Well, I've been off for a while, but that's no reason not to be taking care of myself. I think I actually took the time off to look after myself. There was just too much going on for me to handle it all. So self-care for me was saying "no" to class for a while.'

'That's fair enough,' said Marissa, 'and you're back now, so self-care now means saying "yes" to class!'

'I suppose so.'

'Okay then, how are you going to look after yourself now you're back in class?'

Barbara thought for a moment. 'Good question. I suppose I'll continue with my therapy sessions, and I do journaling. What else...? I like to go for walks, and I try to meditate a few days a week, but I usually get distracted. What about you, Marissa?'

'I don't know actually. I am keeping up with my therapy. I seem to be mostly running from home to work to class, to Cabra, and now to St Mary's. And I'll be offering Reiki sessions now on Mondays, too.'

'Oh? Reiki sessions? What are they?' asked Barbara.

'Yes, Reiki, I suppose, is my main form of self-care, but I've not been doing it as often as I should do. It's a healing practice, it's kind of like meditation, and you can do it for yourself, or for other people. I really need to make more space to do it for myself every day.'

'Sounds interesting.'

'And there's Matt – he looks after me.'

'Matt?'

Marissa blushed. 'My boyfriend. You have been away a while.'

'Yes, I suppose I have, but we haven't talked much in class either, we've all been so busy.'

Marissa nodded. 'Self-care means slowing down.'

'Self-care means saying "no" and "yes" to things.'

'Having a bath is self-care too,' added Marissa, 'its good for the body and mind.'

'Unwinding is self-care – watching a good movie, reading a book, taking some time off from your troubles,' agreed Barbara.

'Yes, having a cup of tea and just sitting in the garden – I love doing that. I never thought of it as self-care.'

'Going to the dentist is self-care. I really need to book an appointment, it's been a year since I went last. Yuk!'

Mr Crowley called their attention back to the centre. 'What did you learn?'

Kelly put her hand up and Mr Crowley nodded for her to speak.

'Self-care means looking after yourself,' she said. 'There's a difference between self-care and pampering. Pampering is luxury, which is nice but not essential. Self-care is essential. Realising this made everything easier for me. I didn't feel guilty then, looking after myself.'

'Very good observation. I think that many people get confused between what is pampering and what is essential. The more people who are able to see the difference, the healthier our communities will become. Well done, Kelly.'

After a lighter session than usual, everyone was in good form while they were packing up and going home. Marissa hung back.

'Mr Crowley, I have a question for you about client work, if that's okay?'

He turned to her with a smile. 'Sure, Marissa, what can I help you with this week?'

Marissa smiled. 'You were right about my client, by the way – it all worked out okay in the end. She was happy, and she focused on something else altogether.'

'Glad to hear it. It's all part of the learning process.'

'What I want to ask you now is, well, it's taking me ages to clock up my client hours. I have access to a room now, I'm renting it for Reiki, but I could also see therapy clients. I'm wondering about insurance. Mr Blakemore told me that I should find out about that. How does it work?'

'It's no problem, just give the address where you're working to the office and ask them to cover you under the school policy.'

'Just like that?'

'Just like that! Just tell the office and you're good to go.'

Marissa felt a huge weight lifting from her chest. 'Thank you!'

'You still need to organise supervision, however, so don't forget.'

'I won't!'

While Marissa was busy at college, Tobermory was in distress. He was pacing up and down in the flat. He really did not like the wrong-thing and it was back, on his armchair, and he really wanted to curl up and sleep in his favourite spot, but he couldn't. Not with it there. It was sleeping in his spot – the cheek of it! And it *might* be looking at him, even though it was asleep. Was it going to pounce? He didn't want it to hurt him again, but he didn't want it here, either.

He gathered his determination, tucked his ears back and approached it quietly. It didn't move, but something about it seemed to change. He showed his teeth, arched his back and his tail twitched. He really wanted to run away, but no, he needed to defend his flat and take back his space. Especially his favourite chair.

Something hazy and translucent rose out of a paper-bound-thing that was on his chair. It drifted outside of it, something rippled and glossy. This paper-bound-thing was something Marissa liked to hold, a lot. Too much. She slept with it sometimes, he wouldn't go near the bed when it was in it. He knew that the paper-bound-thing had something to do with everything. The hazy translucent blackness curled and slithered and spun. It wound and pulled itself out of the paper-bound-thing and hung there, in mid-air, right in front of him just for a moment, before slipping onto the floor.

Tobermory snarled, then pounced on the sticky, black, hazy thing with both paws but it eluded his claws. He lashed out at it, but he couldn't make contact. He refused to give up, but it moved so quickly. He chased it, crept up upon it and slapped it with his paw, but – *How dare you?!* – it bit him on the paw! And not just any paw, but his favourite left front paw. *Ouch!*

He stopped chasing the hazy black wrong-thing and examined his paw instead. He started to lick it. This was the last straw. That thing had to be destroyed. It was nasty. Very, very nasty. And it still didn't smell like anything. BAD NEWS! Even worse than that, it didn't have legs. Imagine that! And he *was* going to destroy it. For sure. But not right now.

Marissa came home tired but happy. She put the kettle on and put her book bag down on the table. She went to the sofa to sit down with a hot cup of camomile tea before bed and noticed Tobermory was there, sitting with both of his paws tucked up underneath his chest, which wasn't his usual way to sit. She sat down beside him.

'Are you okay, baby?'

Tobermory yawned, unfolded his legs and stretched.

'Hello?' Marissa noticed that he had yet another new white spot on his paws, this time it was the left front paw, and this white spot was much larger than the other one was. *That spot definitely wasn't there before. I would have noticed it for sure.* The coarse hairs matched the colour and texture of the streak across his head, but it was a spot, not a streak; it could just be a few grey hairs. *Yes, that's it. Poor Tobermory is getting old.*

She stroked him and he purred, moved over and settled down onto her lap.

CHAPTER THIRTY

Marissa was sitting in an empty room at St Mary's. Her first client of the evening had let her down and she expected Mary R., her next client, to be a no-show also, especially considering she'd walked out on her first session. *'I don't feel like it' – some cheek. Well, I kind of half hope she* doesn't *show up with that attitude... Just as well I brought my assignment with me, at least I can achieve something in the time I'm here waiting around.*

It was time for Mary's session, so Marissa put away her books and went through the motions on the off-chance Mary would actually show up. *I'll give her ten minutes then I'll get back to my essay. It's starting to come together now.*

As she waited Marissa focused on her breath: breathing in counting to four, holding for four, breathing out counting to four and holding for four. She had watched a YouTube video about yogic breathing while doing a little more research on self-care and thought she'd try it. Holding her breath for a count of four was difficult. She tried five, five, five and five, that seemed to work a little better.

She was focusing on her breath when the door opened abruptly and Mary came in. Closing the door heedlessly behind her, she marched to the empty chair and sat down.

Marissa didn't move, just kept to her five, five, five, five breathing, surprised not only at the style of Mary's entrance, but also at the fact that she had appeared at all.

Mary nodded at Marissa in greeting. She was wearing oversized khaki combat pants with big pockets on both legs and a tight-fitting black T-shirt. The long hair on the top of her head was slicked back, showing the short-shaved sides. A buzz cut. A tough woman, not wanting to be messed with. But she had walked out of a session, and that was plain rude. Now that she was sitting in front of her, Marissa realised she was angry with her. The least she'd expected was to be respected in return for the work she was offering for free. She waited, expecting Mary to speak first, but Mary sat waiting for Marissa to open the session. I*'m the counsellor, so I suppose I have to lead this...*

'So, Mary, what happened last week? Why did you walk out after only ten minutes?' *Shit. Well, okay. Let's go there. I have every right to ask.*

Mary seemed affronted to be pulled up on her behaviour. *Is she used to getting her way?* Marissa crossed her legs defiantly and left the question in the room, hanging there between them. Mary would have to answer it if she wanted to make any progress in their therapeutic relationship. *A relationship takes two. I can't work with someone who doesn't want to work with me.*

Mary was looking more uncomfortable now. Marissa continued her breathing practice, counting silently in her mind: five in, five hold, five out, five hold. She could do that for the whole session if she had to. She wasn't going to be negated in a session like that. If Mary wanted to work with her, she had to make an effort too.

'Sorry,' Mary said eventually. 'I just wanted to meet you, that's all. I met you, so I left. I wasn't going to talk to you in our first session. I don't do that, I don't talk in the first session. And I was having a crap day, so I didn't want to sit there either. I needed food. So I left.'

Marissa hadn't expected a 'sorry'. That threw her a little bit. But she was determined to assert her position. 'Thank you for apologising. However, if I am to work with you, I am part of this relationship too. I may be here to listen and support and help you, but I am also a person. So, if you are going to work with me, you need to stay until we both agree that the session is over.'

Mary nodded. 'Point taken.'

'Okay. Apology accepted then.'

Mary looked satisfied, as if she'd just scored a point in a game. Maybe she had. Marissa wasn't sure who had the upper hand. Silence crept in again between them.

It must have been difficult for her to apologise – I'd better make an effort.

'Are you feeling able to talk in this session today then, Mary? We don't have to talk about anything serious, we could just get to know each other...'

'Really?'

'Sure. I get it – you don't know me, you don't want to jump right in and bare your soul. That's cool with me. You want to learn if you can trust me first. That's great. I can tell you what I want, if you like.'

'You want something? From me?'

'Yes. I want two things from you – I want you to be real with me, and you're doing that, so thank you. And I want you to show up. I need the hours for my diploma. I need to get one hundred and fifty hours of client work to qualify, and if you walk out after ten minutes or don't show up, it doesn't help me get what I need. Which is to finish my diploma.'

'Fair enough.'

'I also think we need to respect each other. We have different backgrounds, so we can learn from each other, if we want to.'

'Also true.'

Marissa smiled. 'One of the things they teach us in college is that you can't make any assumptions. If someone says they are feeling sad, you can't say you understand what they're going through. Yes, they may be sad, but sad for them may be very different than sad for you. And if you decide that they're feeling the way that you do when you feel sad, then you're doing them a disservice. So, to start with, I want to know what it's like for you when you feel sad.'

'You do?'

'Yes, I do. I care. Sometimes I care too much. So I don't like it when people don't show up. Here I am, sitting here, caring too much, and people walk out, and people don't show up, and I'm just sitting here... Don't you think that if you know that someone else understands – I mean really understands – what you feel like when you feel sad, that they totally and completely get it, you'll feel a little less sad?'

Marissa was on a roll. She didn't know where it had all come from, but it sounded great, so she went with it.

'Well, Mary, what do you think?'

'Oh, erm, yeah. Yeah. But nobody has ever said they want to know what it feels like when I feel sad.' Mary rocked in the chair and sat on her hands. 'So it's weird. I mean, nobody has cared like that about me. It's strange, but nice if it's true.'

Marissa softened She had Mary's attention now and it seemed that they had broken through something.

'Okay then. Perhaps we started off on the wrong foot, but now we're getting to know each other, yes? You'll only know that I mean what I say with time, but shall we keep going?'

'Yes,' said Mary, a glimmer of a smile on her face. 'Sure. It might be nice, even, to share stuff. To not feel cornered, to feel you're interested in me. Really interested. Yvonne was great, she was. But we didn't talk like this.'

'Everyone is different. And I'm interested in that – in what makes you you and what makes me me.'

Mary nodded her head. Then she said, 'There are a lot of women here, you know. Lots of them, and some of them don't stop talking, but they say nothing – it's all crap, you know. Just what they heard on the radio, or on TV, or stuff like that. They don't talk about real things, like this. I like talking about real things. It feels, you know, right. Good. Like there's more to life than, you know, stuff.'

Marissa nodded her head, just as Mary had been doing earlier. *I seem to copy the body language of the client that's in front of me. But they do say that it helps put them at ease. Maybe it's a good thing.*

'I'm still not ready, though,' Mary said abruptly. 'To talk about what happened to me.'

'You don't have to talk about what happened to you.'

'I don't?'

'No, you don't. Not to me, not ever. I don't need to know. Unless you want me to know, that is.'

'Then why are you...? Why am I...? What are these sessions for?'

'I'm very glad you asked me. These sessions are for *you*, for your life now. To help you with how you are feeling right now, today. With what is going on in your life, so that you can manage it better. We don't need to go back to your childhood, I don't need to know your life story, your favourite meal, or if you like dogs or cats. I don't need to know. But if you're sad, and it's about something that happened in the past, then we can talk about it if you want to. And it might help you make sense of what's going on today, in the here and now. Because how you react to things now can be based on stuff that happened back then. Once you figure that out, connect the dots, you can see the whole picture. That's how you can heal the past and move on with your life.'

That sounds great! Did I really just say that?

Mary seemed to be taking it all in. After a moment she said, 'That sounds ... great. Yeah. So I'm not being interviewed here and I don't need to tell you my life story.'

'No, no, you don't. I don't make a report about you and I don't ever tell you what to do. If you have a crap day and you're hungry, then tell me about it, because that's what I want to know about – what was so crap about your day, what does having a crap day feel like to you, and what can I do to help you so that next time you have a crap day, you can, well, either fix it, or not feel so crap, even though the stuff that happens is crap.'

'That feels so much more ordinary to me. But better than what I thought. See, I thought I had to give you my life history and stuff, you know what I mean?'

Mary sat back in her chair, relief on her face.

'Yeah, I do,' Marissa said. 'But really I'm just here to listen to you. You don't need to impress me. And whatever you say stays in this room. I just want you to be real. I can see now that if you thought all of those things, and had a crap day, and were hungry, you wouldn't want to talk to me. So you were actually very brave coming to see me at all. I want to thank you for apologising to me, and now I'm getting to understand you a little bit, what you did makes sense to me. I understand. And it's okay. I'm not upset with you anymore, and I think we could do some good work together.'

'Okay. Thanks.' Mary was in a more relaxed position in her chair now.

'Yeah. Remember, this isn't a test or an exam. Well, not for you – *I'm* the one who gets tested! I've got an assignment to write and a live assessment to do, and I've got a shitload of client hours to clock up before I get my diploma. You can use these sessions with me for whatever you want – to learn how to relax, how to get more confident, how to start reaching towards your dreams, how to believe that you can have a good and happy life.'

Mary was nodding. She looked softer, more relaxed. 'Thanks. Yeah, I can do that. I feel better now about coming here. I felt on guard, like I was being judged or something, you know. But now I think I see where it all fits in. Yeah. Okay.'

'Okay. Well, Mary, that was really good work tonight. Our time is up now.'

'Jeez, that was fast. Very fast! Thanks, Marissa.'

'Thank you, Mary.'

Mary stood up, went to the door and then turned around. 'Hey, is it okay if I tell the girls about this? About what you said? That they don't have to tell you their life story and stuff? That you want to know what it feels like when they're sad?'

'Yes, please tell them. And tell them that I want to help them realise their dreams, to have more good days than crap days, and that I need the client hours, so I would be very happy if they showed up for sessions with me.'

Mary saluted. 'Will do. See you next week, so.'

'See you next week.'

CHAPTER THIRTY ONE

Marissa phoned the administration at her college, registered her new practice address with them and then decided to join Reiki Federation Ireland and organise proper insurance for the Reiki sessions. That would take a few days to organise, but it was all in motion. Rosemary at the Reiki Federation even told Marissa that she would be able to join them on their RFI stand at the Mind Body Sprit fair at the Royal Dublin Society that October if she wanted to help out. After talking to her, Marissa felt more supported and more confident in moving forward. She had someone booked in for the following week from the ad at the local shop, and Noreen's sister had finally got in touch and wanted a session too. There also was some interest from some of her colleagues at work, Sarah had been raving about her session and talking about having Marissa offer Reiki at work as part of a wellness day in a few months' time.

It was all going so well, but at work time seemed to drag and Marissa found it difficult to sit at her desk. *It's more difficult to be in work now. The more I'm involved in therapy, the more I seem to love it. And I don't love this. Damn, it's only seven minutes past three.*

A few hours later, she was very glad to arrive at the Priory. She took a moment to stand at the entrance and look at the church and the Priory building just beyond it. *I remember when I first started here, I was so unsure of myself. I've really grown. I'm happy! It's great to be happy.*

She made her way through the building and up to her room. Tonight she had three clients lined up, and they might all show up too. *Three is a magic number! Margaret, William and Aisling.*

Margaret was first. She smiled at Marissa when she came in, nodded her head and sat down in the chair. She wasn't wearing a coat tonight. She looked neat and tidy, and her face was softer than usual, the frown lines weren't as obvious.

'Nice weather we're having,' she said. 'I'm sure it's not the beginning of the good weather yet, though. There will be a frost or two before the winter's really gone.'

'Hello, Margaret, lovely to see you. How was your week?'

'Oh, much better, thank you, dear. I did waver a little bit, once or twice, but I realised what I was doing. Disastrous thinking, that's what I've decided to call it, and it doesn't get a person anywhere, not at all. No, I've stopped doing that now, and when I catch myself, I use a... what did you call it?'

'Balancing thought?'

'Yes! That's it. Balancing thought. I have a few more. I wrote them down – would you like to hear them?'

'Yes, I would very much.'

Margaret got out her notebook.

Before she could open it, Marissa asked, 'Margaret, this is our fifth session together. You have a cycle of six, which means we only have one more after tonight. Do you want me to put you down for another cycle, or are you feeling one more session will be enough? And tonight of course!'

'Oh! That was quick.'

'Yes, it was quick, wasn't it! But we have been working hard and you seem to have really turned this issue around.'

'You helped me a lot!' Margaret smiled. 'Maybe a lot more than you realise. No, dear, I don't think I need any more. I'd be happy enough to let someone else take this slot, someone who might need it more than I do.'

'Duly noted, thank you. So, yes, let me hear your balancing thoughts, and we can see if we can come up with a few more of them together.'

William was Marissa's next client. According to her info sheet he was thirty-four, had depression and had been to the Priory three years earlier for two cycles. Before he came into the room Marissa spent some time breathing and centring herself. She sprayed the room with her St Germain. She buzzed him in, and a few moments later, there was a hesitant knock on the door.

'Come in,' said Marissa, standing to attention yet trying not to sound overly enthusiastic. She liked meeting new clients, liked even more getting to know them and being able to help, but she knew that their first impression of her was important. The door opened and William stepped into the room. He was of medium build, with dark hair, and wore a leather jacket, jeans and a sweatshirt.

'Hi, you must be William?' said Marissa. 'Come in. You can hang your coat on the back of the door or put it on the chair. Choose whichever chair you like.'

William sat down and Marissa took the remaining chair.

'I'm Marissa. We have six sessions together, but if we need more I can ask for more at the end of the cycle. These sessions are for you to tell me whatever you want me to help you with, and anything we say here stays between us, unless I believe that you are a danger to yourself or to someone else, then I will have to let my supervisor know.'

'A danger?' William asked in a quiet voice.

'Yes, if you are suicidal, or if you're contemplating hurting someone else, and you tell me about it. I can't keep that a secret, but everything else is just between you and me. Is that okay?'

'I suppose so. They already know I tried to kill myself – my parents, I mean. But that was two years ago.'

He was here three years ago. I wonder why he didn't want to come back here then. Marissa reined herself in. This could be serious territory, she couldn't come to any conclusions yet, and she had to concentrate. She didn't want to miss anything, just in case it was important. She waited to see if William would offer any more information, but he didn't.

'Well, you can talk about that if you want to,' she suggested, 'or you can talk about something different, such as what is going on now for you that made you want to come and get counselling. I'm here for you and there's plenty of time, we're not in a rush. The sessions are one hour long, but you have six of them, or more than that, if we need them.'

William nodded his head. 'Yes, they told me that at the office. Same as last time. It's fine.'

Silence spilled out between them like a wave from the ocean. It retreated, only to fill the room once more, and once more again. Marissa felt she had to intervene.

'So, where would you like to begin?'

'Okay then, I guess I should talk about it. What's the point of coming, if I don't?'

William shifted in his seat, looked down at his feet, then spoke in a low voice that was difficult to hear. Marissa had to lean forward to hear him.

'I was suicidal, like I said, a few years ago. The doctors put me on medication, and told me I'd be on it for life. But when I feel better, I don't need it, so I stop taking it.'

Marissa nodded her head in understanding.

'Anyway, I know I have to try not to do that. This is really embarrassing; I stopped taking the meds a year ago. I'm back on them now – don't worry I'm not going to do anything weird – but I stopped taking them back then, like I said. And they got worried for me, Mum and the doctors, and wanted me to go back on them, but I didn't want to. I had gone to see someone to see if he could get me off them – totally off them, like. He said he could, so I went off them, then I went to see him. He wanted me off them for a month before he saw me, then he was going to work on me. I was hopeful, and believed everything he said, but now I see it was just wishful thinking on my part. I wasn't well back then, and I got real sick from what he did. It took me six months to get over it, it was worse than psychosis. I've had psychosis before. This was way worse.' He stopped talking.

Marissa let his words sink in. There was a lot to it. 'I appreciate you telling me all this,' she said, eventually. 'It sounds as though it was a very difficult time for you.'

William seemed a little more relaxed. 'Yeah, it was tough,' he agreed. 'It took months for me to get back regular again – like, regular sleeps, eating every day.' He blushed. 'Even going to the toilet, but even now, a year later, I'm still not right. I don't know what he did, that guy. But he lied to me, and he hurt me, and I think I could have died. That's what Mum said, though it could be an exaggeration. She does exaggerate a lot.'

Marissa listened, not really sure where to go with what William was telling her. *It's always best to let the client lead. Just listen, You don't need to fix anything,* she reminded herself. She had an urge to put Reiki hands on him. *I'm sure that would help, but maybe it would help me more. I can't believe someone would abuse someone vulnerable like that. Reiki could really help him. But he hasn't signed up for it.*

She decided to say nothing and let him talk on. That was her remit here, anyway.

'Okay, so,' he continued. 'Now you know. I'm not myself yet, but I'm a lot better now, and even if I did feel great, I would still stay on my medication,' He made a fist with his left hand, pounded his chest and said, 'Lesson learned.'

Something inside Marissa sparked into life. 'Do you read Scott Taylor?' she asked excitedly.

William seemed to spark into life in response. 'Yes! that's where the "Lesson learned" fist-pounding thing came from. Don't you like him? He's great!'

Marissa smiled, eyes wide. 'Yes, I like him. He's very good, So his books have been helping you, too?'

'Oh yes. His mindset practice has helped me immensely. I get out of bed now every day, even though I still feel like shit. Oh sorry, I didn't mean to swear...'

'It's okay, you can swear if you want to.'

They both laughed and William softened his body language.

Marissa said, 'It must be difficult for you when you feel bad. Is it physical or mental?'

'Yeah, both. Emotional, too. Some days are worse than others, but it's getting better, though. I don't think I could come here and talk about it if I was feeling as bad as I was.'

'That's very true – you do need a certain amount of energy to be able to talk about what's going on. You're very self-aware if you're able to see that.'

'Yeah, maybe. Sure I've had months to think about it, years even. It's hard, alright. And I'm still not right. But I keep on going.'

'What exactly isn't right for you? Do you want to tell me?'

'Being on medication is never going to be right, is it? But hey, I don't have much choice. I was on medication before, but it's not the same this time. I don't know what that guy did to me, but he fucked something up in me that's never been the same since.'

'Do you want to tell me about him?'

'Yeah, okay. He's a healer, he travels around, you know? You have to know someone who knows someone to get to see him. He has a great reputation. Dunno why, though. I won't be shouting about him, that's for sure.'

Marissa listened to the story of the healer, the session that William had had, and his slow recovery. Then time was up.

'William, I think this has been a very good first meeting. We're getting to know each other and you've really shared a lot of information with me. Thank you so much for your trust. I'll be here same time next week and we can talk some more then, and maybe look at some things that we can do together that will help you feel better.'

William stood up and offered his hand. 'Thanks, Marissa, I do feel better just talking about it. Some of that stuff I'd forgotten – my memory isn't so good. And you like Scott Taylor! So you're okay. See you next week.'

He stood up and put on his coat. On his way to the door he stopped, turned back and asked, 'Do I have time to tell you one more thing?'

Marissa looked at the clock. 'Sure, but I have someone else coming in five minutes.'

'Okay, I'll be quick. It's about my nightmares. I thought if I told you about them now, maybe next time we could work on fixing them?'

'Go ahead.'

William sat back down with his coat still on.

'In them, I can't move. My dreams, I mean. It's like I'm tied up. My hands are tied together, and my feet, and sometimes my hands and feet are tied together and I'm curled up in a ball. Other times, there's something around my throat.'

Marissa's own throat constricted as he spoke, and William rubbed his throat around the same time. 'Strange – as I'm telling you my throat is getting sore.' He rubbed his wrists too. 'Anyway, that's my dreams. There's nothing more that I remember, but I get them two or three times a week, and when I wake up sometimes I feel like I can't breathe. I get scared to go back to sleep. If I could sleep better, I know that would really help me feel better. Thanks for listening. See you next week!'

He got up and left, leaving Marissa three minutes to spare. With William gone she realised the room felt heavy. Her throat was still constricted and beginning to ache. She rubbed her wrists, and realised that William had been doing that before he left the room. She felt incredibly tired and wanted to lie down and sleep. But she stood up and stretched out instead. She had to be awake for the next person.

She clapped her hands really loudly. *Why did I do that? But it feels better, like it helps me to wake up.*

She clapped again, loud and strong. The sound was crisper than the first time, so she did it again a few more times and felt her energy lifting.

She shook herself out and sat down, connected to Reiki and did a minute of self-practice. *See, I do remember to do it. I just need to have more than one minute available to me when I do it...*The buzzer rang. It was Aisling, her last client of the night. Marissa buzzed her in and soon there was a knock on her door. She had met her the previous week, all she did was cry, and didn't speak. *I hope we can make some progress tonight. But I suppose crying is progress too, if you've not been able to cry.*

'Come in. It's good to see you again.'

Aisling came in, closed the door behind her and sat down in the chair that Marissa had been sitting in.

Marissa shivered, but she wasn't cold. 'How are you doing tonight?' she asked, sitting down in the other chair and crossing her legs.

'I'm a little better, thanks,' Aisling replied. 'I wasn't as upset this week. It helped knowing that someone else knows how upset I am.'

'I understand. I'm glad I could help. I'm here for you, you can tell me anything.'

'That's good. Because I wasn't going to tell you at all, but I decided last night that you were safe, that I could talk about it with you.'

'Absolutely. You can tell me anything, but you don't have to if you don't want to, or if you're not ready yet.'

Aisling looked relieved. 'Maybe I'm not ready just yet.'

Marissa nodded. 'Then tell me something else that's going on in your life, something small, so you can get used to talking to me.'

'Thank you, yes, that's a good idea. I can tell you about my cat.'

•

On her way home on the bus, Marissa looked out the window at everyone as they passed by. *Passers by.* She thought of Margaret and the relief she had felt, wondering what was going on in everybody's heads and knowing that she would never know. *I'm learning more about what is going on in people's heads. It can be overwhelming. I'll have a nice hot bath tonight, then curl up with a book. My book.* Something inside her chest eased, and she felt a little bit better.

CHAPTER THIRTY TWO

Olive looked down her nose through her tortoiseshell glasses to study Marissa who squirmed in her chair, and looked down at the floor. 'You really don't look like yourself – you've got black circles under your eyes and your hair isn't as glossy as usual. I thought we agreed that you were going to spend more time being still and doing self-care? I take it from your reaction to my question that you know you still have a ways to go in this regard.'

'Yes, probably,' Marissa admitted reluctantly. 'But that's why I've become part time at work now. It will take some time to get used to it, but I'm going to focus on my client work and take a step back from the office. And college is nearly finished now, so that's another less thing to do. A therapist is what I really want to be, I've just got to settle down with it. With the routine, I mean. I guess it will take some time for me to catch up with myself.'

Olive smiled.

'St Mary's is also new. I'm not sure of myself there. The women are, well, challenging. I'll have to give it some more time. But I'm hopeful. One of the residents, well, she had the wrong end of the stick completely about counselling. I told her that for me, it wasn't about fixing things, but listening. She seemed to appreciate that… I have a feeling I'll have more clients there from now on.'

'That's wonderful,' Olive replied, 'but I still worry about you, Marissa. Honestly, you look as though you've not had a proper night's sleep in weeks. Your eyes … yes, they're bloodshot. Are you sure you're eating properly? You're only as good a therapist as you feel – your clients will know if you're not in a good space. Once *they* start to mind *you*, you've lost the therapeutic relationship. So it's vital that you stay on top of things. And if you're too tired, or not paying attention, you could make a mistake.'

Marissa was silent, wanting to disappear.

'You've gone from having three clients a week to having potentially nine, and you still have your school work, and you also have your day job. And you're not sleeping. What are you going to do to look after yourself?'

Marissa thought for a moment. She hadn't actually made any concrete plans for additional self-care, but yes, she had to admit the sleeping thing was becoming an issue. 'I've been trying out a new yoga breathing exercise,' she said hesitantly, 'but honestly, it's not helping with my nightmares. I keep forgetting to do my Reiki self-practice. I don't know why, but once I do remember, and do it, I always feel better. I'm getting there, Olive, you just need to be patient with me.'

'Nightmares? What of?'

Marissa was silent once more.

'Hmm, dear if you want me to help you, then let me help you. Please.'

Marissa shrank. Feeling told off wasn't something she was good at dealing with.

'I'm just playing Devil's advocate,' said Olive, a little softness coming into her tone. 'Carers must care for themselves, and that means you, especially as you're taking on more clients now. You have to do more self-care. Last time we spoke about PTSD, now I worry about these nightmares.'

Marissa sighed. 'I've not had any panic attacks since I saw you last. I'm sure I'm getting better. And the nightmares, well, It's a feeling, mostly. I don't remember any details about them. But I wake up and I can't shift the feeling for several hours. It's as if I've been fighting something. Struggling with it.'

Olive was silent for once, waiting for her to go on.

'I've just realised, too, Tobermory, he's not been sleeping up in the bed with me anymore. I always slept better with him beside me. I wonder what's wrong with him?'

'Now dear, don't make this about the cat, it's about you.'

'I know. I do know,' she said defensively. 'I suppose that's why I'm telling you what I can tell you, so you can help me move in the right direction. I really want to do it right, but I know I'm not getting it right just yet. I supposed I do need some help.'

'Perhaps you just need to rest and relax a little more. Are you doing anything for yourself, outside of work, therapy or college I mean? I'd like you to plan a nice day out for yourself, by yourself – something that will replenish your soul. Yes, soul work. That's what you need. Think of it as homework for me, if that makes it easier for you. Then you can tell me all about it in our next session.'

'Okay,' said Marissa, wondering what exactly she needed to do, to replenish her soul. She added, 'I'm going to London for a conference in a couple of weeks' time – that'll be fun. I should have time on my own to explore. I am beginning to get excited about it.' Images of what she might do in London suddenly filled her head and she felt a cold rush, similar to nerves, but she knew it was something else. *I am excited, very excited, when I have time to think about it.*

'Oh, that sounds interesting,' Olive said, 'and London is delightful. Who is speaking?'

'Scott Taylor.'

Olive looked intrigued. 'I haven't heard of him. What is his subject?'

'He's written lots of books. I guess he's a motivational speaker, a coach. He has lots of tools and techniques to help people do well, like a success coach.'

Olive raised an eyebrow. 'Success coach? Odd choice for you. I would have thought you would have preferred ... well, never mind. A trip to London to see a success coach. Hmm. Do tell me, Marissa, what is your definition of success?'

Marissa's answer came out as if by rote. 'Success is living your best life now.'

Olive laughed. 'No, dear, I asked you for *your* definition of success!'

'Oh.' Marissa took a few moments to think about it. 'Well, living your best life now? When you're doing everything you dreamed of.' She nodded. 'Like I'm trying to do, by taking on more clients!' her eyes glistened.

'No talk of being happy then?' asked Olive, her eyebrow still raised.

'Oh yes, of course. That's intrinsic to it – when you're doing everything you dreamed of, of course you'll be happy,' agreed Marissa with relief.

Olive didn't seem convinced. She picked up her appointment book. 'Hmmm. Well, I look forward to hearing all about it when you get back. Let's make a time for our next appointment. And please, try to get some sleep.'

Marissa had planned a busy weekend but after the session with Olive, she thought perhaps she should empty her calendar a little. She cancelled her Fri-yay night out with Sarah but kept her dinner-and-a-movie date with Matt, on the Saturday. She spent some of her birthday money on a lovely green cashmere jumper, and she wore it on Sunday to have lunch with her parents. She also bought herself some new covers and sheets for her bed, to encourage herself to have a better night's sleep. *It's something, anyway, which is better than nothing.*

Rose's eyes widened to see her daughter finally out of her black ensemble. 'Green suits you, dear. Very well wear.'

After spending most of the lunch talking shop with Eli and her dad, she felt she was beginning to understand exactly how much organising was required when running her own business. It was so much more than seeing clients – she had to keep records, take bookings and payments, and pay rent to her new landlord. She would probably need to get an accountant for her tax, unless she wanted to do the books herself. Her father offered to explain it to her, so she hung back after they had eaten and sat at the table with him while everyone else went into the front room.

As he explained how to keep books and records, all the while in the back of her mind she was dying to ask him about Louis, about the gambling. She wanted to know if it had really happened as it had unfolded in her Gestalt with Ronan, but she held back. She knew that he'd be embarrassed if it had been real, possibly even humiliated, and if it hadn't been real, he would want to know why she had even thought such a thing was possible. *Anyway, I was satisfied with it at the time, so I need to put my curiosity as to whether or not I got it right, to bed. That's all that is.*

'So, are you going to get business cards made?' he asked. 'I know a guy who is very good. I could get his number for you.'

'Oh, I hadn't thought about that,' said Marissa. 'I suppose it's a good idea.'

'And a website too? What about a Facebook page?' said Eli, barging in and grabbing a biscuit from the saucer on the table.

Marissa looked up at him and sighed. 'You couldn't keep your nose out of this, could you?' She smiled and fingered her angel broach that she had deliberately chosen to wear, knowing that he would be there. Eli winked at her. 'There's so much to think about, so much to do. It feels like I don't know anything.'

'Well, you'll learn,' said Bernie, gesturing to a chair to invite Eli to sit back down at the table and join their conversation.

Eli happily plonked himself down beside them and took yet another biscuit. 'You need a logo and branding, so your website, business card and Facebook page all say the same thing.' Eli scratched his head. 'LinkedIn! I forgot them, yes, you'll need to be on there, too. And Twitter of course!'

Marissa didn't know whether to laugh or cry. Her father seemed to pick up on this. 'One thing at a time, and you have plenty of time. You're seeing clients already, and you can only see one client at a time. You're on the right track. And...' he nodded over towards Eli, 'branding will come in its own time. If you brand yourself too early, before you know what you're about, then you'll be stuck with something that isn't appropriate, and you could be very sorry for it.'

Eli's face scrunched up. 'Yes, Dad, I remember,' he said, chuckling, then brought his hands up to his face, made claws out of his fingers and let out a squeaky roar.

Marissa remembered too. 'Baby dragon! Ha, ha!'

'It wasn't *supposed* to be a baby dragon,' said Bernie, blushing and looking down at the table.

'All those coasters and mugs, T-shirts and, was it a towel?' said Marissa, scrunching up her face to match Eli's. They both started clawing with their fingers at the table.

She let out a squeaky roar, then Eli let out another one, soon both of them were pretending to be roaring baby dragons, clawing and roaring, they looked at each other, then roared with laughter. Soon Eli was laughing so hard he had tears coming out of his eyes. It felt good to laugh.

'Can I sing the baby dragon song?' asked Eli through his hiccups.

'No,' said Bernie, but he was a little more relaxed now.

'How old were we at the time?' asked Marissa once she got her breath back. 'I remember stacks of merchandise in the house. Most of it went in the bin, didn't it?'

'Well, we can't get it right every time,' said Bernie, laughing too. 'Pick yourself up and keep going, that's what my father used to say.' Turning to Marissa, he tapped his nose and added, 'If you do get a logo, make sure you get a professional to design it.'

Marissa loved Mondays now that she didn't have to rush to work. She took her time in the mornings, pouring herself a cup of tea and bringing it back to bed, lying in the warmth of her covers to stretch the morning out a little longer. The covers seemed to help a little, but Tobermory still wasn't sleeping beside her. She couldn't remember her dreams which suited her just fine.

That morning she spent some time designing business cards for herself on a website. She chose a template with a nondescript clipart-style logo of hands and a lotus flower. *It's just for now, it doesn't have to be what I end up with. Just to get started.*

Marissa Rosenthal, Reiki Sessions
Reiki with Marissa

I don't like either of those. And what if I offer psychotherapy too? I can't use the cards for both? That would be a waste.

Reiki and Psychotherapy, Marissa Rosenthal

I don't know, it just doesn't sound good.

Marissa Rosenthal, ~~Reiki Master~~ Reiki Sessions

Reiki Master does look good, I'll have to do Level 3 then. I wonder can I do it without doing that Practitioner Cert that Dolores was talking about?

Marisa Rosenthal
Reiki Sessions and Psychotherapy, Ranelagh.

That will have to do.

She added her phone number and ordered two hundred and fifty cards, just to try them out.

At 4pm, she packed away her books and assignment things and took a few hours to get into the right frame of mind for her first two 'official' Reiki clients that evening. She was a little nervous as she walked, going over the checklist in her mind of everything she needed. She even had brought some small water bottles.

Sam greeted her at 6 on the dot and gave her the room with a nod, and left. Setting up the plinth was a little easier than before, she was getting used to it. Once the chairs had been moved, the stand-light turned on, glasses and bottles of water on the table, blankets on plinth and music ready, she lit some incense for atmosphere and was ready for her clients. She readjusted the blanket on the plinth, and then the buzzer rang. *Good timing!*

The first client of the night was Noreen's sister, Julie. Marissa sprayed her St Germain into the air above the plinth then pressed the button and spoke.

'Hi! Come on in.'

She walked out into the corridor and saw Julie coming in the front door.

'Hi, I'm here for Reiki?' Julie said hesitantly. She was much younger than Marissa had expected her to be, dressed in jeans and a sweatshirt. She looked as though she'd been in the wars. Marissa's first thought was that she wanted to scoop her up, give her a hug and wrap her in a warm fluffy blanket.

'Yes. Hello, I'm Marissa. You must be Julie? Welcome! Come in, let me take your coat.'

They went into the room together. Marissa looked at it with a different eye now that she had a paying client. The room was still darker than she would have liked, but it would have to do for now. The counselling chairs were harder than the ones she was used to in Cabra, or even in St Mary's. *They're not really conducive for an hour's therapy. I must get some cushions for when I start seeing psychotherapy clients in here.* The room otherwise was sparse. There was only one painting on the wall, the window was barred on the outside and the net curtain was dusty. *I really need to spruce this place up a bit.* She brought her awareness back into the session.

After hanging Julie's coat on the back of the door, she gestured to one of the counselling chairs and she and Julie sat down facing each other. *I guess starting with a chat is a good idea? It's what Dolores did with me.*

'Hi, Julie, it's lovely to meet you. I don't know how much Noreen told you about me. Or about Reiki – have you had Reiki before?'

'Hi, Marissa, it's good to meet you too. Yes, Noreen told me you couldn't see me just yet for psychotherapy, but the Reiki might help me relax a little. So that sounds good for now.' Julie smiled nervously.

'Is there anything you'd like to talk about before we start?'

Julie cleared her throat. 'I've been having bad dreams. I can't settle at all at night. I'm hoping the Reiki will help my body relax.'

Marissa nodded, 'The Reiki Federation do say that one hour of Reiki is like a full night's sleep, but of course it will be different for everyone. Let's get started then, shall we? Would you like some water?'

'Yes please.'

Marissa opened one of the small bottles, poured it into a glass and offered it to Julie, who drank.

'Now, if you can take your shoes off, and anything else that might cause discomfort while you're lying down... You can leave your bracelet and watch here. Yes, that's fine.'

Julie got up onto the plinth and lay down. Marissa switched off the ringer on her phone, hooked it up to the speakers and turned on her new Reiki playlist. She placed one of her new fleece blankets over Julie, then stood at the foot of the plinth and connected to Reiki.

Half an hour in, Julie seemed much more relaxed and closed her eyes. After a few moments, Marissa found her mind drifting.

She was on a horse on a cobblestone path surrounded by green hills and a bright blue sky. She wore a heavy blue robe, underneath was a jerkin, blouse and leggings. There was a castle in the distance. It looked medieval, something straight out of a fantasy novel. Marissa felt good riding the horse, sitting tall in the saddle, stirrups beneath her feet.

On the grass at the side of the road, a woman lay wailing, in obvious pain. Marissa felt something twitch in her heart as she rode past. It felt wrong to go past. She pressed her knees into the horse, pulled the reins and turned around fully, then dismounted and approached her, reigning the horse behind.

The woman was doubled up. She wore black robes with a white hood and looked as if she was from a religious order. She couldn't see her face.

'Can I help you?' Marissa asked. 'Is there something I can do?'

The woman looked up at her from underneath the hood. It was Julie.

She winced in pain. 'Please untie me. They're so tight, they hurt,' she pleaded.

Marissa bent over her and saw she was bound hand and foot by coils of heavy rope. She checked in with herself to ask if she could untie her and got a full-body 'yes', tinged with a hint of urgency.

She let go of the horse and knelt down on the grass beside Julie. 'Can you show me what is going on?'

Julie rolled onto her side, then onto her back, trying to raise her hands and feet to Marissa, but she hadn't the strength.

'Thank you. It's okay, I can see now.'

Marissa examined the knots. Julie's wrists and ankles were wrapped in rope tied with an elaborate knot, then they were tied together in such a way that it was almost impossible for her to move. There was no slack, her legs and arms were bunched together.

Marissa pulled out a small sharp knife from a small front pocket in her jerkin. It was silver with a short hooked blade, like a cheese or apple knife, It had an elaborate handle with intricate designs, but there was no time to examine it or ask herself how she knew it was there. She prised the hook in amongst the knots to try to cut the tie between hands and feet, but to no avail. She tried to use the knife as a saw, but the rope seemed to be more effective at blunting the blade than the blade was at cutting the rope.

Julie started tensing up on the plinth and pulled Marissa's attention back into the room. She caught her breath, centred herself and looked at Julie, who still had her eyes closed. She focused on the Reiki light and brought her hands to Julie's stomach, to roughly the same position where the knot she was working on was in her mind. She felt the Reiki flow into Julie; it was as if she was sucking it in. More Reiki poured into Marissa and flowed straight into Julie. It was like putting petrol in a car, only the tank was vast and endless.

I thought these sessions would be easy and straightforward.

Marissa steadied herself on her feet and used her imagination to ground herself through the floor, into the rocks and stones beneath the Reiki room. After a moment she felt like she had her stability back. *I don't like leaving this the way it is. Maybe I should go back into the image and see if I can help her there.* She closed her eyes and went back into the images in her mind.

The ropes seemed a little slacker now, not as tightly knit. In fact, the ropes themselves seemed slightly less dense too. Marissa connected to Reiki and set her intention and will for the Reiki to loosen the ropes. Nothing seemed to be happening, then, after a moment, the ropes started to shrivel, there was a snap and Julie the nun was able to straighten her body.

At the same time, Julie on the plinth's body jerked, as if she was going into a deeper sleep.

The nun's hands and feet were still bound to each other, but at least she wasn't being pulled into such an uncomfortable and awkward position anymore. She was able to sit up. She had tears of gratitude in her eyes.

'But you're not free yet,' said Marissa.

'This is more freedom than I've had in so long. It's such a relief. Thank you.'

'But it isn't enough. At least let me try to release your feet and hands.'

Julie the nun nodded her consent. She had aged; she looked like a much older version of the Julie on the plinth now. But her face was soft. The urgency had left it.

'Feet?' she asked

Marissa focused on her feet. The rope was thinner, but the knots seemed to have multiplied. The knife was lying on the grass. Marissa reached out and grabbed it and saw that it had returned to its former sharpness. Working its point into the tightest knots, she worried at them until she felt something hard within. She prised it open, but didn't feel she was getting anywhere.

In the therapy room, Marissa moved her hands down to Julie's feet and placed one hand on each of her ankles. She then had an idea and drew the Reiki power symbol over Julie's feet.

There was a flash of light and the ropes disintegrated. Fragments fell to the ground, turned black and disappeared.

Marissa, pleased, tried it again for Julie's hands, drawing the Reiki power symbol on them in the therapy room.

There was another flash of light and the ropes around her hands fell to the ground. This time they appeared to turn into snake-like beings and slither away out of sight.

Marissa turned to Julie the nun, who was rubbing her wrists and rotating her ankles. She was standing up now. She took down her hood and she appeared so old she was almost skeletal. She smiled, and then flesh grew on her face, rejuvenating her, until she was the age of Julie on the plinth.

'Thank you, thank you so very much,' she said. 'How can I repay you?'

Marissa smiled. 'It is my pleasure. Honestly, I feel it's my role. No payment is required.'

'Thank you so much. I will be on my way now.'

The images disappeared and Marissa was fully back in her Reiki room. Julie on the plinth was wide awake. She looked the same as before – *no, wait. Her face looks softer. She seems more at peace.*

She opened her eyes, looked at Marissa and smiled. 'I feel better now, so much better. Thank you so very much.'

Marissa was really shaken. She was feeling naïve now, a little bit silly in fact. She had misjudged what she would be doing in these Reiki sessions. She'd thought it would be simply hands on, Reiki flow, hands off. Her mind was frazzled by what happened. She needed time to process it all. *I felt really confident doing what I did, though. I seemed to know what I was doing too... Julie did seem to feel better... Maybe it is okay then.*

She helped Julie off the plinth, and after drinking some more water, Julie paid Marissa the agreed amount in cash. As Marissa accepted the money she felt as if she was split in two. One part of her was observing herself receiving the money, thinking, *I should be really excited and happy. I should celebrate this, my first paying client,* but in reality she was in a daze with the images she had just seen still hovering around her.

Julie left, gratefully.

Marissa straightened out the room and the buzzer rang almost straight away. It was her next client, Annette, who had booked her from the advert in the shop. Marissa was back on duty once more.

The room was warm, Annette was on the plinth, covered in blankets, and the music was playing gently in the background. After about ten minutes, Marissa went into another vision.

Rainbows splashed into rockpools as she deftly avoided the cracks and crevices in the rocky landscape while she chased the child. She lost sight of her behind a boulder, but could still hear her giggling.

'I'm coming to get you...' Marissa sang out as she narrowly missed catching her shoe in a turn of the rock and twisting her ankle.

'Can't catch me for a penny cuppa tea,' giggled the child, her voice leaving a trail behind her for Marissa to follow, like scent from a candle. She turned a corner and she was standing on a beach. There the child stood there too, her pink party frock dishevelled and sandy, hair escaping her Alice band and a big smile on her dirty face.

Marissa caught up with her, knelt down and pulled a handkerchief out of her pocket, and wiped her face clean. 'That's better,' she said, examining her work.

The child shrugged her shoulders, giggled and ran away again.

Marissa sighed.

Annette on the plinth also sighed, stretched and closed her eyes again. Marissa's attention snapped back into the room. She pulled her hands away from Annette to let her settle, and once she seemed more relaxed, she continued with the Reiki treatment.

Oh dear, I was on a journey. It's been so long since I did anything like that, but it felt so good. Why did I stop doing it? It was playful, and light – no harm, nothing scary. But no, I said I wouldn't do this again.

Marissa pushed away the urge to drift back to the landscape and brought her focus back. Annette seemed peaceful and relaxed. *Still forty minutes left in the session. I've got to stay focused and stay right here in the room.*

Marissa brought her awareness to her shoeless feet on the cheap carpet in the room. She didn't like to do Reiki with her shoes on, but her feet could feel the cold coming up through the floor. *I must get some thicker socks. Or maybe a rug for under the plinth. No, that's too much. I could put socks into the suitcase so I'd always have them here.* She rocked back and forth on her feet to keep her awareness in her body. She started to sway and dance a little bit to the soft music she had chosen, and she looked at the clock. It was becoming hard work keeping her concentration in the room while offering a Reiki treatment, and after the session with Julie she felt particularly tired. *I've got to stay* here. *No more of this journeying stuff.* She felt deflated at that. It felt so long since she'd done it, and it had felt good to run on the beach with the little girl. *Why aren't I allowed to journey?*

She pressed into herself, to follow the tracks to answer the question, but reached a dead end. *No point pushing it.* So she stopped.

At the end of the session, Annette was sleepy and grateful. She spoke while still lying down. 'I was having the most wonderful dream while you were working on me,' she said, stretching out on the massage table. 'I was a child again, running around on the beach. I loved that beach. I should go back for a visit sometime.'

Marissa's stomach twisted up inside her but she didn't say anything.

Annette paid her when she was ready to go, and said, 'I feel really peaceful now, calm and quiet inside, like someone turned off a noisy radio that was playing inside my head. I'm ready for a good night's sleep. Can I tell my friends to come see you?'

'Oh yes, that would be great, thank you!'

'Do you have a business card?'

'Actually, no, not yet, I've only just ordered them. But you can give them my phone number? You have it from the advert?'

'Perfect.'

'I'm really glad you enjoyed it. I should have some cards for next time. Thank you so much!'

Annette left and Marissa shut the door behind her. She sat down in the counselling chair, waves of anxiety licking up and down her body, her nerves were frazzled and starting to make her nauseous. *Why do I feel like this? I was certain Reiki wasn't going to be like this.* She shook her head from side to side, as if that would release her from the feelings. It didn't. She texted Matt.

> Hi love, how was yr day? I've just finished the Reiki sessions. Can I call u?

She packed up the room, put her things into the suitcase and shoved it, and the plinth, under the stairs. She stood at the door of her room, wondering if she should use sage to clear it. *I really didn't want to get back to shamanism. I thought I was finished with all of that. Maybe I'll put some sage in my Reiki bag for next time, just in case.*

As she walked home her phone rang. 'Hello? Matt?'

'Hi! How did it go?'

'Erm, it was great. Actually, something happened...'

Matt's breathing changed. 'Are you okay?'

She didn't speak for a moment. There was a sense of 'here we go again' on the other end of the line. *I don't need to tell him everything. No, I'll leave it. It's not fair to drag him into this.*

'Yes, I'm good. I'm so glad I ordered those business cards, Annette asked me for some for her friends. I should have them next week. I didn't think I'd need them for my clients – isn't that great?'

Matt let out a held breath. 'I knew you'd be great at this. Well done you! That's great, you're going to be in demand, I just know it.'

Marissa was walking deeply in a dark forest. It felt dense and maleficent. There were eyes watching her within the darkness in between the trees. She was scared – no, she was terrified. Going into unknown territories.

'Did I say that or did I just hear someone say that?'

She saw a tree that looked familiar. It was a large old tree. It felt welcoming and safe amongst this scary forest. She went up to it to get her bearings and saw there was a mirror hanging on it. She peered into the mirror and saw her own face reflected back to her. Then the reflection changed; the face became that of an old woman with long, slivery grey hair.

'I know you...' Marissa said, pointing to the reflection. 'Where do I know you from?'

The face was smiling at her in a gentle, loving way, and Marissa felt safe. The anxiety trickled away from her body.

'You forget who you are,' Grandmother Medicine Woman said. 'You forget your gifts, child. And you forget us. But we are here, with you, waiting for you. We have every faith that you will overcome this and you will prevail. Love and truth will shine out from you once more.'

The mirror started to sink into the bark of the tree. It became swallowed up by it, then the tree got darker and darker, and roots grew out from it and wrapped themselves around Marissa's legs. Branches grew from the tree and wrapped themselves around her body, wrists and ankles. She felt caught, then a tendril of a vine grew and wrapped itself around her throat, squeezing her tighter and tighter until she couldn't breathe.

Marissa woke up in a sweat. Tobermory was standing on her chest, meowing and pawing at her. He seemed very distressed. She got a shock to see him there, it had been so long. It was dark in the room. She rolled him off her, reached over and pulled her curtain open. Orange-tinged light from the street lamp flooded in and over the bed. She arranged the pillows, sat up and caught her breath.

Rubbing her neck, she reassured herself that she wasn't actually being strangled.

Tobermory was still meowing. She reached over to reassure him too. 'It's okay, Tobes, I just had a bad dream. I'll be okay in a few minutes.' He leapt into her lap and sat upright, looking straight at her. She looked back at him. 'What's wrong, cat? You have been acting strange lately.'

She leaned into him and placed her brow onto his. It calmed her and it seemed to calm him too, but after a moment his tail started to twitch in annoyance at her hot breath on his face. He broke the contact, turned a circle in her lap and sat down, tail flickering, but he started purring too.

Marissa stroked him, noticing once again the large white spot on his left front paw. He turned onto his side, and she shifted down in the bed so they were almost lying down together. She examined his paws and found three more smaller spots that were new, too. She hadn't really spent time with him lately, she'd been so caught up in her own world. And he had seemed to be avoiding her, too.

The texture of the new hairs didn't match the rest of his body. She compared them to the texture of the white hairs across his face, his 'lightning strike', and they were similar.

'I've not seen these before. What are you doing, cat? Putting your paws into the electricity sockets? You're getting lots of these new white patches.. I don't understand. Maybe I should take you to the vet?'

Tobermory's tail was twitching again, but it was softer this time, and he continued to purr.

'Or maybe you are just getting old?'

The dream forgotten, Marissa repositioned herself in the bed and, throwing her arm around her beloved cat, fell asleep.

CHAPTER THIRTY THREE

Marissa woke exhausted and drained, her face plastered to the pillow. Her alarm went off for the second time and she dragged herself out of bed. Her arms and legs seemed to weigh three times as much as usual. Tobermory was already outside.

She plodded into the kitchen and switched on the kettle for tea. She looked around at her flat while the kettle boiled. It seemed different, cold somehow. Like she hadn't been living in it for a while. She took her tea into the bedroom and placed it on her bedside locker, took off her pyjamas and had the hottest shower that she could stand. Throwing on her clothes and draining the last of her now lukewarm tea, she packed her bag for college and left for work.

At work, images of her dream and the Reiki sessions floated in and out of her mind. It was becoming more difficult to push them away. At one point she thought she was wearing the jerkin and leggings from the image, she kept pulling her top down at the neck, it felt like it was strangling her. She visualised a door deep inside her, a door that was big and heavy. It had an iron lock and an iron bar across it. She made sure that it was closed and sealed. A flashing advert on the browser that was open on her computer screen caught her eye. 'Scott Taylor coming to London soon. Get your ticket now!'

An image of Scott Taylor came into her mind, with his blond hair slicked back and his big blue eyes. He was smiling at her and holding out his hand as if to help her over an obstacle in her path. She saw herself taking his hand and he lifted her up. Just then her phone buzzed a text from Matt.

> Hey thinking of u, hope ur good sorry my phone was off last nite, how was ur Reiki session?

She pulled herself out of her reverie with Scott.

It was good, they both said they'd come back. When can I see you?

Matt wrote back:I'm free Wed but ur in St Marys? Friday? I can come 2 u if its easier. Miss u.

Miss u2. yes sounds good. call u b4 Friday xxM

Good luck tonite at assessment u'll B gr8 xx

Marissa was still so very tired. She was already on her third cup of coffee and it wasn't even lunchtime yet. When lunchtime did come around, she sat with Sarah outside the work building in the fresh cold air, sharing a packet of crisps and getting worried about the assessment. She was going to be the counsellor tonight, She would be a client next week.

'I'm the same,' Sarah said sympathetically, licking salt off her fingers. 'Whenever I have an exam, I forget everything, but I think it's nerves. It will be my turn for exams next month. I'm dreading them.'

'Next month? Already?' asked Marissa. 'I thought you'd only just started the course.'

She helped herself to more crisps. They were making short work of the packet.

'I think these packets are getting smaller and smaller,' Marissa added, as she rummaged around for a healthy-looking crisp.

'Or they're putting fewer crisps in them,' agreed Sarah, waiting patiently for her turn.

'Well, I could be getting nervous and looking through textbooks, but that's the thing about counselling – it's not what's in the book but what's inside your head that counts when it comes to live sessions.'

'Ah, Marissa, this doesn't sound like you. You've always been good at this. You'll fly through it.'

'I don't know, Sarah, I'm not feeling as confident as usual. It's like a part of my mind is missing or something. I've been forgetting things, having trouble recalling stuff. I've not been sleeping well, even Olive noticed. And this morning, I was looking at my flat as if I hadn't lived there in weeks. I've really been struggling with the assignment, too. I spent all day yesterday on it and when I'd finished, I reread what I'd written and it didn't seem that I'd got my point across. I'm thinking that I might have to do it again.'

'When's the deadline?'

'Not till the end of May.'

'You've plenty of time, so take a break from it and come back to it again later.'

'I know, that's probably the best idea. I've so much on right now with the new Reiki room and St Mary's, and London is coming up soon too.'

'London? What's London? You're going to London?' Sarah looked as though she'd been slapped in the face.

Marissa blushed. There were no crisps left in the packet for her to hide behind. 'Erm, yeah. I'm going the weekend after next, to a conference. It's all booked and everything.'

'Oh. What's the conference?' Sarah seemed deflated.

'It's Scott Taylor, that guy I was telling you about. The success coach. It's a three-day event, pretty full on. I don't think it's your thing. That's probably why I forgot tell you.'

'But you didn't even me...'

Marissa sighed. 'Yeah, you're right, I didn't ask you. I didn't think of it. Sorry, Sarah. Like I said, I don't know what's going on with me.'

'A weekend in London with you would be fun,' Sarah said mournfully.

'Yes, it would totally be fun,' Marissa agreed hurriedly. 'You and me, shopping and exploring. But I'll be in a conference all day, every day I'm there. So I wouldn't be doing those things this time.' 'Hey, let's book a weekend away together and we can spend the whole time doing fun stuff.'

Sarah arched her eyebrow. 'Seriously, you don't have to pretend you want to spend time with me if you don't.'

'Fuck sake, Sarah, you're my best friend! Of I want to spend time with you. And I'm not making the mistake I made when I was with James – ignoring all my friends for Matt. I do want to spend time with you – I seriously didn't think this would be your thing. And

I seriously didn't even think of mentioning it to you. So don't take it personally, okay? I didn't even ask Matt if he wanted to go with me.'

'You didn't? Wow.'

'Yeah, I know,' Marissa said, sheepishly.

'Okay then,' said Sarah, forgiving her.

'Thanks. Maybe I'm still in a crisis. I don't know. I'm really not myself.'

'Did you really drop all your friends for James?'

There was a significant pause before Marissa answered.

'Yeah, I did. Yeah. And when he left me I didn't have any friends left to support me – well, except for Joanne. She was great. But she's always great. We can go for years not talking to each other and then we come together like we've never been apart.'

'She's your friend from school, right?'

'Yes, that's her.'

'I don't have a school friend like that,' said Sarah, deflated again.

'But you have me now,' said Marissa. 'And I meant it – you are my best friend. And I am sorry I didn't ask you to London. I think the London thing is part of my spiritual crisis.' Something inside Marissa pricked up it's ears with interest at hearing this. She went on. 'I think we should plan a weekend away, just the two of us. It would be really fun. Maybe somewhere sunny?'

Sarah smiled.

Back at her desk after repairing her relationship with Sarah, Marissa felt exhausted. She really didn't want to fall out with her. The realisation that the trip might have something to do with her spiritual crisis explained why she hadn't really talked to Matt about London either. Tim came over with some work for her and she allowed it to keep her occupied until it was time to pack up and head to college. Grabbing a sandwich and a bottle of Diet Coke on the way, she wondered if remembering to eat was self-care or if she had to do better with food, on top of everything else she wasn't doing right.

The mood in college was serious. People were talking in hushed tones, asking each other if they were client or counsellor for the night.

It was going to be a strict schedule with no one allowed go over time. Barbara was just observing as she had to finish her modules during the summer first, so she said she'd cheer everybody on.

They all got tea and sat at their usual table in the canteen. Marissa was going to be on fourth. Her client would be Ronan. He nodded at her from across the table.

'I hope it's not going to be too difficult, whatever it is you're bringing to me later,' she said with a smile, trying to lighten the mood.

'Oh yes, I thought long and hard about this one,' said Ronan with a wink.

'Should I be worried?' Marissa sipped her tea. But she felt herself finally waking up. 'Perhaps,' Ronan said, with another wink. He stood up. 'It's too tempting sitting here with you. I think I should leave, or I may give you a spoiler and spoil it all. I'll see you in the session.' He walked away.

'Wonder what he has in mind?' said Marissa to nobody in particular.

Yvonne replied, 'I've no idea, but he likes to be mysterious, that's his thing. Nothing like a man with a mystery.'

Marissa turned to her. 'Ha, ha, I think I prefer my men transparent. I do like to know what they're thinking, who they're with and what they're doing at every moment!'

'You are joking, right? That would be exhausting, and it sounds like co-dependency to me,' said Yvonne.

'Yes, I am joking,' said Marissa, with a sigh and a giggle. They took their places. Marissa felt her energy levels drop again as she watched the first three sessions before hers. Each session was fifteen minutes, with a five-minute break in between. Ms Greene, Mr Crowley and Mr Hughes, the head of the school, were all there at a top table, with notebooks and pens, writing things down. It was quite disconcerting. Ms Greene had a clock in front of her and was keeping time. They didn't give any feedback at all, just, 'Thank you, next.'

It was soon Marissa and Ronan's turn. She pushed down her anxiety as she took her chair. Ronan nodded as he took his seat opposite her. It didn't all hinge on this particular assessment; they had a track record, and the assessment was a small percentage of the overall diploma. But she couldn't help but be nervous, and the energy of the room reflected her nervous energy back to her.

'Whenever you're ready, Marissa,' said Ms Greene.

Marissa took a moment to breathe, then she opened the session. 'Hello, Ronan. I'm Marissa. I'll be your counsellor this evening. We have fifteen minutes together. Anything you say to me is confidential, unless I believe that you will cause yourself or others harm, then I will have to inform my supervisor. But I will tell you if that's the case, and we can discuss that too. So, this is your space to talk about anything you wish. What would you like to talk about today?'

Ronan shifted in his chair and cleared his throat. 'I've not told anyone this before, so I hope it's okay to talk about it with you tonight.'

Marissa's hackles went up. 'If you feel you want to talk about it, that's okay, but please make sure you look after yourself. Even though this session is confidential, I want to draw your attention to the reality that we are in a room filled with counselling students and lecturers, and this is an assessment, so, even though I said at the beginning that what you say is just between you and me, be aware that they will hear it too. If you do want to go ahead, for the benefit of them all, and for you, I'll ask them to enter into our contract of confidentiality, so that whatever you say doesn't leave this room.'

Ronan seemed taken aback by this comment, but then he seemed to relax. There was a ripple in the room too. Being brought into the session wasn't something the 'audience' was used to.

'Yes, Marissa, you're right,' Ronan said, 'and that's what I like about you – you keep it real. And this is real, and I feel it's okay to talk to you about it. I thought about it for a while before I decided to bring it up. I think it would be good for me to talk about it here.'

Marissa nodded and left the space silent for him to go on.

'I'm having trouble with our assignment,' Ronan said. 'I've been having trouble in college in general, actually. And it's making me frustrated.' He paused. 'It's not the practical work – I like the practical work – it's the writing and the reading.' He looked down at his feet. 'I'm dyslexic,' he said.

Marissa could hear the in-breaths of some of the people in the room. She waited to see if there was more, but Ronan was silent, so she asked, 'How are you feeling, telling me about this?'

'Relieved, actually. It makes it more solid for me. I've been thinking of it as a handicap, and it has held me back in life quite a bit, but I've been determined to do this diploma, so I've not let it stop me.'

'You said earlier that you'd been frustrated and you'd been having trouble with the assignment. Do you think me knowing that you're dyslexic will help relieve some of your frustration around it?'

'Yes. We've been doing a lot of opening up to each other, the group, in the classes. I've been struggling with opening up too, and I felt this was my last opportunity to do it. To open up, I mean. It's a relief, to get it over with.'

Marissa smiled. 'I hear you on that one. We all have our own struggles – I think everyone is struggling with something. It does help, though, when you don't bottle it up, when you tell someone.'

'Yes.' Ronan seemed a lot more relaxed in the chair now, his face wasn't as tight as it had been before. 'I've learned a lot of tricks to get by in my life with dyslexia, but there's no trick when it comes to writing an assignment. The last one we did, I didn't feel as much pressure, perhaps because I had more time with it, or it was a slightly easier topic, or I didn't care as much. This one is harder.'

Marissa waited a moment, checked the time that they had left, found there were eight minutes and thought she'd take it a little deeper. 'You're saying that you care more this time about getting it right, so you're finding it harder to do the assignment?'

'Yes, exactly. It's important to me to get it right. I want to do a good job. I like counselling, I'm good at it, and I didn't think I'd like it so much.' He looked around the room to acknowledge his classmates. 'It was difficult enough at the start, being in the minority with the men,' there was a hushed giggle in the room, 'and I didn't care as much about the course. "Sure, if it was gonna work, it was gonna work," I thought. But as time passed, the work became more important. Now I'm nearly qualified, and I really want to get it right.

Especially as there are fewer men counsellors than women out there. Well, it seems that way, if the class ratio is anything to go by. And sometimes a man has to talk to a man, you know? I think I'd like to be there for those men.'

Marissa let his words take up the space in the room and gave him some time to settle with his emotions.

'I do feel better getting this out there,' he said. 'Thanks for listening.'

'That's what I'm here for,' said Marissa. 'But I'm also wondering if there's anything that we can discuss together in the few minutes that we have left that will make the work easier for you. Or perhaps changing your attitude to the work would help make it easier for you?'

'How do you mean, "changing your attitude to the work"?'

'Well,' said Marissa, thinking of something she'd read in one of the Scott Taylor books, 'when you think of the assignment, how big a challenge does it feel to you? A walk in the park, a trek through the forest, or a hike up a very big mountain?'

Ronan laughed and rubbed his hands together. 'Ah, a hike up a very big, very icy, very steep mountain, with no snow boots, or ropes. And on my own, with nobody to help me if I get caught or stuck on a ledge.'

Marissa nodded her head. 'That sounds dangerous and scary.'

'Well, it hasn't felt dangerous, but it has felt scary alright.'

'What if you didn't feel alone? Now that you've told me about it, you're not alone.'

'Yes, that's true. It's like telling base camp that you're going, and if you don't return, they can send out the helicopter!' He smiled.

Marissa smiled back. 'Yes, I suppose it could be like that. What if you got some help? Who could you ask to help you? So you're not climbing alone.'

After a moment Ronan said, 'You know, just knowing that ye all know now, it feels as though the mountain isn't as high as it was.' He turned and acknowledged the room, and the compassion that came back from the group was palpable.

'That's good,' said Marissa, feeling emotional, but staying in the moment.

'I suppose I could ask for an extension too, if I needed one, so I had more time.'

Marissa nodded. 'What happens to the mountain in your mind, when you factor in the extra time?'

Ronan took a moment. 'It levels out a bit. And the ice melts a little bit too. It feels better in here, in fact.' He pointed to his stomach.

'So you've been feeling anxious, too?'

Ronan nodded his head.

'Okay. So you'll ask for an extension if you need one, and we all know now that you're having difficulty with it. Let's come up with some more support for you, before we finish here.'

'I could tell my wife,' Ronan suggested. 'She knows I have dyslexia, of course, but she doesn't know I'm struggling so much with the assignment. She could read it for me – what I've got so far, I mean. And if it makes sense to her, I guess that's going to help a lot. She's offered to help before, but I've been stubborn. You know, men!'

There was a slight ripple of laughter through the room; it really felt as though everyone was on Ronan's side.

He smiled. 'I'll take her up on her offer to help me.'

Marissa held steady and didn't fall into the laughter trap. 'Does she know how important the diploma has become to you?'

'I think she knows, but I haven't actually told her. I'll tell her tonight.'

Marissa nodded. 'So, how does the challenging mountain look to you now?'

Ronan thought for a moment. 'Well, I've got a home base,' he nodded at Marissa, 'and the mountain has levelled out, and my wife will be there to hold the ropes if I lose my foothold. It feels a lot better now. Thank you.'

'Time,' said Ms Greene.

'Thank you, Ronan. I hope this session has helped you.'

'Thanks, Marissa, I think it really has.'

At the end of the night, when they were packing up to leave, Ronan came over to Marissa.

'That mountain thing, that was really helpful, thank you.'

Marissa gave him a friendly punch. 'Hey, you, bloody typical to bring up something big like that in such a tight space, and involve everyone in it too.'

'Ah, that's me. Drama queen supreme. But I knew you could handle it,' he said, 'and handle it you did.'

'You are anything but a drama queen. And I meant what I said, I'm always here to help you, if you need me,' said Marissa. 'Hey, as well as being part of your base camp, I can read your assignment too, if you want, before you hand it in.'

'You'd do that for me?'

'Of course I would. It would be my pleasure.'

Ronan smiled. 'Thanks so much, that would be really great. I think that mountain has suddenly turned into a walk in the park.'

'It always helps to talk.'

'That it does. Maybe one day you'll talk about your stuff, too.'

He walked away, leaving Marissa with a strange feeling in the pit of her stomach.

CHAPTER THIRTY FOUR

Marissa sat down in her armchair of choice in the room in St Mary's. The room was slightly chilly; it was more clinical than Cabra, white walls and big glassy windows gave it a hospital feeling. It just wasn't lived-in enough yet, the walls had lost their new-paint smell, but they had a glossy sheen when the light shone on them. *It doesn't feel as though much has happened in this room, yet. Maybe a room feels more lived-in when some drama has unfolded within it.* Marissa shivered. She was expecting another no-show. *Six client hours spent in this room, with only three I can actually use. That's a 50% success rate. And almost as many hours spent on the bus to get here and back again.*

She rearranged the items on the table in front of her: a candle, a little clock and an empty terracotta dish, which was quite pretty, but didn't seem to serve any particular purpose. She could feel the anxiety beginning to build in her stomach, so she pushed it down and focused on her breathing. She was just getting it in hand when there was a knock on the door. Marissa jumped, then stood. She really had believed nobody would show up. 'Come in?'

The woman who entered was quite young, it was difficult to tell how old she was. She was very slim and wore a pink tracksuit with a hoodie top that had kitten ears sewn into it. Her hands were deep in her pockets.

'Hi,' she said in a small voice. 'Mary said you were cool, so I thought I'd come today.'

'Hi,' said Marissa, standing up. She referred to the client sheet she had been given by the office. 'Maria?'

'No, Maria's not here anymore, she left. I'm Lucy.'

'Hello, Lucy, I'm very glad you came. Have a seat.' Marissa gestured to both chairs and Lucy chose the one that she hadn't been sitting in. Marissa sat back down again.

Lucy looked at her feet, pulled her hands out of her pockets and rubbed her face. Marissa gave her some time to settle into the room and get used to being opposite her. She opened the session with the usual contracting, and then asked, 'Have you been to a counsellor before?'

'No,' said Lucy, after a moment. 'I've never.'

Marissa nodded. 'Well, all I'll do is listen, if you want to talk.'

'Talk about what?'

'Well, anything you like. You can tell me how you are feeling, what it's like for you to be here, or why you're here in the first place.'

'Oh. Okay.' Lucy seemed dreamy, not really present. Then something shifted and she became more solid. She looked Marissa in the eye and said, 'I'm here because of Peter, my ex. He hurt me. I had nowhere else to go.'

Lucy shifted in her chair. For a moment Marissa thought she was going to disappear again, but she stayed present. 'Mary said I should talk about it, I should tell you what happened. I'm not sure, though, if I'm able to put it into words.' She seemed to be trying to break through something.

Lots of patience with this one, give her space, let her take her time.

'That's okay,' said Marissa gently. 'You don't have to tell me everything today, or even at all. But if you want to tell me about your ex, maybe you could describe him to me. If you want to, that is.'

'I could do that, yeah.' Lucy shrank back once more into her chair and looked distant once again. Some time passed.

Marissa thought it might help her relate to Lucy better if she knew how old she was, but although that information, was usually on the contact sheet, she didn't have it. *I never realised how valuable that could be for counselling. It isn't really the place to begin now, though.*

Marissa went back to the subject at hand. 'Tell me about when you first met Peter?'

'Yeah, okay.' Lucy smiled and stretched out in her chair. 'He was so beautiful, I couldn't believe it when he said he wanted me. He played in a band, he saw me the first night, he knew I fancied him. After the concert, he took me to his boat.'

She pulled a lock of hair out from under her hoodie and started twisting it around her finger.

'It didn't feel good there, it felt dirty or something. I mean, it looked clean, he had just had it done up. But there was something about it that felt really bad. Like I knew I wasn't safe there. I don't know how I knew, and he was really nice and all when we first met. But I should have known to leave right away.' Lucy drifted away again.

After a moment Marissa asked, 'Do you want to stop?'

Lucy came back, focused and said, 'No, I want to tell you. You're right, it will be better if someone knows what really happened.'

Marissa nodded. *She doesn't seem lucid, she's drifting in and out of reality. I wonder, has she taken anything?* She pushed that thought aside. She wasn't sure where to go with that, and she wasn't trained to deal with drugs. *I guess I'll just work with what she's happy to talk to me about.*

'Tell me in your own time. We have plenty of time left, and we always have next week, if you want to come back.'

Lucy seemed to drift away again, but after a moment she snapped back into the room. *I do think she has taken drugs of some sort. Either that, or she's traumatised. I guess that's also possible.*

Lucy took a deep breath, then began to speak. 'Yes, you're right, I do need to talk about it. I guess I was starstruck. He was the guitar player, the band was well known, I'd bought their record. And there I was in his boat. He said it was a barge. It was a really shabby barge – all blue and red and the paint chipping off, but he lived in it and I thought it was so cool that even though it felt bad, once I got there like, I ignored the feeling. He had a big sofa, and a bookshelf, and a bed. A double bed.' Lucy shrank.

Marissa held back. She wasn't going to force Lucy to talk before she was ready.

Lucy sighed and sat back in her chair. A tear formed in the corner of her eye. 'Yeah, I knew I should have run as soon as I got down there. But he locked the barge door and then it was just us.'

Marissa shook her head, then stopped herself. *I don't know what the best thing to do is. Maybe she just wants to talk about it. I need to stay non-judgemental. No sympathy, just empathy.*

'I kept telling myself he was so nice, so attractive, dreamy even. Nightmare more like.' Lucy stopped talking and drifted again, then came back to Marissa. 'I don't know why I kept going back to him. There was something about him, I've got to admit it. Even though I knew he was bad for me. After he raped me the first time, he was so lovely to me, so kind and gentle, and I did fancy him. I guess I convinced myself it wasn't rape. He walked me home, said he wanted to see me again, and he *was* beautiful... I wondered what such a beautiful man would see in a girl like me. So, yeah, I saw him again. And again. He was like an addiction. I'd sneak out of the house when everyone was asleep, get my bike out and cycle to the canal in the dark. I had a dynamo. I used to think it was exciting. I'd lock the bike first, catch my breath, then jump onto the barge and knock on the door. He'd be waiting for me. He always seemed happy to see me. And it was nice too, for a while.'

'You're doing great.'

'Thanks,' said Lucy with a shiver. 'Then he locked me in the boat one night, tied me to the bed. He left with his mates, went out drinking, left me there for hours. Came back then, said he was sorry, was so nice to me. And I forgave him. I'm such an idiot. But that wasn't as bad as the times when he hit me. I don't think I want to talk anymore about it today.'

Lucy was shaking. Her whole body shivering, but the room wasn't cold.

Marissa looked around and saw there were blankets folded on a shelf just beside one of the bookcases. She got one of them, opened it out and wrapped it around Lucy's shoulders.

'Thanks. Can I have another one please?'

'Of course.'

Marissa got a second blanket and placed it on top of the first. Lucy started rocking back and forth in the chair. Marissa sat down opposite her.

'Are you okay? Does this happen a lot?'

Lucy nodded. 'Yeah, I get the shivers when I get stressed, but they soon pass.'

I could give her some techniques to use for stress, but maybe today should just be about talking, getting her story out. I could do Reiki for her too, but it isn't appropriate here. Marissa's hands started itching, as if they were pleading with her to be placed onto Lucy, but she held them back by sitting on them.

Lucy seemed to be calmer in the blankets. After a few minutes she took the second blanket off.

'I'm a little hot now,' she said, apologetically.

'That's okay. you do what you need to do,' said Marissa compassionately, releasing her hands.

'Thanks. I feel safe here, with you, It's okay isn't it, to tell you anything?'

'Yes, you can tell me, or not tell me. We can just sit here too, if that's what you want.'

'I'd like that. Let's sit here for a while then.'

After a few minutes Lucy took the blanket from her shoulders and settled it on her knees. It was a fleecy blanket, pink. It looked very soft.

'It's nice here.' Lucy said. 'They have nice things. I have a blanket like this in my room.'

'How long have you been here?' asked Marissa.

'Oh, a few weeks. I think. I can't tell, it's hard to keep track. But not very long really.'

Marissa had so many questions, but she didn't want to ask any of them in case it upset Lucy. *This is what person centred really means. It's actually very difficult to do. Perhaps I should give it more credit as a way of working.*

They sat together until the end of the session.

'It's time now, Lucy,' Marissa said. 'I need to end the session with you, as I have someone else coming next.'

As she was getting up, Lucy said, 'Thanks. It's nice to sit in here – it's a lot more peaceful than out there with the others. I can think in here. With you just sitting there, it's easier for me to think. It's good. And I'm glad I told you. It was nice to talk about Peter, when I talk about Peter with the others they all jump down my neck about it, or they tell me what a bastard he was. I know what he was, but I did love him, too. Yes, it was nice to talk about him and remember how beautiful he was. I'll come back next time.'

'Thank you for sharing all that with me Lucy. I know it's hard to talk about something difficult, especially when you're upset.'

'Yeah. Thanks again.'

Marissa was left feeling upset at seeing Lucy so upset. *I think I need to talk to Audrey about Reiki. If only I could offer it... But maybe that's just me being uncomfortable with someone's difficult feelings and story. That guy Peter sounds terrible. I wonder what else he did to her? It doesn't bear thinking about. Not my business. I can't be curious. I need to park this until next time.*

Getting up, she walked around the room to try to clear her head. She opened the window to let some fresh air in and she sprayed her St Germain. *This bottle is getting used up, I need to get some more.*

There was a knock on the door and Mary R. came in confidently with a smile on her face.

'How's it goin'?' she asked, sitting down in the chair that Marissa had just been sitting in. She crossed her legs. This time her pants were black and white camouflage print, but still combat style, with large pockets on the sides. She was wearing a white sweatshirt and her hair was growing out a little, which made it a little softer. Her skin was tough, wind-beaten; she looked old before her time. She had yellow on her fingers – she was a smoker. *You wouldn't want to mess with her. You'd want her on your side in a fight. There's me being judgemental again.*

'Hello Mary! It's nice to see you today. Thanks for suggesting to Lucy that she should come to see me.'

'No bother,' Mary said, folding her arms and sitting back in the chair. 'So, did you get more client hours?' she asked.

'Yes, thank you. And thanks to you, I've now got two more.'

'Three, if Loretta shows up after me,' said Mary with a nod.

'Oh, you've talked to her, too?'

'Yep.'

'Okay then, thank you.'

'I talked to everyone. That I knew, that is. My girls. We stick together, me and my girls.'

Marissa waited to hear more.

'We've got to look after each other, you know. Who the bloody hell else will, if we don't? In here, though, we're safe. It's cool here. But out there,' she pointed out of the window, 'who the feck knows what's coming? That's one thing I didn't have before here.'

'What's that?'

'Friends. Good, solid, dependable friends. I do now. I've got some good friends now, from this place.'

Marissa waited for more.

'Yeah. We're gonna get a place together and keep an eye out for each other. It'll be great.'

'Sounds great,' said Marissa. *Oh, but maybe I shouldn't have said that. Perhaps it's a bad idea... I need to keep my mouth shut.*

Mary R. nodded. 'Yeah. So you have to sign some form or other that says I'm making progress, after four sessions. like. So, am I making progress?'

'Sure, you're talking more now to me. But you've not told me how you feel today.'

'You've not asked me!'

Marissa grinned. 'So Mary, how do you feel today?'

Mary uncrossed her arms and legs, set her feet on the floor and leaned forward in the chair. 'I'm crap today, Marissa. But I'm still here.'

'You're still here,' Marissa reflected back to her.

'That I am.'

'So what does "I'm crap" mean? To you, I mean?'

'Oh. I never really thought about it. Okay then. I'm not sleeping good, I'm bored in the classes, and I hate the food here. I've got to get more cigarettes. I'll do that after this session with you.'

'But how do you *feel*?'

'I told you, crap.'

'Crap – does that mean sad, angry, frustrated, anxious? Or are you in physical pain?'

'Yeah, all of that, I guess. I don't have words for it. Crap means crap. Like dogshit, I suppose. You get it on your shoe and you want it off. It's smelly and disgusting.' Mary laughed. 'But I'm not smelly.'

'Do you feel disgusting?' Marissa asked, feeling on the edge of a dangerous precipice.

Mary sat further forward in her chair and looked Marissa in the eye. 'Do *you* think I'm disgusting?'

'I'm going to be real with you, Mary, and tell you the truth, okay?'

Mary's lips went tight, and she pulled back from Marissa, as if expecting to be reprimanded.

'I don't think you're disgusting, but I am a little bit afraid of you. I want to help you, but I'm not sure how to do it. We have different backgrounds. I think I've had more support in my life than you've probably ever had. So I can't pretend I understand you, because I don't. I need you to teach me what it's like to be you. I want to help you, but I can't if you don't let me. And before I've even helped you, you've already helped me by sending your friends to me. Thank you for that. I want to do something for you in return. So I wonder if you're telling me that you think you're disgusting. People say that type of thing and I don't let them get away with it. I don't intend to, anyway. I can assure you that you're not disgusting And perhaps it would help you a little bit if you knew that someone didn't think that. And maybe you wouldn't think it anymore and that would make your life a little less, well, crap.'

Mary looked taken aback. 'Wow.'

Marissa was silent, letting Mary make of it what she would.

'Wow, wow, wow. Bow, wow, wow!' Mary stood up and rubbed her hands on her head as if she was drying her hair with a towel. Her head was red when her hands moved away. She approached Marissa with a threatening stance. She flinched but held her ground. Mary laughed, went back to her chair and sat down with more open, approachable body language than before.

'Okay, Miss Marissa, you want to understand me, you want to help me and make me feel a little less crap.'

'Actually, I don't want to make you feel anything – you're gonna feel whatever you feel – but yes, maybe I can ease things so that what you are feeling is a little more pleasant.'

'Cool,' said Mary. 'And yeah, I had zero support from my family growing up. For most of my life. Yeah, I've been on my own. That's why I like having my girls now. It's gonna be great.'

'So should we start again?' asked Marissa.

'Sure.'

'So, Mary, how are you today?'

'Well, I'm feeling interested. Yes, that's it. I'm interested and intrigued as to how you are going to help me. And knowing that you really mean it, and are interested and intrigued by me, has made me feel a lot less crap today.'

'I'm very glad to hear it.'

Mary told Marissa a little bit about her childhood and family life. She insisted on shaking Marissa's hand before she left the room. *Two down, one to go. Wow, that was tough, but I think I broke through something there.*

Marissa looked at her client sheet. Loretta was her last client of the day.

Just on time, there was a knock on the door. Marissa stood and opened it, with a tired smile on her face.

'Come in. You must be Loretta?'

The woman nodded. She was in her mid to late thirties, with long straight blonde hair and blue eyes.

'Please, choose a chair.'

Marissa contracted with her, and then an awkward silence fell between them.

Marissa studied Loretta. She wasn't as butch as Mary R., or as slight and vulnerable as Lucy. Loretta reminded her of Katie at college. She looked like she knew her own mind, but she seemed deflated and a little drawn. But looks are always deceiving.

'What would you like to talk about with me tonight?' she asked.

A few moments passed. Marissa softened her body and breathed, unfocused her eyes. The image of Loretta in the chair in front of her rippled for a moment. She appeared to have bindings around her neck. *Was that a collar? No, it's gone now, I must be exhausted. I'm imagining things.*

'What do you want to know?' asked Loretta. At the sound of her voice, the room came quickly back into focus.

'How are you feeling?' asked Marissa, trying to shake off the image of the collar. *So strange.*

'Sad.' Loretta nodded her head. 'I wish things were different, but they're not. Wishes are for losers.'

'Wishes are for losers? Where did you hear that?'

'One of the girls said it during dinner. Wishes are for losers. I always make a wish. I suppose I'm sad because, well, it means I'm a loser.'

A phrase from Marissa's Scott Taylor book entered her mind. 'You can wish, and you can ask, but if you don't make the moves, you'll have nothing to show.'

'What's that?'

'It's from Scott Taylor. He says you've got to make the moves. Wishes are good, because they show you what you want. But nobody is going to give you what you want if you don't ask, or take action.'

'Oh, I've not heard of him. Is he good?'

'Yes, very good. What kind of things do you wish for, Loretta?'

'A decent night's sleep to start with,' she said. 'And I want what's best for my kids.'

'Tell me about your children.'

'Yeah, okay. Aaron's five, Ava's three and Barry Jr is eighteen months. I've got them all here with me. They're in the crèche. I'll get back on my feet soon, and get a place for us, and it'll be great. That's what I wish for – a home, one where I can put the heating on and not worry about the cost, with a few toys for them and maybe a TV, and dinner on the table every night. It's not that much to wish for.'

Marissa nodded her head.

'Barry used to give us all that, until his drinking got bad, then we couldn't stay. He would hit me. I'd get over it. But one night he hit Ava, poor mite, that was the last straw. So I took 'em and brought 'em all here. Been here ever since. We'll get our own place as soon as I can get it sorted.'

'I can see why you wish for that. It's hard work bringing up three children on your own.'

'Damn right it is. Damn useless husband no good son of a you know what. Making life harder for everyone when it's damn hard enough already. But enough about me. Thinking about it makes me angry.'

'I can understand why you'd be feeling angry. But we have lots of time left, and this whole session is about you.'

'It is?'

'Yes, totally. You can talk about whatever you want here with me.'

'Oh, yeah. Yeah, okay.'

'So what do you want to talk about?'

'Dunno. What should I talk about?'

'There are no shoulds,' said Marissa, quoting Ms Greene, 'but you could talk about Barry, about feeling angry, or about what you're feeling now, in this moment.'

Loretta sat up and slapped her thigh. 'What's the effin' point of that? It won't change a damn thing.'

'No, but it could change how you feel about it, or give you some new ideas so you can take those actions to go with your dreams, to get some results.'

'Results would be good. Yeah. Okay. Let's do it.'

It was a long bus ride into town through still unfamiliar streets, and even though she had done it several times, Marissa still felt uncomfortable alone in the dark. She listened to music with her headphones on and sat downstairs on the bus so she could be closer to the driver in case anything happened. Being in St Mary's with all those women made her feel quite fragile and vulnerable in herself. *Some women put up with so much grief from their men. I did well with my Matt.* She took out her phone and sent Matt a text: love you babe xx

Her phone rang. 'You okay, Marissa?'

'Matt! Hi. Yes, I'm okay. You?'

'Yes, I'm good. I was worried, you sending me a text like that. You've not done that before. Where are you?'

'I'm on the bus coming home from St Mary's. It's been a long day. All those women, Matt, with their nasty boyfriends and difficult husbands, it made me appreciate how lovely you are. I just wanted to say it to you, that's all.'

There was silence on the phone for a moment.

'Yes, it must be hard for them,' Matt said eventually. 'The women, I mean. Hey, thanks. thanks for saying that. I miss you. We spent a lot of time together and now the past few weeks both of us have been very busy. When can I see you again?'

'Saturday? Friday night? I'm free all this weekend.'

'So am I. Yeah, my place or yours?'

'Tobermory is still acting strange – can you come over to me? I don't want to leave him on his own.'

'Sure. We can go somewhere nice, maybe on Saturday. See you Friday after work, so.'

'Yes, we can get a pint somewhere.'

'Mmm, now you're talking.'

CHAPTER THIRTY FIVE

'And this is Thomas, and this one is Gertrude, and here's Kevin and I on our twenty-sixth anniversary.'

It was Thursday in Cabra, and this was Margaret's last session. She had brought a photograph album with her to show Marissa, who smiled as Margaret leafed through the photographs.

'And this is Sarah.' Margaret became very quiet. She turned the page. 'And Sarah and me. There's Sarah and Thomas, and look, there's all of us together. That was Kevin's fortieth birthday. It was a lovely day.'

Marissa peered at the photograph, Margaret looked so young, and so happy.

'Who's Sarah?'

'She is – was – my daughter. She died. She was hit by a car when she was cycling home from school. It was ten years ago. She was only twelve.'

And with that, everything fell into place. Marissa suddenly believed she understood where Margaret's disastrous thinking had come from. 'Do you want to talk about it?'

Margaret was still leafing through the photographs. She looked up at Marissa. 'Oh. No, dear, it's all water under the bridge now. Water under the bridge. She was a darling, my Sarah. So bright, so much promise. Anyway. Water under the bridge.'

Margaret closed the photograph album and put it on the floor beside her handbag. She folded her arms and looked at Marissa, waiting for her to say something.

'You never mentioned her before,' Marissa said softly.

Margaret stayed silent.

'How do you feel, now, after showing me the photographs?'

'I'm not sure. I wanted you to see my family, my life. Because we are finishing up now, I suppose. You said it was our last session tonight?'

'Yes, yes, that's right.'

Margaret nodded 'Yes. So I wanted you to see. Her. Sarah. So you know I'm not mad.'

Marissa sighed. 'You're not mad, Margaret. You're probably still grieving, even though it was a long time ago.'

'I always wondered, you know, why they never had a name for parents like us. Parents who lose a child. You never lose them, they're always right here.' She placed her hand on her heart. 'It doesn't get any easier. I suppose I was distracting myself with ... what did you call it? Disastrous thinking.'

'I understand. You didn't expect her to die.

'Yes, that's right. It happened all of a sudden, out of the blue. Not ever something I expected. It wasn't right. Made me lose faith, in everything. Anything could happen out of the blue, to the others too.'

'Yes, I understand,' said Marissa.

'Sometimes I spent hours wondering what it would have been like if she hadn't died.'

Marissa waited for her to say more, but she seemed to have drifted off somewhere. After a few moments, though, she smiled.

'Life is precious,' she said. 'That's the most useful thing that anyone said to me, around that time, when she died. 'Life is precious, we need to make the most of it.' It's fine now, to say that, but at the time, I didn't want to hear it.'

Marissa nodded.

'In fact, it made me want to punch him, that priest. The one who said it. He'd never know what it was like to lose a child. But he was right. But he was right, unfortunately. Life *is* precious, we just can't see it sometimes.'

'Yes, we can't see it, maybe more often than not. But we're human, Margaret, and we get caught up in the small things, the wrong things, the discomforts of life. We forget the big picture at times.'

'So true. We do. I need to stop doing that and remember what is important. Thomas and Kevin, they're still here. And Gertrude too.

I know I need to make the most out of life while we are all here. We never know what's going to happen to us, or to the ones we love.'

'Completely true,' said Marissa. 'You've done amazing. Well done. You can come back to the Priory anytime if you need more support.'

Margaret studied Marissa's face. 'You know, I feel much better for having talked to someone about this. Thank you again for all your help.'

'And thank you for working with me. Perhaps I'll see you again sometime, Margaret. But I hope you never need to come back.'

Margaret laughed.

Marissa centred herself and got ready for William's session. He was right on time.

'Come in,' she said, and he did, taking the chair he had sat in the week before. He looked very smart, hair slicked back, his leather jacket shining where the light hit it. He smiled at Marissa.

'Marissa, isn't it?'

She nodded. 'Yes, that's right.'

'You can call me Will, if you want to.'

'Would you prefer it if I called you Will?'

He cocked his head on one side. 'Well, it's a little less formal, I suppose.'

She smiled. 'It is, isn't it? Okay, Will it is. Do you want to take your coat off? Great. Okay then. What would you like to talk about with me this evening, Will?'

William settled back down in his chair after hanging his jacket up on the back of the door. 'I mentioned to you last time about my dreams. I didn't say how often I had them, or how I felt afterwards. I think it could be useful to talk about that, because I haven't told anyone before.' He leaned in. 'You're the first person I've told, actually.'

'Okay, sure, we can talk about your dreams.' Marissa pulled away a little in her chair without realising it, hoped he didn't notice, and shifted so it looked like she was just making herself more comfortable. 'When was the last time you had one of these dreams?'

'Last night, or should I say this morning. I usually seem to have them in the waking hours, you know, just early in the morning, before it's time to get up.'

Marissa nodded. 'Do you want to tell me about it?'

'It was pretty bad. They're getting worse. More violent, this week, actually. I'm wondering if it's because I told you... It's like telling you makes me accept that I'm having them, so they have more of a hold over me now. Maybe. Anyway. This sounds ridiculous, doesn't it?' William laughed. He continued, 'When I wake up from one of these dreams I feel like I'm being strangled. Sometimes I wake up coughing uncontrollably and I have trouble breathing.'

'That sounds scary.'

William looked Marissa in the eye. 'I don't want to scare you, but I need to talk to someone about them. I know they're only dreams, but they seem more sinister, stronger than only a dream, if you know what I mean?'

Marissa nodded. *Oh yes, I know, alright.* She felt a creeping sensation over her body, but shrugged it away. *This is Will's session. I need to be here for him. My stuff doesn't matter, right? I put my stuff outside the door, I'm here completely for my client. Even if it makes me uncomfortable. Really, really uncomfortable.* She shivered. She felt on a knife's edge. She looked at William who was waiting for some sort of acknowledgement from her. She pulled her energy in and made the effort to continue.

'Yes, I think I do know what you mean.' The feeling of wanting to run out of the door began to subside. 'It might be useful for us both if you could explain, in your own words, how it feels when you're in the dream, so that I have a better understanding, if that's okay?'

'Yes, yes, it's okay by me.' William sat back in the chair and sighed, crossing his legs, as if he had to put some space between himself and Marissa while he gathered his thoughts.

'The colours are vivid,' he began. 'The golds are more golden. The sounds, I can hear them. In my head, like it's real or something. Some dreams are in black and white, some are grainy, but these are in full colour, high density, like a film. And they stay with me for hours afterwards, sometimes days. Like flashbacks, as if I was really there again.'

At the word 'flashbacks', Marissa remembered Joy had also called her dream memories 'flashbacks', but calling them 'episodes' had seemed to suit them better at the time. *I wonder if they're the same thing. But why would they be the same? That's ridiculous. But my dreams feel like that too, sometimes. And in my dreams ... and I wake up...* A cold sweat drenched Marissa's back. *And I can't remember my dreams right now, but I usually can remember them...*

William was still talking. 'I used to only have one or two every couple of months, but in the last few weeks, I've had them almost every night.'

Marissa decided to stay silent so he could continue. She found herself pushing her feet into the ground to steady herself and bringing her awareness to her breath.

'I'm always tied up in them,' William explained. 'No, that's not true – one time I was tying someone else up. I was enjoying it too, until I realised what I was doing, then I screamed in horror and woke up.' He scratched his head in thought. 'It wasn't waking up *per se*, more like I pulled myself out of it.' He nodded his head as he agreed with himself. 'Yes, sometimes I realise what is going on in the dream, while I'm still dreaming it, and it's like I don't want to be there. I know it's a dream, and I'm still asleep in it, but I have to get out of it. It's like I pull myself out of it.' He turned to her. 'Do I sound crazy? I'm not making this up, it feels very real to me.'

Marissa was really on edge now. Prickles of fear bit at her lips, waves of anxiety moved up and down her legs. She took a breath out and responded. 'You don't sound crazy, no. They sound like lucid dreams.'

'Lucid dreams?'

'Yes, they're documented in the literature.' *Good, yes, let's bring it back to academic work, to psychotherapy.* 'I've had quite a few lucid dreams myself.'

No, wait – I don't want to tell him too much, especially now, as I need some space to figure out what is going on. I'm here to listen to him, that's what I'll do. I don't need to fix anything. Just listen. That feels better, taking the pressure off myself to do anything really helps.

William sat up straighter in the chair, excited. 'You have? Oh that's wonderful – I mean, it's great that it's not just me then. I don't know anything about dreams really. That's why I wanted to come here. To talk about the dreams. I don't know what they mean, or if they mean anything at all. When I wake from them, I feel weird. It's hard to describe. It can be different every time, but it's almost as if a little piece of me stays there, in the dream world. And there's a little bit less of me here, in the real world. I know, it's crazy – "dream world", "real world", what am I like at all? Hey, I'm probably not describing this very well.'

He smiled apologetically at Marissa, but she was taking him very seriously now. She remembered something she had read ages ago in the shamanic book that Olive had given her about soul loss. *Is Will suffering a form of shamanic soul loss? I don't know enough about this. I wish I knew more. It's so hard to sit here and not help. How could I...?*

Suddenly, Marissa felt she'd been hit by a brick wall, walloped in the chest. Winded, she froze in the chair.

'Are you okay?' William asked, concerned. 'I didn't mean to upset you.'

Marissa gasped for breath, let go of the thoughts around shamanism and came back into the room. The colour came back into her cheeks.

'Yes, yes I'm fine. Thanks for asking.'

William still looked concerned. 'Are you sure? Would you like some water?'

Oh no, he's minding me! That's the biggest no-no in psychotherapy. He won't see me as someone able to help him now that he's helping me. I've failed him. Oh no. There must be some way to turn this around, to get my credibility back.

She blinked to refocus her attention back on William and smiled at him. 'Sometimes I get caught up in my thoughts. I have to pull myself back here to be the therapist.' She blushed. 'I'm still only learning. I'm really fascinated with what you're saying, I want to know more, and I'd really like to help you. But I need to remind you that I'm still in training, and this sounds serious.'

'Yes, you're right, I forgot. I thought I could talk about anything.'

'Oh no, you can! Absolutely you can talk about anything. But I might not have the answers for you. At least if you tell me, you'll know that someone else knows, which is a good start. I don't know if I can fix this, but maybe together we can come up with something that will help you manage it better. Would that be okay?'

William thought for a moment. 'I don't know what I expected from you. Yes, I suppose you're right, in a way. I thought you would be able to take the dreams away. But maybe nobody can. I'm disappointed, but that's my fault.'

'Sorry about that. Psychotherapy has its limitations, and a new therapist has their own limitations too.' Marissa felt relieved. *It's good to make that clear. Yes, it's not my responsibility to heal him. I can't rescue him, it's not up to me what happens to him, I'm only talking to him, and only for one hour a week at that.* Something tight around her throat released. It was very subtle, she barely noticed it.

William had been thinking about what she'd said. 'Okay, yes, you're right. And I can't afford to see a consultant, but hey, from what you say, maybe they wouldn't know what to do with me either.' He laughed apologetically. 'So, yeah, maybe it would be worth a try, with you, I mean, to see if there's something we can do together that will make it easier. But it's difficult for me to accept that I'll have these dreams forever.'

I can work with this. 'Ah, but you probably won't have them forever, they will fade with time as you become engaged with something new. Let's look at that. Tell me, how long have you been having these dreams?'

William hesitated. 'I think I've always had these – lucid dreams, as you call them. But not like these. Never as violent, never as suffocating. The quality of these dreams is different. When I was a young boy I used to dream I was surfing. I'd be up on the surfboard, and a big wave would knock me over. I loved those dreams – they were vivid, with strong colours, and I could hear the sound of the sea. It was almost like I was really there. When I fell into a wave, I'd wake up feeling drenched. But of course there was no water, it was just a dream. I would always feel happy, though, after those dreams. I got really good at surfing – I'd combat one wave, then another would come and I'd combat that one too. Yeah! When I woke up, I usually felt great.' He was smiling as he remembered.

'As a teenager, they got a little darker. I dreamed that someone was following me for a while. It seemed very real to me and I'd wake up a little freaked out. But it wasn't as vivid a dream as the one about the waves. It stopped, but around the time of my diagnosis for depression, these strange dreams were happening. Then I got the medication, and all my dreams stopped.' He seemed to drift off for a moment, then he came back to the room. 'Do you think the dreams are connected to not taking the medication?'

'Honestly, I'm not qualified to say, and I don't want to jump to conclusions or assume anything. Have you ever kept a dream journal?'

'Yes. A good few years ago, but then I got bored of doing it.'

'What if you just made a note in your calendar – you have a calendar?'

'Where I keep track of my comings and goings?'

'Yes, that's the one. What if you just mark the days when you have a dream, so you can track how often you really have them? You don't even have to write down what the dream was, if you don't want to. And then you can see what you've done on those days, or on the day before. Maybe there's some reason, some trigger, that's creating them.'

'That's a good idea. I can certainly do that, especially if I don't have to write the dream down. I can just put a tick in a box, so to speak, and that's great, because I don't want to go back and remember what happened.'

'Well, it's nearly the end of our session now, Will,' Marissa said, 'but I just want to ask you, how do you feel about your medication? Are you on it at the moment?'

It was William's turn to blush. He looked down at his feet. 'No. No, right now I'm not taking it.'

'Are you supposed to be on it? Do you think it might help with the dreams?'

'I don't know. I'd rather not go back on it. I know I'm supposed to and all, but I don't like how it makes me feel – just emotionally levelled out. Not happy and not sad. Feeling sad is shit, but I like to feel happy sometimes.'

'Okay. Well, I'm not saying it's a good thing or a bad thing to take the medicine or to choose not to take it, it's totally up to you, but if your doctor thinks you should still be taking it, it might be worth thinking about.'

William nodded.

'Okay, I'll see you next week, so. Thank you for telling me about your dreams – well, not about the details, but about how they make you feel. It's a good start. For next week, I'll have a think about what I can do for you that might help, and in the meantime, you keep track of whether or not you have a dream, and maybe next time we can talk more about what happens in the dreams themselves.'

William shook his head. 'I don't know if I want to tell you.'

'Okay. Just remember I can handle it, if you do want to tell me.'

I wonder if I really can?

'Okay. Thanks, Marissa.'

William got up and offered her his hand to shake, then got his jacket and he was gone.

The candle on the table flickered as he closed the door.

CHAPTER THIRTY SIX

She was back on the cobblestone path. It was crowded this time. She was walking with a group of people. No, she was shuffling, not walking. There was no horse. Her feet hurt. Her whole body hurt.

'Come on then, hurry up.' The man's voice was loud behind her. She was surrounded, crushed by people walking closely beside her. They all wore dark tunics and black trousers, and their feet were bare, dirty and had many cuts, some of which were oozing blood. Her feet were also cut and bruised. They didn't look like her feet... She realised they were bound at the ankles by a thick heavy rope, which continued up, bound her hands and was wrapped around her neck. It chafed as she moved. She tried to turn her head, but she felt a slap and saw white stars.

'Keep moving,' said the voice.

She realised she was hungry. She looked around her at all the faces. They were all terrified...This was wrong, so totally wrong, this was completely and utterly wrong. She felt a heavy weight on her chest. Was she having a heart attack?

Meow!

She opened her eyes to find Tobermory sitting on her chest. As soon as she did, he leapt off of her, as if chasing a mouse. Marissa felt the room spinning around her, she felt very groggy. She needed to wait a few moments before she could sit up. There was some water on her bedside locker and she reached for it and held it, looking at the water. She drank it. As flat as it was from the night before, the feeling of something in her mouth helped bring her back into the room.

What the heck was that? She rubbed her eyes, and with great effort swung her legs over to the side of the bed and placed her bare feet on the cold floorboards. She rubbed her neck, relieved to find no rope around it. *That felt so real. I half expected it to still be wrapped there. I wonder is this the type of dream that Will is having?*

She wanted more water, and tea. It was 6am, but she didn't want to go back to sleep again. She walked heavily into the kitchen, her body feeling like she was dragging sacks of potatoes tied together behind it. She filled and switched on the kettle and opened the back door for fresh air and light. As she did this she and almost tripped over her Scott Taylor book on her way to the sofa. *Who left that there? I was sure it was on the table.* She picked it up and Tobermory meowed loudly again, then ran out the door into the garden. *What is going on with that cat?*

Just as she settled on the sofa the kettle was boiled, but she stayed where she was, book in hand. She pulled a throw over her legs and another over her shoulders and opened the book to the back page, where it gave details about the event in London.

I can't believe it's next weekend! It's going to be so great!

Her heart lifted and the dream was completely forgotten. She read Chapter Fifteen once more, because that had the story of how Scott had helped his father when he thought he had lost everything due to alcoholism. *Such a good person, helping his father... He's helped so many people, he's even helped some of my clients without even knowing it!* She giggled. *Scott where would the world be without you?*

> *And so my father got his life back on track, with my help, we were able to save his house and he never drank again. Remember, my friends, what you are doing now counts more than what you did back then.*

After a non-eventful day at work and some giggles at lunch with Sarah, Marissa looked through her wardrobe back at her flat to choose something nice to wear on her date with Matt. She was really looking forward to seeing him; it had been a whole week. Pint? was his text. She laughed. *Men! He'll probably show up in jeans and a sweatshirt, but I'll make the effort, I want to look pretty for him.*

She put on a new orange blouse that she had bought for London, then went through several of her skirts, they all seemed too formal, or didn't match the orange. In the end she decided to wear the black jeans as the blouse set off the colour of her dark hair, and he hadn't seen it before. She put on some eye make-up and chose the little sparkly bag that she had acquired for the Christmas party. She fed Tobermory and locked the door behind her.

That wrong-thing was definitely going to die today, especially since it had just nearly killed Marissa. That black sticky translucent thing, whatever it was, really had to go, Tobermory was certain of it. But first he had to eat his dinner; a cat needs its strength.

He had tracked it down and he knew it was back inside the paper-bound-thing, and up on a shelf with the all other paper-bound-things. Tobermory was a clever cat, he knew exactly which one it was. There was still no smell, but yes, he understood how it was, now.

Once he finished his dinner and cleaned himself thoroughly, because he was a well-mannered cat, he jumped up on the shelf to seek it out. There were so many of them! Which one was the nasty one? He was certain that he knew before, but now he was up here, they all looked the same. He could still feel that wrongness, though, so he knew it was close.

He pawed at one of the paper-bound-things. It didn't move. He tried another, and another. They seemed jammed in together. But then he noticed there was a space on top of them, just underneath the shelf above. Yes, that would do nicely, He crawled into it to get on top of them all. He just about fit and it would be a good place for a nap. Yes. No! Wait, there was something to do first.

Tobermory pushed at one of the paper-bound-things from above, mewing at first softly, then much more loudly as he became more confident, his pawing becoming stronger until all the paper-bound-things moved together, and then one gave way, then another, then suddenly most of them fell, spilling out onto the sofa and the floor, making such a loud noise that Tobermory squealed in fright and fell as well, landing on the sofa on his paws, exactly as a cat should land.

He quickly composed himself and leapt gracefully down onto the floor. So many paper-bound-things were lying around him that the colours swam before his face. He was sure the nasty one was there, but there were so many, he couldn't work out which one it was. Deciding he didn't like any of them, he peed on the one that was closest to him. *There, that sends the message. Leave my human alone.* Then he went into Marissa's bedroom and curled up on the new duvet cover, and went to sleep. His work was done, for now.

It was after midnight when Matt and Marissa came back. They practically fell through the door of the flat, they were kissing and laughing so much. They had had a lovely evening together. Not bothering to turn the light on, they went straight into the bedroom, throwing their coats onto the floor. Marissa thought she smelled something acrid, but they had had a lot of beer, so she dismissed it as her imagination. She slept through the night, dreamlessly, her arm thrown around Matt.

The next morning Marissa awoke to find her entire bookshelf strewn across the sofa and the floor. Most of the books had fallen onto their sides, but some of them had fallen face forward and had opened, crushing some of the pages. There was definitely a smell of cat piss.

'Tobermory! Did you do this? What is going on with you?'

'What's up?' asked Matt, putting on his shirt as he came out of the bedroom. 'Oh dear. What happened?'

'I have no idea. No, I do have some idea. It's Tobermory. He's been acting very strange lately. Look, he's even pissed on one of the books!'

She held up Maslov's *Hierarchy of Needs* by her fingertips. The stained cover reeked of the piss that had been absorbed by the pages.

'I'll have to throw this one out,' Marissa said reluctantly, 'and it was so expensive too. It cost me €80 for college. Damn it.'

'Maybe you can save it?' said Matt, coming over. 'I'm sure there's something you can do.'

'Fuck sake, Tobermory, what the hell has gotten into you?' Marissa looked around for the guilty party, but he was nowhere to be seen. She sighed. 'You can put the kettle on if you like, Matt. I think I'll put this book outside to dry. Maybe it won't smell so bad once it's had an airing.' She opened the back door and a guilty cat shot outside before she could catch him.

Matt started picking up the books and putting them back on the shelf. The Scott Taylor book caught his eye, it had become very tatty. He opened it to a random page and saw scribbles and notes crammed into the margins, words underlined, and some kind of shape, like a symbol made of circles and inverted triangles, scrawled in biro obscuring some of the text. He took a breath, then turned the pages of the book to see more symbols, whatever they were, scrawled on most of the pages. He didn't know what to think. He shivered as he turned to a blank page between chapters and saw it drawn clearer there. He flicked back to the pages he had already seen and realised that it was in fact the same symbol, drawn over and over again, in various sizes.

'Hey, Marissa, I thought you didn't like symbols?'

Marissa came in and snatched the book out of Matt's hand. 'Oh! I was just doodling. It's nothing. Nothing at all.' She put the book quickly back on the shelf, snug between two other books. 'I wonder what has gotten into that cat?' she said angrily.

'I wonder what has gotten into my girlfriend, wondered Matt, taking a step back.

As they put the rest of the books back, he kept an eye on her, his lips tight.

Finally Marissa turned to him and smiled, looking as if nothing strange had happened. 'Let's go somewhere nice today! The sun is out. It looks cold, but it could be a good day. What do you think?'

Matt took one more look at the tatty book nestled up on the shelf, and then he looked back at Marissa. He shivered again, then shrugged his shoulders and decided not to pursue this until he could figure out what was going on. 'I'll take a shower and then we can decide where to go,' he said. 'Is there any hot water?'

'Yes, of course. You go ahead.'

Marissa put the kettle on.

They had a lovely walk in the gardens at Powerscourt, but Matt couldn't get the symbols in the Scott Taylor book out of his mind. They were violent somehow, distorted, swirling together, disturbing. Yes, they were deeply disturbing. As they were settling down to lunch, he couldn't help but ask, 'What was that symbol you were drawing in that book?'

'Which symbol?' asked Marissa, nonchalantly.

'Come on, you know exactly what I'm talking about.'

'Oh. In my book. Yes. I think I was just working something out.'

'On every page?'

Marissa shrugged her shoulders and took a sip of her coffee. 'Maybe.'

Matt closed his eyes and counted to five. He opened them again. 'Marissa, what the heck is going on?'

She stiffened, then softened. 'I don't know,' she whispered.

'You haven't been yourself for a while,' Matt said gently. 'Have you taken on too many clients too quickly?'

'Yes, maybe that's it,' agreed Marissa, hoping that would stop this line of questioning.

But Matt took a breath, then in his kindest, most compassionate tone he said, 'I'm not stupid, love. I know you had a big fright earlier this year and I know how hard it's been for you not to continue your training with Séamus.'

Marissa shivered at the mention of Séamus's name, but stayed silent.

Matt went on, 'And now you seem to be obsessed with this Scott Taylor. Yes, now that I say it, I realise that is exactly what's going on – an obsession. You've always got his book with you – beside your bed, in your handbag. I've not seen you without it lately. You've never shown it to me, and now I can see why. You've been forgetting things, you've not looked healthy, you're not sleeping well. You've hidden it well. Maybe even from yourself. But now I see it, and I can't unsee it, and I don't like it, not one bit.'

Marissa just sat there, biting her lip, waiting for him to finish.

'Don't you have anything to say?'

She shook her head.

'I don't think you should go and see him next weekend,' Matt continued. 'I think you should cancel your trip. Really. I don't like what I saw in that book. It scared me. If I'm honest, I think you need to get some help.'

Marissa looked down at the table, still biting her lip. She started to wring the tablecloth in her hands.

'Did you go to see Dolores? You didn't, did you?'

Marissa stayed looking down, wringing the cloth.

Matt slammed his hand down on the table. 'Damn it, Marissa, I don't understand what is going on here! Something feels really, really wrong.'

Marissa was still silent, but tears started to fall from her eyes. One landed on the tablecloth with a thump.

Matt pulled back a little. 'Hey, I didn't mean to get angry with you. I'm worried, that's all. I love you, I care for you, I just want what's best for you. But I don't know what that is. And you don't seem to know either.'

Marissa was crying properly now, her whole body shaking, not caring who saw her, just feeling the relief of getting out the pent-up emotions.

Matt got up from his chair and sat down in the chair beside her, turning her to face him. He unwound her hands from the tablecloth and held them. But she still couldn't speak.

'Listen, I know you gave up shamanism,' Matt said. 'I think you need to give up this Scott Taylor person too. He sounds great on the outside, but there's something strange about the whole thing.'

Marissa stiffened. 'No,' she said quietly.

'What do you mean, no?'

'No, I won't give him up. I'm so close to going to London next weekend to see him. I have to go. I need to go.'

Matt pulled away. 'I don't recognise you when you're like this. You're really not yourself.'

Marissa started shaking. 'Please, please don't go. Don't leave me.'

Matt leaned back towards her. 'I'm not leaving, love, I'm just very concerned. This isn't right. Can we get some help? Would you go and see Dolores for me? Before you go to London?'

'Yes, yes, I will. I will go, I promise. Just don't leave.'

'I won't leave. I'll stay tonight too, if you want. But let's talk more about this, okay?'

Marissa nodded, blew her nose and composed herself. *Matt could leave me, he really could leave me over this. I have to make it right. I don't want to lose him.* 'Don't get angry at me. I've been lost... I'm stuck, I agree there's something not right. I've been having a very hard time, trying to keep everything going. Inside I feel like a volcano about to explode.'

Matt pulled away again, looking concerned.

'Don't worry, it's not you,' Marissa said hurriedly. 'I don't want to hurt you.'

'I know. But I'm having trouble seeing you like this.'

'I'll be fine. I will, I promise. I know I will. I just need to go to London. It's important.'

Matt nodded. 'Okay, I'll come with you then.'

Marissa froze. '*No.* Please. *Don't* come. I don't want to be always needing you. I have to do this on my own. Whatever it is.'

Matt moved back to his side of the table, but he kept one of Marissa's hands in his own. 'Just remember I have no problem going with you, if it's that important. We can talk about this again.'

Marissa's coffee had gone cold, but she took a sip from it anyway. She turned to Matt and gathered herself and said, 'It *is* important. I don't know why, but I need to do it on my own.'

'Maybe it's a dark night of the soul that you're going through,' said Matt, mostly to himself this time.

'I heard that,' Marissa said, 'and it could be true – yes, a dark night of the soul. Olive said I had to do something for my soul. What *is* the dark night of the soul?'

'It's something that happens just before a transformation,' Matt said. 'All the hidden pain and darkness within comes up to be released, because you can't hold onto it anymore. At the point of release, the soul expands. It feels like a death, but then it transforms into something more – the next phase, growth. It's an idea from alchemy. I've read a few books about it.' He blushed. 'Actually, it's from a computer game that I liked to play, one based on Dungeons and Dragons-type stuff. But it seems to fit.'

Marissa nodded. 'I like that idea. Transformation. I'm transforming.'

Matt seemed happier now.

Hopefully that's the end of that conversation. What am I transforming into? And will I even recognise myself? Do I know who I am right now? And how could I hide something from myself?

'Stop this stupid carry on,' said a voice deep within. 'You know damn well who you are. You are distracting yourself from your quest. It's time to be who you are and shed off this nonsense for once and for all. And if you aren't going to do it then we'll make sure it happens, whether you want it to or not.'

Marissa ignored this and turned to Matt. 'Let's go back into the gardens while it's still sunny. I really loved being beside the trees. And then we can go back to the flat and I'll cook for you. Cook properly this time. What would you like for dinner?' She put on her sweetest voice. 'I can make a roast chicken?'

'Now that sounds great,' Matt said, relaxing a bit. 'Roast potatoes too? With peas, carrots and gravy?'

'Anything you want, love – a proper home-cooked meal, and a movie too. You can choose the movie.'

'Lovely jubley,' he said, rubbing his hands together in anticipation, but still feeling wary about what he had just seen.

CHAPTER THIRTY SEVEN 

The rest of her time with Matt passed without a hitch, or so Marissa thought. The hiccup seemed to have been smoothed over, the tension was relieved and they had a lovely dinner. The movie was funny, and the next day they went for a walk in Stephen's Green before she walked him to the DART station around lunchtime. Afterwards, she strolled back through town, looking to pick up something for herself for dinner later on.

The weather was warming up, the sun was out and she relished the stretch in the evenings. She fancied some wine so she got a bottle of white to go with her dinner. Sitting in her little garden on her chair, stretched out, cat purring at her feet, glass of wine in her hand, Scott Taylor book on her lap and London to look forward to, life was good.

The next day, Marissa woke early for work, then realised that she didn't have work to go to. She got up slowly and spent time finishing off her assignment, deciding not to send it into college just yet. *Better to hold off and wait a few days so I can look at it again, just to make sure it reads well.*

She had two people booked in for Reiki later that evening. *I can start looking for psychotherapy clients too. Eli said I needed a website – maybe I can look at other people's...* Some time later, she became overwhelmed and decided that wasn't for now.

I'm the client tomorrow for the college assessments. What will I talk about? She was preoccupied with this conundrum for another hour or two, not really sure what to settle on. *Why is being a client so much harder than being a therapist?*

On her way to the shop for milk and bread she visited a few of the local shops and pinned up some of her business cards which had arrived the week before. They were okay, they'd do for now. She noticed that there were many other cards there too, they all looked similar to hers... *Mine don't stand out at all, why would they want to come to me over all the other ones? I guess I will need to improve on what I've got. Well, at least I've made the effort. Now I really do need to get my act together and get a website sorted out.*

The evening was fast approaching. Marissa ate the leftovers from last night's dinner, fed Tobermory, got her bag with her Reiki things and went over to her Reiki room to prepare for her clients. *I guess I shouldn't call it my Reiki room if I'm going to have psychotherapy clients in here soon... What should I call it?*

She got there on the dot and this time she could definitely hear voices inside the room. *I must see if I can book the whole day. That would give me more space and time in between clients.* She could see the door handle turning and then Sam opened the door and nodded to her as he said goodbye to his client and walked him to the front door.

'I need a moment to get my things,' he said, and went back into the room.

Marissa waited, becoming more agitated with every minute he was in there.

'Now, all you need to do is breathe and relax, and let the Reiki do the work.'

Christina smiled. Marissa connected to her Reiki light, used the opening symbol and let the energies flow. She realised that she was feeling tight and stressed, even after having more than twenty-four hours to herself, so she imagined herself as an onion and the Reiki peeling away the layers of stress around her. She drew the peace symbol over zzzzzzzzzzzz, and begin laying her hands on her. She drew the peace symbol in the air beside the plinth too, a large one. She imagined it there, glowing with the Reiki light. Then she stepped into it and felt something release in her shoulders. The music track she was playing changed to something velvety, and she swayed her hips to it, allowing the energies and the music to move deeper within her body, through it and outwards, towards her client. She closed her eyes and danced while she placed her hands on and over Christina's body.

She felt herself walking on a knife edge, dancing on it, getting too close to something dangerous. It was taking all of her strength to stay centred. One misstep, one hair out of place, and something would be destroyed. She felt a presence in the room behind her, dancing with her. It felt good, warm, almost sexual. She forgot she was working on someone and leaned slightly back, as if knowing a dance partner would hold her, catch her if she fell into him. She felt herself relaxing even more, her hips gyrating more openly, moving in wide circles, as if teasing. She imagined hot breath on her neck, someone leaning in to kiss her. Christina moaned on the plinth and shifted her body. Marissa's attention faltered. She realised where she was and brought her focus back to the work. The music played on and she felt a warm liquid inside her body, something opening, releasing inside. She felt calm, centred, strong.

'That was amazing,' said Christina, as she put on her coat. 'I'm glad I'm not doing anything else tonight, I'm going straight home to bed.'

Marissa nodded to her and gave her her change. 'Perhaps have something to drink first. Not alcohol, though.'

Both women giggled.

'Yes, camomile tea would be good, I think,' Christina said.

'I hope you sleep very well. You know where I am if you need more.'

Marissa felt more open and relaxed than she had in a long time. She didn't question what had happened, just focused on preparing the room for her next and last person of the night. She hadn't heard from Matt all day, but that was okay.

The buzzer buzzed.

'Hello?'

'It's me, I'm here.'

'Eli! You came!' Marissa pressed the buzzer and Eli entered the building. Marissa practically ran out to see him. 'I'm so glad you made it! I wasn't sure, from your answer, if you wanted to come.'

Eli raised an eyebrow. 'Hey, sis, it's not my cup of tea, but it's important to you, and Dad was raving about it, so I thought I should at least try it.'

Marissa led him into the room, which smelled of incense.

'Were you smoking something in here?' he asked with a grin.

'Ha, ha. No, you know I don't smoke.'

'Only kidding. It's nice. A little small.'

'It's my first room, and it's not really mine, I just have it for a few hours on a Monday evening. I want to take it for the whole day, but there's someone in ahead of me.'

'I know someone who might have something more suitable for you, if you're interested,' Eli suggested. 'It's a little further away from your flat, though. It's across town, actually. But it would be your space, if you wanted it.'

'Oh, that could be interesting. I don't know if I'm ready for that yet, though. I have to get a few more clients first, and some regulars. Maybe in the autumn.'

Eli nodded. 'Fair play, sis. Got to hand it to you, you've been working hard to get this sorted out. Well done.'

'Thanks, bro. Now, you're here for Reiki, so take off your shoes and lie down on the plinth. Please.'

As Eli bent to take off his shoes, Marissa changed the playlist to something a little less yoga-like. *I'll try some classical guitar. That might help me keep my focus.*

'How's Carol?' she asked, as Eli got up on the plinth.

'She's good. She seems to be over the worst of this latest bout of morning sickness. I don't know why they call it that – she's been sick pretty much all day, and into the night too. I don't know why it's come back either. She thought it was all over with already.'

'Oh, I'm glad she's feeling better. That must be rotten.'

Marissa took a moment to connect to Reiki and opened the session, starting at Eli's feet.

'Are we starting now?' he asked.

'Yes. Can you tell?'

'Yes. It feels weird. I can feel something where you are, but something at my head too.'

'Yes, that's the energy.'

'I don't know if I like it, though. It's weird.'

'Give it a few minutes. Just breathe, close your eyes and relax.'

Eli settled on his back and Marissa placed her hands on his ankles. His leg spasmed and he sat up. 'No, I don't like this...'

Marissa pulled back. 'That's strange. Maybe it's just you releasing something?'

'Like what?'

'Stress? Have you been very stressed lately?'

'Have I what? Jeez, Marissa, you know how wound up I can be. Work has been mental, and with Carol, the baby coming... I'm more stressed than usual, yes.'

'I'll see if I can go a little lighter on you. Give it another try?'

'Okay.'

So how do I go lighter? Reiki isn't something you can turn a dial with.

Marissa closed her eyes and imagined a rushing river, then she imagined it becoming calmer and narrower until it became a stream. She put her hands on Eli again and he lay back once more, but held himself stiffly nonetheless.

After a few minutes, he seemed to relax a little bit, but after a time he started stiffening up once more. Marissa stood back from him and held her hands in his field instead of on his body, but he didn't relax.

'This isn't working for me, Marissa,' he said in a disappointed tone. 'I just have a strong feeling that I need to get away from you, which is very strange. Can you stop?'

Visibly hurt, Marissa pulled away completely.

'Ah, that's better,' said Eli, relieved, getting up from the plinth.

'I don't understand,' said Marissa.

'I don't either,' said Eli, 'but I feel so much better now that you've stopped. Maybe it just isn't for me. Can we get a coffee or something instead? I've not seen you alone for ages and it would be nice to catch up.'

'Okay.'

Deflated, Marissa turned off the music.

'Here, let me help tidy up.'

'Thanks. I've nobody else coming, so yes, thanks.'

'I remember this suitcase,' said Eli as he folded the blankets and placed them into it. 'Do you remember that trip to Spain? How old were we?'

'I think you were about five. How do you remember that?'

Eli laughed. 'That was the time I nearly drowned. I don't think I'd forget that in a hurry.'

'Oh God! Yes, I remember. Mum was in an awful tizzy. It was just a big wave though. It knocked you down, you floundered and Dad picked you up by your pants and took you straight back into the water again. I remember how upset you were, You were so afraid, you didn't want to go back in.'

Marissa laughed. Reminiscing eased the disappointment of the session.

'I really thought he was going to kill me,' said Eli, in all seriousness.

'He just wanted to make sure that you wouldn't be afraid of the water. It was important. I understand why he did it.'

'I understand now too, but at the time it was terrifying.' Eli zipped up the suitcase. 'This goes under the stairs?'

Marissa nodded. 'I guess we don't really see what is happening when we are experiencing it. That's why they say "with the benefit of hindsight".'

'I guess so.'

They finished packing up the room, Marissa locked up and they walked out into the twilight.

'It's great the days are getting longer now. I much prefer the light to the dark,' said Eli.

'Most people do,' said Marissa. 'I don't think I know anyone who likes it the other way round. Did you drive?'

'Yeah. Do you want a lift back to your place? Or shall we go grab a pizza somewhere?'

'Mmm, pizza sounds great.'

'I know a really good place.' Eli opened the car door. 'Here, get in, I'll drive us.'

After chatting over pizza, and ice cream for dessert, Eli left Marissa at her door and went home to Carol.

Why didn't he like the Reiki? I don't understand.

Marissa put her Reiki bag in the cupboard and settled in for the night with her book.

CHAPTER THIRTY EIGHT

There was a subdued atmosphere in the classroom. Nobody was getting their results, and nobody expected to. Some people had handed in their assignment and were just staying to watch the assessments to be polite. Others were biting their fingernails, waiting for it to be their turn.

Marissa had her assignment in her bag but she had decided to drop it in at the end of the month, closer to the deadline, as it still didn't feel finished to her. As it came closer to the time for her to be on, this time as client, she felt her nerves building. As usual, she had trouble coming up with an issue. Her counsellor was Suzanne from the Thursday group.

It was time. She stood up, brushing off her pale blue, below the knee, A-line skirt. She was wearing black tights and black Mary Jane shoes, and her top was also black, but a blue skirt was a nice change. She had been trying on outfits for London – *Only a few days to go now!* – and her wardrobe didn't seem as drab as usual.

With a sinking heart, she made her way heavily up to her chair on the dais. Suzanne was already there, dressed smartly and wearing make-up, her slightly too long bob sweeping over her face. She kept tucking the front part of her hair behind her ears, unsuccessfully.

'Hello, welcome. Do take a seat.'

'Thank you.'

Marissa sat down and Suzanne sat opposite her.

'I'm your counsellor for today. We have fifteen minutes and everything you say will be completely confidential, just between us. What would you like to talk about?'

Suzanne smiled and tucked her hair behind her ear once again, a shaky hand betraying her nerves.

'Hi, Suzanne.' A moment passed. Marissa swallowed. 'Erm, okay. I want to talk about a dream I've had.'

Suzanne's lips tightened. Dreams could go either way – they could open a door to further introspection, which wasn't particularly good for a fifteen-minute session, or they could have an obvious resolution, which would lend itself nicely to the allocated time. Suzanne was hoping it would be the latter.

'It's bothered me, the dream,' Marissa began, 'and I've had it more than once. it seems so real at the time that I wake up covered in sweat and have difficulty breathing. I know, when I wake up, that I've been dreaming it, and sometimes in the dream I know it's a dream. But most of the time I don't realise that I'm dreaming, and it's like I have to relive the whole thing again.'

'How do you feel after you wake up?' asked Suzanne.

'Troubled and emotional. And the worst part is that I don't actually remember the dream. It's like I've forgotten something, or made a mistake and can't remember what it was. Or I've lost something. Or been tied down and unable to escape. I don't know what it is.'

Suzanne seemed troubled, and Marissa realised she should have taken this to Olive, not to a trainee counsellor, especially one doing her final assessment. She had to turn it around.

'Anyway' she added, 'I was wondering what you could suggest I do to have a better night's sleep. And what I could do to help myself remember the dream, so that I could maybe take it to my personal therapist at a later date?'

Suzanne relaxed. That was something that she certainly could do.

After Marissa's session there were only two more, and then class was over.

'I can't believe this is it,' said Katie, 'our last class together as a group! It won't be the same next year, there will only be one group doing the degree.'

'Well, I'll be there,' said Emmet enthusiastically.

'And so will I,' said Yvonne. 'How about you, Marissa, have you decided yet?'

Marissa nodded her head. 'Yes, I think it makes sense to keep going, and it will give me more time to catch up on my hours.'

'Yay!' said Katie. 'So we'll be together, anyway. How about you Ronan? Barbara?'

Ronan was slow to answer. 'I think a diploma will do me for the moment,' he said finally. Marissa felt disappointed. She really liked Ronan and couldn't imagine the class without him.

'I'm going to try to catch up over the summer,' said Barbara, 'and hopefully then I'll be in class with you again in October.' She leaned in to Marissa and whispered, 'Are you okay, Marissa? You don't seem your usual bubbly self.'

'Yes, I'm fine, thank you,' Marissa answered curtly. 'Maybe a little tired. Yes, that's it – I'm tired.'

'Pints?' asked Emmet, rubbing his hands together in anticipation.

'Why not?' they all said gleefully. It was really the end of term, the end of the diploma, the end of a chapter of their lives. The degree course would be different – much less practical work, more theory, and exams instead of assignments. But it was only one year and then they would have another string to their bows.

'I'll have two degrees,' said Marissa, thinking out loud.

'Will you really?' said Katie. 'You know, I'm glad that we'll nearly all still be together. I'd miss you.'

'Ah sure we'd meet up at our accreditation ceremony in a year or two,' said Emmet, knowing he was pushing his luck.

'Cheers!'

+++

After fifteen minutes waiting for Lucy, Marissa was just about to chalk her up as another no-show when there was a knock on the door.

'Come in.'

Mary stuck her head around the door. 'Hi, it's me. Lucy overdosed last night. She's in the hospital, so I thought I'd take her place.'

Marissa's heart leapt. 'Oh! That's awful. Come in, Mary.'

Mary strolled in, hands thrust deep into her the pockets of her grey hoodie. She wore matching tracksuit pants and white runners, and her hair had been freshly buzz cut, including the top of her head, so there was nothing to flick out of her eyes. She sat down in the chair opposite Marissa, lips smacking with chewing gum. Reaching forward, she took a tissue from the box on the table, put her gum into it, balled it up and threw it at the wastepaper basket and missed.

She turned to Marissa. 'So, how's it goin'?'

'How are you feeling, after Lucy and all?' Marissa was still trying to get her head around the news.

'Grand. Shit happens. She was miserable, it was obvious. She wanted to get back with her ex, but he was the reason she was here in the first place. Bastard. She's under age. She dropped out of school, went missing, you know?'

'No, I didn't know.'

'Yeah, she was missing for a week. They found her on his boat, took her back home, and a few days later they caught her climbing out the window of her bedroom, on the second floor, going back to him.'

Marissa was wondering how much of this was gossip and how much was true. And what happened next. It wasn't her job to know, but she wanted to know.

'Anyway, the parents called the Gardaí and the ex was put on warning, then probation, then they made him move the boat, but he wouldn't. Big fight, made the local papers. She was a wreck, fought with her parents over it, somehow she ended up here. She should have been in the hospital in the first place. I think she's a little psycho, myself. Anyway, she'll be fine.'

'Well, thanks for filling me in,' Marissa said. She turned her attention to Mary. 'So this is your session now.' She looked at the clock. 'We're starting at 6:25, so we can run till 7:25, which gives you the hour. Is that okay?'

'Yeah, grand,' said Mary, rocking a little in her chair.

'Good. Okay then.' Marissa felt herself back on stable ground. 'So, what do you want to talk about tonight with me?'

Silence.

'Last time you told me a little bit about life with your parents. This week, would you like to talk about your hopes and dreams?'

'Hopes and dreams – *ha!*' said Mary 'What do I have to dream about? Stuff that will never happen.'

She got up and started pacing the room. She wandered to the bookshelf and ran her finger over the spines of the books, looking at their titles.

She turned to Marissa. 'I'm in the literacy class here. That's why I'm staying. But it's very slow.'

Marissa nodded. 'You're frustrated because you feel you are not making good progress?'

'No progress at all. I'm tryin', really I am. I dunno. You seem to have it easy – you're in college and all, with your degree and your counselling training. What do I have?'

'Potential, you have potential,' said Marissa. 'I know, from what you've told me, you didn't have as good a start in life as I did. But you have a chance now to make it work for you.'

Mary sat down again and rubbed her head. 'Sorry. I don't mean to be angry with you. Yeah you're right. Frustrated – that's the word. But I'll get there. Maybe when I see girls like Lucy fucking it all up for themselves, I realise what a knife edge we're all standing on at times.' She looked out the window wistfully.

'You could tell me more about that, if you wanted to?'

Mary looked at Marissa. 'About the knife edge?'

She nodded her head.

'I dunno what to say. It's a good place, this. But I've been here too long. I need to be out there, having my own life.'

'I'm only new here,' Marissa said, 'as you know. So I'm not sure what you need to have achieved before you can go back out there. Can you tell me?'

'Yeah. You need to be clean – off drugs – and have somewhere safe to stay, where you won't be attacked or messed up. I've been off drugs now for three years, so that's not a problem for me. But I've nowhere to stay. I'm on the list for a house, but I won't get it for a while. Anyone with kids comes first, and there are a lot of people out there with kids. So I need a job, so I can pay for a place myself. And to get a job, well, I need the literacy, don't I?'

'And you're having trouble with literacy.'

Mary nodded her head. 'It just won't go in. Must be 'cos I'm older. It's easier to learn stuff like that when you're young. I have to read five books and write an essay about them, and I just can't seem to read any of them.'

'Yes, it is harder when you're older,' said Marissa. 'I find it difficult to learn new stuff too, unless I'm really interested in it.'

'I'm not interested at all!' said Mary. 'All the books they have me reading are so boring. *Moby Dick.* I thought it would be about... Well, it wasn't about that at all. Just some guy fishing. I'm fed up with it.'

Marissa tried not to laugh. 'Can you choose the books?'

Mary nodded.

'So why don't you pick another book? One that does actually interest you? There are so many books out there, I'm sure you could find *something* that makes you want to read it.'

'I suppose. What books do you like?'

'I've been reading a lot for college. I'm just finishing now, so I guess I'll have more time to read novels and stuff. I've been too busy lately, though, with work, study, workshops and stuff.'

'That sounds like a lot.'

'Yes, but when you enjoy it, it's easy. That could be the key for you: to read stuff you enjoy. Maybe I could help you with that. What type of things are you interested in?'

Mary looked out the window again, then back to Marissa. 'Food. I love food. Cooking. Oh yeah, I want to have my own kitchen again, cook my own dinner.'

'Sounds good. I'm sure there are books about food you can read.'

'Recipe books?'

'Well, there's more to food than recipes. You could read about sustainable farming, about the lives of famous chefs, about the history of different types of cooking...'

'Oh, I don't know about the history, but the farming could be interesting. I'd love to have a garden.'

'Would you? Well, you could get a gardening book too. How many out of the five have you read so far?'

Mary blushed. 'None, actually. I was going to skip the assignment, but then I'd fail the course.'

'Now I understand what's so frustrating. But if you choose books about things you're interested in... Cooking, gardening, what else?'

'Motor racing. I like that.'

'That too then. Pick books that you want to read. That could change everything for you.'

'Yeah. It could be good, alright. Then I'd get the assignment, get my cert and I could start looking for a job.'

'See, we *can* talk about your dreams – you want to get your cert, get a job and then get a place of your own, with a kitchen where you can cook your own meals and a garden where you can grow herbs for cooking!'

'That sounds really good, yeah, but it's small really. I didn't think you'd count that as a dream.'

'Why not?'

'Well, it's ordinary, isn't it?'

'Maybe so, but so many people don't have that. Having your own place, having a peaceful life – you can dream about having that and then work towards it. It might not be grand compared to, say, the guy who created the internet, or someone who wants to travel around the world, or be in the *Guinness Book of Records*, or the Olympics. But I think having your own place, a kitchen to cook your own food, and maybe a garden, too, it sounds like a lovely thing to work towards.'

'Yeah. If you put it like that, then yeah. It's a good dream, and one I could have. I feel better now.'

'Small things, day-to-day things, I think they're the most important things.'

Mary nodded. 'Sure. What else would you be doing with your time?'

Marissa smiled. 'Exactly.'

Loretta was a no-show, but Marissa felt was getting somewhere with Mary. *I'm not sure if I like working in St Mary's, though. The women here need a session every day, especially if they're only here for a couple of weeks. They can't really go into process if they only have one or two sessions. Poor Lucy, I hope she's okay. She was acting strange the last time, I did think she may have taken something then. Shit! Maybe I should have said something to Audrey about it. Oh no! What if the overdose is my fault because I didn't say anything? No, it couldn't be. I didn't do anything wrong... she didn't say she was going to harm herself... We didn't even get a chance to get to know each other. I hope she is going to be ok. Maybe Olive is right, maybe it's all too much. I really need to sleep tonight.*

She got home, got her suitcase out and started packing for London.

CHAPTER THIRTY NINE

'I can't believe you're really going to London without me!'

Marissa couldn't tell if Sarah was teasing her or genuinely upset. She sighed. 'Look, like I said, let's plan a weekend away, anywhere you like, just the two of us.'

'Paris?' asked Sarah, with wide, hopeful eyes.

'Sure, why not, we could go to the Louvre, drink wine on one of those long boats on the river and visit the Eiffel Tower.'

'And we could have coffee and real French croissants, and go dancing in the Moulin Rouge!'

'I don't know if you can actually dance there,' said Marissa with a smile.

'Well, they did in the movie...' Sarah looked puzzled.

'Anyway, I'm back in work next Tuesday,' Marissa said, 'and I'll tell you all about London. Or I could meet you for lunch on Monday, or you could come for another Reiki session on Monday night. I still have appointments free.'

Sarah turned to her. 'I know, I know. I am joking with you. Promise!'

Marissa sighed. 'You really had me going there for a minute.'

'Look, I think it's great. You should be able to go to workshops and things for your studies. I'm really glad you're going. Hey, this time two years ago you wouldn't have been able to do this, you know. You've really gotten so much more confident than you were even one year ago.'

Marissa thought about who she had been and who she was now. 'I still have a way to go, though. I was very nervous the other night, being a client in front of everyone in class...'

'Yes, but it's not about you being the client, not really, it's about you being the therapist, and you're great at that.'

Am I, though? Marissa's heart sank. She was still feeling bad about Lucy. *I'm not sure I'm any good at this at all.* 'I don't know,' she said. 'Honestly, I've still got so much to learn. But I'll keep trying. I keep having no-shows at St Mary's, but I have three clients tonight at Cabra and it seems better when they come regularly and I can get to know them a little bit.' *Yes, I didn't know Lucy at all, really.*

Sarah guessed what she was thinking. 'It's awful about that girl,' she said, 'but it's not your fault. You only saw her that one time – how could you know what was going on in her head?'

Marissa smiled. 'Yeah, I am upset over that. But you're right, I didn't know her, or how to deal with it, or how bad it really was. She didn't talk to me about how she was feeling,' She was beginning to have a pain in her stomach when she thought about Lucy. 'I just wonder if I missed something. When I contract with someone new, I keep saying, "If you're going to harm yourself or harm someone else, I may have to tell my supervisor," but I didn't tell anyone. I wasn't sure, though. And she never told me. They're not always going to tell you they want to do harm, are they? I suppose saying what I say might even put them off telling me.'

'You are supposed to say it, though, aren't you?' said Sarah.

'Yes. I guess you're right, it's part of the job, and I'm not going to be able to help everyone, especially the people who don't let anyone help them.'

Sarah shrugged her shoulders and smiled. 'That sounds right to me. You can't expect to fix everyone.'

'I don't expect to fix anyone. But I do want to help everyone.'

'Fair enough,' said Sarah, turning to go back to her desk. 'If you didn't want to help, then you wouldn't be doing it. And you did your best – you can't do better than that. I'm sure she will be alright, she's in hospital now, which is the best place for her. She's off your plate now, so let it go. Now, I'm looking at what is on *my* plate, I've got to get ready for a management meeting.' She giggled. 'It's great sitting in with the other managers and having them take me seriously. I suggested something last week and they put it on the agenda for today, so I had better prepare. I do enjoy being listened to.'

'Sarah,' said Marissa.

Sarah turned back around.

'*I* do listen to you, even though at times it might not seem that way.'

'Thanks, and I listen to you, too. And we can plan Paris when you get back next week.'

Marissa smiled. 'Yes, let's do that. Let's really do it!'

Marissa sent her last email for the day and shut down her computer, watered her desk plant and pushed her chair under her desk. She wouldn't be back in the office until Tuesday. She waved at Tim and Noreen as she left, and they waved back with smiles.

Yes, work is done and my work is beginning. London tomorrow – I can't believe it, I'll actually get to meet Scott Taylor at last, and be with people who understand! Just to be in the room with him is going to be so amazing!

With a smile on her face and a big bursting heart filled with joy, she grabbed a sandwich, Diet Coke and packet of Tayto for later and caught the bus to Cabra.

She got off the bus a little early and walked the last few stops to ground herself. The excitement was mounting in her body and she needed to stay level-headed for her clients. She was like a fizzy drink that had fallen off the shelf, the pressure building up inside her was immense. *After the last session, I can allow myself to get really excited. I've got to keep it down for now. Excitement and nervousness are quite similar, aren't they? I guess it could be difficult to tell them apart, but this is definitely excitement right now.*

Marissa went into the building in Cabra and made her way upstairs, prepared her room and lit a candle. She had a new client today, Niamh, then William and Aisling. Aisling had been coming for a couple of weeks now, and she hadn't said anything yet, just sat and cried. *Poor Aisling, I don't know if these sessions are helping her at all. She tells me she feels better afterwards, though.*

Marissa sat down, pushing her two feet into the ground, breathing and pushing away imaginings of her coming trip.

Ten minutes past the hour, she was feeling Niamh wouldn't show, and then the buzzer rang. She went downstairs to meet her.

'Hi. Sorry I'm late.' A dark-haired young woman with a large handbag and many shopping bags was standing at the front door, wearing a red scarf and hat and a shiny red raincoat. She smiled apologetically, looking quite burdened by her load.

'Hi. You're Niamh?'

The woman nodded.

'Come on up to our therapy room.'

Marissa led the way, and when they got there, she opened the door and they both went inside.

'You can put your bags down here, if you want, and hang your coat up on the back of the door.' Marissa waited for Niamh to organise herself. 'Choose any chair you like.'

Under the coat, Niamh was dressed casually, in jeans and a long-sleeved top with a pattern on it. She chose the chair that Marissa had been sitting in and Marissa sat in the opposite chair.

'Hi,' Niamh said. She had big blue eyes, her skin was clear and she looked around twenty-five years old.

'Hello again! I'm Marissa. We have six sessions together.' Marissa contracted as usual, wincing slightly as she mentioned the part about self-harm, and then waited for Niamh to talk.

'Hi,' said Niamh said again, shifting in her chair.

Marissa waited a little longer, giving her some space.

Niamh took a breath. 'I have anxiety. All the time. I'm finding it difficult, at the moment, to do anything.'

Marissa nodded. 'Are you anxious right now?'

Niamh nodded.

'Okay. We'll go slowly. What does your anxiety feel like?'

'I don't know. It's in my stomach. Sometimes I feel sick. It's difficult to talk about it.' Niamh winced and looked down at the floor.

'Is there anything in particular that makes it worse?' asked Marissa.

'Yeah. I figured it out. The worst thing right now is being in work. Going to work. Just the idea of work. Everything to do with work. I'm feeling it now very strongly, just talking to you about it. It's getting worse now.'

'Take a moment. Breathe. Slow down your mind. Are you able to do that?'

Niamh shook her head, 'No, my mind is going crazy. The thoughts are coming so fast I can't even hear them.' She was getting paler and seemed to have shrunk into the chair.

'Let's look at the things here, in the room with us,' suggested Marissa. 'Is that okay?'

Niamh nodded.

'Here's a candle. Here's a table. A carpet.'

Niamh's eyes found the items.

Marissa continued with this for a few moments, then asked, 'Better?'

'Yes, a little.'

'I have a really good one you can use, if you like, if it gets bad. Look!' Marissa held out her hands. 'Here are my hands.' She stroked the back of her left hand with the index finger of her right hand. 'Here is the skin on my hands.' She wiggled her index finger, 'This is my first finger.' She wiggled her middle finger. 'My second finger.' She turned her hand palm upwards. 'This is the palm of my hand. Here is a line on my hand.' She turned to Niamh. 'Do you see what I'm doing? Can you try it?'

Niamh held out her own hands. 'This feels a little silly.'

'Yes, it does feel silly, but it works. It takes your attention away from spiralling thoughts and brings it to something in the present moment that is not a threat to you. And you always have your hands handy, so to speak, so you can do this any time you need to. Go on, try it. You don't have to say anything out loud if you don't want to.'

'Okay.'

Niamh looked at her right hand, then touched the skin on the back of it with her left index finger. She jittered when she touched herself, but then seemed to settle a little. She turned her right hand around and touched the palm with her left index finger.

'Now, do it slowly, methodologically,' Marissa suggested. 'That's right. Does it help?'

Niamh smiled. 'Actually, yes, it is helping.'

'That's great. And when you get bored of your right hand, you can do the other hand!'

Niamh's smile widened.

'And here's another idea. Look,' Marissa drew on the back of her hand. 'This is a "M". This is an "A". This is a "R". You can spell words out on the back of your hand, one letter at a time, and focus on that. I'm spelling my name, but you can spell out anything, like 'Calm down" or "It will be okay." You try it?'

Niamh nodded and she drew a letter on the back of her hand.

'The key is to do it slowly, and to bring your mind, your whole attention, to what you are doing. In fact, you don't even have to spell out words if you are very anxious. You could do numbers and count up to ten or higher, if you need to. See how long it takes you to feel better.'

'That sounds really good.'

Just then, Niamh's phone rang loudly from inside her handbag. Niamh jumped with fright then blushed. 'I'm so sorry!' she said, and fumbled through her bag to find her phone. The ringing became louder as she pulled the phone out of her bag. Marissa sat patiently, waiting for her to turn it off, it took a long time. Niamh was so jittery she had trouble finding the ringer.

'I'm so sorry,' she said again, apologetically. 'I should have turned it off, I totally forgot to.' She put the phone down into her bag again.

'Yes,' said Marissa, 'This is time for you, so you need to make the space for yourself, the phone does need to be off so you know you won't be disturbed.'

Just then the phone vibrated loudly in her bag, a text, possibly to let her know that she had a voicemail. Niamh jumped again, but not as strongly as before. She didn't move to turn off the vibration. *She didn't actually turn it off, did she, just set it to vibrate. She's too afraid to set a boundary for herself? Or maybe she's not used to doing it.*

'I'm just wondering, Niamh, why you didn't turn the phone completely off? Or even to silent with no vibrations?'

Niamh was silent herself for a moment. 'I don't know, actually. I don't think I've ever done that.'

Marissa nodded. 'Silence is good. Even with the phone on vibrate you can still be disturbed. Just something for you to think about? I know it can be difficult but it will help your anxiety levels. So I'll give you some homework to do – firstly, think about switching off vibrate on the phone, and then turning it onto silent, maybe for one hour each day? Make that your hour of the day. You can do anything during that hour – watch tv, go for a walk, even have a nap. But try to actually do it. And the exercise we just did would be good for you to do, too. Anytime you feel anxious this week, bring your awareness to your hands. Draw numbers on the backs of your hands, spell out words, and do it really, really slowly. Or you could look at the things around you, if that's easier to do. See what helps you the most. Counting is good, you can notice how far you count until you feel better. If you get used to doing it, the count you reach may get lower each time you try. It would be a good experiment, wouldn't it?'

Niamh nodded. 'It sounds like a lot to try, but I've not tried anything before. I like the idea of an hour for me. And the exercise, I will definitely try it. Thank you.'

'I look forward to seeing you next week to hear about how you got along with it.'

Niamh left feeling happier. *One down two to go. I don't remember learning that technique anywhere, though. Maybe it was inspiration! I should try it myself, an hour a day for me sounds wonderful!*

William was due in next. Marissa got up and jiggled her body about a little bit to clear the air. *The room feels stuffy, I wish I could open the window.* She sprayed her St Germain and then the buzzer rang. She let William in. He was smiling when he got to the room.

'Hi, Marissa, can I come in?'

'Oh, yes. Please do. How are you doing tonight?' *Shite! Those dreams, I need to pull back a little bit. I'm not here to fix or change him, just to listen. I'm just a counsellor. That's all I am supposed to do.*

'I'm feeling much better. The dreams have subsided a bit, they're fuzzier, not as violent. It's as if they're happening in the distance and I'm watching them instead of being in them. It's meant that I've been sleeping better.'

'Oh I'm so glad.' *And very much relieved.* 'Tell me more.'

William took his chair. 'Well, I don't know what happened, or why. Maybe you knowing about it changed something?'

Marissa smiled. 'Yes, maybe. They do say that having a witness or an observer can change the behaviour of what is being observed.'

'Yes, that's quantum physics! A wave changes into a particle when someone is looking at it, or is it from a particle into a wave? Oh, yes, and Schrödinger's cat. Do you know that one? There's no observer in that case. As far as I know, the question is whether a cat inside a box is alive or dead, because of a random radioactive event that might or might not have happened.'

Marissa's head began to spin.

Back at Tobermory's flat it was getting dark. Low evening light streamed in from the window over the bed, making patterns across the duvet. The paper-bound-thing had been left at home today and was open, face down on the bed. Tobermory had been putting this off. He knew he had been. But his paw... His body remembered the electric shock of the contact with the wrong-thing and shivered. But it was still in his space, and the black hazy nasty thing that lived inside the paper-bound-thing *was* getting nastier. It was NOT allowed. He decided he never had a better opportunity than right now. He switched on his senses, then caught a scent of something possibly delicious coming from the kitchen... No. He would do this first, then he would eat. It will be his reward.

His back arched, he stretched out his claws, admiring each one. Nice and sharp. Good. It was time. He slowly approached the wrong-thing. This was definitely it this time. It was going to die.

He wondered why it wasn't running or hiding from him. He got closer to the bed, and closer again, then sprung up onto the furthest corner of the bed from the paper-bound-thing. It still did not move. Maybe it didn't see him? That could work to his advantage. He was still for a moment, then readied himself, positioned for the kill. He wiggled his pelvis, body low, tail flicking from side to side, and waited, and waited, and... The moment was ... *now!* He leapt onto the book, claws gaining purchase on the pages. He ripped and tore at them.

Feeling braver now, he bit in with his teeth too, venting all of his anger and rage. He tore and ripped and ripped and tore at the paper-bound-thing until the bedroom was filled with flying bits of paper and scraps of notes and words, and all that was left of it was a torn cover and spine, and some glue and the ends of some of the pages.

He stopped. Exhausted. He looked around. Was it gone? The wrong-thing? The bad black nasty thing? It hadn't seemed to be inside that paper-bound-thing at all. But he'd still done a good job. Yes, he'd done well. Proud of himself, he went to the kitchen, found what it was he had smelled earlier, and ate it. Nice. Then he padded into the living room, jumped up onto his favourite armchair, curled up and fell asleep.

Aisling shivered in the chair. Marissa really wanted to put a blanket around her and offer her Reiki. Aisling hadn't talked yet about what had happened to her, but it seemed she was about to. Marissa was getting antsy. Her thoughts kept drifting to her packing. *What have I forgotten? Have I got a phone charger? And my toothbrush, and my face cream...? Sure if I forget anything, I can buy it in London. London, yay! It's tomorrow, I can't believe it! So excited. Shit. Aisling.*

Aisling looked up apologetically at Marissa. It wasn't going to be tonight. *Maybe I should count to myself, slowly in my mind.*

As soon as she said goodbye to Aisling, something inside of Marissa released. Her whole body felt electrified. This was it! She was free, all she had to do was pack and go! Well, she had to wait till the morning to catch that flight, but still, it was only a few hours away.

When Marissa eventually got home, it was pitch dark. She put on the kettle, made a cuppa and brought it into her bedroom where she discovered her Scott Taylor book torn completely to shreds. The sight was shocking to her - bits of paper all over the floor, inside her half-packed open suitcase, and all over the cover of her bed. All that was left was the cover and some scraps of pages and glue. She put down her tea and saw that her hands were shaking. She picked up the biggest part of the cover that was left and turned it over to see

Scott Taylor's torn face still smiling at her, regardless of claw marks. She shivered, then got angry. She marched into the living room.

'Tobermory! Was this you? Why did you do this?'

Tobermory didn't move. He was sleeping peacefully in his chair. Marissa noticed his white streak and the new white dots on his paw glowing in the light from the street.

'Cat!'

Tobermory ignored her completely.

Marissa took a paper bag out from under the sink, collected up the scraps of paper in her room and bagged them all. She felt surprisingly calm as she cleaned up her room. *What has gotten into him?* She held the torn cover in her hands once more, looking at the angry claw marks. *Very angry claw marks...* Downhearted and still puzzled, she put the cover in the paper bag with the rest of the book and deposited the whole lot in the bin outside.

She came back into her flat and looked at Tobermory, who was still asleep. He looked so peaceful and gentle. *Do I really know him at all? What is going on? Why is he acting so weird? He's never done anything like this before.*

Well, it doesn't really matter anyway. I can pick up another book at the airport. And maybe he'll sign it for me! Probably better to give him a fresh book to sign. Yes! London is going to be bloody amazing.

She went back into her bedroom, finished packing and set her alarm for the crack of dawn. She couldn't sleep with the excitement.

CHAPTER FORTY

Marissa locked the door behind her, threw on her daypack and walked to the airport bus stop, her cabin bag sized suitcase bumping on its wheels behind her. It was 5am. She had woken up every hour during the night to check the time, each time she lay back in her bed and closed her eyes, but her mind had been racing so much, it was difficult to relax.

Marissa hadn't travelled on an aeroplane alone before. She checked and rechecked her passport and reminded herself that she had actually locked the flat door and that the stove, and the heating, were off. *And Michelle will feed Tobermory. I'm only going for a couple of days, it'll be fine. Scott Taylor is on the main stage at 2pm. Today! It's today!* She would get the Gatwick Express to Victoria, and her hotel was just around the corner, which was just around the corner from the conference centre. It would all work out beautifully.

The bus came. Everyone on board looked sleepy. Marissa was wide awake now, looking at Dublin lights in the early morning. The roads outside the city were busy; at the docks, there were so many cranes, so much activity. *There are more people than just Uncle Louis making money from the Celtic Tiger.*

The airport was straight forward, checking in was easy and her suitcase was exactly the right size, so it didn't cause any problems. On the plane, Marissa closed her eyes and they took off. It was an uneventful flight and they landed on time with a fanfare as the airline gave themselves a pat on their own back.

Gatwick Airport was busy. Marissa felt a little lost looking for the Gatwick Express. She was hungry, too; she hadn't eaten anything so far that day. She went into M&S and realised that she hadn't brought any sterling with her, but they took her Irish bank card. She grabbed a fruit salad, sandwich, crisps and a can and then found the sign for the

Express train. On the way there was a bookshop – yes, there was his latest book, and now she had that, too. The queue for train tickets was almost as long as the one for the bus in Macchu Picchu.

Eli was right. I'm glad I bought my ticket online and printed it out. She was able to scan the barcode and find the right platform, and within ten minutes she had a seat on the train. *This is like clockwork!* She put her suitcase on the shelf above her head, daypack by her feet and unwrapped her sandwich. She placed her brand new Scott Taylor book on the table too, and sat back in the chair, excitement bubbling inside her for the day ahead.

Thirty-three minutes later the train pulled into Victoria station. Marissa was packed up and ready, got off the train and followed the exit signs, then all of a sudden found herself outside in the sunshine. The traffic was whizzing past and she stood there for a while, getting her bearings. The street signs, the traffic lights, even the cars seemed different from home. She pulled out her phone and opened Google Maps. Yes, there she was, and there was the hotel. It was easy to follow the instructions and walk there. It only took twenty minutes. *I'll be seeing Scott Taylor soon! Wow, I wonder if I'll get to actually meet him in person. Or will he have lots of bodyguards like he does on YouTube?*

The woman at the reception desk was very helpful and Marissa found her room without a hitch. She put her keycard into the slot and the lights came on. She lifted her suitcase up onto the big double bed and lay down beside it with a huge grin on her face. She looked at her phone. The battery was nearly completely drained. It was noon; she had two hours before kick-off. She wanted to get there early. She wasn't tired at all, she had gone into overdrive. Plugging in her phone to give it a boost of power, she unpacked and put her pyjamas under her pillow.

She texted Matt: I'm checked in already! It was easy peasy. Scott is in 2 hrs! Txt u later xx

She saw the bubble activate, and within seconds she received a reply: Gr8 news love, enjoy urself, see u in a few days xxM

So now what? I have three days alone with myself. I'm sure the conference will keep me busy, though.

While waiting for her phone to come back to life, she flicked through the TV channels and settled on a documentary about the British Museum. *Wow, I could actually visit the British Museum! But I'll be much too busy.* She was getting antsy waiting for the phone so she washed her face and then checked the battery level again. *38%. Well, that will have to do! I want to get outta here.*

She put what she needed into a smaller handbag that she could wear across her body, under her coat, unplugged the phone from the charger and closed the door behind her, forgetting the keycard. Thankfully the door didn't lock. She opened it again, got the card and heard the click as she closed the door behind her. She slid the keycard into the slot in her phone case, then changed her mind, and put it into her wallet and into the bag. *Right. Let's go!* She put the conference centre details into Google Maps, and off she went.

She was getting the hang of it now, following the left and right turns dictated by Google looking at her phone as she walked towards her destination. She wasn't the only person doing this, so she didn't feel like she stood out too much. *What else is in London? What else could I visit? I never even thought about that! I don't know if I could manage to get anywhere else. I'd love to go shopping, there are so many amazing shops here.* Her heart skipped a beat, as she realised that London had many shops that Dublin didn't have. *It would be such fun, I could get some new clothes, something colourful! And something nice for Sarah... Oh dear! My bag just isn't big enough! Doesn't matter, I'm here to see Scott.*

She passed a massive poster and her heart leapt: it was Scott Taylor's face, larger than life, advertising his event. *I'm coming!* And then there was another one, and another... *Nearly there... The anticipation is killing me!*

She turned a corner and there was a long queue of people, all talking excitedly. *Can they be waiting for it? It's not even 1 o'clock yet!* She leaned into the person who was last in the queue. 'Are you here for Scott Taylor?'

'Yes! Isn't this so exciting?'

'Yes! I can't wait to see him!'

Marissa took her place in the queue, ignoring her growling stomach, she had forgotten about lunch and she had been up since 5am with hardly any food, but it didn't seem to matter. The excitement was infectious, everyone was smiling and laughing together, strangers were becoming friends and Marissa felt light and vibrant in herself each time they moved closer to the door. Then a sudden thought struck her: *Oh no! Do I have my ticket?!* She reached into her bag and felt it with her fingertips, right beside her passport, where she had placed it. *Jeez, Marissa, chill. It's cool. You've got this.*

The queue moved slowly but it didn't matter, ever step was a step closer to Scott. When Marissa got to the front at last, she had to show her passport and her ticket, then her hand was stamped and she was given a plastic wristband, which she was to wear for the whole three days. Her body recoiled at it's touch, but she pushed the feeling aside.

'Welcome to the greatest event of your life!' the woman checking the tickets was beaming with enthusiasm, even after seeing so many people. 'Gate forty-two, show your ticket to the usher and you'll be shown to your seat.'

Marissa followed the path into the grounds of the conference centre, wide-eyed, looking for signs of her gate. Finding it at last, she showed her ticket and entered the arena. It was huge, bigger than anywhere she had ever been before, and it was filling up with people. There were two stages, one smaller one in the middle of the room and a large stage at the front, joined together by a catwalk. Marissa looked again at the seat number on her ticket and went to find her place. She was about ten rows from the centre stage and could see it clearly, but she wasn't so sure if she could see anything if it was on the main stage. Then she realised there were big projection screens on either side of that stage. *So I will see him wherever he is! This is like a rock concert!*

Seats were filling up fast, the ushers were bringing people in. *I wonder if Dave made it. He was right, I'd never find Dave in here!*

All of a sudden she felt woozy. It was almost time for kick-off, but it was her body that was kicking off. All at once she needed a drink, she realised she was starving, her throat became dry, her head started swimming, she felt nauseous, she felt faint. *I need to get out of here.* The urgency to leave was pressing down on her so strongly she couldn't breathe. She was in the middle of the row, it didn't matter, she had to go. She left her coat on her seat and pushed her way out, past all the people who were still settling in. Some seemed helpful, others annoyed at her for making them get up again so soon. But she got out of the row and stood in the aisle and caught her breath.

Looking up, she saw that there was tiered seating above her, and that was filling up too. *How many people are coming? Oh my God! I have to get some air.*

She followed the marked path and found a door that brought her out to the auditorium. There were stands selling water, food, books, T-shirts, sweatshirts... *It really is just like a rock concert. I didn't realise he was such a big name.* Once she gathered herself, she went to a stand to get some water.

'Ladies and gentlemen, please take your seats. The event is about to begin.'

Marissa stayed at the stand and was able to pay for the water with her card. She got some peanuts too. That was all they had.

Thankful, she made her way back inside. The person at the entrance checked her wristband and let her in. Her row was full now. She had to climb over people who once again expressed their frustration with her as they stood up and she pushed past them to get to her seat.

I made it!

The lights went down. She opened her water and took a gulp. Music came on and everybody screamed.

It was certainly unlike any psychotherapy workshop Marissa had ever been to before. Not that she had been expecting it to be the same, but what she wanted was to spend time with Scott Taylor, learn from him, see him in action. Instead, the opening session ran for four hours straight, with Scott only making his appearance in the last hour. The first three hours were spent dancing, shouting positive affirmations, and building up anticipation for the man himself. It was exhausting. There were three hosts, all of whom had worked with Scott personally. Each had a rags to riches story which they shared tearfully with the audience, claiming, 'He's the man!' And the audience shouted it back to the hosts. Marissa was phasing out. She didn't chant along with them.

Where is he?

Marissa looked around her at the audience. Everyone was entranced, eyes wide, lit up. It was contagious. She surrendered to the noise, the energy, the music. Soon she was up dancing with everyone else, shouting, 'He's the man!' And, 'Yes, I can!'

When Scott eventually came on stage, he was wearing a black cloak. He crept surreptitiously up the catwalk and stood unnoticed for a few moments before opening it, displaying the bright shining silver on the inside and catching the spotlights dramatically. Underneath, he was wearing a flashy silver suit and tie, He stood 6ft 2 inches and was built like a sports star. His photographs didn't do him justice, and it was nothing like seeing him on YouTube. His blond hair was slicked back and his eyes sparkled. He had the charisma. He looked radiant. He said nothing, just stood there in the lights.

The music stopped and the crowd went wild, Marissa included, calling his name over and over again. 'Scott, Scott, Scott...'

Somewhere in Marissa's mind she felt herself being jerked backwards, like a child who had wandered too close to the water's edge being pulled back by a parent. *What the heck?* As Scott stood there on stage with a big smile on his face, soaking up the energies of the crowd, Marissa felt a strong presence behind her, and an image of Bear came into her mind. *Bear? Is that you? Oh my dear friend! I've missed you so much!* Her heart opened to him, like a flower that had been frozen melting in the sun, all the petals completely unfurled, and the fragile beauty within revealed itself. At the same time, something nasty and black, something malicious and evil, was pushed out of her body. Scott's spell was finally broken. *All these people! I need protection!* Marissa imagined a blue cloak being placed around her. Something deep within her closed back up again and she felt sealed and settled.

Marissa looked at the man on the stage and did a double-take, as if he had just appeared there, which, in essence, he had. He was just a man on a stage.

She looked around her with new eyes. *Everyone adores this person, but he's just an ordinary person, he's just a man on a stage.* She shook her head, as if waking from a dream, and realised she'd been standing up for the last two hours and her legs were tired. She sat down in her seat and her view of the stage was blocked by the crowd. She leaned into Bear, and felt him leaning back into her. *I've really missed you so much my friend.*

'Are we there yet?' Scott asked. He was wearing a microphone headset and his voice was loud in the PA system, echoing off the walls and bringing more roars of excitement from the crowd. He still hadn't moved from the spotlight, and he was smiling, really milking the moment.

What am I doing here? Why did I need to come all this way?

Scott spoke again, but Marissa couldn't see the stage. She felt she should make the best of things, seeing as she was there, so she stood up once more, despite her tired legs. The crowd were still chanting Scott's name. She looked at him, remembering who he was.

Ah, yes. Well, I'm here, I might as well enjoy myself. But isn't all of this ridiculous? She started to laugh. *These devoted followers – it could be a cult. Lights and music to draw you in... I'm so glad it hasn't worked on me.*

Scott was on stage for an hour, but he didn't really say anything, other than encouraging the crowd to be the 'Best that you can be' and telling them that tomorrow they would do some work together, that he was in the business of success, the business of changing lives, and that he wanted to work with real-life people from real-life situations, so he was going to invite people from the stage to work with him.

Then the lights came on. The auditorium seemed very ordinary. It took a good forty-five minutes for Marissa to get out of the arena and onto the street outside. The crowds were huge, and so was her relief at getting away from them all. She felt Bear standing beside her and her tired body was very grateful for the love that surrounded her.

Walking back to her hotel she passed an Italian restaurant. She hadn't eaten since the sandwich on the Gatwick Express, so she went in and got a table. Her phone was completely dead, her head and body were still reverberating from the sounds of the concert. *No, it wasn't a concert, it was an event. What exactly* was *it?*

She ordered spaghetti Bolognese with cheesy garlic bread and a Diet Coke. While waiting for it to arrive, she found images of the day flashing through her mind. It was 6pm now and her body really ached. *Tomorrow will be different. He'll be working in a one-to-one situation and that's what I want to see. That's why I came, isn't it? To understand how he works.*

The food came, and as she ate, she felt heavier and heavier, as if she had returned from a distant planet and was getting used to gravity again. Lifting her loaded fork to her mouth became effortful, and after she had cleared half of her plate, she became very sleepy. Somehow, she managed to finish everything, pay and leave.

The sun was going down now. The street had an evening vibe to it – people moving about, going places for food, for fun. *I've finished my dinner already and it's still so early, there's so much to do in London, I should go do something. But I've no energy for it.* She had an urge to lie down. Thankfully she recognised the street she was on from earlier in the day and was able to find her hotel without help from Google. Each step became more of an effort, and when she made it to the elevator and pressed the button for her floor, she closed her eyes as it went up and was reluctant to open them when the doors opened. She practically crawled to her room and fell onto the bed.

When she woke up, it was almost 10pm. *No point going out now.* She was groggy and still in her coat. Still feeling heavy, she roused herself, peeled off her clothing, plugged in her phone and ran a bath. She hadn't brought anything nice for the bath water and there was only a bar of hotel soap in the room. *I'll pop into a shop tomorrow and get a small bag of Epsom salts.*

Sitting in the clear water, soaking in the heat, she came back to herself. She closed her eyes again. *Thank you so much Bear, I guess you rescued me. I really needed some help back there. These past few months have been very strange. I wish I understood what really happened to me.* She went over the images from the very long day, revisiting the moment when Scott Taylor had thrown open his dark cloak and revealed himself. She remembered his smile, his big, wide, beaming smile, and how she'd even seen the colour of his eyes before the crowd had stood up and screamed in joy and blocked her view. It was as if he was a diamond and everyone wanted him. *A little too much? A lot too much? I don't really understand it.* She sank back under the water and stretched her legs out. This bath was bigger than the one in her flat; it felt good to stretch out, and her tired legs really needed it.

She remembered her book then, torn and tattered to bits around the room. *Tobermory! He knew! How did he know? And there I was, so angry at him! Dear, dear sweet clever cat, I'm so sorry I was upset with you.* She was overcome with emotion. She got out of the bath, drenched in emotion and wrapped herself in a towel. She picked up her phone and saw it was charged up enough for her to phone Matt. She got a deep pang of remorse for all she had put him through, and a sudden ache to hear his voice. She couldn't find his number quickly enough.

He picked up after the third ring. 'Hello, love, how's it going in London? I didn't think you'd phone! I wanted to give you some space to work this all out so I didn't text. It's lovely to hear from you.'

Marissa melted, her voice quavered as she replied, 'Hi! Oh, I'm so glad to hear your voice. It's not what I expected, Matt. And I'm so sorry for what I've put you through, the last few months and all. I don't know what happened to me.'

'Marissa? Are you okay?'

'Yes, Matt, very okay. Probably more okay than I've been in a long time. I think I might know what was going on. But I'm still working it out. It's weird here, not what I expected at all.'

'You do sound better, it's like you're yourself again. Thank God for that. What's weird about London?'

'Yes, I do feel like I'm myself again. London is great, the event though, it's very weird – I was there for four hours today and Scott Taylor only showed up during the last hour. He just stood on the stage, basking in the crowd's admiration and not actually saying very much. Everyone seems, well, glued to his every word. And then it just ended! I was exhausted afterwards. Come to think of it, I'm still quite tired.'

'That is weird about Scott, he sounds more like a showman than a therapist...'

'Yes, I'm not seeing anything therapeutic here at all. But he does say he's a coach, not a psychotherapist. I guess the word "coach" could mean anything. There's something more going on here though... I don't know what it is. But I want to stay and find out.'

'Maybe it will get better tomorrow. If not, you can always leave and wander around the city, that would be fun too.'

Marissa hadn't thought of that. 'I'll give it a chance tomorrow,' she said. 'I was so keen to come, after all. But somehow, now that I'm here, I don't know why I felt that way at all.'

'That happens sometimes,' Matt said reassuringly. 'But either way, it's a good experience for you. You're back Sunday evening, right?'

'Sunday night. It's a full day tomorrow, but Sunday is just a morning session and my flight's at five.'

'Perfect. I miss you. Do you want to do a distant Reiki share? We can send to each other at the same time.'

Marissa's heart opened for the second time that day. 'I would love that. We haven't done that in ages! Can you wait a few minutes so I can be in bed properly?'

'Sure. I was just going myself, so I'll text you in ten minutes and we can start the Reiki then.'

'Cool.'

'Bye!'

Matt hung up, Marissa busied herself brushing her teeth, preparing her clothes for the next day and putting on her pyjamas. She got into the bed. Phone back on charge by her bedside, alarm set for the morning, she switched off the lights, leaving the curtains open. The room wasn't so dark that it was uncomfortable. She felt safe and confident. She was looking forward to the event the next day, and to the good sleep the Reiki share would bring.

She was back in the audience, at the moment where Scott opened his black cloak and stood sparkling under the spotlight. The audience was roaring their approval, Scott was basking in it and Marissa felt herself shrinking, becoming smaller and smaller. Scott turned and looked straight at her and the crowd seemed to melt away, so it was just him and her.

He was magnificent on the stage and she was so small, who was she to question any of this? He was smiling and he was beautiful, alluring, drawing her in. He walked towards her and held his hand held out in invitation. She took it – how could she not? He pulled her up onto the stage and held her close.

Music started playing and then they were dancing. Sparkly lights were thrown around the room from a mirror ball, she was wearing a silver sequinned tight-fitting dress and high heels, and Scott was holding her close. It was dazzling, everything was blurry except for him. He was so real, so present to her. She could smell his aftershave, she could feel his body pressed up against hers, she could feel the tension between them, she could feel stirrings within, she could feel herself being drawn to him...

Then she felt that jerking movement again, as if she was being pulled backwards by the neck and she fell down on her backside.

She was sitting on the grass by a lake, still in her dress. Scott was nowhere to be seen.

Marissa woke with a jolt, feeling very thirsty. It was 2am. She got up and poured herself some hotel bottled water. She stood at the window, looking out onto the street. The beautiful white buildings around her reminded her of the scene in the old movie *Oliver Twist*, when they sang 'Who will buy?' She drank and absentmindedly rubbed her neck with the hand that wasn't holding the glass. She noticed the wristband around her wrist and shivered, filled with a sudden urge to rip it off. She pulled and pulled but it wouldn't budge. She couldn't find anything in her room she could use to cut it off. She reluctantly got back into bed, trying to ignore how the wristband made her feel. *Bear? Can you come and mind me tonight? Archangel Michael? I need some protection. Please come.* She settled underneath warm covers and slept once more, dreaming of her bear.

CHAPTER FORTY ONE

After an all-you-can-eat breakfast at the hotel, Marissa made her way early to the arena. She was under no apprehensions now; it was an arena, it was an event, and it wasn't what she had expected. She was going to make the most of it. And if she could, she was also going to find out why the crowd were so enamoured with this man. She bought a sandwich and a drink at a stall on the way there, remembering the length of yesterday's queues.

Her wristband got her inside straight away. There was already a queue in the auditorium, a long line of people waiting at a table which had piles of books on it. Some of them were looking through the books on the table, deciding which ones to buy, others already had books clasped to their chests. *I guess he's doing a book signing?*

There were quite a few helpers at the table. Some were taking money, and one person was taking the books from the customers, stamping something on the inside cover and then giving them back. Marissa watched him do this several times. Everyone seemed delighted. *That's a bit strange. It isn't a signature - is it a voucher or something?* She waited until someone with a stamped book looked approachable.

'Hi!'

'Oh, hello.'

'You're getting your book stamped! What is it?'

The man smiled, his face lit up with joy 'Yes! It's Scott's special signature message. It's fabulous, isn't it?' He opened the book up and Marissa saw what looked like a signature, and a few marks, like kisses. *No, that's not what they are.*

'What *are* those marks below his name?' she asked.

'Oh, that's his secret symbol! Isn't it unusual? I guess it's not really a secret if so many of us have it, but it's just a bit of fun, I suppose!'

Marissa peered at the symbol again. Her heart thudded and her body pulled into itself, like a snail going into its shell. She had seen that combination of triangles and ellipses before, but she wasn't sure where. She wrenched herself away from the book and caught her breath.

'He designed it himself! Isn't it so unusual?'

Marissa nodded and walked away, giving her body time to come back to itself again. *Bear, are you with me? I need your help again.* Something in her relaxed. She looked back at the table and did a double-take – that wasn't a helper at all, it was Scott himself! Why hadn't she noticed it was him? No, it wasn't Scott at all, but he did look very similar to him. Why didn't she notice this when she was closer? This was, like Alice said, getting curiouser and curiouser.

A woman's voice came over the PA system. 'Please take your seats. The event will begin in ten minutes.'

Marissa sat, quite contained, with her plain black notebook and blue and red biro out on her lap, and Bear standing behind her. She waited. The excitement in the audience was borderline hysteria by the time the lights and music came on, followed by the man himself.

It was a dramatic entrance. Wearing a gold suit this time, Scott walked down the catwalk and waved to everyone from the middle stage. The audience roared, stood up, waved, screamed and whistled. It seemed to go on forever. Still in her seat, Marissa felt an urge to put her hands over her ears. She was just about to do so when the music stopped. Then Scott spoke.

'Sit, sit,' he said with a smile. 'Sit please, everyone. We have all day together. We have work to do.'

Marissa sat up. *Thank God! Finally!*

The crowd sat.

'Hello, London! Now please, stay in your seats! Until I tell you otherwise!'

There was laughter.

'I am here to serve you. I want to see you all successful, happy, living the life of your dreams. I want you to get whatever it is that you want. I want to help you make your dreams come true. Not just the big ones, but the little ones too.'

Someone from the back of the room shouted, 'I love you Scott!'

He smiled. 'I love you too!' He turned to the people behind him, his every move shown on the big screens. 'I love you all. That's why I'm here! So! Who has travelled a long distance to get here?'

There was cheering, and hands being raised, and the cameras ran the length and breadth of the audience. People cheered to see themselves on the big screens.

'And who lives just next door?' Scott said with a smile. 'Come on, Londoners! Show yourselves!'

There was a Mexican wave of hands and more screaming.

Marissa just sat there. She had given up all hope of learning a new technique; she was just here for the ride now. She attached her pens to the cover of her notebook. She didn't think she'd be needing them after all.

'So!' Scott said. 'Let's talk! What stops you from realising your dreams? What gets in the way of getting what you want in your life? Even the little things? What do you think it is?'

Many people offered reasons, shouting them out.

'I can't hear you from up here,' Scott complained. 'I'm gonna come down to you.'

They went wild again.

Helpers with microphones appeared and Scott interviewed four people from the floor. They spoke for about ten minutes each, telling the story of why their dreams had never come true.

This is tedious.

Scott climbed back onto the main stage.

'Do you want to know what these people have in common? What all of you have in common, all of you whose dreams aren't reality?'

'Yes!' shouted the crowd.

'A lack of persistence. And a lack of faith. Lack, people, lack – it's what destroys dreams! But that's why you're here – we'll turn your lack into abundance, your poverty mindset into prosperity. Because winners think, *Yes, I can,* and when they fail, they don't give up, they persist. They get back up off the floor, after a little cry – which is okay, by the way. We all need to cry from time to time. But then they get back on their feet and they try again. And again, and again, until they get what they want. Because dreams take effort, you must persist. You must believe that you *can*. Say it with me: "Yes, I can!"'

'Yes, I can!'

The positivity, the flow of emotion, Scott's charisma... Marissa found herself whispering, then saying out loud, 'Yes, I can! Yes, I can!' along with everyone else.

'Would you believe I didn't think I could do it?' Scott asked. 'It took me years to learn how to pick myself up, how to motivate myself. I got there at last. But it wasn't enough for me to have my dreams fulfilled, not while so many other people around me were grieving for theirs. I thought that maybe my dreams weren't the real reason why I'd done it, maybe it was the process of success that I needed to learn. And so I did, and now I'm here, sharing it with you, my success protocol. Because success isn't always money in the bank. Success is how you feel about yourself. Success is happiness, success is joy, success is loving your life. What is success??'

If there was any doubt in the crowd as to what they were to chant, the screens on the back wall dispelled it all, displaying the words in big letters: 'Success is how you feel about yourself. Success is happiness, success is joy, success is loving your life.'

At the break there was a massive exodus to the bathrooms. Marissa stayed where she was. The music was still on, the room was busy, she had the whole day. She checked her phone and texted Matt:

It's mad here, ur right, I'll just enjoy it for what it is.
have a good Saturday xx

Echoes of Peru came back to her. Enjoying Macchu Picchu for what it was had brought her so much relief. *I must be doing it again, letting my expectations take over.*

The man who had been sitting beside Marissa came back and she stood dutifully so he could get to his seat. He busied himself rearranging his coat and pulled out a packet of hard sugar sweets.

'Would you like one?'

Marissa smiled at the kindness. There wasn't a lot of it going around as far as she could see. But she really didn't want one.

'No, thanks. I'm good.'

'What brings you here to see Scott?' the man asked, unwrapping a sweet and popping it into his mouth.

'I'm a psychotherapist – well, I'm training to be one – and I read a couple of his books and found them very good. So I thought I'd come to see him in person. I didn't know what to expect, but I didn't think there'd be so many people here.'

The man smiled. 'Yes, it's wild, isn't it? This is my third time. I've been to see him in Manchester and Edinburgh, and I've got tickets for Birmingham next month. I'm Jeff, by the way.' He held out his hand.

'Marissa.'

They shook hands.

Marissa asked, 'Is it different each time? I mean, with Scott?'

'Yes! It's always different, but it's quite similar too, in a way, I guess I miss some things and I need to hear them again. Like reading his books over and over – I read *Success Principles* till it fell apart!'

That was the book that Dave gave me. I think mine fell apart too.

Jeff had been thinking. 'Manchester *was* different. I went two years ago. It wasn't making dreams come true then, it was about a prosperity mindset! Yes, that's what it was about.'

Marissa studied him. He was quite young, about the same age as Dave, wore casual clothing and looked very clean and groomed. 'What keeps bringing you back?' she asked.

He shrugged his shoulders. 'It's fun, you meet some fun people, and Scott is amazing. He always has something to say. I learn a lot from him.'

People were beginning to file back into the room. Marissa and Jeff stood up to let the people back into their row.

'And,' said Jeff, as they both sat down again, 'something amazing always happens to me after an event. I can't explain it. It's like winning the lotto, but not as big... Like winning a raffle – yes, that's it. You always walk away a winner. Nothing bad about that, if I say so myself.'

The lights were going down again. *Nothing bad about it? I don't know about that, Lotto tickets cost money... What's the price of winning here?*

'Now we're going to hear some success stories from some of my clients.'

Scott welcomed them onto the stage. Cue stories of rags to riches, interspersed with motivational slogans, chanting (with help from the big screens) and more emotive music.

Just before lunch the music got louder and the dancing lifted the energy to the max. Everyone danced out of the arena to get lunch with 'Yes, I can!' running through their head.

The queues for food were literally out of the door. Marissa left the building and went to the grassy area in front of the main entrance, where she found a small courtyard.

She sat on a bench and unwrapped her sandwich, thankful she had thought ahead. Three women were there too. They seemed to know one another and were talking about how great the event was.

Something was playing on Marissa's mind. Was it just Jeff who had amazing things happen to him after the events with Scott?

She leaned in. 'Hi! This is my first time. Have you guys been to see Scott before?'

The women looked up, wide-eyed and enthusiastic. *They look as though they're in love!*

'Oh yes,' one of them said, 'we've all been more than once. This is my third time, and Jessica's fifth!' She nodded over to her friend, who was nodding in enthusiasm, her mouth full of food that she had also brought with her. 'Isn't Scott amazing?'

Marissa nodded as well, feeling it was easier to agree. 'Actually, I heard something from someone else today,' she said, 'and I was wondering if it was the same for you. Do you mind me asking?'

'Not at all, go ahead,' said another woman. 'Always happy to help!'

'This man I met said that something amazing always happened to him after coming to see Scott ... He said it was like winning a raffle.'

Jessica held up her hand and showed Marissa a sparkling diamond ring. 'Yes, Pete proposed after the last event and our wedding is next week! I thought I should come here for luck, just to make sure it all goes as planned!'

'Wow. Congratulations!'

'Yes, me too,' said another woman. 'I got an inheritance not too long after the Manchester event last year. It was enough to pay off my mortgage, and we even went to Crete for a holiday! I didn't even know my elderly cousin that well, but he left me everything! Ooh, the rest of the family were mighty pissed off!'

Curiouser and curiouser. Marissa looked around at all the people, wondering how so many of them could randomly have something amazing happen to them and attribute it to Scott's events. *Weird. No wonder they are all so happy to be here.*

'What about you? What are you going to wish for?' Jessica asked Marissa.

'Wish for?'

'Yes! It's part of it! He will ask you to wish for something... You'd better get your thinking cap on!'

Marissa really wasn't sure she liked this idea. Her grandfather used to say, 'There's no such thing as a free lunch,' and that had stuck with her. She imagined him now, shaking his head. What would he say? She imagined him speaking to her. 'Poor misguided fools, what is the cost? Selling your souls for a few years of happiness perhaps?' Something inside her flashed like a light, like fire. *What's that?* She replayed the image of her grandfather saying 'selling your souls'. *Are these people selling their souls? Is that what's really going on?*

She showed her wristband at the door and found her seat once more, but she was feeling shaken. *Selling your soul, I guess it is possible. But to whom?* As the voice over the PA gave the five-minute warning, she felt someone poking her shoulder. She turned around, but the people behind her hadn't taken their seats yet. She turned back towards the stage again and felt the poking again. She turned once more, but there was nobody there. She shook her head, but then she felt pressure, as if someone was lightly pressing her chest. *What's going on?*

People came back, the lights went down and the music started once more. The crowd was screaming and Scott came back on stage.

'What is your dream?' he asked. 'What is it that you wish for?' His liquid gold voice was hypnotic, resonating around the room. Lights started flashing, strobe lighting appeared, emotions were heightened, the crowd was hyper-excited. Then the main stage lights were dimmed and a massive spotlight followed Scott's every move as he ran up and down the catwalk, back and forth, asking, 'What is your dream? What do you wish for? Do you want it? How badly do you want it?'

People in the crowd were shouting answers, getting louder and more urgent and frantic.

Marissa felt waves of anxiety flood her system. It was becoming difficult to breathe. She looked around. Was it the lighting that was so upsetting? Was it the darkness? Was it the people chanting, 'Scott, Scott, Scott'? Whatever it was, it was like being trapped inside a nightmare.

It is a nightmare... Wait, the energy here, my nightmares... There's something the same about it. She looked around again and everyone she saw seemed to be bound, hand and foot.

Is this anxiety playing tricks on my mind or is everyone really bound? And the bindings, they look just like the ones in the images I saw in the session with Joy ... and Julie... Oh God, Will, and Loretta too? Oh my God! She blinked. She was seeing something now. It was overwhelming.

Are those really bindings around their necks? Wrists? She blinked and looked again. The strobe lights made it very difficult to see. She felt lost, ungrounded, at sea in a storm, with waves crashing over her. She was shrinking. *It's like those dreams! But this is real. And I have to get out of here, just like I had to cross my lake. I need to call on my power, I need to connect to my inner strength and wisdom, I need to call for help. Great Serpent! Emelda! Grandmother Medicine Woman! Help me!*

She dove deep, deep down into her intuition, her body sense. As she tapped into it, gave permission for it to open, all the tension of the last few months fell away and for the second time that weekend she felt flowers opening, rivers gushing through her, her body opening, so much love, so happy to feel her presence. *'My child, I have missed you, missed you so much. You are so loved. You have come back to us.'* As Marissa heard the words in her mind, she still felt her chest was caught in a vice, but somehow she returned to her own sense of who she was. She asked her body, her heart, her inner knowing, *Are they bound?* A full-body 'yes'. *Is Scott doing this to them? 'No. Not Scott. Only through Scott. It is Him.'*

Then she could see everything.

Some of the people in the audience had gags over their mouths, some had blindfolds over their eyes. It was difficult to believe, but the images stayed clear. Jeff, beside her, had bindings around his neck, wrists and feet, tied together with plenty of slack. He didn't know it. He was bound and totally oblivious to it, shouting out to Scott, who was still running around on the stage, asking for wishes.

Marissa wanted to tell him, to try to wake him up, but she couldn't speak. She opened her mouth, but nothing came out. She felt the sense of urgency she'd known before, huge and crushing, pushing at her blood and bones. *But I need to help them.*

But there were too many of them, Marissa was overwhelmed. She couldn't breathe.

After a moment, she felt more in control of herself. *Right, I've had enough of this. I've seen it now, there's nothing more I can do. I can't help them. Not now, anyway. That's it. I have to go.*

With all of her strength she called out loud, 'Archangel Haniel, Archangel Michael, Archangel Metatron!' She called their names three times, then, 'Please come! Help me. Bear, I'm so sorry. I didn't mean to leave you. I won't do it ever again. Please come, please help. Emelda, Grandmother Medicine Woman, Sachamama, please help me. Great Serpent Sachemama, help me!'

She felt hot sweat pouring down her back, trickling into her jeans, down her front and into her bra. She looked at her own hands. There was no bindings, she hadn't made a wish. *Thank God.* But she still couldn't move. 'Emelda,' she whispered, 'help me. You were right. Grandmother, help me. Get me out of this please.'

Scott was moving up the catwalk towards the main stage, microphone in hand, asking people for their wishes, promising them anything they wanted, if they'd only say it out loud. His hair was slicked back, his eyes wide, and his face, it seemed familiar now, not quite Scott, closer to – *Martin? Is it him?*

He stopped right in front of Marissa, singling her out from the crowd, just like in her dream. He looked her in the eye, his face contorted, his dark fiery eyes sparking memories of Cabra, memories of that time in her room, and Marissa was paralysed. The world stopped, faded away, and it was just the two of them, in the audience and on the stage, Marissa and the demon, face to face. She half-expected him to speak to her, to call her by her name... She looked straight back at him.

'Great Mother Isis, please, I implore you to help me. Help me and I will come back to you. I will claim my name and I will stand and fight. Please just get me out of here.'

Suddenly he was gone, over to the other side of the stage, voice pounding out of the PA system, 'What do you wish for? What do you want?' The world was back, the audience was roaring, she couldn't see the bindings anymore.

A strong, graceful and loving presence swept itself around Marissa, the paralysis left her and a voice inside her head said, '*Move. Fast. Now.*'

She grabbed her bag and coat and pushed her way down the row of people, stepping on toes, pushing past knees, almost tripping over handbags. She was out, almost free. No one paid any attention to her; everyone had their eyes on the stage. She craned her eyes but yes, she could no longer see their bindings. They were just people, albeit hysterical people, mesmerised by a man on a stage.

'That's no man. Girl, get the hell outta there now!'

Marissa ran, ran out of the door, out of the exit and out onto the street. Seeing a taxi, she flagged it down, sweat pouring off her, heart racing, mind racing.

'Where to, love?'

'The British Museum, please,' said Marissa, saying the first thing that came into her head.

'Okey dokey.'

The driver made a U-turn and sped off.

Marissa remembered a time when a sparrow had flown through the window into her mother's kitchen. Her mother had been so gentle trying to usher the bird back outside again, but it kept flying towards the window and missing it altogether. It sat on a rolling pin for a while and then was up again, flapping and making a ruckus, and not seeing the window. Her father saved the day. He came in, saw what was going on and found a burlap sack with potatoes in it. He poured the potatoes out into a bowl, and when the bird stopped moving once more, he threw the bag over it. The poor bird was hysterical, but he was able to pick up the bag with the bird inside it and carry it gently out to the garden, where he placed it on the ground. The bird flew up and out, and kept going.

Marissa sat in the taxi feeling just like that bird, trying to catch her breath as she swept past Buckingham Palace and through the streets of London.

CHAPTER FORTY TWO

The taxi driver left Marissa at the gate.

She only had a £20 note. 'Keep the change.'

He was delighted. 'Thank you, love.'

Marissa went through the iron gates and stood in front of the steps of the British Museum for the longest time. Her head was spinning, her stomach nauseous, her hands and arms trembling. She wasn't sure why she was even there, but it was definitely better than where she had been.

A cold breeze blew on her face and her trembling hands felt clammy. She sat down on the steps in a patch of sunlight to catch her breath. It wasn't that cold in the sun, but she shivered as her body cooled down, regulating itself so it could return to normal body temperature.

There were quite a few people around – families with children laughing, a group of tourists with an English-speaking tour guide. It felt surreal to Marissa, even though it was so ordinary. She felt woozy, she needed some space to gather herself. She stayed there for about twenty minutes and her heartbeat slowed down, but when she closed her eyes, her mind flashed images of what she had just experienced. She pushed them out. She needed to think now, to make sense of it. She looked down at her wrist and saw the band there. She picked it off, curled it up and put it in her pocket.

It was him, wasn't it? He's right here, in London, and all those people are bound to him. So obvious now that I've seen it. It's horrendous. What do I do about it? What should I do?

She imagined herself at her lake, by her mountains. 'Ausangate,' she whispered, and tears came to her eyes. Oh, how she missed her mountain, and how her mountain missed her too. She felt its presence come in strongly and surround her, tall, strong and proud.

The feeling of that magnetic charisma and strength took her back to Peru, when the dawn was breaking. She felt taller, calmer, more like herself than she had felt in months. *I am a shaman. I claim my space in the world. Yes, that feels right. Everything is back in its right place.*

She felt a pull to go inside the museum. *Not now...* She pushed it away and stayed with her images of the lake, the mountains... There were no stepping stones, no guides, no serpent. She felt a pull in her centre, drawing her up and into the building. She shrugged her shoulders, got up and slowly walked to the entrance. One of the women standing at the doors said, 'It's free, luvvie, go on inside.'

'Thank you,' Marissa replied, and entered the building.

The atrium was something to behold. Marissa gasped. It certainly wasn't what she had expected from a heavy stone building with Doric columns. Light streamed in from every angle through the glorious glass ceiling, fanned by steel beams throwing shadows onto the floor. In the centre there was a wide sweeping staircase. Marissa was glad she had come, if only to see this space. It felt light. She smiled.

I am safe here. He's not here, he's busy with all of his people, his minions. I can rest now.

She started walking, just following her feet, not having anything particular in mind. In fact she didn't know what was on display, and she didn't care. She was just relieved to find somewhere she could gather herself again.

She found herself standing in front of an obelisk. It was covered in hieroglyphs, and right on the front of it, so that you couldn't miss it, was an ankh. 'Of course!' Marissa closed her eyes and took a breath, feeling supporting, calming energies rushing in and around her. She felt home at last.

Thank you, Isis. I know it was you who got me out of there safely. Maybe you even brought me here. I really am grateful.

She stayed, looking at the fine detail on the obelisk as she processed the serendipity of it all. Then, when she was ready, she walked around the exhibit, examining the mummies, the remnants of tombs, taking in details of the fading colours, the other stone obelisks and the remains of a civilisation which had been swallowed up by the passage of time. A wave of sadness washed over her. *So many items, so much richness, a lost time. Why is it all here? In London? Doesn't it belong to the Egyptian people?*

The sadness became heavy in her and she needed to sit down. She found a bench and was about to squash herself in beside an older woman, but the woman decided to get up just as Marissa was about to sit down. With the bench to herself now, Marissa closed her eyes. She wanted to talk to Isis again.

'Yes, I agree, these items, fragments, they belong to my people. But this is not the discussion we need to be having in this moment.'

Marissa looked around her. She was in a beautiful open room, sitting at a table. Light streamed in from gardens surrounding it on all sides. It's not a room, it's a tent, or a marquee?

The marquee was white and both the table and the marquee were lavishly decorated, the table filled to overflowing with white and golden plates of food, small cakes and dips and breads, olives, pomegranates, dates, figs and honey. There was a beautiful white teapot which had rings of gold in the centre of the table, and two matching teacups on saucers.

'Shall I pour?' asked a smiling voice.

Marissa looked up at the woman speaking. It was the great Goddess Isis. She was stunningly beautiful, with ivory skin and thick black hair which was tied on top of her head and adorned with golden ornaments. She wore a golden dress and had many bangles on her arms, and a large golden ankh around her neck. This time she did not tower over Marissa, instead they were sitting together at the table just like ordinary women having tea.

Isis smiled, parting perfect lips, and said, 'You did well to get out of his lair in one piece. You did that yourself – I just gave you a small shove to get you started.'

She lifted the teapot, which looked incredibly heavy, and poured tea into both cups, then put it back down onto the table. Taking a small spoonful of honey from the honeypot and stirring it into her own cup, she nodded to Marissa to take the other cup, which she did.

'Milk? Honey? Help yourself to whatever you wish. Now, dear, we really must talk.' She sipped her tea. 'I want you to tell me everything. Make

your report to me, Marissa Tori Scarlett Lightbringer, and then we will make some plans. You have a lot of work to do.'

Something warm and soft brushed past Marissa's legs and she jumped.

Isis laughed. It was a warm, musical laugh that lifted Marissa's soul. She looked down and saw an exceptionally large, exceedingly elegant jaguar looking up at her. Jet black, except for a sliver streak across its face, and several white spots on its paw. He had deep green eyes and wore a golden collar around its neck, he was at least twice as big as her own dear cat at home, but wait, something about the tail was familiar? Yes, there it was, that twist. It couldn't be, could it? Was this Tobermory, as a Jaguar? Her heart opened and she felt love gushing through her body.

'Tobermory! It is you! Thank you so much for helping me, you probably saved my life and I didn't even know it.'

He looked at her and twitched his tail as if to say, 'Of course it's me. Silly humans never see anything of great importance until it's staring them right in the face.'

Marissa knelt down to him and threw her arms around his neck. He licked her face, pulled out of her embrace and walked away.

'Ah, you recognise him,' said Isis as Marissa sat back at the table. 'Good. He has been with you before, over many lifetimes.' She beckoned, and Marissa realised there were girls standing in the entrance of the marquee, waiting. 'Bring the kitty some cream please, then leave us.'

Isis turned to Marissa. 'They mean well, but cannot be trusted. He has ears and eyes everywhere.'

A large golden bowl filled to the brim with cream was delivered for the large cat, then the girls were dismissed, and it was just Isis and Marissa. Isis waited patiently in silence. Marissa looked at her as if asking permission to speak.

'Yes,' Isis said, in golden honey tones. 'Tell me.'

Marissa described the event, the bindings, the hysteria. Isis was silent and nodded. Marissa described her client sessions, how she had found similar bindings in some of her clients. 'Now it makes more sense to me,' she said.

Then she talked about Martin, about meeting the demon and how afraid she'd been. She explained how she'd turned away from shamanic work and how her guides had tried to tell her it wasn't the energy work at all, but she hadn't believed them. 'I should have listened.'

Somewhere on a distant plain in another dimension, Emelda stood up in excitement and punched the sky, saying, 'Yes! I told you so!' but was quickly hushed and shushed by Grandmother Medicine Woman, who was also watching the interaction between Marissa and Isis through the reflection in a scrying bowl beside the lake. She pulled Emelda back down to sit on the rock beside her, narrowly escaping being punched in the face by Emelda's rising excitement.

Marissa told Isis how sad she had been, how she had felt she had cut off a piece of herself by not going to the workshops, by not connecting to her guides. She started to cry (Emelda was crying too), but she kept talking through the tears, telling the goddess about how she had tried to convince herself that Reiki wasn't shamanism, but really she had known better and had been hiding things from herself to suit herself. She realised Matt had been right, and that he really did love her, because he'd stayed. She told Isis everything. About the symbol and the book, about her dreams and the people selling their souls for wishes. About Scott Taylor coming into her dreams, trying to seduce her. 'Yes, he really did do that, didn't he? The cheek!'

She felt better upon unburdening herself and the Great Goddess was patient and kind and had all the time in the world. When she had finished speaking, she felt spent, like a container that had spilled all of its contents out onto the floor. She crumpled then, feeling an urge to throw herself at the goddess's feet. She got down from the table onto her knees and cried, and asked for forgiveness. She didn't care how it looked, or what the goddess thought about her now.

Marissa was crying real tears, and people in the museum were walking by, not knowing whether to offer help or not. She caught herself and calmed herself, not wanting to make a spectacle of herself, but not wanting to leave the journey either, not wanting to leave Isis.

She closed her eyes again and she was back with Isis once more, but this time she was no longer on the floor, but seated at the table.

'There, there, now. Drink, drink, it's good for you. And it's good to get it all out, and everything you say, everything you have told me, is important, is a part of this. I feel your guides acknowledging us, and I see you making connections that you did not make consciously before. That time is over now, now you can consolidate. Grow stronger. Together we will mend the chinks in your armour so you become whole.'

'I see you, Tori, and I understand now why you brought your incarnate, Marissa, with you when you came to visit me. She has awakened, I see her transformation and she is coming into herself. This is very interesting. I don't recall this happening in many thousands of years. It must be the convergence, the preparation for the new consciousness.' She sipped her tea and nodded to herself. 'Yes, that must be exactly what this is. So interesting.' She turned to Marissa, who wasn't sure if she was Marissa or Tori. 'Come, I must show you something.'

Marissa felt lighter, unburdened. All the heaviness was gone and she was seeing herself in all of her fullness for the first time. Life had been exhausting; keeping everything split and separated, locked behind a closed door, had taken more energy than she'd realised. She didn't want to do it anymore. This is who she was, and she liked it. Why did she need to hide herself from herself? Or from anyone else? She stood to follow Isis and shook out her long limbs. Ah, yes, my arms and legs are longer and harder here, as if I am an athlete, or a warrior...

She followed Isis out of the room, through a beautiful garden and into a small pyramid. They went down a staircase which led to a dark corridor lit by torches, They walked for quite a while, the pyramid was bigger on the inside. It was as if they were in a labyrinth, but Isis knew where she was going.

They came to a passageway which led down a smaller corridor to a blind ending. There was a tall man standing there, arms crossed, waiting for them. The torches threw his shadow on the wall. It didn't match his human form: his silhouetted head was bird-like, yet to look at him, he had the body of a man.

'Is this her?' he asked Isis.

She nodded and turned to Marissa. 'Tori, you know Thoth. Marissa, this is my teacher, he has asked to be introduced to you. He will be sharing his wisdom with you. Do not be afraid of him. He is mysterious, but the wisest being in the universe.'

Thoth nodded.

Marissa bowed.

Thoth gave thanks to Isis. 'Marissa, it is good to meet you. I look forward to our discussions together.' He nodded once more at them both, then left.

Two silver javelins were hanging criss-crossed on the wall beside them. Isis touched the centre where they crossed, and the wall opened.

Isis led Marissa inside. 'Welcome to my weapons room,' she said, running her finger along the glass cabinets on the wall. They held axes and bludgeons, heavy scythes and lances. On the opposite wall there were shields of various shapes and sizes, and there were bows, whips, clubs and maces hanging from the ceiling. A great double-bladed axe caught Marissa's eye. It shone brightly and looked menacing, and incredibly sharp.

'Sharp enough to slice a hair lengthwise into quarters,' Isis laughed. 'You remember using that one, Tori? We had such fun, remember? Oh the good old days. But it isn't these weapons that you need now. Times such as these call for something different. The reckoning is coming. The timing of your transformation is exact. Come now, my girl.'

She led Marissa to the back of the weapons room, where there were various chainmail shirts, breastplates and suits of armour on display, also in glass cabinets.

Isis walked around thoughtfully, hesitating between one thing and another until she settled on a silver chainmail body suit which had ornate floral decorations on the seams. Isis opened the cabinet, lifted it out and nodded for Marissa to raise her arms, which she did. Isis placed the chainmail suit on Marissa, over her clothing. It felt big and heavy at first, but then it shrank and dissolved through her clothing, to fit around her body snugly. It was as if she wasn't wearing anything at all.'

'That will stay with you, always. But the armour you must choose to wear it when you need it.

Isis lifted the lightest silver armour out of the cabinet and handed it to Marissa, who put it on herself. Again, it felt heavy, but adjusted itself so that it felt light. Isis nodded in approval before going to a bench and choosing a helmet.

'This one,' she said, and placed it over Marissa's head. Just like the other pieces of armour, it reshaped itself around her body until it fit her perfectly. Isis smiled. Marissa moved her arms up and around, and didn't feel awkward at all. The armour fit her like a second skin.

'Oh, wait,' said Isis, and opening a drawer in a cabinet, she pulled out gloves. 'These for your hands,' she said.

Marissa offered her hands and Isis slid them on.

'Perfect. No more chinks in your armour.' Isis stood back and looked Marissa up and down. 'And there you are. Oh wait, you need your sword. Then you will have arrived.'

Marissa followed Isis into an ante-chamber and then a smaller room, dominated by a single display cabinet attached to the back wall. Inside the cabinet was a massive sword. There were symbols engraved on the handle and the blade was inlaid with gold and silver. Wrapped around the hilt was a leather thong. The blade was as thin as ice, but Marissa knew it was strong, powerful and incredibly sharp. She felt an affinity with it right away.

Isis enjoyed watching her reconnect to her old friend. 'Yes, I kept it all these years,' she said. 'I knew we would need it. And here you are, reunited.' She snapped her fingers and the cabinet opened. 'Go on, take it. It's yours.'

Marissa approached the cabinet, looking at the magnificent weapon in awe. She had never seen anything like it, not even in any of the movies she had seen with Eli. But the Tori part of her recognised her old friend and was yearning to touch it again. She reached out and the sword glowed softly as her hand got closer to it. She pulled her hand away and the glow dimmed, then she reached closer again and it brightened. She touched the hilt with her index finger and a spark flashed between her hand and the sword, which lit up like fire. It frighted and excited her at the same time.

'It does feel familiar.'

'What are you waiting for?'

'Marissa is getting to know us,' she said, hearing the difference in tone and confidence as she spoke. She touched the sword again, this time leaving her finger on it. The glowing settled down and she felt her armour glow in response.

'Go on, take it out of the cabinet,' said Isis, gently. 'It's yours.'

Tori reached for the hilt of the sword with both hands. She expected it to be heavy but it felt light. When she held it, the hilt seemed to shift to accommodate her fingers. Her grip felt as snug as her armour.

She took the sword from the cabinet and held it high. Energy poured through her whole body and she felt her spine straighten and her body grow taller. She felt the fear she had been carrying had left her and a piece of her *soul had returned. She kept the sword high, relishing the feeling of strength that had been missing for so long. She felt powerful, and she didn't ever want to feel any other way.*

Finally she lowered her arm, turned to Isis, fully armoured and weaponed, and bowed.

'Your majesty, I am your servant. I am at your service.'

'Then let's get that bastard for once and for all.'

Marissa opened her eyes. For once, she knew what she needed to do.

· + ✦ · ✶ ✦

Find out what happens next in the final instalment
of The Inner Compass Trilogy - BOOK 3

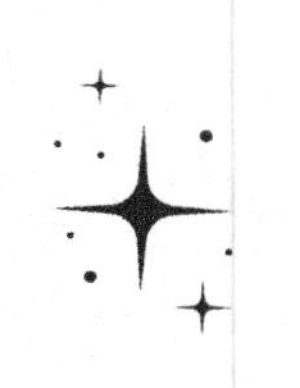

ALSO BY ABBY WYNNE

BOOKS

The Inner Compass Trilogy
The One Day at a Time Diary
Planting the Seeds
Heal your Inner Wounds
How to Be Well
The Book of Healing Affirmations
Energy Healing Made Easy
A–Z of Spiritual Colouring Affirmations
Spiritual Tips for Enlightenment
Energy Healing for Everyone

SELF-PACED HEALING PROGRAMMES

Heal your Inner Child
Heal your Inner Teenager
Creating Good, Strong, Energetic Boundaries
5 Days to Raise your Vibration
Rise Above Anxiety and Fear
High Frequency Lightworker Healing Intensive
How to Be Well Part 1 (based on the book How to Be Well)
The Anxiety Playbook
Programmes are added on a regular basis.
Visit www.abbysonlineacademy.com to find out more.

ABOUT THE AUTHOR

Abby Wynne is a bestselling author and healer living in Ireland. She blends Shamanism, Psychotherapy and Energy Healing to create a unique way of working which she shares with the world through her many offerings. You can join Abby for a live or self-paced healing programme, take part in one of her live group monthly healing sessions, or join her healing circle. Visit her websites www.abby-wynne.com and www.abbysonlineacademy.com

Printed in Great Britain
by Amazon